Praise for
DragonQuest

"Donita K. Paul's *DragonQuest* is a rich tapestry of creatures, characters, and adventure. A whimsical allegory, casting bright light on ultimate truth."

—LYN COTE, author of the Women of Ivy Manor series

"You never know what to expect in a magical world full of creatures like mordakleeps, blimmets, and doneels. But one thing is sure: this grand, fantastical odyssey of Kale the Dragon Keeper will sweep you off your feet."

—ROBERT ELMER, author of the Hyperlinkz fantasy series for kids

"Shut your eyes, hold your breath, and plunge into the unshackled imagination of Donita K. Paul! In *DragonQuest,* Kale's journey of self-discovery continues through a succession of adventures and mishaps that leave you grinning with breathless, page-turning anticipation. I am in awe of Donita K. Paul's intricate world-building that can rightfully stand alongside master storytellers Lewis and Tolkien. There is so much depth of heart to this fantastic adventure that it's difficult to say what I most enjoyed. This book is a fantasy must for the very young at heart, no matter your age."

—LINDA WICHMAN, author of *Legend of the Emerald Rose*

"Donita K. Paul's *DragonQuest* continues the story of Kale and her well-drawn compatriots, who set out on yet another quest in service to God by serving His people. Cleverly and compellingly wrought, *DragonQuest* is a terrific sequel to *DragonSpell* that is sure to delight readers of all ages."

—KATHLEEN MORGAN, author of *Giver of Roses*

DragonQuest

Donita K. Paul

WaterBrook
PRESS

DRAGONQUEST
PUBLISHED BY WATERBROOK PRESS
12265 Oracle Boulevard, Suite 200
Colorado Springs, Colorado 80921
A division of Random House, Inc.

The characters and events in this book are fictional, and any resemblance to actual persons or events is coincidental.

10 Digit ISBN 1-4000-7129-1
13 Digit ISBN 978-1-4000-7129-6

Published in association with the literary agency of Alive Communications, Inc., 7680 Goddard Street, Suite 200, Colorado Springs, CO 80920.

Library of Congress Cataloging-in-Publication Data
Paul, Donita K.
    DragonQuest / Donita K. Paul. — 1st ed.
      p. cm.
    ISBN 1-4000-7129-1
  1. Dragons—Fiction. 2. Quests (Expeditions)—Fiction. I. Title.
  PS3616.A94D727 2005
  813'.6—dc22

                                         2005005027

Printed in the United States of America
2007

10 9 8 7 6 5

This book is dedicated to these first readers,
who "test" my work for me:

Mary and Michael Darnell
Jason McDonald
Alistair and Ian McNear
Claire and Rachael Selk
Amy Stoddard
Sarah White
Michael and Rebecca Wilber

Contents

Acknowledgments ❧ xi

Vendela Surprises ❧ 1

The Goose and The Gander ❧ 9

The Mural ❧ 16

Summoned ❧ 21

Expectations ❧ 27

Attack! ❧ 34

Poison ❧ 40

Regidor ❧ 46

Paladin's Visit ❧ 52

Research ❧ 57

Left Behind ❧ 64

Joining the Battle ❧ 70

Another Plan ❧ 75

Lesson One ❧ 80

The Company Assembles ❧ 87

Wizardry Lesson Two ❧ 92

Peace? ❧ 98

Mother ❧ 104

Hidden Talents ❧ 111

A Mixed Bag of Comrades ❧ 117

Two Tricksters ❧ 125

A Different Direction ❧ 133

Last-Minute Changes ❧ 139

The Journey Begins   144

Feast of Friends   149

Ambush   154

Stranded Travelers   160

Quartered with the Enemy   166

Dirt   173

Meech Dragons   179

Prushing   184

Getting Down to Business   190

Foray into a Den of Evil   195

A Brawl   202

Missing Person   207

Finding Dar   211

Good News, Bad News   216

Legend of the Past   221

Ardeo   228

A Light on the Subject   233

Homecoming   239

Mother?   245

Good Night   253

Morning Surprises   260

Breakfast   266

A Peaceful Interlude   271

Wayfarers   277

Confrontation   284

Plans to Proceed   291

Building the Gateway   298

In Enemy Territory   ❧   305

Mother's Love   ❧   312

Gathering Together   ❧   316

Another Mother's Love   ❧   321

Treachery   ❧   328

Action   ❧   334

Test of Fire   ❧   338

Where Is Home?   ❧   345

Glossary   ❧   350

Acknowledgments

Because iron sharpens iron:

Margie Barritt
Dudley Delffs
Evangeline Denmark
Jani Dick
Michelle Garland
Dianna Gay
Cecilia Gray
Michelle Griep
Jack Hagar
Beth Jusino
Christine Lynxwiler
Chip MacGregor
Paul Moede
Sandra Moore
Jill Nelson
Shannon McNear
Jeanne Paton
Kathryn Porter
Armin Sommer
Faye Spieker
Stuart Stockton
Case Tompkins
Ahneka Valdois
Brenda White
Laura Wright

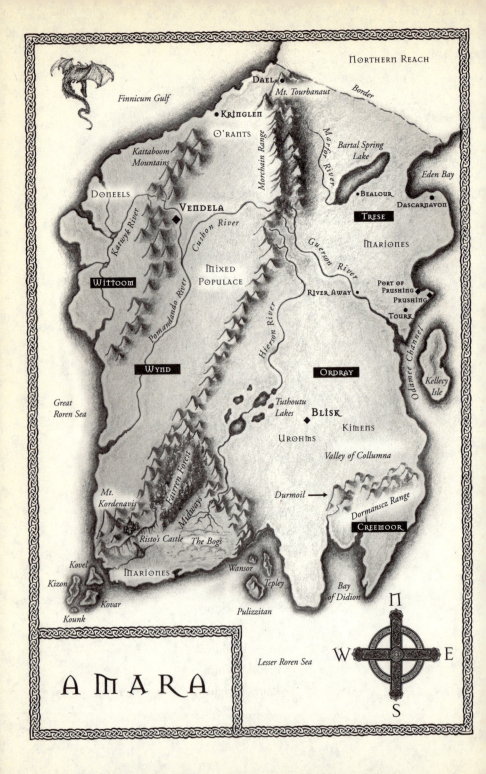

Vendela Surprises

"We're going to get in trouble," Kale muttered. She'd lost sight of her doneel friend Dar in a Vendela market. Amara's capital city teemed with people from each of the seven high races. Kale found the throngs fascinating and intimidating.

She inched past two women, a marione and an o'rant, haggling over the price of a brass candlestick, then ducked as a man swung his arm out, gesturing to three men listening to his tale. She bumped into a kimen, said, "Excuse me," and moved to the middle of the street.

I should have stayed put. I should have turned away and marched right back into The Hall. But no! Dar says let's go explore, and I follow him.

Kale detoured around a fruit cart. As an o'rant, she was taller and slimmer than the mariones in the crowd. Much taller than the kimens. A good two feet taller than Dar. But her height hadn't helped her keep an eye on the doneel.

She shook her head at the confusion in the street. People seemed either in a hurry to get somewhere or else planted firmly in one spot so she had to squeeze around them.

Dar's nimble ways are to his advantage in these huge streets. I keep getting jostled and shoved aside.

Dar! she shouted with her mind. She listened, expecting him to answer with a thought as clear as if he spoke in her ear. Mindspeaking was a gift she had recently developed, and it still surprised her. It also puzzled her that Dar technically could not mindspeak. She talked to him and listened to him with her mind, but he could not start a conversation.

Kale spotted Dar's furry head, ears pricked up in excitement and a grin spreading across his face. He stood on something, she couldn't tell what, and waved his hat above the crowd. He'd found a long red feather and two creamy white ones to stick into the dull brown band of the lee-cent hat.

Heads turned to size up the image of a somberly clad leecent wearing jaunty feathers. Some smiled. Her own uniform was partially hidden by her moonbeam cape.

"We're going to get in trouble," she grumbled again.

Dar dropped out of sight, and Kale zigzagged through the milling shoppers, trying to get to him. The carts full of trinkets, clothing, and gadgets caught her eye, but she didn't stop. She must catch up and per-suade Dar to go back to The Hall.

Of course, he said I didn't have to come with him. But when he headed out the east gate instead of through the west portal, I followed. When will I ever learn?

Kale gave a little hop, trying to see over the heads of the gossiping matrons in front of her. She spotted the tall red feather in Dar's hat.

Too late to change my mind. I'd never find my way back through these city streets by myself.

She pushed aside a niggling suspicion that she probably could find her way to The Hall. True, all the roofs of the city were the same azure blue. But many spires and turrets in a vast variety of shapes and colors studded the tall buildings like jewels. She recognized quite a few landmarks even though she could not name them.

Each afternoon, Kale spent time admiring the metropolis outside her window. She was supposed to be reading, actually studying. But she'd never lived in a city. The view intrigued her more than the books.

Three azure towers spiraled above The Hall compound, a clear globe floating between them. Even now, she looked over her shoulder and saw one of the distinctive blue towers rising above the buildings.

I could get back.

But she didn't really want to return yet. She'd chosen the east gate and freedom from monotony, just as Dar had. The west portal led directly into the back quadrangle of The Hall. The old abbey and its complex of buildings were the center of spiritual and intellectual renewal for the entire continent. Kale and her friend trained for service to Paladin in a many-windowed edifice where great scholars roamed the corridors.

Kale and Dar had been residing in The Hall for two weeks. In those two weeks, they'd gotten uniforms and instructions—two sets of the tan and brown leecent uniforms and a dozen lists of instructions, rules and regulations, edicts and codes of ethics, orders, injunctions, and decrees. They'd finished the last orientation class that morning and had been given the afternoon to relax.

Kale and Dar had called two dragon friends. Responding to the strong mental connection with their riders, Merlander and Celisse had flown in from the hills.

They had swooped out of the sky and landed in the dragon field. Merlander's scales flashed brilliant colors while Celisse's ebony and silver scales looked subdued and elegant.

Kale stroked Celisse's long neck and felt some of her tension drain away. Without words, they exchanged details of the past two weeks. All dragons and their riders shared a special bond, stronger than friendship. She was tempted to climb on Celisse's back and ride far above the city, forgetting all about lists of rules and stacks of books.

Too soon, Dar and Kale waved good-bye to the dragons. With a swoosh of large, leathery wings, Celisse and Merlander rose above the flowered meadow. The two spiraled upward in an airborne dance, twirling and passing back and forth until they were specks high above the dragon field. Kale watched them head out toward the mountains and then looked with displeasure at the many buildings surrounding her. The field seemed a part of her old life. The Hall offered a very different future.

A brick wall, not a wooden fence, hemmed the beautiful field. Dar nodded his head toward the imposing barrier. "Let's go," he said.

Beyond that wall, the city beckoned. Sights the country-raised o'rant girl had never seen filled the bustling streets. She wasted no energy resisting Dar's suggestion to go explore.

And it was fun! She didn't gawk like a complete gaperlot. She'd seen urohms and kimens and tumanhofers before. But she still watched in awe as a group of towering urohm soldiers passed by.

Her knees almost buckled when a small creature slammed against her lower legs. Her cape tightened around her body, seeming to draw itself closer in a protective clutch. She staggered, caught her balance, and looked down.

A doneel child's furry head barely reached her knee. The tiny girl grinned and winked one eye under her fluffy eyebrows. "Sorry, mistress."

Mistress! I'm not old enough to run a household. I haven't got a gray hair on my head nor a wrinkle on my chin. I'm only fifteen summers.

The child reached up and put her grubby hand in Kale's.

Doneels prided themselves on their appearance. Yet this poor urchin had somehow missed that point. Kale examined her more closely. The child had a doneel's flair for bright, fine clothing, but this getup had been scavenged from refuse bins. The girl wore a yellow silk blouse many sizes too big, cinched at the waist with a man's purple necktie. Garish green pantaloons peeked out from the skirtlike hem of the blouse. Slippers, decorated haphazardly with discarded buttons, covered the girl's feet.

A toothy grin on the small doneel's face charmed Kale just as easily as any Dar had ever used. She found herself smiling back.

"Thief! Pickpocket!" A shrill voice pierced the babble of the marketplace. The hand in Kale's squeezed convulsively and then let go. Kale looked up at the commotion. In that moment, the girl disappeared.

Three mariones, in city guard uniforms, appeared among the crowd. The men's powerful muscles strained against the fabric of their gray jackets. Bright yellow epaulets and corded trim did nothing to make them look more congenial. Kale had only met a few mariones who had any cheer in them. These guards wore typically sour expressions and marched unhurriedly to do their duty.

A red-faced tumanhofer merchant followed, shaking a pointed stick in the air. "She's a pest, a nuisance, a blight on the market." The short, round man rushed ahead of a guard and thrust his wooden stick between two crates belonging to a vegetable vendor. "She's quick, sneaky, and looks as innocent as mumfers in a flowerpot."

The tumanhofer's head swiveled on a thick neck as he vigorously searched among the market stalls. He banged his crude weapon on an upturned barrel and then stood on tiptoe to peek inside. Whirling about, he scowled at those watching. His look accused them all of hiding the vagrant child. He shook his fist at several men who grinned at his anger, then still bristling, he stomped over to confront the lead guard. He waved his stick in the man's face.

"You catch that child and put 'er in an orphanage. Better yet, send 'er into the country. Find a small village as many miles from 'ere as you can."

Grunting, he went back to poking his stick into any little hole he saw. "It'll do 'er good to be a village slave. Train 'er up in service and righteousness instead of letting 'er run wild."

The man's words caught at Kale's heart. She'd been raised in an obscure marione settlement as a village slave. In fact, she would still be there if she hadn't found a dragon egg and been sent to Vendela. Kale looked around quickly, wondering where the urchin had gone.

A whiff of hot air and dust swirled around Kale's legs. The moonbeam cape relaxed. Kale furrowed her brow, trying to figure out the odd occurrence. Why had the cape tightened around her? Why had it then loosened its hold? She suspected she still didn't know all the mysterious properties of the wondrous garment.

Granny Noon, an emerlindian wise woman, had given Kale the cape. The cloth repelled water, didn't tear, and sloughed off dirt. She could deposit any number of things in its special hollows without creating bulges or any additional weight. Granny Noon had sewn pockets for the eight dragon eggs Kale had carried. Two had hatched.

She counted the cape as her own personal treasure, even though it was cream-colored and rather plain. The gift had been from someone who treated her kindly, and she had not received many gifts in her life. This gift was wondrous in other ways as well. If she stood very still in a dimly lit area, the cape acted as camouflage.

She watched the guards as they moved among the gaily dressed shop-pers, searching several booths. Turning her eyes away, she admitted to her-self she didn't want to see them capture the little doneel. She moved in the direction she had been going before.

Dar? Dar? No answer. *That's odd. He must be preoccupied.*

She jumped when his voice entered her thoughts.

"Kale, I found the inn."

The Goose and The Gander?

"None other."

Kale smiled. A kind old farmer had once told her about the inn and a woman named Maye. She wanted to meet the lady.

"Can you find me?" asked Dar.

Not in this crowd.

"You can't follow my thoughts?"

Dar! Kale bit down on her exasperation. *I'm getting better at this mindspeaking, but there are hundreds of people. Every one of them is think-ing up sufficient noise to rattle the windows. It's hard to hear you. Vendela's entire population is buzzing around your words with their scattered thoughts.*

"Humph!" The doneel paused. *"Are you still in the market square?"*

Yes.

"I'll come back and get you."

Kale grumbled under her breath, "He wouldn't have to come back and get me if he hadn't run off in the first place."

Thanks. She muttered the word in her mind.

"You're welcome."

Dar's chortle echoed after his polite answer. Kale knew he'd heard the sarcasm underlying her thanks.

She glanced at the city guards going from one merchant's stall to the next. The little culprit seemed to have given them the slip.

Roaming around the square, Kale examined the merchandise—finely woven material from the southern provinces, glazed pottery from the hills of Blandel, and intricately sculpted stone statues. She paused to run her fingers over a glossy purple fruit she didn't recognize. A tart, lemony smell tickled her nose. A tug on her cape brought her eyes down to a small figure hiding under the wooden counter. Two big eyes stared mournfully up at her.

"Help me?" The whispered voice barely reached Kale's ears, but the frightened look in the doneel child's eyes reached her heart.

She glanced over her shoulder and saw the guards approaching. One surveyed the crowd as the other two systematically inspected each booth. Kale waited until the marione scanning the marketers turned his head away. Quickly, she opened her cloak and signaled the child to come. The little girl hopped out of her hole between baskets of fruit and attached herself to Kale's leg like a monkey.

As a leecent, Kale had vowed ten days before to uphold justice in the name of Paladin. Instead, she walked across the square to a booth that had already passed the guards' inspection. Pretending to examine trousers and blouses in the merchant's display, Kale reached out with her mind to speak to the fugitive she harbored.

What did you take?

"You can mindspeak!"

What did you take?

"A pickle."

Kale looked over her shoulder at the guards moving to a cart filled with bags of grain.

"I'm Toopka. What's your name?"

Leecent Kale.

A rough hand slammed down on Kale's arm and spun her around.

"This one 'ere!" With a stubby finger pointed up into Kale's face, the shopkeeper spewed out his accusation. "She's the one. She's got that pickpocket under 'er cape. They're in league together."

"Master Tellowmatterden, she's one of Paladin's," said the guard with a captain's insignia on his collar.

"Ha!" the tumanhofer merchant growled. "She's stolen one of their uniforms, more likely."

"Here now!" Dar's voice rose above the murmuring of the crowd. "That's no way to treat a servant of Paladin."

The shopkeeper thrust Kale against the captain's broad chest. The guard seized her arms in a no-nonsense hold.

Tellowmatterden rounded on Dar. "A doneel! The child's a doneel. Arrest 'im. He's the one trained 'er to steal."

Dar pulled himself into his most dignified stance. His glare should have made the peasant merchant tremble. "I beg your pardon." He turned to the guard in charge. "This unfortunate incident can be easily unraveled. May I suggest you send for a representative of The Hall? Leecent Kale is, indeed, in Paladin's service, as am I."

"Stuffed with feathers, they both are!" screeched the merchant. "Who ever 'eard of a doneel in the service?"

Dar ignored the man and spoke with solemn politeness to the guard holding Kale. "Should we take our business out of the streets, Captain?"

"That's right," the shopkeeper's voice boomed. "Take them down to city jail."

"I think," said Dar, still amiable and soft-spoken, and still talking only to the captain, "a nearby inn would be more appropriate while we wait. It would be less embarrassing for your superiors if you were to settle this without involving the court."

The captain eyed the calm doneel and the red-faced tumanhofer. He nodded toward his companions. "We will escort these two to The Goose and The Gander. Hamwell! Off to The Hall. Get someone to come vouch for them."

2

The Goose and The Gander

Three doors stood open at the front of the bustling inn. Above the left one, a sign read, "The Goose," and a white bird wearing a bonnet looked down with beady eyes on the entryway. Above the right door, a similar sign, "The Gander," pictured a large goose with his mouth wide open as if he squawked a greeting.

The middle door led into a hallway dividing the inn into two parts. Through this entry, Kale could see to the back of the building and into a garden. She followed the captain and Dar through the arch and down the dim passage.

The light weight on her leg shifted, and Kale felt the doneel urchin crawl higher, past her knee. Toopka grasped Kale's tunic. Kale clutched one edge of her open cape and pulled it closer to the other side. She looked around. No one had noticed the small bulge moving up the side of her body under the moonbeam cloth.

What are you doing? she asked Toopka.

"*Looking in all these pockets.*"

Stop.

"*There's no harm in looking around.*" The child moved across Kale's back, hanging on to the sturdy material of the leecent uniform. "*Did you know it's kinda light in here? Lots of pockets, too, some big, some small. I could sure use a cape like this. When I first reached in, the cape nearly snapped my hand off, like it was alive.*"

It's not alive.

"*Here's a bigger pocket.*"

Don't! The bulge disappeared from Kale's side, and she could no longer feel the little girl's hands and feet digging into her. *Toopka!*

Kale stopped in the hall and closed her eyes, willing her thoughts to reach the little doneel's mind.

The marione guard bumped into Kale. She ignored the man's impatient words. Her eyes flew open.

Nothing! Oh no! Kale's hands searched around her waist, trying to locate Toopka. *She must have gone into a hollow pocket. Is that safe?*

The guard prodded her back. Kale marched on. Four more steps and she emerged into the courtyard of the inn. Tables and chairs sat under shade trees, and a wild array of scarlet, gentian, and cobalt flowers bloomed in scattered beds. People relaxed with trays of fruit and tiny sandwiches set before them. Mugs of drink and delicate cups of tea also graced the tables. Serving maids scurried to and fro, providing for the customers' comfort.

Again Kale patted the side of her tunic, hoping she would feel the small form of the child. The fabric lay flat against her hip.

Dar! I've got to talk to you.

"I'm listening." He stood looking up at the captain of the guard and seemed engaged by what the man was saying.

Toopka went into a hollow inside my cape.

"I take it Toopka is the name of the pickpocket."

She took a pickle, and I doubt she found it in someone's pocket. What's going to happen to her inside the hollow?

"I don't know. I've never been in one myself, and right offhand, I can't think of anyone who has."

Gymn has.

"Ask him."

Kale looked back at the two guards and the sour-faced, grumbling merchant. She almost stomped her foot in exasperation. What could she do with them looking on?

Dar, the little girl could be in trouble.

"And then again, she might not. Probably not, I would think, if Gymn has been in and out of those hollow pockets."

But he's a dragon, and she's a—

The memory of the doneel child's frightened eyes sprang up to accuse her. What in Amara would the little girl encounter in that mysterious hollow?

Untying the top of the cape from around her neck, she stepped over to the nearest empty table. She swung the cape off her shoulders and laid it inside out on the bare tabletop.

"Here now!" the tumanhofer merchant objected. "Whatta you doing?" He and the guard moved closer.

At the sound of his bellow, Dar and the captain turned to watch, as did every other person in the garden.

Two minor dragons, neither one bigger than a kitten, popped out of the cape and ran around the tabletop. One sparkled in purple hues, and the other shimmered green. They did a couple of flips in the air and chirred with delight.

"Gymn, Metta," said Kale, "I've lost a little doneel girl. She went into a hollow."

In a flash, the two dragons disappeared into the folds of moonbeam material. The green one's head sprang forth again without any evidence of success. The purple dragon reappeared more slowly. Clenching a bright yellow sleeve in her teeth, Metta struggled with a flailing arm. Kale reached into the hollow and helped pull the squirming doneel free of the cloth.

"Ha!" The merchant slapped his stick against his hand. "You see. The o'rant hid 'er in 'er cape!"

A woman's voice, strong and commanding, resounded over the crowd. "You be quiet, Henricutt Tellowmatterden."

"Maye Ghint, ye be 'arboring a thief and a pickpocket, a band of renegades, a swarm of stealing scum, a—"

"Nonsense!" A statuesque o'rant woman pushed through the crowd.

She took a quick look around at those assembled. "I see customers disturbed by your noise. I see my serving maids neglecting their duties. I see city guards and two of Paladin's servants, and a starved doneel child." She turned to face the shorter, broader tumanhofer. "And I see a scalawag who likes to clamor and snort to draw attention to himself."

"You can insult me all you want, Maye Ghint, but I *will* see justice done. This little wretch 'as been stealing me blind."

"After your gold, silver, and jewels, is she?"

"No," blustered the merchant. "A pickle today. Yesterday, a loaf of bread. The day before, a link of sausage *and* a ripe parnot."

"Oh dear, Master Tellowmatterden." Maye shook her head in mock sympathy. "I'm so sorry to hear you've come upon hard times. I had no idea your prosperous business had fallen into such a decline that the loss of one pickle, a loaf of bread, a piece of sausage, and a bit of fruit would spell your ruin."

"See 'ere, Maye Ghint, a thief is a thief whether she steals half a green pickle or a whole pink pig." He shook his stick at Kale. "And those that aid and abet 'em are just as bad."

Maye Ghint turned her stern gaze upon Kale.

The woman's speculative stare raised a blush to Kale's cheeks. She tried to assume an air of confidence but knew she must look like a clown. She'd hastily thrown on her cape, and it hung cattywampus. She cuddled a shivering doneel child against her chest. Perching on her shoulders, two dragons each held a tuft of Kale's hair in a forepaw. She'd tried to break them of this habit that began when they came to The Hall. Not only did it look silly, but occasionally they pulled.

And if that weren't enough, Gymn had knocked her leecent hat crooked when he flew up. With one hand, Kale straightened her cap. She nodded to the owner of the inn and smiled.

Tellowmatterden cleared his throat and took a step toward the guards. "She's obstructing justice, that she is!"

The captain grimaced. "Would that be Mistress Ghint or the leecent who is obstructing justice, Master Tellowmatterden?"

"Why, they both are, come to think of it. Ye should arrest 'em all. Haul 'em before the magistrate."

The captain narrowed his eyes. "I'm thinking of the law that says a citizen shall not slander nor malign, but allow truth to be established without rancor."

Tellowmatterden's face screwed up in a fierce glare. His lips pressed together in a straight line, and he said no more.

The captain confronted Kale. "Did you know this doneel child was the one sought by the guard?"

"Yes sir."

"And you hid her?"

"Yes sir, but from the merchant, not the guard."

The man wrinkled his brow. "How is that?"

"I didn't think it out exactly, sir. But I didn't want the angry man to hurt her. I thought I could figure how best to help her once the immediate danger had passed."

Kale glanced at Dar and Maye Ghint. Both wore approving expressions, which gave her courage.

"I knew I could consult at least two people who have more experience than I do." She nodded toward Dar. "My friend served as adjunct to Paladin before we came to The Hall. He's given me good advice in the past." She nodded to the proprietor of the inn. "The man who brought me to Vendela a year ago, Farmer Brigg, told me if I ever got into trouble to find Maye at The Goose and The Gander."

A look of interest crossed the matron's face as her features softened.

Kale hunched her shoulders and sighed. "I wasn't really thinking all this when I took the little girl under my cape, but Paladin once told me that I had acted well when I acted quickly, and I guess that gave me confidence. And the criminal…"

She held the little girl away from her for just a moment to show the unthreatening nature of the small culprit. Toopka whimpered pathetically and ducked her cute, furry head, a gesture bound to appeal to the sympathies of those watching.

"Well, Captain," Kale continued, "she didn't seem to be a dangerous sort who needed to be apprehended at that very moment."

The guard's stony expression chilled Kale. She suspected she'd be hauled off to court.

After a long moment, the guard's narrow eyes shifted right, then left. In a lowered voice, he said, "You've met Paladin?"

Kale nodded. "Twice."

"Ha!" The tumanhofer glared up at the captain. "Don't listen to 'er lies. Take 'er to the jail. Put 'er before the magistrate."

"I would be that magistrate." An older emerlindian man stood at his table, leaving his afternoon tea unfinished. He cast a long, thin shadow across the lawn. His intelligent face was darkened with age. His brown eyes glittered cold, holding no humor. "I've had quite enough of your loud posturing, Tellowmatterden."

Maye Ghint stepped forward. "I apologize that you've been disturbed, Magistrate Hyd."

The man held up his hand, and she was silent. He looked at Kale. "Young lady, come here."

Kale obeyed.

"Who gave you the cape?" he asked.

"Granny Noon."

"A moonbeam cape *cannot* be stolen." He stated the fact with a powerful voice that reached those all around. His eyes remained on Kale. "What is your name, child?"

"I am Kale Allerion. Leecent Kale."

The man's eyebrows twitched upward, and a new gleam entered his eyes. "You will do well to follow closely the teachings of Paladin and remember Wulder in all your dealings."

This phrase was often spoken among those at The Hall. Kale nodded obediently.

Magistrate Hyd lifted a hand and pensively stroked his smooth dark chin. He studied Kale until she wanted to squirm under his gaze.

Finally, his eyes shifted to Toopka, and he spoke. "Are you an orphan?"

She gave a quick nod and clung to Kale, her fingers tightening on the cape.

The magistrate's attention came back to Kale. "You will take the doneel child as your charge."

Kale jerked at the command. "But—"

"Dar will assist you."

"Excuse me, Your Honor," Kale tried again. "But I—"

"You are fully capable of this charge, Kale Allerion. Do not turn back what has been given you."

"Yes, Your Honor."

Magistrate Hyd looked over her shoulder. "I believe an escort has arrived from The Hall. Good day, Kale."

"Good day, Your Honor." Kale turned away as the magistrate sat back down.

Maye came forward to offer fresh hot tea and nordy rolls, warm and fragrant from the inn's oven. The guards put a hand on each of the disgruntled tumanhofer's arms and guided him toward the door. Dar watched with a pleased grin on his face. As Kale turned her head to see the guards escort Tellowmatterden through the center doorway, she lost her own smile. Next to the inn stood the representative of The Hall.

Kale caught a groan before it escaped her throat.

Lehman Bardon, the only o'rant in The Hall who treats me like I don't exist. He never speaks to me. He looks right through me when we pass in the corridors. And now he looks like he swallowed a drummerbug. What else could go wrong?

3

The Mural

Bardon bowed in the magistrate's direction and then nodded to Kale and Dar. Kale wondered how anyone could gaze upon the festive garden with so little interest. Guests and serving maids wore colorful attire. A sweet fragrance rose from the flowers. Guitarists provided lilting music. Lehman Bardon looked as if nothing made any impression on his wooden soul.

Kale frowned at the grim lehman.

Dar raised a hand, acknowledging the escort from The Hall. "One minute, Bardon," he said. "I wish to thank the magistrate for his intervention."

Well now, Bardon can't like that. Dar is only a leecent and Bardon is a lehman. Surely, Dar should have called him by his title. And shouldn't a leecent jump to do whatever a lehman wants?

Kale watched Bardon's face for a reaction. Not a muscle twitched. He nodded solemnly and stepped out of the way of a maid carrying a tray of tall glasses.

Hmm? Our teachers keep reminding Dar of his new humble rank. But I bet Bardon lets Dar do what he wants, then reports his misconduct. He's an official monitor, and everyone says that's just a fancy name for a snitch.

Dar approached Magistrate Hyd and engaged the man in conversation. As a diplomat for his region, Wittoom, the doneel had traveled to every large metropolis and visited the courts of many rulers.

Kale admired Dar's way with words. He could talk to a turnip farmer, a wizard, or a king and never utter an inappropriate comment. Dar could act like a noble, fight like a knight, and play like a peasant. He enjoyed everything he did, and he did most things well.

Gymn and Metta flew off Kale's shoulders. She was about to call them back when she saw what had attracted their attention. A serving maid stood in the window of the Gander with a platter. She put it down on the broad sill, and the dragons landed on either side.

The blond maid dipped a curtsy to the small dragons and giggled when they inclined their heads toward her, thumping their tails once in a friendly greeting.

"The mayor in the town where I grew up had a minor dragon," she said. "She was blue and predicted the weather."

Someone called from inside the inn. The maid smiled at Metta and Gymn. "Enjoy your treat." She glanced up at Kale and winked before returning to her duties.

Dar was still talking to the magistrate. Bardon stood stiff and unyielding. So, holding the doneel orphan close, Kale joined her dragons. She saw the maid had placed a mound of pudding in the middle of the plate and sprinkled it with shaved cardonut. It looked like an island covered with grass in the middle of a brown lake of ale. With typical dragon enthusiasm for food, Metta and Gymn lapped at what was called poorman's dessert.

"I'm hungry," said Toopka.

Kale patted the small child's back. "I thought your tummy was full of pickle."

Toopka flashed a mischievous grin. "That was an hour ago."

"Stealing is not right."

"I know." Toopka's face fell. "Most of the grocers leave food behind the stalls for those who have to forage. Master Tellowmatterden doesn't." A grin peeked from under her furry top lip. A twinkle lit her eyes. "And he hollers so loud and gets red. It's fun to watch him stomp around."

"It *is* still wrong to steal."

"Paladin says to feed the orphans and widows."

Kale wondered if that was written in one of the books that sat on her desk in The Hall. "Even if he does," she said slowly, "you should take what is given to you. You shouldn't steal from Tellowmatterden."

"I wish you would quit calling it stealing. It was more for fun than stealing."

"If it's stealing, it has to be called stealing."

Toopka gave a great sigh and laid her head on Kale's shoulder. "I'm still hungry."

A serving maid passed by just at that moment. Kale suspected Toopka had timed her declaration. The young woman stopped, picked a delicate finger sandwich off her tray, and handed it to the little doneel. Toopka accepted it with one of her winning smiles and a polite, "Thank you." She nestled in Kale's arms and chewed with contentment and a great deal of lip-smacking.

Leaning against the wall next to the window, Kale surveyed the people around her in the garden. A marione family with small children sat at a table. The father said something, and the others laughed. Their relaxed, friendly faces reminded Kale of the mariones she had met at Lee Ark's home. Unlike the people in River Away where she was raised, these mariones enjoyed each other and life in general. Even though they lived in the shadow of the evil wizard Risto's domain, Lee Ark's family still managed to smile.

Gathered around another smaller table, four kimen women and several children sipped their tea and ate spicy hard cakes known as daggarts. Kale sniffed the air, wishing she could smell the fragrant morsels. Instead the strong odor of malty ale from the dish at her elbow assaulted her. Wrinkling her nose, she frowned as her dragons slurped the treat.

A roar of laughter from inside the Gander caught her attention. Through the window she saw a dozen men lounging around rough wooden tables in a dim room. A cold fireplace stood against one wall, and a mural covered another. Kale leaned in for a better look.

In the tavern in River Away, there had been a similar mural. Kale had thought nothing of the picture. But during her adventure, a quest to find a meech egg and deliver it to Wizard Fenworth, she had found herself in a real scene that looked very much like the picture on that tavern wall.

She squinted at the mural inside the Gander. A boat moved across dark waters. A tapered line of light from a full moon made a path across the water and illuminated the prow. Two figures sat at the front. One looked like her friend Dar. Kale moved to the open door of the Gander. She had to see who else was in the boat.

With Toopka's thin arms snug around her neck, she slipped along the wall of the busy room. On the other side of the mural wall, the hallway passed through the center of the building. The painting covered the entire length. Gently rolling waves extended from one end to the other. White foam capped some of the waves.

Only in the center had the artist strayed from the persistent, repetitive blue-green waves. Here moonlight danced over the waters. The boat edged into its glowing beam.

She examined the people in the boat. A doneel sat in the prow with a small bundle on his knee. A kimen sat straddling the front tip of the small vessel, with his legs dangling above the water. His clothing either glowed white or reflected the moon. Behind the doneel sat a larger figure in a gray cape. This person leaned against an old man, bearded and wearing a wizard's hat. With their heads together, they seemed to be whispering. In the widest part of the boat sat a urohm who dipped one oar into the waves. Beside him sat a marione and a young o'rant, both of whom applied their muscles to the other oar.

The light did not reach the back of the boat. Kale moved closer, trying to make out the images in the shadow behind the huge urohm. Possibly a tumanhofer with kimens around him. If so, the kimens had not illuminated their clothing. A fine lady sat beside the squat man who had to be a tumanhofer.

"Why are you looking at that?" asked Toopka.

"It's like a painting I saw before."

"Another boat?"

"No."

"A lake?"

"No. It was a mountain pass."

"This isn't like a mountain pass."

"No, but the people look the same."

"Leecent Kale?"

"Yes?"

"I think we better get out of here."

Kale became aware of the silence. She straightened and turned to view the room. The serving maids had stopped in their journeys back and forth to the kitchen. Every man sat or stood motionless. All eyes bored into Kale.

"This is the men's side of the inn," whispered Toopka.

Faced with more than a dozen glares, Kale swallowed hard.

Toopka's little fist shook Kale's collar. "I really think we better get out of here," the doneel hissed. "Now!"

Kale gave a brisk bow to her statuelike audience. She had seen Dar do the elegant motion many times. Only when *she* did it, the gesture felt jerky. Sidestepping along the wall, she came to the corner of the room and had a clear shot to the back door. She hustled toward the bright rectangle of sunlight.

The closer she got to the opening, the faster her feet hit the clapboard floor. Her steps echoed as if she were crossing a wooden bridge. Her lungs ached as she reached the door, and she realized she'd been holding her breath. Gasping, she swung around the corner and out into the crisp, clean air. She also smashed headlong into a broad chest.

A quick step backward put her in the doorway. She tilted her head and saw the obstruction. Bardon. Lehman Bardon. With a face that would freeze water.

4

SUMMONED

Bardon parted the market crowd with a firm step forward and an occasional, "Excuse me." Dar ambled along behind, but Kale kept close to Bardon's back so people wouldn't converge again before she had a chance to get through.

Toopka slumbered on Kale's shoulder. The little girl wasn't worried about what would happen once they reached The Hall and had to face the dean of leecents. Inside Kale's cape, Metta and Gymn had tucked themselves into their pocket-dens. The minor dragons were content, their bellies full of poorman's dessert. They hadn't been humiliated by the scene at the Gander.

Kale, however, was worried about the interview with the dean. Her cheeks warmed every time she recalled the shocked expression on the faces of the people at the inn.

How was I supposed to know the inn had been divided into three parts over two hundred years ago? One side for women, one side for men. I didn't know the terraced garden is for families. And I don't think it was obvious, no matter what Bardon says.

Bardon stopped suddenly, and Kale ran into his back. He tipped his hat and bowed to a marione matron, allowing the woman to cross his path. He continued on without a word to Kale.

Manners! He's got manners for some, but not for me. Why does he treat me like a blattig fish?

She glanced over her shoulder. Dar tipped his hat to the same matron and then to another. The ladies rewarded him with friendly smiles.

Hmm? Dar and Bardon both have manners, but Dar has something else, too.

Kale's head swiveled back and forth as she tried to observe both young men at once. Dar's actions were graceful in comparison to Bardon's stiff movements. The doneel's face beamed with friendliness and goodwill. Kale couldn't see Bardon's expression, but she knew well the determined look about his eyes and mouth.

So does the way Dar acts toward people bounce back at him? He smiles, so people smile in return?

All the way to The Hall, Kale watched the two men interact with those they passed. It kept her from dwelling on the unpleasant reception she expected in the dean of leecents' office.

Two guards beside a high-arched entry gave them sober nods, signaling them to move on. A footman opened the great front door and quietly instructed them to proceed immediately to the high chancellor's study.

The high chancellor! Not the dean?

Kale looked back at Dar, hoping he could explain.

Why? she asked, making sure that only he could hear. *We couldn't be in* that *much trouble.*

Dar's eyebrows shot up, and he shrugged. *"I don't know. Seems to me like a lot of hullabaloo for a simple walk in the city. Let me do the talking, Kale."*

Gladly!

Bardon led them up a wide, curving staircase and into a long corridor. Sunlight streamed through elaborate stained-glass windows, making a mottled patchwork of bright colors on the polished marble floor. Portraits of countless dignitaries from The Hall's illustrious history looked down on the procession approaching the high chancellor's quarters.

On either side of one of the many mahogany doors, two men stood waiting. One wore the simple garb of a house servant. The other wore the uniform of The Hall guard. Bardon stopped a few feet from the door.

"We're expected," he said. "Lehman Bardon, Leecent Kale, and Leecent Dar."

The guard remained motionless, but his eyes roamed over the small party. Evidently he saw no reason to challenge them.

The footman bowed and opened the door. In a clear voice he announced their arrival. A rumbling bass answered, one Kale had heard intoning words of wisdom almost every morning at chapel.

"Come in, come in."

No anger heated the simple command. Kale relaxed and walked into the room, expecting to see High Chancellor Grand Ebeck looking staid and solemn. The black emerlindian had lived long and gathered much wisdom.

"Here they are at last." The deep voice rolled across the room.

Smiling broadly, High Chancellor Grand Ebeck stood beside the window, bright sunlight outlining his thin form. He wore long, sweeping robes of wispy purple, gold, and royal blue stripes. His ebony hair flowed over his shoulders, almost reaching the lush carpet. He held a book in one hand and a large mug in the other. The scent of eberbark tea filled the room.

Kale smiled. Then her eyes shifted to the person beside High Chancellor Grand Ebeck, and she let out a squeal.

"Librettowit!"

Kale forgot the decorum expected of a mere leecent visiting the high chancellor's quarters and rushed across the room to embrace the sturdy tumanhofer. Toopka squirmed and protested softly, but Kale paid no attention.

She and Librettowit greeted each other with laughter and hugs and questions tumbling out too quickly to be answered. When that round of greetings subsided, Dar joined them, and they began again.

Kale watched Librettowit with a grin on her face she couldn't subdue. The tumanhofer cleared his throat, peered over his glasses, and inspected his young friends. He looked much as he always had, a bit grumpy, a bit curious, a bit impatient. He was a very dependable tumanhofer.

"Now who is this ragged little beasty looking something like a doneel?" Librettowit patted the sleepy-eyed child on her back.

"Toopka," said Kale. With a sigh of relief, Kale realized she had landed in the right circumstances to have all her troubles undone. Grand Ebeck and Librettowit would help her. She couldn't think of anyone other than Paladin to whom she could turn with this predicament. These two scholars, both men of wisdom, both compassionate and discerning, would rescue her. They'd know what to do about the mess this morning's venture into the city had created.

Kale smiled at Librettowit. "We haven't had a chance to give Toopka a bath and new clothes, but we will as soon as we get back to the dormitory. It's a long story, but Magistrate Hyd put her into my charge, and I don't know exactly what I'm supposed to do, but Dar is to help me. I don't even know if the rules of The Hall allow us to have an orphan under our care. There's probably a regulation against it, don't you think? I've read more rules and edicts and orders of conduct than you can imagine, but I don't think even one mentioned an orphan."

She turned to High Chancellor Grand Ebeck. "I don't want to cause any more problems, Your Grace, but under the circumstances, I can't abandon her. I would appreciate your counsel."

As she said the last bit of her speech, Kale realized it sounded almost as good as anything Dar would have come up with. He had said to let him do the talking, and she had really meant to do just that. But she hadn't done so badly. The first part of what she said had rushed out and sounded a bit garbled. But the last part was fine. She had pulled herself together and made a decent plea.

High Chancellor Grand Ebeck put a hand on her shoulder. His eyes held no humor, only gentle patience. "It won't be a problem, Leecent Kale. You will not be staying at The Hall."

Her mouth dropped open. A large lump formed in her throat. She tried to swallow and come up with a protest. Her mind spun, but her lips would not move.

What have I done that's so bad? I know I'm not a very good student. I could try harder. Is it because we went into the city? Is it Toopka? Or because I went in the wrong side of the inn?

Toopka's small hand patted Kale's back. Kale hugged her warm little body, comforted by the child's sympathy.

"Oh my, oh my." Grand Ebeck's gravelly voice rumbled about her ears. "Do not be so distressed, little Kale. It is not due to your insufficiency, but rather your ability. You are needed. My dear friend Librettowit has come to fetch you at Wizard Fenworth's request. The meech egg has hatched, and Fenworth can't do a thing with it, or *him,* rather."

The emerlindian glanced over at the librarian and gave him a wink, then he patted Kale's arm and continued. "His name is Regidor. He is all that we would expect a meech dragon to be—intelligent, capable of speech, maturing rapidly, showing signs of great talent, and stubborn. Ah yes, irrefutably stubborn."

Alarmed, Kale turned pleading eyes to Librettowit. "What am I supposed to do?"

He cleared his throat. "I, of course, will help you all I can, Kale. But I must admit that so far my attempts to reason with and guide Regidor have met with less than satisfactory results."

Oh my, if Librettowit and Wizard Fenworth can't handle this Regidor… "Why me?"

"You carried the meech egg. It quickened because of your contact. During the time it incubated, your dragons guarded the egg. In short, Kale, Regidor is attached to you, not Fenworth. It is obvious to us now. You are the one who can befriend him. Indeed, affinity for you has already been accomplished, and most of his disruptive behavior can probably be accounted for by his need to have you at his side."

A slight pressure from Grand Ebeck's hand turned her to face him.

"Kale, you must go. Fenworth is old. This disturbance in his life is causing him to weaken. He is distraught."

"Aggravated," put in Librettowit.

High Chancellor Grand Ebeck took his hand from her shoulder. "Dealing with a stubborn meech has made Fenworth a bit disagreeable."

The librarian clenched his fists. "Cantankerous, surly, crotchety, petulant, hot-tempered. Disagreeable? Ha! Impossible!"

Grand Ebeck regarded the fuming tumanhofer with sympathy.

"We will do what we can," he assured him and turned back to Kale. "Our council judged Fenworth to be the best equipped to handle the meech dragon and the important role Regidor could play in Risto's defeat. Perhaps we did not consider Fenworth's advancing years as carefully as we should have."

He looked out the window for a moment, his expression grave, his eyes sad. At long last, he sighed, then shook himself as if a shiver had gone up his spine.

"We will need the wizard and Regidor in the months to come," he said. "A great evil is brewing in that nest of vipers under Risto's command."

He clasped his hands behind his back and solemnly looked into her eyes. "You will leave immediately. Accompany Librettowit back to The Bogs and lend what assistance you can."

"Toopka?" she croaked.

"Toopka will go with you."

"Dar?"

"He will remain here and finish his training to serve Paladin."

"My training?"

"You will enter your apprenticeship to Fenworth. It is premature, but you were always meant to be a wizard. You will do well."

She blinked. She could not think of one thing to say. She felt the two little dragons thrum with excitement under her cape. Toopka gave her neck a squeeze and giggled.

Grand Ebeck continued. "Librettowit will oversee your scholastic advancement."

She nodded.

"And Bardon will accompany you. He will instruct you in the art of defense, which would have been part of your training here at The Hall. He will also report back to the dean of leecents, keeping him informed as to your progress."

One word sprang up in Kale's mind with a whippish hiss. *Snitch!*

5

EXPECTATIONS

Bardon stepped forward. "Excuse me, Your Grace. I don't see how I can accompany Leecent Kale and also finish preparations for knighthood."

High Chancellor Grand Ebeck grasped the front edges of his silken robes, resting his hands against his chest. "Time enough for that after you've been on your own, away from The Hall for a while."

Kale watched Bardon out of the corner of her eye. She knew some of what the other students said about him. Bardon had been left at The Hall by his father when he was just six years old, two years younger than most candidates were when they entered training. He was a few years older than Kale, so that meant he'd been here at least a dozen years. The Hall was his home, and everyone said he took his obligation to fulfill his father's will seriously. In fact, they said that was why Bardon was such an unyielding, tiresome bore.

The muscles in Bardon's neck tightened. With the same talent that enabled her to mindspeak and find dragon eggs, Kale could feel the other o'rant's tension. Sympathy for him invaded her heart. The emotion surprised her for only a moment. When she'd been a slave, there had been plenty of times when those in charge dismissed what she wanted to do as if it were nothing. People at The Hall were supposed to be more sensitive. They followed Paladin.

Kale's eyes sought the face of the wise emerlindian chancellor. Surely he understood that Bardon would take this order to leave Vendela as punishment.

Grand Ebeck showed no awareness of her outrage or Bardon's dismay.

The high chancellor picked up his book. He paged through the volume, stopping to scan an entry and then moving on.

Her eyes went back to Bardon. A red flush stained his pale cheeks. Black eyebrows drew together over those blue eyes that so often looked cold and distant. A muscle in his square jaw worked, and Kale suspected his teeth were clenched like a bodoggin's grip on his next meal.

High Chancellor Grand Ebeck made his next pronouncement without even looking at either o'rant.

"You aren't ready to go on, Lehman Bardon."

Kale heard Bardon's sharp intake of breath. *Oh no! He hadn't known he didn't qualify.*

"There is nothing more we can do for you here. You might as well make yourself useful to Wizard Fenworth for the time being."

She chafed at the high chancellor's words. *That's just cruel. Granny Noon would never have been so mean. Maybe men who are grands aren't as kind as women. I don't think Grand Ebeck's so terribly wise after all.*

His voice droned on. "Perhaps in a year or two you can reapply for candidacy."

Oh, that's nice! She couldn't help the sarcasm spicing her thoughts. She pressed her lips into a tight line to keep from saying something she shouldn't. She could feel Metta and Gymn turning around and around restlessly in their pocket-dens. They always picked up on her emotions, and she on theirs. If she didn't tamp down her anger, they might come out hissing and stomping and ready to fight.

Librettowit came to her side and put his hand on the arm that held Toopka.

"Go pack your belongings. Meet me at the entry to Trell Tower before the next chime of hourly bells."

With a wrinkled brow, she tried to determine the sense of such a command. "We aren't going to the dragon field? Celisse is not taking us back to The Bogs?"

Librettowit shook his head. "I came through a gateway. We'll be home again in Fenworth's castle this afternoon."

"But Celisse—"

"—will fly to join you." He patted her arm. "Don't worry so, Kale. We will have a pleasant summer. Studying, training, good company, good music, good food. No quests, no adventures, just the camaraderie of intelligent, reasonable, compatible people. Once you have Regidor in hand, life will be comfortable once more."

Dar cleared his throat. "Sounds idyllic."

She had known Dar long enough to read the caution in his eyes. She wanted to quiz him, but the high chancellor interrupted.

"Well now," he said, "we all have things to do. Leecent Dar, I wish to have a word with you. Lehman Bardon, you will also need to pack and meet with Kale and Librettowit. Off with you now." He gestured with a dark, wrinkled hand toward the door.

The door behind them opened even though the footman could not have heard their dismissal. He jumped to bow them out.

Bardon inclined his head to Grand Ebeck and said, "Good day."

The high chancellor nodded absent-mindedly and murmured the correct response. Carrying Toopka, Kale followed the lehman out of the room.

As soon as the door closed, she hurried to catch up to Bardon.

"I'm sorry," she said.

He didn't slow his pace. "For what?"

"That you don't get to begin your apprenticeship."

"Wulder's timing is best."

"That's what people say when they don't understand why things happen." She wanted to tell him about Paladin's explanation to her of Wulder's perfect timing. She believed the saying was true, not just a platitude.

She opened her mouth, eager to relate the images Paladin had put before her, but Bardon's gruff voice pushed her enthusiasm aside. "That's what people say to help them accept what has happened. It works, Leecent Kale. Excuse me. I have a lot to do."

He quickened his pace and left Kale trailing behind.

"He's mad," said Toopka.

"He didn't say he was mad." Kale turned down the hall leading to the main staircase.

"He's still mad."

"Yes, probably. But he doesn't want us to know."

"We know anyway."

"Yes, but let's pretend we don't. I think he's embarrassed as well as disappointed."

Kale and Toopka reached the bottom of the grand staircase and crossed the wide foyer to the front doors, where a footman bowed them out of the building.

Outside, the sun shone brightly on the azure towers. The translucent globe floated fifty feet in the air, unmoved by the breeze fluttering the banners on each of The Hall's turrets.

"Can I have new clothes?" asked Toopka. "I'd like new clothes."

"I don't think we will have time."

"A bath? I'd like a bath, inside, with smell-good soap. Maybe pink soap."

"As soon as we get to Wizard Fenworth's castle. He has a nice tub. Actually, it's a huge wooden bucket. But hot water comes out of a reservoir in the treetop. The sun warms the water. I don't know about pink soap."

"I was thinking I didn't want to leave Vendela. I have friends here, you know. But maybe this will be fun. I've never been on an adventure."

"We are not going on an adventure. Adventures are not fun," said Kale as they crossed the courtyard. "I know. I *have* been on one."

She walked briskly to the dormitory, aware of the curious glances from fellow students. Once within the doors, she sprinted down the empty hall, up three flights of narrow stairs, and into the room she shared with five other girls. No one was there.

"I guess that's good."

"What's good?" asked Toopka. She craned her neck around, trying to see everything.

"No one's home, so I don't have to explain why we're leaving. Sit here, and don't touch anything." She deposited the little doneel on her own cot.

"Is there anything to eat?" Toopka slipped off the bed and headed for a chest of drawers.

"Toopka!" Kale snatched her up and put her back on the cot. "We aren't allowed to have food in the rooms."

Toopka squirmed toward the edge again. "That doesn't mean there isn't any."

"Stay where you are. I'll find you something to eat but not right now. I have to pack and get to the tower."

Toopka's face folded into a grumpy frown. Kale ignored her and opened a drawer. She stuffed clothes into the hollows of her cape. When she glanced at the doneel again, she saw Toopka's eyes had grown large, and her mouth hung open.

"You're putting all those things in that pocket I went in?"

"Yes."

Kale dropped to her knees and pulled a shallow box from under the bed. Toopka lay on her stomach and peered over the edge. Kale continued to pack. When she'd emptied the box, she stood up and pushed it back under the bed with the toe of her brown boot.

"Let's go."

"Aren't you going to take the books?" Toopka nodded toward the clutter on the desk beside the bed.

"No. Wait until you see the castle. It has rooms and rooms full of books."

A sharp rap on the door sent Kale to answer.

"Dar!"

"I brought some clothes for our little friend."

He entered the room and placed a folded stack of clothing on the bed beside Toopka. She squealed with delight and rummaged through the pieces, cooing as she shook out a white shirt embroidered with an ivy vine. Metta and Gymn emerged from the cape, flew to her side, and examined her new possessions.

Kale studied the furry face of her friend. "What did Grand Ebeck want to talk to you about?" she asked.

"Oh, he wants me to attend a dinner tonight. A doneel diplomat will be trying to influence a regional governor to increase trade with their district. Dull, political stuff."

"I don't think I like Grand Ebeck as much as I did before."

"He doesn't particularly care whether you like him or not. He was more interested in softening your attitude toward Bardon."

"What?"

Dar plopped down on the bed beside Toopka and helped her lace up a boot she'd found.

"Diplomacy. He detected your dislike of Bardon and set about constructing a situation in which you would side with him."

"That's sneaky."

Dar shrugged and concentrated for a moment on getting Toopka's tiny foot into the other boot. "If he had told you to consider Bardon a comrade, you would have resisted. However, when he revealed Bardon's weakness and need for a friend, you jumped right in. He counted on your noble instincts."

"How does he even know I have noble instincts?"

Dar rolled his eyes and commenced working the laces through the boot's eyelets. "He's a grand. He knows. He wanted you to discover for yourself that you could feel sympathy for Bardon."

"A lot of good it did. Bardon didn't want to talk to me."

"Maybe not, but now there is a chink in your prejudice against him."

"Prejudice! I'm not prejudiced!"

"Your opinions of Bardon are formed out of gossip and surface impressions. That's prejudice."

Toopka looked up from her new boots. "If it's prejudice, it has to be called prejudice."

"Very wise," said Dar and chucked Toopka under the chin.

Kale glared at both doneels. She inspected the little black boots on the child's feet. They fit well.

"Where'd you get these clothes?" she asked Dar.

"I've been collecting some things to send to my sister's family. One of the reasons I wanted to go to the market."

Kale thought about the huge family Dar claimed and felt a sudden loneliness. Dar was like a brother, and she didn't want to leave him.

The doneel stood and squeezed her arm. "You'll be all right, Kale. You have lots of family now in the form of good friends. And two new additions as of today, Toopka and Regidor. You'll be too busy to miss me."

"Are you sure you don't read my mind?"

Dar just laughed and moved to the door. "You'd better hurry." He went into the hallway, then turned, laying a hand on the door frame. "You will do well to follow closely the teachings of Paladin and remember Wulder in all your dealings."

Not trying to hide the grin on her face, Kale answered in mock approval. "Don't *you* sound proper all of a sudden."

"Exactly!" Dar winked and saluted. "And Kale?"

"Yes?"

"Give Bardon a chance."

6

Attack!

Kale and Toopka waited at the base of Trell Tower. Toopka played among large round boulders ringing the turret. Embedded in the boulders, millions of quartz chips glistened in the afternoon sun. At night, these sparkles glowed blue.

Toopka skipped from one rock to the next with the same natural agility Kale had seen Dar display. Kale smiled as she watched the little doneel. As a slave, Kale had been strong from her work but not particularly nimble. She'd spent part of her first quest falling on her face.

With a quick look around, she noted the Torsk Tower clock gave the time as five minutes to the hour. The courtyard was empty. She hopped up behind Toopka.

"Better run. I'm going to get you!"

Toopka squealed. Metta and Gymn emerged from Kale's cape in a flurry of bright wings and joined the chase. They bombarded the little girl, getting close enough to ruffle her hair with their wings. She flinched the first time they swooped over her head, but batted at them playfully on the following charges.

Even with the dragons on her side, Kale had a hard time keeping up with the surefooted doneel. Kale hopped off the boulders and ducked into the tower doorway. The recess of engraved stone hid her as she prepared an ambush.

She waited for the child to pass her hiding place and then pounced. She snatched Toopka off the boulders. With the little doneel tucked under one arm, Kale tickled her with her free hand. Metta and Gymn circled above, letting out trills of encouragement. Kale laughed almost as hard as her captive.

She saw his boots first. The soft brown leather gleamed in the sunshine. His feet were twelve inches apart, his toes pointed straight ahead, his legs rigid. One hand gripped the handle of his tote bag, and the other rested on his hip.

Even though Kale had quit tickling, Toopka still squirmed. Kale put the doneel down on the grass before looking into the ice blue eyes of Lehman Bardon.

She tried a smile. "Ready to go?"

He nodded and looked away. Gymn and Metta landed next to Toopka.

"I'm hungry," announced the child.

The dragons raised their voices in a series of shrill notes. Kale interpreted the dragons' emphatic chorus of chirps. They reminded her she had promised to find the little girl a snack.

Bardon reached into a pouch hanging by a leather strap over his shoulder. With two steps, he crossed to the tiny child and handed her a packet.

Toopka grinned as she unfolded the layers. "Thank you. Ooh! Daggarts!" She took a big bite and then broke off a piece for each of the dragons.

Bardon straightened and looked at Kale. "You didn't bring any food for the journey?"

"No."

"We may have some distance to go once we exit the other side of the gateway."

"Librettowit said we would be at Fenworth's castle this afternoon." Kale shrugged. "I didn't think about food."

"You are honest."

She didn't know how to answer. She turned away from Bardon's steady gaze.

Hoping Librettowit would rescue her from this uncomfortable situation, she searched the pathway from The Hall. If the tumanhofer would just hurry so they could go to the gateway and leave.

"I noticed when you spoke to Magistrate Hyd."

She looked back at Bardon with her brow furrowed. "Noticed what?"

"That you're honest."

"Well, honesty is good, isn't it?"

"Indeed. Article six—'Truth upholds the community of Paladin.'"

Metta landed on Kale's right shoulder and Gymn on her left.

"Trouble," she said as the dragons' anxiety penetrated her thoughts. She glanced around the peaceful garden. Toopka stood in the middle of a flower bed, clutching a fistful of prize blossoms. "Oh no!" Kale took two steps forward, then stopped. Gymn's agitation had nothing to do with the child. The minor dragon pinched Kale's shoulder with his rear claws. His sense of danger raged through her mind.

Kale glanced at Bardon to see his eyes riveted upward. Following his gaze, she saw the transparent sphere floating above them, the surface skittered with tiny bursts of lightninglike energy. The air crackled, and the hair on her arms stood up. Trumpets resounded around the perimeter of The Hall compound.

"What is it?" she asked Bardon.

"A threat to the city."

"What?"

"Watch the sphere."

She squinted, keeping her eyes trained on the globe above them. A haze appeared in the center, then cleared. A three-dimensional image formed, showing a formation of dragons in a cloudless sky. This picture disappeared, replaced by an image of an ugly creature. Large black wings canopied over a small body. A myriad of tentacles writhed snakelike out the sides. Clawed legs hung beneath. The beast floated more than flew.

"Attack by air," said Bardon. "Creemoor spiders."

From a distance, she heard troops of Paladin's warriors gathering in their squads. Boots pounded on the walkways. Men shouted orders. House servants scurried past them in a sudden frenzy of activity. A young man dressed in a lehman's uniform rushed up to Bardon, delivered a brief message in a low voice, and darted off.

"We must go." Bardon took her arm and pulled her toward the tower door. "Toopka, come."

The child scurried across the courtyard and flung herself on Bardon's back.

Bardon's hold on Kale's arm tightened. He dragged her through the wooden door. "My orders are to see you to safety."

Dark dragons dotted the sky. Bundles dropped from their backs as they passed over the city. The objects plummeted a distance, then wings opened. The spiders glided in spirals toward the ground.

Kale leaned out the door and looked up. Directly above, a score of Creemoor spiders floated toward The Hall.

"Librettowit!" she protested.

"He's coming. You must get out of the open."

"If there's to be an attack, I can help. Gymn's a healing dragon. We may be needed."

She struggled, but Bardon's strength far outmatched hers. Toopka screamed and pointed out the door.

A spider landed in the gravel pathway to the kitchen gardens. The small stones scattered under the impact of eight shell-hard legs. The spider scuttled forward with almost delicate steps, making a critch-critch noise as the pointed claws kicked gravel. It stood for a moment as if on tiptoes and let out an eerie wheeze. Tentacles waved out from its round body, looking like skinny tongues licking the air.

Two hall guards charged into the garden with lances. The Creemoor lowered its round body to the ground and sprang at one of the guards, wrapping eight legs around the man's body. Hindered by the tentacles lashing out at his spear, the second guard circled with his lance raised until he got an unobstructed opening. He thrust his weapon into the spider's shiny black back. Thick gray fluid spurted out. The hall guard jumped away from the noxious fumes and horrid slime. The creature let go of his first victim and whirled around to attack.

Another guard ran up, pulled his sword, and slashed downward, severing a row of tentacles and three legs. The appendages writhed on the ground. With the soft critching sound of its pointed claws upon the gravel, the spider advanced toward the second guard.

Beyond this terrible skirmish, Kale saw Librettowit running from the mansion just as Bardon tugged at her arm.

"Wait!" She pulled away and ran out the door with her small sword drawn and ready.

A Creemoor spider thumped to the ground before the tumanhofer. Librettowit's sword was longer and heavier than Kale's, but the tumanhofer was only head and shoulders taller than his opponent. He hacked at the beast in front of him. The spider snapped at the tumanhofer. The click-click-click of the pincers plus the critch of its other legs on the gravel path made a muffled drumbeat over the background sounds of battle. Shrieks of terror, the clash of arms, and the grunts of both man and beast came from every direction.

Kale crept up to the Creemoor spider attacking Librettowit and jabbed her sword into the back of the creature's head. Foul-smelling gray liquid squirted over her hand and stung. Despite the pain, she withdrew the sword and thrust repeatedly.

One of the spider's tentacles whipped out and encircled her waist. The moonbeam cape hissed at its touch, and the tentacle jerked away. She sprang to the side to get away from the stench as well as the waving arms of the beast. Gymn and Metta swooped in and spit in the many-eyed face of the spider. Their green and purple saliva blinded the creature. It backed away into rosebushes and became entangled in thorny branches.

"To the tower!" yelled Librettowit.

She turned and saw Bardon combating two more Creemoors. She and Librettowit, along with the dragons, raced to his side. Battling the spiders, they inched toward the open door of Trell Tower. Each time they succeeded in felling a beast, another joined the fray.

Her arms ached, and her hand felt on fire. At least the long tentacles released her as soon as they felt the hissing burn of the moonbeam cape. Once a spider caught Bardon by his foot. Librettowit hacked away the thick tentacle. Twice Librettowit had to be rescued from the grip of a beast.

Turning toward the tower, the tumanhofer saw another attacking spider in his way. He charged forward, swinging his sword.

"One obstacle after another," he grumbled. "This is why I prefer a quiet library!"

They killed three Creemoors in the fierce struggle and made it to the door. Bardon slammed it shut before another onslaught.

"Where's Toopka?" The question wheezed from Kale's throat.

Bardon answered. "I told her to climb to the top of the tower."

"Oh dear," panted Librettowit. He leaned against the wall and struggled to get his words out. "There are eight gateways at the top. If she goes through one, we'll never find her. You two go on. I can't just now."

Kale sprinted to the staircase winding up the sides of the tower. The iron steps rang under her boots. Bardon's footsteps echoed in a rat-tat-tat behind her. Light filtered through narrow windows placed at intervals up the climb. The wall shimmered with an eerie blue glow.

Metta, Gymn, fly ahead and see what Toopka's doing. Keep her out of the gateways.

The minor dragons darted past, ascending the stairwell faster than the two o'rants could. Kale opened her mouth to call out a warning to Toopka to stay away from the gateways, but she had no breath to spare.

Her lungs strained, ready to burst. Her hand burned. The horror of battling Creemoor spiders still sent blood pounding through her veins. She was glad Bardon had been there. If not for him, she and Librettowit would have been torn apart.

Halfway up, she heard breaking glass and Toopka's scream.

7

Poison

Around the next turn of the staircase, Toopka's tiny body hung from the wall. Her open mouth no longer emitted a scream. Beads of sweat and tears rolled down her furry cheeks. Her eyes scrunched so tightly that Kale knew she was alive.

Behind Toopka, a Creemoor spider hissed, only its four-part mouth visible in the narrow window. A snakelike tentacle held the little girl captive.

Hanging on to the outside of the tower, the Creemoor had reached through and nabbed the small doneel. With its tentacle wrapped around her, it could not draw back through the tight opening.

Bardon pushed past Kale and slipped the point of his sword between the window casing and the tentacle. When Kale realized what he was doing, she also jumped to help with her short sword. The Creemoor's grip loosened. Toopka gasped for breath. Kale dropped her sword and caught the doneel just as Bardon severed the tentacle.

Toopka threw her arms around Kale's neck and squeezed, howling in her ear. "Run, Kale, run!"

Kale patted Toopka's back and crooned. "We'll be all right. There's no place to go right now, Toopka. And Bardon is here to take care of us." Kale focused on the child rather than the appendage squirming among shattered bits of glass on the steps.

The stench of Creemoor spider filled her nostrils. Something brushed against her shoulder. Her cape sizzled. With a start, she clambered up the staircase, away from more tentacles worming through the small window.

Bardon hacked at the threatening spider with his blade, methodically lopping off one snaking tentacle after another. With the tip of his sword, he pushed the stinking spider arms over the edge of the staircase toward the center of the tower.

Clawed legs critched against the outside of the tower as the spider shifted its body. A pincer thrust into the building and snapped viciously. With two hands on the hilt of his sword, Bardon raised his weapon and brought it down.

With each slice of the blade, the stink from the beast grew in the close quarters. Kale ducked her nose down against Toopka's furry head. The child now sobbed, her face hidden against Kale's shoulder. She'd let go of Kale's neck and covered her ears with her hands.

The spider hissed. Its hard legs snapped with each movement. Against the outside of the tower, it critched against the stone. Bardon dispatched a second leg, and then the creature fell away. One moment the Creemoor menaced them through the window. The next it was gone.

The stench hung in the air. Kale thought she would faint. Toopka had never felt heavy before. Now her weight made Kale's arm and shoulder sore.

"Go on to the top of the tower," ordered Bardon. "I'll go back down and help Librettowit climb these stairs."

"I'm coming. I'm coming." The tumanhofer's wheezing voice drifted up the metal staircase. His footsteps echoed in a slow cadence. He huffed between phrases as he trudged up the steps. "I'm not as young as I used to be. I never was suited to fights, adventures, quests. I'm a librarian, after all."

Bardon wiped his blade against the sole of his boot. He then pointed the tip toward Kale's dropped weapon. "Pick up your sword, Leecent. Clean the blade. We must hurry."

Holding Toopka in one arm, she bent and stretched out her injured hand to follow his orders. She swallowed hard at the sight of her skin, red and blistered and already oozing pus.

"You've been poisoned!" Bardon came to her side and took Toopka.

"I don't feel anything anymore," she tried to reassure him. "It burned at first, but now it doesn't hurt at all."

"That's bad, not good. Get that green dragon to work quickly before the infection travels up your arm."

Librettowit appeared from around the corner and sat down a few steps below them. He pulled out a large handkerchief and wiped sweat from his reddened face. He frowned up at them. "A Creemoor got her?"

"I'm fine," Kale protested, but her head felt light, and her chest tightened. She tried to take a deep breath, but her lungs refused to expand. A searing pain greeted the effort. She concentrated on breathing in and out, short, quick puffs.

Bardon put Toopka down. The child huddled against the stone wall of the tower. Kale wanted to speak, but her tongue had grown dry and too big for her mouth.

Maybe I don't feel so well after all.

Librettowit, there's something wrong.

The tumanhofer rose quickly and clambered up the last few steps.

"The poison is already past the arm. She's mute." He glared at them all. "Bardon, pick her up before she falls over. Gymn, ride on her chest and see what you can do to help. We must get her through the gateway and to Fenworth."

Bardon sheathed his sword. He scooped Kale into his arms as if she weighed nothing and charged up the metal steps. The clatter of his boots hurt her ears.

Gymn landed on her. His feet bore down as if he were digging his claws into her skin. Kale knew he weighed less than Toopka. The minor dragon wasn't causing the pain. It was the poison.

She felt Gymn's sympathy and concern coming through to her mind, but she couldn't feel the soothing effect he usually had on her nerves. He lay down and stretched out, covering as much of her as he could with his tiny body.

I can't feel it! The panicked thought circled in her brain. *I should be able to feel his healing. He's trying to heal me, and I feel nothing! I can't feel it! I should be able to feel the healing.*

She looked up at Bardon's chin. The muscle in his jaw worked.

She closed her eyes. *Paladin, you said you would be watching out for me. Do you know what's going on?*

Bardon stopped. Kale forced her eyes open and looked around. Without moving her neck, she could see little. Her muscles ached, all except her arm. Her arm felt nothing. Her vision blurred. No, she could see well enough, but the space between her and the walls shimmered in places.

The lehman had carried Kale into the center of a round room. The walls slanted inward to a point above their heads. On the outside, each of The Hall's turrets looked as though it were crowned with an onion, a golden bulb tapering up to a spire pointed heavenward.

The air quivered. Ripples of iridescent colors radiated from the wooden floor to the curving ceiling. Gateways! Side by side, in a ring around the room, there were gateways. How would Librettowit know which one to go through?

Bardon's arms tightened around her.

He's nervous. Why is he nervous? She knew the answer. *He's never been through a gateway. Toopka hasn't either. Is she scared? I've got to tell them it's all right.*

Her lips would not open. Her tongue took up her whole mouth. It was harder to breathe.

Hurry, Librettowit. Hurry!

Kale heard the near hysteria in her plea to the tumanhofer. The top of his cloth hood appeared above the hole in the floor, and he climbed the last few steps with Toopka in his arms. He glanced at Kale with a worried eye but quickly looked away.

I know I'm dying, she told him.

"Not yet, you aren't! Fenworth will have my hide if I don't bring you to him."

Toopka whimpered. Metta landed beside her on Librettowit's shoulder and sang gentle, melodious notes designed to pacify her fears.

It's all right, Toopka. We're almost there.

The little doneel's frightened eyes turned to Kale, and a small smile quivered at the corner of her thin black lips.

Bardon shifted from one foot to the other. His eyes darted around the room, flicking from one gateway to the next, never resting on any of the shimmering spots for more than a second.

It's all right, Bardon. The light clings to you when you walk through, and the air squeezes, but it only takes a second. Take a deep breath first and blow out as soon as you're through.

"You mindspeak!"

He said it out loud. His chin whipped down. His widened eyes met hers.

She tried to smile, but her face would not move. She no longer felt the pain in her shoulders and neck. She could no longer feel Gymn pressing against her heart. Bardon had said no pain was bad, not good.

It's all right, she told him. *Let's go.*

"This way," said Librettowit. He pointed to the floor in front of one of the gateways.

Bardon's mind registered the letter *s* for south, and Kale read his momentary relief that the tumanhofer was not choosing a gateway at random. Then she felt his renewed fear of the unknown as if it were her own. She'd learned much about controlling the influence of others' thoughts and emotions. She'd learned to keep herself protected from an overload of sensations emanating from those around her. The poison sabotaged her efforts to put up the guards.

I don't think I'll make it, Bardon. I'm too weak.

The muscles in his arms tensed. He barked an order. "You will make it, Leecent Kale." Renewed resolve coursed through his body and transferred to Kale.

A sigh of relief caught in her throat. The small choking noise captured Librettowit's attention. He turned back and scowled at them. Without a word, he hastened his departure.

The light in the gateway sparkled as Librettowit stepped into it with Toopka. The shimmering glow clung to them both for a moment, and then he passed through, out of Kale's sight. Metta flew into the portal and disappeared too, in the slow, distorted way Librettowit had.

Bardon took a deep breath, tightened his grip on his burden, and plunged ahead.

Kale saw the explosion of tiny lights around her. The air pressed in all around. She could not breathe.

Only a second. She repeated the words several times. But only a second was a second too long.

8

REGIDOR

Wailing. Long, loud moans. Sobs.

A hiss vibrated in the air. "Sh! Sh! Sh!"

Kale tried to open her eyes. She wanted to protest. *It's not me. I'm not crying. Don't shush. I want to sleep.*

— ⚬ —

Crying. Soft, muffled whines. Sobs.

"Blasted, caterwauling beast! Go for a walk."

Metta sang sweet songs. The melodies soothed Kale's raw nerves.

The bawling subsided to gentle weeping.

— ⚬ —

Shivers racked Kale's body.

"Ah! That's the end of it now. She'll live." Wizard Fenworth's voice crackled next to her ear.

Another blanket covered her shaking body. Kind hands wiped perspiration from her brow.

"Get that sniffling, whining creature out of here!"

She smiled. Fenworth was crotchety indeed.

— ⚬ —

Kale did not want to open her eyes. She knew she could, but it felt wonderful to just lie on the soft cushions.

I'm in Fenworth's castle, and I'm safe.

She could smell the woody fragrance of the walls and floor and ceiling. She'd been in this castle before. A tangle of massive, hollow trees composed the wizard's castle. Large limbs encompassed hallways leading from tree to tree. In each towering tree, rooms stacked one on top of another, each slightly smaller than the one below. Circular stairs carved out of wood spiraled up through each room.

Fenworth owned a world-famous library. More rooms held books than beds. Pillows stuffed in niches and comfortable chairs scattered throughout each room offered abundant places to curl up and read. The beds were either hammocks hanging from the walls or rowboatlike frames made of what looked like gnarled roots. Colorful cushions filled these knobby platforms to the brim.

Kale breathed deeply, relishing the earthy odor and knowing that when she did open her eyes, she was as likely to see a fox or an owl as a person in the room.

Gymn snuggled on the pillow with his chin resting on her shoulder. His healing powers flowed through her. Only a comfortable feeling of laziness kept her in bed. Vaguely wondering how long she'd been ill, she stretched her legs out straight and then rolled onto her side. Gymn shifted with her.

Metta sang. Her voice energized the air in the room. As always, the dragon sang in syllables with no recognizable words. A ripple of music touched Kale as gently as a mother's loving hand. She could imagine the mother she'd never known stroking her cheek, teasing her to awaken.

Even without lyrics, the cheery melodies echoed through her thoughts, taking away some of her lethargy. She pulled her mind out of a pleasant drifting and puzzled over Metta's song.

What is that tune?

She remembered one phrase: *monkey tree.*

And then a few lines:

climbing and jumping and scrambling around.
They flip and flop

and skip and stop,
but ne-ver touch the ground.
Da-dee-da-da
dee-da-dee-da-dee,
orange and purple monkeys in the monkey tree.

What are the words for the da-dee-da-da part?

Kale furrowed her brow and concentrated on her surroundings. Something was not exactly as she expected it to be in Fenworth's domicile. She shifted slightly on the bedding and sighed.

Someone held her hand. Small fingers lightly clasped her palm. Toopka? No, the hand was too big for the tiny doneel and too small to be Librettowit's or Wizard Fenworth's. Too rough to be her friend Leetu Bends's hand. Too scaly to be Bardon. Scaly?

Kale's eyes flew open.

A diminutive creature, a little bigger than Toopka, sat beside her on the bed, peering at her with impatience. His trousered legs were crossed, and his pointy toes wiggled restlessly on his bare feet.

He wore a tan linen shirt, open at the neck and showing a pale blue, scaly chest. His chin jutted out a bit more than an o'rant's, and his wide mouth definitely sported thin reptile lips. His nostrils were slits instead of round holes, and his squarish nose dominated his face. Black oblong pupils slanted across his green eyes, and instead of hairy eyebrows, his face folded in a lizardlike brow. His hairless head and neck were shaped like an o'rant's but were covered with lustrous blue scales without visible ears. He leaned forward at the waist, staring at her.

Out of his toothy mouth, a bass voice rattled from deep within his chest. "She's awake." The creature's delighted cry sounded like it belonged to a blacksmith.

"Regidor?" Kale asked.

"That's me. You've been asleep forever." The childlike words in the voice of a grown man made her laugh.

Gymn and Metta spread their wings and took to the air. They flew into the space above her head and did an acrobatic dance. She listened in on the jumble of excitement in their minds. To her, it was as if they were both speaking at once. Their thoughts bubbled with anticipation. The two tiny dragons zoomed out the open window, intent on telling the others that she was awake.

"Fenworth's mad," said Regidor. "But that's all right. He's always grouchy. Librettowit brought you through the gateway, and Fenworth fixed you. I've been playing with Gymn and Metta. Toopka taught me to play marbles. I taught her the letters I know. I know all of them. She doesn't know how to read yet, and she's old. We're friends now."

"How long have I been asleep?"

"Forever."

"Oh yes, you said that before."

"But now you're awake, and we can be friends. We're going to learn to be wizards together, if Fenworth doesn't throw me to the mordakleeps first."

Kale sat up and looked at Regidor's hand still resting lightly in her own. Four fingers and a thumb. Narrow nails that just missed being claws. *So this is a meech dragon.*

She looked into his friendly, eager face. "Wizard Fenworth won't throw you to the mordakleeps," she assured the young creature. "He doesn't like mordakleeps."

"I know." Regidor shrugged narrow shoulders. "When he says that, I go climb in the branches. Later he makes tea and daggarts. He makes good daggarts. And nordy rolls. I like nordy rolls."

"I don't remember Wizard Fenworth cooking much."

"I know." The dragon shrugged again. "That's because Dar was here. I know all about Dar and the quest for the meech egg. The meech egg was me. And Wizard Risto. Risto is bad. And Librettowit burns things, because he reads instead of stirring. I'm going to learn to cook. I can already make tea. If you bring Fenworth a cup of tea when he's cranky, he says, 'Thank you.' He does it to model good behavior. Librettowit says they have to model good behavior. I have to *do* good behavior but not model it, because there is no one to watch me modeling. Except now maybe I will model good behavior for Toopka."

"You don't have to model good behavior for me." Toopka entered the room and bounced onto the bed, scooting up close to Kale's other side and glaring at the meech dragon. "I have excellent manners for a street urchin. Bardon said so."

Regidor shook his head. "He was just being nice."

"Was not!"

"Was so!

Kale sat up. "Enough foolish arguing."

The two stopped glaring at each other and turned frowning faces to her. For a moment she frowned back at them, not because of their quarreling, but because she had just heard herself sounding exactly like Mistress Meiger, the woman who had overseen her life as a slave.

A light tap on the door drew their attention. Bardon stuck his head around the wooden frame, and when he saw her sitting up, he came in.

"You're looking better." He stopped at the foot of the bed, towering over them. "Are you hungry?"

"Yes!" said Toopka, springing to her feet and dancing among the cushions that made Kale's bed.

Kale and Regidor laughed, but Bardon scowled at the little doneel. "I was speaking to Kale."

Toopka turned her expressive face to Kale. Her ears twitched. "You're hungry too, aren't you? I can go to the kitchen and bring you a tray. There's all sorts of wonderful food in the pantry."

With a gloating smile, Regidor waved a finger at her. "Fenworth told you to stay out of the pantry."

Toopka addressed her adversary, her small fists propped on her hips. "That was to keep me from having too many snacks. Getting food for Kale is different."

Regidor let go of Kale's hand and swung his legs toward the floor. She stared at his tail. It protruded from a slit in his neatly sewn trousers and seemed much too big for the meech dragon's small frame.

With a swish of the awkward tail, Regidor knocked several cushions to the floor as he scooted off the bed. Stepping over them, he headed for the door.

"You'd drop the tray," he said over his shoulder to Toopka. "You're way too puny to carry a big tray. I'll help you."

Toopka scrambled to catch up, sprinting over the covers and leaping off the end of the bed. As they reached the door, she slipped her hand into the meech dragon's. With her head tilted, she grinned at him. "Do you smell nordy rolls too?"

"Yes, and Librettowit said there is parnot jelly in the top cupboard."

"The top? How we gonna get it?"

"You leave that to me. It will take ingenuity."

The two friends turned the corner into the hall.

9

Paladin's Visit

Kale shook her head in disbelief.

A meech dragon is not at all like what I expected.

She noticed Bardon staring at her.

He's as rude as ever!

She tried to think of something to say. Her mind was still too fuzzy to come up with much of anything. *I wish he'd go away.*

She nodded toward the door where Regidor and Toopka had exited. "How old is he?"

Bardon shrugged and stroked his chin with his long fingers. "About five weeks."

"That's incredible!"

"No, typical."

She shook her head. "I used to take care of babies in River Away. Babies do not talk at five weeks. Babies do not walk at five weeks. And he said he taught Toopka her letters."

"He's a meech. It's typical for a meech to mature rapidly."

Kale flopped back on the bed, suddenly exhausted. She let out a moan.

Bardon moved swiftly to the side of the bed and took her hand. "Are you all right? Should I call Gymn and Fenworth?"

She opened her eyes and frowned at him. "No, I just realized I'm supposed to 'guide' Regidor, and he's probably much smarter than I am."

Bardon released her hand as suddenly as he'd grabbed it. "More than 'much smarter.' He's a genius. But he's still just a child. He needs a friend."

"I can't do this, Bardon." She put both hands over her eyes as if she could hide.

"Of *course* you can do it," he barked at her.

The contrast from the more relaxed tone he'd been using shocked her. He sounded like the Bardon who ordered leecents around at The Hall.

Kale dropped her hands and glared at him. "How can you say that? I don't have any training. I was a slave. I don't know anything about anything, and I especially don't know anything about meech dragons."

"Librettowit will help you with knowledge." Bardon paced around the room. "Paladin gave you this job, so you can do it. Wulder will supply the means."

She wanted to argue, but weariness from her illness cloaked her with despair. A tear escaped and rolled down her cheek. She brushed it away, checking to see if Bardon had noticed. Fortunately, he had stopped next to a large knothole window and stared out.

Kale closed her eyes again, hoping she could sleep. She tried to remember what her dreams for the future had been when she lived in River Away as a village slave. Surely it had been something about growing up and getting married and having a home of her own. She remembered wanting a kitten.

Never had she wanted special talents. She never dreamed of walking hundreds of miles to go to the biggest, most important city in the realm. Paladin and Wulder were only names people used in storytelling. Now she'd been to the capital city and a lot of other places as well. She'd met Paladin and experienced Wulder's presence on more than one occasion. She'd met people from each of the seven high races and more creatures from the seven low races than she ever wanted to meet.

Somehow, she was no longer a slave, but a leecent. She had a destiny, which once she thought was thrilling, but now she often thought was uncomfortable. Having Paladin claim you as his own meant you had to deal with grumbly wizards and tumanhofers, hard-nosed lehmans, precocious meech dragons, and street urchins. Being a slave was simpler.

She had no desire to cope with Regidor's needs, Bardon's stiffness, and Toopka's odd perception of right and wrong. Kale was supposed to go to The Hall and train for service to Paladin. Instead, she went on quests, had adventures, got attacked by Creemoor spiders, and ended up in a wizard's castle in The Bogs with too much going on to learn anything!

"Kale?" Bardon's voice interrupted her list of complaints.

"Hmm?" Maybe if she acted as drowsy as she felt, he would go away.

"He was there. Do you remember seeing him?"

She opened her eyes. "Who?"

Bardon whispered the name. "Paladin."

Kale shivered in response to Bardon's reverent tone. In the past, when she'd met Paladin face to face, she, too, had been awed by his presence. "Where?"

"In the gateway."

"That's impossible. A gateway is too narrow. You step in. You step out. There isn't enough room to meet someone."

"He was there."

Bardon turned to look at her, and when she saw his face, she believed him.

Several emotions caught her by surprise. A touch of anger made her clamp her lips together.

Why didn't Paladin wait until I could talk to him? He'd know how much I want to see him again.

Through her nose, she took a deep breath and blew it out slowly.

When I met Paladin, I felt wonderful. Bardon looks worried. She sent him a cross look, but he had turned away again. *What's the matter with him?*

She tried to keep the irritation out of her voice when she spoke. "What happened?"

"He put his hand on my shoulder, and I could breathe. He touched your head, and I could see you were breathing again."

"What did he say?"

"That you would live. That we had work to do."

Kale watched Bardon's face and realized he was laboring to keep that blank mask covering his emotions.

Is he excited? Scared? No, Bardon wouldn't be scared. Maybe nervous, but not frightened.

"Is that all?" she asked.

Bardon sighed. "No."

She waited only a moment. "Well, are you going to tell me?"

"He told me to be courageous. That Wulder is always with us—and some other things just to me."

Kale lay quietly, wondering what she should say.

Bardon cleared his throat. "He said to trust him."

She nodded.

"He said to trust you."

Her eyes grew big, and she smiled.

"Kale?"

His tone of voice wiped the grin from her face. "What?"

"He knew."

"Knew what?"

"That I'm afraid. Not just afraid, right then, of going through the gateway, but afraid of leaving The Hall. Afraid of doing something different from the way I'd planned to spend the next few years."

Kale gasped. "Me too! Oh, Bardon, that's funny!"

"Funny?" His face clouded over, and he gave her a dark look.

"Yes! Don't you see? We're so different, and yet we both are afraid. I sometimes make it sound like I'm angry, but I'm really afraid. Just now I was griping to myself about having to be here instead of at The Hall."

Bardon took several long strides and crossed the space between them. He towered over her with his arms akimbo.

"I'm not a coward," he said. "I don't want you to think that. The mordakleeps and fire-breathing dragons, evil wizards, grawligs, and bisonbecks are foul creatures to be fought. I'm trained to fight. I excel with a sword, spears, and a bow and arrow. I'm not afraid of combat."

She spoke softly. "You're afraid of not being good enough. That's what I'm afraid of. Paladin gave me a job to do, and I'm afraid I'll fail him."

Bardon stared at her for a moment and then nodded in one hard movement. "True."

"He said to be courageous, and Wulder is with us."

Bardon nodded again.

"Maybe we should think of that as 'Be courageous *because* Wulder is here with us.'"

Bardon continued to look at her without speaking, but his face began to relax.

Kale said, "I won't tell if you won't tell."

He frowned.

"That we're afraid," she explained.

Bardon grimaced. "Paladin knows."

Kale plunged ahead with what she wanted to say. "That's all right. And maybe after a while, we'll get as brave as we're pretending to be."

"Maybe."

A crackly voice from the door interrupted them. "Good, then, that's settled." Wizard Fenworth tugged at his beard. He dislodged a tiny bird, and it flew out the window. Fenworth watched it with a puzzled air, then shook himself as if ridding himself of the distraction. He grinned at Bardon and Kale, then rubbed his hands together. "Now we can explore the Creemoor caves and find out who sent those spiders to plague Vendela."

10

RESEARCH

"Research." Librettowit thumped his tankard down on the kitchen table. "That's what's needed for a venture like this. Research, plenty of research and planning."

Kale watched the tumanhofer with interest. She lounged on a sofa in Fenworth's large common room. Metta sprawled on her lap, and Gymn snuggled on her shoulder against her neck. Every once in a while, the small dragon raised his rough chin to rub affectionately against her cheek.

Librettowit's commentary on what he already knew about Creemoor continued. He talked of the wind-sculpted towers above ground and the catacombs carved by underground rivers long gone, the history of desolation, and hungry creatures desperately seeking food and water.

"There's a lot more information needed to aid in this proposed quest." The librarian eyed the dozing wizard. "Caution, prudence."

Librettowit grumbled under his breath, but Kale heard him. "Treachery brews in Creemoor."

He sipped from his tankard and raised his voice. "I'm as eager as anyone to dig out any bit of information. Of course I want to discover who instigated the spider attack on Vendela. But I've a librarian's soul, and I prefer to find out by some means within the strong walls of Fenworth's extensive library."

Librettowit turned his short body on the wooden stool and surveyed the room. Regidor sat on the sofa with Kale, his tail pulled around and into his lap where he fingered the scaly ridges. Toopka had been tucked in for the night in a hammock strung between beams opposite the kitchen end of the common room. Bardon sat in a corner next to book-cases and a branch of bright lightrocks. He was reading a book called *Knights in Service.*

Fenworth snoozed. He sat in a comfortable chair with a yellow light globe suspended in the air over his right shoulder. One hand held a mug, and an open book rested in the other.

Kale watched Librettowit study each of his comrades in turn. She wondered what he was thinking but refrained from reaching into his thoughts. It was bad manners to eavesdrop on private musings. She averted her eyes when the tumanhofer turned his gaze on her, but she still felt a subconscious blush under his scrutiny. She deliberately focused on the homey room.

Pools of cool blue light emanated from lightrocks hanging in fixtures from the wall and sitting on tables. Breezes freely came and went through the open windows, large round holes in the tree walls. The damp air carried the tangy fragrance of swamp flowers. Night birds hailed one another as the moon rose over The Bogs. Kale relished the peace.

Truthfully, I'm siding with Librettowit. I don't want to explore the caves of Creemoor. For one thing, I don't feel strong enough. Gymn's healing has always been quicker than this.

She rubbed her hand. The skin itched.

I wonder if something is wrong this time. It's been hours now since I awoke, and I still feel like I fell out of a treetop. My arm's weak, and it aches.

Librettowit cleared his throat and wagged a finger at the wizard. "Mind you, Fenworth, I am *not* tagging along to be your portable encyclopedia. I'll give you facts, maps, and the probabilities, but I am *not* going with you. I'm a librarian, after all, not a knight or a wizard or an adventurer."

Toopka leaned forward and almost fell out of the hammock. She swung precariously for a moment before her bed settled into a steady rhythm and she could ask her question.

"Who will tell us stories if you don't come along?"

The tumanhofer offered her a fierce growl, but the child just giggled.

He drew his brows together more fiercely. "You're not going either, so it's a moot point."

"Who will sing?" she persisted. "You sing all the old, *old* folk songs. Metta only knows them if she gets them from you. It will be boring without you and Metta singing after supper."

Regidor got up from the sofa. His bulky tail knocked over an end table piled with books. While everyone in the room held their breaths, he sat down beside Librettowit without toppling anything else.

Fenworth harrumphed. Opening one eye, the wizard glared at the mishap. The table righted itself. The spilled books leapt back into neat stacks.

With none of his usual buoyant attitude showing on his face, Regidor studied his folded hands. His shoulders slouched as he sighed heavily.

Librettowit ignored Fenworth and placed a hand over Regidor's. "Don't worry about him. Truth be spoken, you've done the old man a world of good."

Fenworth grumbled something about "old man" and pointedly stuck his nose into the small volume of woodland lore he held.

Librettowit chuckled. "A month ago it would have taken Fenworth fifteen minutes of concentrated effort to recall the backup spell. Now he does it without thinking. All because of you, Regidor." He patted the dragon's hand once more. "You're good for him. Keeping his mind sharp."

"Harrumph!" Fenworth put his mug down and turned a page.

"Am I to be left at home?" asked Regidor. "Do I have to stay with Toopka?"

"You *get* to stay with me, my boy," said Librettowit. "We'll study geography. Maybe do some traveling through the gateways. Learn a bit about our country. Go to a festival or two. Autumn is a good time for traveling—weather's not too bad and lots of harvest galas happening all over the place."

Regidor pouted. "I want to go on the quest."

"Me too!" Toopka rocked her hammock wildly.

Metta and Gymn sat up abruptly and let out a trill. Kale forced herself to concentrate. The dragons' thoughts pushed into her weary mind.

"Celisse?" Kale straightened. The little dragons leapt into the air and flew out the open window into the night.

"Celisse and Merlander!" Kale exclaimed and struggled to her feet. A smile spread across her face as she went to the window and peered out. The limbs of Fenworth's castle obscured some of the sky, but she could see twinkling stars and the moon's soft glow on the towering bog trees.

Kale crowed. "And Dar! Dar's coming too!"

Toopka twisted over the edge of her hammock, dropped to the floor, and trotted across to the window.

"Where? Where is he?" She pulled on Kale's sleeve. "Lift me up. I want to see."

Bending to pick up the child with her stronger arm, Kale shook her head. "You can't see him. He's far away, riding on Merlander. They have to land outside The Bogs, and Dar will walk in."

"The big dragons won't come here? Why not? Is Fenworth mad at them, too?"

Regidor jumped out of his chair, knocking it over, and shouldered his way into a position where he could look out the window. Kale had to step aside.

Bardon looked up. "Bad manners, Regidor."

The dragon muttered, "Excuse me."

He poked his nose out the window and sniffed. "I don't smell anything but The Bogs. I smell sweet mallow vine, water, wet wood, water, and more wet wood. I don't smell any other dragons. Or this Dar person, either."

"He's too far away," said Toopka. "Kale said so."

"Then how does she know he's coming?"

"The little dragons told her," Toopka said, sticking her chin out.

"Yes, that's right," said Kale. "But I can also feel their presence."

"Teach me to do that," demanded Regidor.

"Manners," said Bardon.

Regidor turned to glare at the lehman. "It's a waste of time to put in all those extra words just to sound good."

"If you want to be in service to Paladin, you must follow his example. Article seventeen—'gracious in every word.'"

Exasperated with Bardon's rules, Regidor hissed through thin lips, "Please, teach me to do that!"

"I don't know that I can, Regidor," answered Kale. "It's a talent given to me by Wulder. Leetu Bends taught me how to use it, but Wulder gave the talent to me first."

"How do I know if He gave it to me?"

"Well, close your eyes, then try to reach with your mind to things that are beyond this room."

The meech dragon obediently closed his eyes and stretched his neck out through the window. "I don't think this is working."

"Be quiet. Give it time."

"It's not working."

"You aren't being quiet."

"Do *you* have to be quiet?"

"It works best when I'm quiet."

A moment passed.

"I still don't think it's working."

She clamped her jaw shut, biting back a sharp retort. Regidor was just like the small children she had tended as a village slave. "You have to wait two whole minutes before you can say it's not working again."

Regidor's eyelids wrinkled as he squeezed them tighter. His thin lips clenched in a determined grimace.

Kale gazed out the window with a contented sigh.

Hello, Dar.

"Hi, there. Guess I'm not going to surprise you."

I'm surprised. I'm also glad you're coming, but why?

"We had a battle against an onslaught of Creemoor spiders right after you left. I happened to be in the thick of things and got a medal for bravery. Seems kind of ridiculous to give a fellow a medal for trying to stay alive."

Oh, Dar! That's wonderful. Now they must realize doneels are capable of being warriors. Now they won't be so reluctant to allow you to train at The Hall.

"Actually, I'm not going to continue training there."

But that's what you've wanted for half your lifetime. You told me so yourself.

"Paladin said the medal shows I don't need the training, and he has another job for me. He gave me an honorary commission. You may have to call me 'sir' now."

Kale laughed. *Sir Dar?*

"Exactly."

What is the job?

"Determining the intent of Risto's two henchmen, Burner Stox and Crim Cropper. They've been involved in some mighty peculiar enterprises of late. Maybe even the spider drop on Vendela."

We were there.

"When the spiders attacked?"

Yes, we hadn't gone through the gateway yet. I was poisoned, and it's taking a long time to get well.

There was a pause. "Kale, very few victims of Creemoor spider poison survive."

Paladin helped—and Gymn and Fenworth.

"I'm glad you made it. We're landing now, west of The Bogs. We'll camp tonight, and I'll walk in tomorrow. I can't wait to see you, my friend."

Give Celisse a hug for me. I've already greeted her and Merlander. I wish I could fly out to meet you all.

"I am not going to hug Celisse, but I'll give her a pat and maybe scratch behind her ears."

Kale laughed again. It was going to be good to have him around.

"Mordakleeps!" screeched Regidor.

"Where?" Kale searched the shadowed landscape outside the castle window.

"Not here. There. Where that man Dar is and the two dragons."

Dar! Kale screamed the warning with her mind.

"Mordakleeps!" came the doneel's cry.

Fenworth came out of his chair in one swift, powerful motion and stretched a sinewy arm into the air. "To the rescue!" he shouted, and the room began to spin.

LEFT BEHIND

Beams of light surrounded them, shining brighter and brighter until Kale had to close her eyes and duck her head. Strong winds rushed through the room. Kale put her arm around the meech and pulled him to the floor. She crouched there with Regidor and Toopka.

"Now this is more like it!" shouted Fenworth. "First, off to rescue the doneel, and then on to the caves. Spiders, beware!"

One after another, smells rose around them and then blew away. A flower garden, a bakery, piney woods, and apple cider vinegar.

Fenworth sounded very close. "Did that doneel fellow say he was east or west of The Bogs?"

Kale tried to yell "west," but a rush of wind filled her mouth and stifled her shout.

"West, you say, Kale? I believe you're right. West makes sense. Thank you, my girl. Be good now. We shan't be long."

Librettowit wheezed near her ear. "Let go of me, you confounded wizard."

Fenworth didn't answer him, but a trumpet blew the quick notes of a charge, and the wizard's voice rose above the quacks and brays and oinks of barnyard animals. "Prepare for battle, Bardon!"

"Yes sir," the lehman answered.

His voice sounded muffled. Kale felt as though she was floating in a vast empty space but knew better than to open her eyes. The light still turned her eyelids blood red with its brilliance.

The light began to fade. The force of the wind eased. Normal swamp noises filled the night air. Kale opened her eyes, expecting to be in a field just outside The Bogs.

Beneath her knees, broad planks formed a solid floor. Her body curved over the huddled figures of Toopka and Regidor. She patted their backs and straightened up.

"It's all right now," Kale said, but she glared at her surroundings.

Flames crackled in the fireplace. Bardon's book lay open on the floor. Librettowit's mug still sat on the kitchen table. The wizard's hat was gone from the hook by the door, and so were the three men—Bardon, Librettowit, and Fenworth.

"We've been left behind," said Regidor.

"No!" hollered Toopka. She scrambled onto the windowsill to peer out as if she could see Wizard Fenworth departing with Librettowit and Bardon. "No, no, no! This is my first adventure. Kale, do something!"

"What?"

"Take us there. You're a wizard."

"I'm a wizard without any training. I can't take us anywhere."

Regidor pounded a fist in the palm of his other hand. "Then we'll walk. If Dar could walk in, we can walk out."

"Through The Bogs?" Kale's voice squeaked. "At night? With mordakleeps attacking?"

"I'm not afraid of mordakleeps," said Regidor, planting his fists on his hips.

"Me either." Toopka jumped down to stand beside her friend, mimicking his stance and his obstinate glare. "You chop off their tails, and they die. I'm not afraid."

"Listen to me." Kale stood and faced the two children. "Mordakleeps are dangerous. They don't *let* you chop off their tails. They try to surround you and cut you off from everything. They're fierce and fast and deadly."

Regidor ran to the kitchen and grabbed a meat cleaver. Toopka followed and soon waved a paring knife in front of her tiny figure.

"We'll go without you," she said.

"No, you won't."

Kale brought images to her mind that she suppressed at all other times. Mordakleeps had attacked while she was traveling with Dar and Leetu Bends. She projected to these would-be child warriors the images of dark, oozing creatures looming out of the trees.

Kale remembered black shadows rippling and becoming hideous monsters. Their bloblike heads silently wagged back and forth. As the mass of dreadful shadows became more distinct, she saw that each mordakleep had two thick legs and a thin tail disappearing through the leaf floor of cygnot planking.

The mordakleeps trudged silently toward their victims. Small red eyes glared from gray hollows. Grotesque mouths chomped, and green tongues flicked over sharp, yellow teeth and thin lips.

The mordakleeps' great weight made the cygnot planking undulate like waves on an ocean. Kale waited for a monster to lumber close enough for her to hit. Two more mordakleeps emerged through the cygnot floor. Kale's attention focused on the ugly black slime menacing her. In spite of its size, the monster twisted and turned cleverly.

Along with the hideous vision of the swamp creatures, Kale conjured up her terror and desperation as she and her comrades battled a force much stronger than their own. When she reached the despair she had felt at the end of the struggle, she jerked away from the emotions, cutting short the glimpse of horror she had given Regidor and Toopka.

Toopka clasped Regidor's arm with both hands, her eyes wide with fear. Regidor looked pale but stood straight, clenching his jaw.

Toopka shuddered. "They're bigger than I thought."

Kale opened her arms, and the doneel ran to her. Scooping the little girl up, she hugged her close. "Who told you about mordakleeps?"

"Sittiponder. He's an orphan tumanhofer, and he used to live in the mountains, and he knows all sorts of stories about mordakleeps and grawligs and bisonbecks and all the seven low races and all the seven high races, too. He sits under the wooden steps of an old warehouse near the docks. He'll tell you a story if you bring him something to eat. He's blind."

"Oh dear," said Kale.

"Harrumph," said Regidor, sounding exactly like Fenworth. "Seems you better learn to read so you can tell if his stories are true or not."

"Oh, pooh on your old reading. I don't have to read 'cause you'll read stories to me. It'll save time if only one of us is in charge of finding the best books."

"I won't always be around."

"Why not?"

"I'm going to grow up."

"Well, I'm gonna grow up too."

Regidor shook his head. "I'm going to grow up fast, and you're going to grow up slow. Pretty soon I'll be an adult, and you'll still be a baby."

"That's not true!"

"Yes, it is."

"Can't be. I'm already not a baby."

"You're the one clinging to Kale's neck."

Toopka squirmed out of Kale's arms and plunked herself down on the floor with her fists on her hips. "If we were in Vendela, you'd need me to take care of you. You wouldn't know where to get food or where to sleep or who to avoid to stay out of trouble. You'd be hopeless unless I took you by the hand and led you around."

"Stop!" Kale shouted. "This is foolish arguing. Only fools argue foolishly, and you aren't fools. Not another word out of either of you!"

Another quote directly from Mistress Meiger's lips, but Kale was too agitated to care. She strode across the room and sat down in Fenworth's chair. With her elbows on her knees, she put her chin on her fists.

"I'm going to try to find out what's going on."

Regidor and Toopka followed her. They stood on each side of the armchair, watching her with wide eyes.

"You shouldn't sit there," said the dragon. "Fenworth gets hopping mad if he finds me in his chair."

"Please be quiet," Kale answered. "I'm concentrating."

"What are you concentratin' on?" asked Toopka.

"Dar."

Regidor dropped to the floor and sat crossed-legged by her knee. "Are you mindspeaking?"

"No, just trying to see what they're doing. They're fighting, and they don't need me talking to them." The rapid succession of images she saw in her mind was hard to sort out. Questions from Toopka and Regidor interfered.

"Regidor, close your eyes and see what impressions you pick up. Toopka, be quiet for a bit."

Toopka put her elbows on the arm of the chair and put her chin on her fists, mimicking Kale.

Kale couldn't touch Wizard Fenworth's mind at all. She knew from past experience that he guarded his thoughts with a powerful spell. When she sought Librettowit, she found a mixture of rants against mordakleeps and the wizard. Lehman Bardon's mind was almost devoid of thought, but she could feel energy flowing into decisive moves of combat. He performed with drilled precision. Dar fought from beneath a protective shell, his movements not as regimented as the warrior trained at The Hall.

It was easiest to touch the minds of Metta, Gymn, and Celisse. Metta and Gymn flew in sweeping dives, spitting thick gobs of caustic saliva they used in battle. Each minor dragon became increasingly frustrated as their weapon proved ineffective against the mordakleeps. Celisse, with the minor dragons, fought from the air. Her attitude was ferocious but also cautious. She used her powerful tail to batter the monsters. The dragon Merlander stood beside Dar.

Regidor nudged Kale's knee. "Fenworth is trying a dehydration spell."

"You can mindspeak with the wizard?" Kale focused on the meech dragon's face.

He closed his slanted eyes and pursed his thin lips. He nodded in answer to her question. "It won't work. He wants to cast the spell around each mordakleep's tail and sever the connection with the swamp water. It won't work. It takes too long."

"Can you help him?"

Regidor's expression twitched in annoyance. "No. I don't know how."

His eyes popped open, and he stared at Kale. One word came out of his mouth in a horrified hiss. "Blimmets!"

Kale stood up. Regidor sprang to his feet beside her.

Toopka grabbed Kale's leg below the knee and squeezed as if nothing would pry her loose.

"I can't sense them," Kale said, her voice shrill with fear. "Where are they?"

"Coming to join the fight." Regidor's grim words sent a shiver down Kale's spine.

"Are you sure?" she demanded. "No one controls blimmets. They tunnel through the earth at random and come forth to devour anything alive only when they're hungry. They couldn't have a goal. They're almost mindless."

"They have a goal. It's our friends."

"It's impossible."

Kale didn't want to believe the destructive horde of weasel-like creatures could actually search for victims. She reached out and put a hand on Regidor's shoulder, wanting to give him a shake to make him change his opinion. As soon as her fingers rested on his shoulder, a sensation hit her thoughts with whirling intensity. She saw the squirming mass of dark bodies burrowing rapidly toward the field west of The Bogs. She felt the blimmets' collective desire to consume dragon flesh.

"We have to help. We have to warn Dar and the others."

Kale leaned her head back and screamed. "Wulder, help!" In the same instant, she knew what He expected. Wulder had chosen her to be that help.

"No, no, no." She beat clenched fists against her thighs.

"Open your hand, Kale, and I will hold it."

Kale sucked in a surprised breath. The voice belonged to Paladin.

12

Joining the Battle

"It's up to us," Kale declared.

She looked from Toopka's wide eyes and open mouth to Regidor's serious expression.

"Regidor, tell Fenworth the blimmets are coming."

"How?"

"Mindspeak. You can do it."

Regidor dutifully closed his eyes and scrunched his face into his thinking grimace. A moment later his eyes popped open. "I did it!"

Kale hugged him and then dropped to her knees. She focused on the patch of worn floorboards in front of her and concentrated.

What should we do? If only Dar or Leetu were here.

Kale shook her head in frustration. "We have to think of a way to help."

She looked from Toopka to Regidor. Both shrugged.

"Water," Kale said as a memory struck her. "Fenworth drowned the blimmets when they attacked our camp."

Regidor's face brightened. "There's water in the swamp."

Kale nodded. "We have to figure how to dump it on them."

"Buckets!" said Toopka, bouncing on her toes with excitement.

"Too small," said Regidor.

"Weather," said Kale.

"Weather?" Toopka's and Regidor's voices harmonized, with Regidor's bass almost burying the little doneel's squeal.

"Yes!" Kale clapped her hands together. "Fenworth used a storm."

Regidor ran out of the room. His footsteps rapidly pounded through a hallway and then faded away as he ascended one of the many spiral staircases. Soon the soft tattoo thudded back through the hollow branch corridor, becoming louder as he jumped down the stairs. The meech returned to the common room, holding a huge volume bound in exquisite blue leather and two smaller tomes covered in what looked like moss.

"Weather spells." He huffed as he dropped the heavy books on the short table between the sofa and the armchairs.

He opened one of the smaller volumes and leafed through the pages. Kale bent over the largest, running her finger down a lengthy table of contents. Toopka picked up the smallest and held it against her chest, her thin arms cradling the valuable book.

Tears swam in her eyes. "I can't read," she moaned.

Regidor curled a lip and spoke through clenched teeth. "That one has pictures."

"Oh," said Toopka and clambered onto the nearest chair. She nestled in and reverently opened the small book. "Ooh, pretty. A rainbow."

"Look for something helpful," barked Regidor.

"Dumping water," she muttered, and with a scowl examined the pages.

In the book Kale held, the chapters were in alphabetical order. She thought about turning to "Chapter 3: Clouds," but scanned further down. Hurricanes seemed too big for two apprentices who hadn't even had one lesson from the master wizard. A short chapter, "Lightning," attracted her attention just because it was short. She didn't stop to figure out what "Noisy Weather" might be. "Rain" stood out in bold letters, but a title a few lines down caught her eye.

"Tornado!" Rapidly, she turned the pages, searching for number 549. Toopka slipped off the chair and hopped to her side.

Regidor cheered. "We can suck up water from the swamp and dump it on the blimmets."

"Yes, yes!" Toopka jumped up and down, clapping her furry hands.

Kale found the chapter and began to read. A frown tightened her face.

"I don't understand all of this," she said.

"We don't have to," explained Regidor. "Fenworth says Wulder does all the work anyway. Being a wizard means understanding His creation and working with His universal laws. Fenworth says Wulder has systems for everything, and they always work."

Kale shook her head, not bothering to ask for explanations. She kept reading. Toopka continued to hop beside her. Regidor moved to Kale's other side to peer at the pages. She slowly skimmed the brown words in fancy script, faded by time.

"Here it is," she jabbed her finger at a paragraph beginning with, *Waterspouts are developed by creating a low pressure area over dense moisture and surrounding it with a strong circular wind.*

"The swamps are dense moisture," said Regidor.

"What's a low pressure area?" asked Kale.

"I don't know."

"How do we make circular wind?"

"I don't know."

"Stirring!" said Toopka.

Her toenails clicked on the old wooden floor as she ran to the kitchen table. She brought back Librettowit's abandoned tankard with a spoon and placed them on the table in front of Regidor.

"Stir!" she commanded.

Regidor grabbed the spoon and whirled it through the creamy white liquid. The sweet smell of mallow rose from the tankard.

Toopka climbed on the table and knelt, her head bent, nearly touching Regidor's.

"See," she said. "The middle is low, and the mallowsap is going round and round."

Regidor nodded. "But I don't see how this is going to help."

"Just concentrate," said Kale. "Imagine the wind going round and round over the swamp, just like the mallowsap in the cup."

Toopka closed her eyes along with Kale and Regidor. In just a moment, Kale felt a burst of energy tingle along her spine. She opened her eyes to see Regidor's eyes blink rapidly as if he had just felt something truly startling.

"Something happened," he said.

Kale nodded, hoping he wouldn't ask *what* happened, because she wasn't sure.

She looked around the room. Everything seemed normal, from the glowing lightrocks to the small fire in the hearth.

"What do we do now?" Regidor asked.

Kale rubbed her sweaty palms over her breeches. "See if you can pick up from Fenworth's mind what's going on there. I'll concentrate on the dragons."

She reached with her mind to Gymn and found him hiding under a bush. Terror shook his little frame in fierce tremors, but it wasn't the mordakleeps causing him to cower. A violent wind had plucked him from the sky and hurled him to the ground. Metta, too, sought refuge. She burrowed into the soft wood of a fallen log. Celisse flew rapidly away from the storm, climbing higher and higher, seeking safety.

"Oh no," gasped Kale.

Regidor cast her an uneasy glance. "Fenworth is still concentrating on that dehydration spell."

"Where are the blimmets?"

"Close, but they haven't broken to the surface yet."

"The winds are battering our friends." Kale wrung her hands. "We didn't think of that. The storm will kill the blimmets, but it might hurt Fenworth and everybody else."

Regidor squinted as if he could see something far away. "The tornado is moving slowly, slower than the blimmets."

"How do you know?"

Regidor shrugged his thin shoulders. "I can feel it. I can sense the movement of the blimmets, the commotion at the battlefield, and the tornado's path."

"What's gonna happen?" Toopka squealed, bouncing on her toes and flapping her hands in front of her.

Regidor answered, "Tornadoes travel across the countryside and wipe out what's in front of them." He frowned at Kale. "Maybe we could stop it."

Toopka wailed. "But we were gonna drop the water on the blimmets."

"We can't do both," said Kale. "We can't drown the blimmets without hurting our friends."

13

ANOTHER PLAN

Kale ran her fingers through her hair, grabbing hold and pulling as if she could yank the answer out of her head.

"We have to get the water above the blimmets. If the tornado's above them, maybe the wind won't blow everyone to smithereens."

"How? How? How?" Toopka hopped with each word.

"Stop jumping," barked Regidor.

"Jumping!" said Kale. "Regidor, imagine the tornado jumping! Hopping in the air, like Toopka." She clamped her hands on his shoulders and gave him a shake. "Think of the tornado jumping into the air over the field and hold that thought. Hold the tornado in the air."

Kale grabbed on to the image with her mind. As soon as she touched the energy of the storm, she knew it had already weakened. Their skills were not developed, and their minds certainly were not disciplined for such a tremendous task.

"Oh, Wulder, help."

Regidor squeezed her arm. His clawlike fingernails pricked her flesh. His voice came out in a gravelly whisper. "The tornado is above the field. The blimmets are almost directly below and tunneling upward."

"Hold the tornado," begged Kale. She felt the energy of the whirling storm seeping away from her. "We have to control the tornado. Wait until the blimmets break the surface, then release it." She moaned. "It's falling apart, unraveling."

"Hold it, Kale! The blimmets are almost to the top."

"It's weakening. I can't."

"Just a few more seconds."

Kale begged Wulder to take over. *I can't do it. I'm not strong enough. Wulder, I can't.*

"Now!" screamed Regidor.

Kale collapsed on the floor and felt the tornado give way to a cloudburst.

"What's happening?" cried Toopka.

Regidor gave a hoot of triumph. "The blimmets are drowning. As they come out of the dirt, they get hit full in the face with water, tons of it."

"Tons?"

"Well, maybe not tons." He looked at the tiny doneel with annoyance, and then his face relaxed into a jubilant grin. He grabbed Toopka and whirled her around the room, dancing a jig and hollering. His long tail knocked over smaller furniture, but the clatter only added to the joyful noise.

Kale took deep breaths and scooted to sit with her back against Fenworth's chair. She reached with her mind and checked each of her comrades. Everyone was drenched but healthy. She even touched Fenworth, reassuring herself that he was alive, even though she could not delve into his thoughts.

They're safe. Thank You, Wulder.

A frisson of fear gave her goose bumps.

"Regidor?"

The dragon skipped to her side and plopped down on the floor, sitting in his favorite position with his legs crossed.

"We did it, Kale."

She shook her head. "Where are the mordakleeps?"

Regidor closed his eyes, and a puzzled expression wrinkled his scaly brow.

"They're strong. Stronger than before. The hurt ones are well again. Uncut, unbruised."

Kale dropped her head into her hands. Not wanting to listen, she slid her palms over her ears. She still heard Regidor's deep voice.

"Everything is wet and *that* helps *them*. Fenworth is still working on the dehydration spell. It's almost finished, and he's going to cast it around their tails, one by one."

Regidor grabbed Kale's hand and pulled it away from her ear. "Listen, Kale. Fenworth knows we brought the rain. Listen, he's mindspeaking to both of us."

She inclined her head and heard the wizard's crackling voice.

"Clever, that was. Unasked for, of course. Unneeded, for sure. But good thinking on your part if not exactly thought through. Now, children, let's see if you can follow directions. I doubt it, but we'll try. I'm altering this dehydration spell. Tricky business, throwing in a switcheroo at the last moment. But I'm a wizard, you know. Quite experienced at adaptation.

"Now listen carefully, my inexperienced but worthy apprentices. Think of each of us here. Not the mordakleeps, of course. Not the blimmets, either, come to think of it. But us! Think wet on the inside, dry on the outside. Normal in and out. Got that?"

Both apprentice wizards nodded as if the old man stood beside them.

"We can help, Kale." Regidor squirmed closer to her side and threw his arm around her shoulders. "Fenworth says we can help."

"Me too," said Toopka and flung herself into Kale's lap.

"Here goes," said Regidor, his voice rising in excitement. "He's going to release it."

"Are we helping?" squealed Toopka.

"Yes!" shouted Kale and Regidor in unison.

Kale squeezed Toopka's hand gently. "It's kind of like mindspeaking. We're all connected, and Wulder's part of it too. He's the biggest part. Do you feel it, Toopka?"

Before she could answer, a shiver zinged through the three huddled on the floor. With their arms around each other, the power sprang from one body to the next, linking them as it sped several times in a circle. Exhilaration filled Kale as the intensity ebbed away.

"He did it!" cried Regidor. "He dried up everything. The rain, the field, their clothes. The mordakleeps are dying."

"Why?" asked Toopka. "Did he cut off their tails?"

"No. Their tails are shriveling and breaking off. The water's all gone, and their tails have to be in water because mordakleeps have gills and breathe like fish. The gills are in the tails, but now the tails are on dry land. Oh yuck! Dead mordakleeps kind of drip into the ground." He wrinkled his long squarish nose. "Their bodies lose their shape and dissolve into a mass of icky goo when they die."

A giggle escaped Kale's throat. A tear ran down her cheek. She remembered the last time she'd battled mordakleeps. The slimy creatures oozed into the forest floor, leaving noxious fumes behind.

Giddiness followed relief. Kale leaned her head back on the seat of Fenworth's chair and laughed. Soon Regidor and Toopka joined her with wild cackling and hiccupped giggles. Kale tried to stand, but laughter weakened her knees. She collapsed in the big chair and wiped tears from her eyes. Toopka and Regidor rolled on the floor around her.

"Harrumph!" Wizard Fenworth stood in the door. His dry hair stood out wildly around his head. He clutched his hat in his hand and shook it at them. Minnows flew all over the room and flopped around wherever they landed. Fenworth frowned at the wiggling mess, waved his hand about in a distracted manner, and the tiny fish disappeared.

The old wizard refocused on the three youngsters, glaring fiercely. He started to shake his hat again, thought better of it, and instead shook the crooked branch he carried in the other hand.

"That's my chair, and I have need of it. Away with you. What are you doing up? Sleep. No one sleeps at a decent hour anymore." He stomped a foot. "I'll have discipline from those under my care. An apprentice should show respect. Two apprentices should show twice as much respect. Out of my chair. Away to bed with all of you. You'd think this was a holiday."

Kale heard Librettowit muttering behind Fenworth. The tumanhofer shoved the wizard unceremoniously to the side and forced his way into the room. Dar and Bardon followed, stopping to remove their boots caked with dried mud.

"Tut-tut, oh dear." Fenworth peered into his hat, shook dried leaves from the crown, and placed it on the hook by the entryway. A couple of mice dropped from his cloak and scampered out the open door. "We've company here and more coming."

"Who's coming?" asked Toopka.

The wizard growled, glared at the child, and pointed his bony finger her way. Toopka's small frame rose into the air and floated across the room, landing in the hammock she called her bed.

"Tut-tut. Tomorrow, child, tomorrow."

The lights went out, and Kale found herself in her own bed with the cover tucked around her.

How did I get here? Fenworth! I'll never sleep. I'm too excited. I want to talk to Dar. I even want to hear what Bardon has to say about the battle with the mordakleeps.

In the background, she heard Toopka. "We didn't get a bedtime snack."

Regidor's voice rumbled from some distance away. "You ate before you went to bed the first time."

"But this is the second time. We didn't have a second bedtime snack to go with the second bedtime."

"I'll fix you a second bedtime snack in the morning. You can have it for breakfast."

"Promise?"

"Promise."

Kale smiled and rolled over. She closed her tired eyes. They were suddenly too heavy to hold open. The adventure seemed like something from a book. But no, it was real. She and Regidor had done something spectacular.

It's a shame I don't know how we did it.

She rolled over and pulled the blanket up to her chin.

"I didn't even get to say hello to Dar," she grumbled and promptly fell asleep.

14

LESSON ONE

"Time!" Wizard Fenworth entered the room lined with bookcases and stood with his hands folded over his beard.

Just minutes before, the wizard had hushed their excited chatter and banished them to a library.

"Lessons first," he'd said, quelling their desire to go over the spine-tingling details of the night before.

All the occupants of the room raised their heads from the books they held and stared at Fenworth. Librettowit looked annoyed. Excitement quickly registered on Toopka's and Regidor's faces, a bit of wariness on Dar's and Bardon's. Kale tried to touch the wizard's mind to see if she could pick up a clue as to what he meant.

"Tut-tut, Kale." He shook his head at her.

She looked down, slightly embarrassed but unrepentant. *He's not really mad at me.*

She heard his distinctive chuckle in her mind and looked up to see him wink in her direction. She smiled back.

Fenworth clapped his hands together and then rubbed them together vigorously. "What do you say? Shall we begin?"

Librettowit cleared his throat. "That depends, Fenworth. What is it you propose to begin? Preparations for noonmeal? A quest? The laundry? Research into the geographical structure of Mount Kordenavis?"

The wizard frowned. "At times, Wit, you are entirely too frivolous for a librarian. I refer to the apprenticeship, of course."

"Of course." The tumanhofer nodded and returned his attention to his book.

"Kale, Regidor, come." The wizard grabbed the edge of his cloak and swirled it around him, turning in place. "Toopka and Bardon, you may accompany us."

Toopka sprang to her feet, tossing her small book on the table in front of Regidor.

Bardon slowly stood. "I'm not a prospect for wizardry, sir. I've no talent."

"No sense?"

"No sir. I said no talent."

"No talent! No sense! Nonsense. Come, my boy. You may observe."

Bardon closed his book, *Knights in Service,* and placed it carefully on Librettowit's table.

"On your feet, Kale, Regidor. We depart."

They followed Wizard Fenworth onto the wide branches serving as walkways around his tree castle. They had to trot to keep up with the old man's long, purposeful stride. He led them to the front door and into the common room.

Kale leaned against the doorjamb and watched Fenworth, Toopka, Bardon, and Regidor. Bardon had immediately settled in one of the chairs in the sitting area. Regidor balanced on his toes, his attention riveted on the wizard. The wizard stood next to the worn kitchen table, patting his long beard. Toopka hopped onto a three-legged stool, put her elbows on the table and her chin in her hands. Her eyes were glued to the old wizard. Clearly, she thought this would be more interesting than Regidor's lessons on reading.

"Regidor," Fenworth commanded, "get us a bowl big enough to put our little doneel in."

Toopka's eyes widened, and she sat up straight, placing her hands demurely in her lap.

"Our first lesson in wizardry"—Fenworth looked purposely at Regidor and then at Kale—"will be transforming existing material supplied by Wulder into a different form."

Toopka slid off her seat and edged toward the door.

"Stay, my little Toopka." Fenworth bestowed upon her his most charming smile. "You will be needed."

Toopka shook her head warily. "Librettowit's gonna help me write my letters."

"You told Regidor at breakfast you had learned them all."

Toopka gulped, took a step closer to the door, and nodded. "All the capitals." Her bobbing head stopped midmotion and became side-to-side denial. "I'm not doing very well with the small ones."

Fenworth gestured for her to return to her seat. "Time enough for that later. You'll learn a bit here, being in the thick of things."

Fenworth perched on a high wooden stool and folded his arms into the sleeves of his loose silken robe. His face twitched in annoyance, and he brought out one hand. A gray mouse dangled by its tail from his long fingers. He leaned over, set the animal on the floor, and waved his hand in a wide circle over the cowering creature. "Begone!"

The mouse scurried away.

Fenworth resumed his posture on the stool, with his arms crossed and hidden in his robe. The color of the fabric shifted from red to orange to purple and settled in a blue darker than the evening sky. A myriad of twinkling stars dotted the robe. A few pinpoints of light dusted his shoulders, but as the material flowed to the ground, the stardust grew more dense until the hem glowed brightly with starshine.

"We will need," said the wizard in solemn tones, "the fine powder ground from the annual grasses of the class of Triticum. And three ova of *Gallus domesticus.*"

Regidor narrowed his eyes. "We need flour and three eggs."

Kale listened as Fenworth gave convoluted instructions and watched Regidor assemble the ingredients for an ordinary cake. She had seen women in River Away bake just such a cake.

Sighing, she relaxed against the frame of the door and let her gaze roam the room. Bardon soon picked up a book and didn't even pretend to be interested in the cooking class. Regidor nodded seriously at Fenworth when given instructions, then winked at the doneel child at every chance. Kale moved quietly into the room and sat beside Toopka.

"He was just fooling." Toopka gave her a toothy grin. "I'm not going to be part of the cake."

Kale nodded. She couldn't see that this baking had any wizardry to it. She watched all the more carefully to see how Wizard Fenworth might surprise them with a twist of magic in the making of one two-layered round cake. Nothing but the extravagant names he gave for ordinary baking powder, butter, sugar, and vanilla was any different from the way any marione mistress put together a cake for Sunday dinner.

While the cake baked in the old oven, Kale, Toopka, Wizard Fenworth, and Regidor sat around the table playing benders.

Toopka's cards kept falling out of her hands. Regidor patiently helped her sort them and get them back in order.

"She's won," he said as he again helped rearrange her hand. "She has each of the seven high races and two wizards."

"Two wizards, you say?" Fenworth rubbed the beard at his chin. "An excess. One wizard suffices for almost any task. Kale, take the cakes out and let them cool."

The wizard rose from the table and put the cards back on the shelf. Standing over the cakes, he rubbed his hands together.

"Shall we have mallow or cream frosting?"

"Chocolate!" squealed Toopka.

"Very well." He went over and sat in his large cushioned chair, nodding to Dar and Librettowit as they entered. "Dar, be a good fellow and teach them how to make frosting."

Soon the wizard was snoring as the group around the table measured and stirred.

"Do we get to eat it when we finish?" asked Toopka.

"Of course we do," said Regidor.

Librettowit shook his head. "Maybe not."

Both Toopka and Regidor stopped to stare at the tumanhofer, disbelief written clearly on their young faces.

Librettowit cleared his throat. "Remember Fenworth said we had company and more company coming. He could intend this for our guests when they arrive."

Toopka leaned across the table, eyes bright and a grin touching her black lips. "Who's coming?"

Librettowit cast a sidelong glance at the sleeping wizard and lowered his voice. "He hasn't said, but it stands to reason that if you're about to embark on a dangerous quest, Paladin would send warriors."

Bardon dropped his book in his lap and sat up with a jerk.

Fenworth's snores ceased abruptly. Without opening his eyes, he spoke. "Supposition. What need have we of Paladin's warriors? We have a wizard, two apprentice wizards, two strong, able men, and a librarian."

"Not me," objected Librettowit loudly. "Count me out. I'm staying with the books and the comfort of home. I'm not going questing."

Kale remembered the fiasco of their attempt to create and control a tornado. The creating part had gone all right, but nothing afterward had gone as planned. "Pardon me, Wizard Fenworth, but I think your two apprentices are inexperienced."

"Nonsense!" Fenworth stood, stretched, and turned to the table. He came across the room and stood, patting his beard. "Tut-tut, you have no confidence in yourselves. You've already had your first lesson in wizardry."

Toopka's face folded into a fierce scowl. "Baking a cake is wizardry?"

"Oh dear, oh dear, I see you don't fully comprehend."

"It's just a cake," said Toopka. Her words directly reflected Kale's thoughts.

"Harrumph. Toopka, when you turn and look at the counter, what do you say then, dear little doneel?"

All eyes shifted to the plain wooden counter along the kitchen wall. There sat another cake, the exact duplicate of the one they had just made.

Fenworth's eyes twinkled as he watched the expressions on their faces. "And then there's the cake on the table in front of Bardon."

Again, everyone in the room turned as one to see a third cake, which had appeared out of nowhere.

Regidor harrumphed. "That still doesn't mean Kale and I can make cakes appear all around the room."

"It doesn't?" Fenworth tilted his gray head to one side as if considering the matter. He stood that way for almost a minute, long enough for a vine to shoot out a tendril from his beard. "Are you sure, Regidor?" He considered the young meech dragon. "Have you tried?"

Regidor's eyes narrowed in suspicion. He shook his head slowly.

Fenworth clapped his hands together, a smile breaking across his wrinkled face. "That does it, then. You must try. Tut-tut. Can't say you can't until you've tried. Kale, come here and stand next to Regidor."

Kale hurried across the room and stood shoulder to shoulder with her fellow apprentice.

Now he's going to teach us! She grinned at Dar across the room.

"Close your eyes, both of you," commanded Fenworth. "Picture in your mind the milk and eggs being stirred into the flour and baking powder.

"A batter forms. Since this is one of Wulder's principles, there is nothing you can do to stop this particular combination from turning into cake batter."

Kale heard Bardon come to stand behind her. She inhaled the citrus smell of another o'rant. All her people carried the same tart fragrance.

Do all my people have an innate ability to perform wizardry? Could Bardon be an apprentice too?

"Tut-tut, your mind is wandering, Kale."

Kale squelched the annoyance she felt. Bardon's presence had distracted her. She paid strict attention to Wizard Fenworth's deep, rough voice.

"Imagine pouring the mixture into pans and placing them in the oven. Yes, yes, that's right. The heat causes the batter to rise and solidify, another handy edict from Wulder.

"Think, think, children. What comes next? Oh dear, oh dear, don't jump ahead to the frosting, Regidor. Cool your cake."

Kale heard Bardon expel a breath of air and felt the hair on the back of her head stir.

I will not *let that bothersome lehman get me in trouble. I* will *pay attention to my teacher.*

"Wizardry is all a matter of appreciating Wulder's creation, taking the time to understand the intricacies of the universe and then applying that knowledge. Quite simple, really.

"Slowly, slowly, step by step. Wulder has established what will go together and what will not. You are merely following His directions."

Toopka's high-pitched squeal pierced the room. "Oh! Look! Look!"

Kale opened her eyes. Two more cakes sat on the table beside the first.

"Excellent!" Fenworth beamed and clapped his hands. "Enough wizard's cake for company, I should say. Unless Paladin sends us more than one urohm."

15

The Company
Assembles

The guests did not arrive that evening, which meant the cakes could not be eaten. Fenworth finally relented and cut one cake into nine small pieces. The eighth piece was shared by Metta and Gymn. The ninth piece was given to a big blackbird named Thorpendipity, who landed on the windowsill when Fenworth whistled.

Toopka went to bed grumbling over the cakes going stale and woke up with a bad stomachache. A second cake had disappeared during the night, with only a few crumbs left to testify to its former existence. Those crumbs dotted Toopka's bed covers.

The only ones awake to witness the little doneel's suffering were Dar, Kale, and the minor dragons. Dar shook his head and put a small copper teakettle on the old stove.

"We'll scold you," Kale said, "after you're well enough to listen. I've got something Granny Noon gave me. It'll make you feel better."

"I won't *ever* eat a whole cake again," promised Toopka. "I won't *ever* eat *anything* again."

Gymn curled up on Toopka's shoulder while Kale fetched the moonbeam cape and spread it out on the kitchen table. She reached into a hollow and handed a packet of dried, pink leaves to Dar to brew.

"Something is wrong," she muttered, running a hand over the front pockets. Six of them held unhatched dragon eggs.

Toopka groaned loudly. Kale ignored her and took out the eggs, one by one, placing them carefully on the inside folds of the cape. The sight of the eggs struck awe in Kale's heart. Paladin had charged her to tend the unborn dragons and raise them once hatched. She'd even been called the Dragon Keeper. The responsibility seemed too enormous for a former slave girl.

The fourth pocket held a stone, not an egg. When Kale saw the irregular shape and dark gray color, she dropped the offending rock on the table and moved on to the last two pockets. In only a few seconds, Kale looked with dismay at the row of eggs. She had five dragon eggs and one smooth stone.

Toopka's groaning subsided to a whimper.

Dar came to stand beside Kale, putting a comforting hand on her stiff arm. "Nothing can be stolen from a moonbeam cape. Did you move the egg?"

Kale shook her head slowly.

"Then the only way it could have been taken is if you allowed someone to ride within the cape, and that someone took the egg."

Toopka's noise ended abruptly.

Dar and Kale both turned to look at the forlorn figure huddled beneath a light blanket in her hammock.

Kale took a step toward the doneel child. The little girl's ears perked upright on top of her furry head, and she dove beneath the covers.

"Toopka and I," said Kale as she continued walking, Dar beside her, "went for a walk several days ago. It began to rain, and Toopka rode back under my cape."

Dar put his hand on the blanket and tugged, but Toopka held fast from underneath.

"I'm sick," she wailed.

Dar growled. "Because you got up in the middle of the night and stole a whole cake, it seems you are still a common street thief."

"I didn't steal the egg." The muffled protest quivered.

"Then where is it?"

"I just wanted to see a baby dragon hatch. I didn't mean any harm."

Kale patted the trembling hump of blanket. "The egg has to quicken before it begins the hatching process."

Toopka's eyes appeared at the edge of the covering. They were big and full of wonder. "It quickened."

Kale stifled a moan. Paladin had trusted her with the eggs. If this egg quickened under the warmth of Toopka's body, who would the egg bond to? Kale could only imagine the kind of mischief Toopka and a young dragon could instigate.

Dreading the answer, Kale asked, "Who quickened the egg, Toopka?"

"You did."

"Me?"

"Yes, it's under your pillow."

With a flutter of leathery wings, Gymn and Metta raced out of the room.

Toopka sniffed and ducked her head. "I thought you'd be mad at me if I held it until it quickened. I was right, wasn't I? But you're mad anyway, so I guess all that figuring out how to do it without getting into trouble didn't work. I won't bother figuring next time."

"There better not be a next time," warned Kale. "Why didn't I feel the egg?"

"Because I put it under your pillow after you went to sleep and took it out before you woke up. Only last night, when I came back in here, I saw the cakes on the counter, and I was just going to have one piece, but it was so good."

"And this morning," said Dar with a shake of his finger, "you were too sick to retrieve the egg."

The chittering of excited minor dragons interrupted Dar's lecture. Gymn entered the room doing aerobatics accompanied by wild, shrill whistles. Metta followed more sedately. Her wings whooshed the air in a steady rhythm. Between her front legs she held the missing egg.

Kale stretched out a hand. Metta landed on her wrist and placed the egg in her upturned palm. For a moment the egg lay cool against her skin, then it began to warm. A slight tingle raced up Kale's arm, and in her hand, the egg began a gentle thrum.

Metta scampered to Kale's shoulder, singing a song of joy in her soft, cooing voice.

Kale smiled. *Yes, the egg has quickened. And it already connects to me. I can feel its life.*

She rummaged through a hollow in her cape and came up with the same red pouch Mistress Meiger had given her to carry the first dragon egg she'd found. She slipped the egg into the safety of the soft cloth and hung it around her neck by the leather thong. She tucked it under her blouse.

"Attention! Attention!" Wizard Fenworth's voice boomed from behind his bedroom door. "Does no one around here pay attention to details? We could be surrounded by the enemy, overwhelmed by evil, blasted to smithereens by ravagers of utmost depravity. Attention to your surroundings, that's what's needed. We could be undone!"

Bardon, Regidor, and Librettowit barreled into the room from one of the corridors just as Fenworth's door banged open.

A frisson of apprehension raised bumps on Kale's arms and shivered her spine. She looked around the room at the faces of her companions. Bardon glared, his hand on the hilt of his sword. Librettowit looked annoyed. Regidor had a silly grin on his face. Dar scowled, and Toopka dove beneath the covers again.

A knock brought all eyes to the massive front door.

"See?" Fenworth whispered. "Didn't I tell you?"

Bardon drew his sword and approached from one side of the room as Dar armed himself with two bejeweled daggers and came at the door from the other side.

Kale reached with her mind to discern who stood on the other side. She gave an exclamation of surprise. "It's Leetu Bends and Lee Ark!"

Librettowit threw the old wizard a look of disgust.

Fenworth bristled, shaking his robes around him and clasping his beard. "I never said the enemy was here. I merely noted that no one was on guard. Our guests have arrived, and they very well could have been a troop of bisonbecks. Intentional attention to detail is essential in all quests. All quests at all times!" He raised his eyebrows and looked down his nose at the occupants of his common room. "Someone open the door."

Librettowit stomped across the wood floor and threw open the door.

"Greetings," he said and promptly stepped aside to allow the two soldiers of Paladin's forces to come in.

Lee Ark entered the room with Leetu following. His brown uniform covered a short, bulky body typical of the marione race. His forthright stride proclaimed power of muscle and confidence in leadership.

Leetu's slight feminine form was likewise clothed in the earth tones of Paladin's army. Kale hoped she would have the chance for a long talk with the young woman who had guided her through the initial stages of her last quest. She counted Leetu as a real friend.

I'm glad you're here. Kale spoke directly to Leetu's mind.

Without an outward flicker of acknowledgment, the emerlindian answered. *"Friend, we have another adventure ahead of us. Paladin issued a call for warriors and for you in particular."*

Kale nodded and carefully watched her comrades from the previous quest.

Both the officers were of the same height, yet Lee Ark embodied tension and a lethal force waiting to be unleashed. Leetu displayed grace and tranquility.

They answered Bardon's salute with a tap of a fist to the chest, Lee Ark's sharp and Leetu's casual.

"Welcome to my castle." Wizard Fenworth stepped forward and clasped both of Lee Ark's arms at the elbows. Lee Ark grasped the wizard's lean forearms.

"I bring urgent news," he said.

Fenworth nodded. "Yes, yes. Urgent, deadly, insidious. The world is in peril, and we must rise against evil." The old wizard released the general and patted him on the shoulder. "Tea and cake first, don't you think?"

16

WIZARDRY LESSON TWO

"Now, the universe, children, is made entirely out of three things." Fenworth dusted crumbs from his beard and dislodged a lizard. The creature grabbed a chunk of leftover dessert and darted under the wizard's chair. Ignoring the skittering reptile, Fenworth looked around the table where the members of the quest had assembled for tea and cake.

"Three things so small that they cannot be seen by the eye of anyone but Wulder."

Librettowit nodded in agreement and sipped his tea.

The wizard closed one eye and stared with the other at a point above the empty cake platter. A cloud of green mist formed, hovering over the middle of the large wooden table. Its color faded to white, and then an image became clear as wisps of cloud drifted away.

Kale watched the translucent, three-dimensional picture of a bowl tilt slightly so they could all see the creamy batter within.

"Harrumph." Fenworth cleared his throat and patted his beard. "This is batter for pancakes."

Toopka licked her lips.

"Add three eggs," said Fenworth. Three eggs floated into the image, tapped on the side of the bowl, and emptied with a plop, plop, plop into the batter. The shells disappeared. A wooden spoon stirred. "And now you have batter for crepes."

The spoon lifted and thin batter dripped into the bowl.

"Add flour," said Fenworth. Two glass cups of flour appeared over the bowl and dumped their white powdery contents into the batter. The spoon stirred. "And you have cake batter. Add more, and you have dough for daggarts." Another measuring cup came barreling out of nowhere and jettisoned flour into the bowl. The moment the glass cup was empty, it shattered, but the smithereens vanished into nothing.

Fenworth cleared his throat. "You see how changing the amounts of the ingredients changes the substance?"

Kale nodded her head but had no idea how this related to the three very small things Fenworth said made everything in the universe.

"Wulder took three ingredients and made the world," continued the wizard. "Of course, He also created the three ingredients. One is ozoic, the second is azoic, and the third is ezoic."

The picture above them changed to three round dots, one red, one blue, and the other white.

"In the first element we will examine, we have one ozoic and one azoic."

The bowl reappeared, and the red dot and blue dot fell into it much as the eggs had.

Except he didn't crack them on the edge. Kale suppressed a giggle.

"Don't let your mind wander, Kale," the wizard's voice entered her thoughts, reprimanding her.

Yes sir.

The bowl disappeared, leaving the two colored dots suspended in midair, clinging to one another. The white dot circled the pair.

Librettowit looked up from his mug. "A simple substance. Same three ingredients which make up all substances, only in different combinations. A wizard, with the right knowledge, can call together ozoics, azoics, and ezoics."

Fenworth harrumphed and glared at the librarian. "My lecture, I believe, Wit." He patted his beard and a slew of dots shot out from the grizzly curls to join the picture above the table.

"When a *wizard*," Fenworth cocked an eyebrow at Librettowit and continued, "places these zoics in close proximity with each other, they assume the positions that Wulder has ordained and become the substance they are meant to be."

Dar slurped his tea and ignored Leetu's frown at his manners. "Only Wulder can create the primary ingredients."

"Of course!" The wizard nodded. "And they can only be combined in a mode prescribed by Wulder. A wizard is only as great as his understanding of the complexity of Wulder's established order. Within those parameters, a wizard can do almost anything."

He heaved a melancholy sigh and shook his head. His shoulders drooped. His gaze lowered from the busy image hanging over the table to the empty plates and scattered crumbs.

"Where Risto and his comrades have gone astray," Fenworth said, "is in the belief that they can create primary ingredients. And that they have no need of following Wulder's dictums."

Kale forgot the swirling dots above the table and eyed the wizard. *He looks old—and tired—and so very sad. Is he sorry for Risto? No, that couldn't be. He's mourning for all those who have lost loved ones at Risto's hand. He's sorry for the pain Risto has inflicted on others. He can't be sorry for Risto.*

Fenworth shrugged. As he looked back at his picture hanging above the table, his expression brightened, and he clapped his hands.

"It's gone," said Toopka.

"No, little one. I've replaced the illusion with reality. Now, in its natural size, only the eye of Wulder can behold it. But wait, I am adding to it."

Over the table a gleam of light reflected off a narrow strip of metal that had not been there seconds before. The metal expanded and took shape.

Toopka clapped her hands and bounced in her chair. "A blade!"

"Yes," said Fenworth. "All made from the same configuration of zoics you observed before. Then you couldn't see them because they were small. Now there are so many of them you can see the form I have created. I will add other configurations to make the hilt."

No sooner had he spoken his intention than a dark mass began to form at the blunt end of the shining sword. A hilt took shape with gold swirls embedded in a leather grip and a large ruby at the pommel. A gold emblem of Paladin's army shone on the crossguard.

Fenworth reached up and plucked the sword from the air. He presented the sword to Bardon, but Bardon did not raise his hands to take it.

With his eyes fixed firmly on the magnificent sword, the lehman said, "I cannot, sir. It is a knight's sword, and I have not earned the right to carry it."

"You will need it on the quest."

Kale held her breath. *Fenworth's giving Bardon permission to take the sword. Should he take it? Will he?*

Bardon squared his shoulders and stood from the table. "It would not serve me if I carried it under false pretenses."

"Aye," concurred Lee Ark. "Paladin will provide him with the appropriate weapon should the need arise. The boy does well not to take the offering."

Kale saw the approval in the general's face and hoped Bardon saw it too. But when she reached with her mind to tell him, *Good job,* she was met by a swirling mass of dark emotions. She backed off, and her glance swept around the table. Tension visibly stiffened the postures of her comrades. Everyone waited. All eyes watched the wizard and the young lehman.

Fenworth ignored Lee Ark's interruption and continued to watch Bardon's stonelike expression. Only the lehman's eyes hungered for the sword.

"You desire the sword just as you desire knighthood."

"Yes," said Bardon.

The sword shrank until it fit in the palm of the wizard's hand. He tucked it in a pocket of his voluminous robes. "I shall keep it for you."

"I'll not be a knight, Wizard Fenworth. Grand Ebeck said as much at our last meeting."

"Really?" The wizard turned to stare at Librettowit. "Oh dear, tut-tut. No, I don't think you have that right. Oh dear, no, no, not right at all."

He clapped his hands together and rubbed them with enthusiasm. He moved around the table to slap one firm hand on Regidor's shoulder and reached for Kale's. She braced herself against the strength of the blow and even then bent under the wizard's heavy hand.

One minute I think he's a doddering ancient, and the next I think he could beat Brunstetter at arm wrestling.

"Right you are, Kale, my dear. I am indeed a doddering wrestler of many weighty things. Not Brunstetter, I think not Brunstetter."

He squeezed his fingers into her shoulder and beamed at his two apprentices. "Now that your lesson on elementary wizardry is firmly established in your minds, shall we proceed with our quest?"

"No!" shouted Librettowit. "We must organize, gather pertinent data, assign responsibilities."

Fenworth looked astonished. "But Librettowit, that is what I have just done."

"Only in your mind, Fenworth."

"No, no, Wit. Didn't I just explain that until one masters certain knowledge one must content oneself with being a follower and not a leader? I carefully explained the complexity of what must be learned and that such knowledge is attainable."

"Only in your mind, Fenworth."

The wizard looked confused, but before he could voice an objection, the librarian pressed on. "We now have seven comrades, two children, two minor dragons, and an unhatched third, and four major dragons to consider."

"Four?" Fenworth wrinkled his brow.

"Celisse, Merlander, and the two dragons ridden by Lee Ark and Leetu," Librettowit explained. "And that reminds me, Lee Ark has information of import." A hopeful tone slipped into the tumanhofer's speech. "Perhaps his message will put off the quest to Creemoor."

"I'm afraid not," said Lee Ark.

All eyes turned to him. He stood and placed his fists upon the table.

"Paladin has given us a rescue mission. Our goal is to pull a longtime friend out of Burner Stox's clutches. Until recently this devoted o'rant was relatively safe within Risto's stronghold." He paused, and his gaze shifted to Kale. "Your mother is in danger, Kale. She has one more task to perform for Paladin, and we are to be at hand when it is completed. We will then bring her out of Creemoor to safety."

Kale's breath carried a quiet question. "My mother?"

Lee Ark nodded. Kale turned to look at Dar. He gave her a gentle smile and a reassuring wink. She then looked to Leetu. The emerlindian's eyes held a sparkle of joy in her otherwise serene expression.

But a question marred Kale's anticipation. It hung in her mind like a black thunderhead. *Who is this "mother" who left her child in slavery?*

17

PEACE?

They traveled on dragons to the Valley of Collumna. Frigid air blasted them as they flew over the southern branch of the Morchain Range. Kale wrapped Toopka inside her moonbeam cape, keeping both of them warm. The little doneel pushed her head out to see the magnificent snow-covered peaks.

Kale noted the splendor of the dragons. The sun glistened off their scales, making them look as if gemstones covered them from head to tail. Their huge wings beat in rhythm. The thurumph of each stroke underscored the whistle of cool wind.

Celisse moved her strong, ebony wings in perfect synchrony with Merlander's glistening red wings.

Leetu, with Librettowit, Bardon, and Regidor riding behind her, rode just ahead on a massive blue and green greater dragon. Lee Ark, with Wizard Fenworth snoozing in a passenger basket, flew on another of the larger dragons. This one carried even more supply bundles than the first.

Lee Ark rode point, and Kale gathered from his position that he was in charge of the expedition. She looked at the marione's square shoulders and thick neck, his black, windblown mane, and pictured the kind, serious expression that dominated his features. Everything she knew about him made her feel safe under his command.

Kale put her hand out to rest on the silver scales of Celisse's shoulder. Beneath her palm the dragon's powerful muscles rippled in a majestic rhythm. She trusted Celisse to fly straight and true.

A sigh escaped her lips as she stroked Celisse's strong neck just above the collarbone. *We're on our way. Another quest. Another adventure. Part of me would like to stay at home, safely reading about others' escapades. That part is like Librettowit. But I also felt a thrill when the dragons took off from the ground, and we were on our way. That's more like Dar.*

She looked once more at her companions. Her smile widened into a grin.

The excitement continued to bubble inside her as she looked down on the verdant valley. Their first stop would be where the smallest and largest of Wulder's creations lived side by side. An adult kimen could sleep in either the hat or the shoe of any grown urohm. The two races had a long history of working together.

Dar?

"Yes?"

Do you think we'll see Brunstetter? Do you think he'll come with us?

"We might. He might."

Gazing across the wingspans of the two dragons, Kale encountered Dar's furry grin. The wind ruffled the white linen cravat at his neck and sent the tails of his fancy jacket trailing behind him.

Kale scowled. *What's so funny?*

"You didn't want to come on this little excursion."

This part of the excursion is to a land I've heard about all my life.

"In fairy tales and legends."

Yes! And I'm anxious to find out what is truth and what is make-believe. A year ago I thought gateways weren't real.

Dar's face tightened into a frown. "Some of the things we'll find to be real won't be very nice."

I know, but that's later, when we cross the Dormanscz Mountains into Creemoor. All the stories about Ordray are fun. And Fenworth says we have to wait here until Paladin sends reinforcements and gives the order to rescue my mother.

With the last two words, Kale shifted her eyes away from Dar. She didn't want him to see how important it had become to her to find her mother. She had a lot of questions, but most of all, she wanted to know what kind of mother hers would be.

In the village where she was raised, the mariones showed little affection for their offspring. Parents spent a lot of time training children but very little time enjoying them. The mariones she had met in Lee Ark's home, though, hugged and laughed and played games together.

She forced her mind away from the disturbing image of a mother who ordered her around like Mistress Meiger.

Her friends, all but Fenworth, sat at attention, eagerly watching the beautiful landscape below. The slope of the lead dragon's wingspan tilted, and Lee Ark guided the small company northward. To the right, Kale caught glimpses of blue-green water along the horizon.

Again, the lead dragon banked, and the troop turned more to the east.

They set down in a pasture through which a stream flowed. Meadow grasses swayed in a pulsating breath of warm air, greeting them with the scent of flowers and fertile earth. Walking away from her friends, Kale followed the sound of water splashing over rocks.

She stopped in her tracks when she saw a miniature three-tiered waterfall. The water flowed over the ledges in an even stream without froth and foam at the base of each diminutive fall. At other points along the brook, water swirled and bubbled as the flow hit rocks and roots. But the water over the falls unnaturally bent to the angles without any disturbance.

"Kimen falls," said Lee Ark from behind her. "An amazing sight, isn't it?"

"I've heard about them in songs sung at the tavern, but to see one…"

Gymn and Metta flew from her cape with squeals of delight. They landed in the water and let the stream carry their tiny bodies over the falls. With musical trills, the two minor dragons rose from the water and flapped their leathery wings, showering droplets about them.

Toopka struggled against the confines of the cape and broke away. In only a minute, she had her tiny boots and socks off. She shed her clothes down to her white drawers and splashed into the stream with the dragons. She floated on her back and bumped down the steps like a child on a staircase.

Kale looked up at the general. "Did the kimens make this?"

"No, this is impossible," answered Lee Ark with a smile. "Impossible creations spring from the hand of Wulder."

Metta and Gymn teased Toopka by darting at her and shaking water-soaked wings above her head. They tired of the game long before the little doneel and took off looking for a place to sun themselves. They flew around the bare branches of a tree and chittered as if discussing this new oddity.

The rootup tree looked upside down. A dense bush surrounded the base. From the center, leafless branches reached upward, intertwined tightly. From a distance, they appeared to be a solid trunk. At the top, these limbs spread apart, just like a root system waving in the gentle breeze.

Toopka came dancing over the green grass, doing a shimmy every few steps to rid her fur of water.

"I like it here," she announced as she grabbed her shirt and scrubbed her face dry.

"I like it here too." Kale rested her hand on the pouch hanging from her neck. The egg within thrummed, reflecting her present mood.

By the time the sun slipped behind the Morchain Mountains, the party of travelers had settled in around a blazing campfire. Leetu Bends had taken the larger dragons off for a feed and returned to eat her own dinner cooked by Dar. Songs and stories followed the meal. Dar played a number of instruments with Metta's cooing voice harmonizing.

The music fascinated Regidor. The meech dragon insisted on holding each instrument as Dar put it down and pulled another out of his bags. He concentrated on Dar's every movement and mimicked him when he had a chance. Remarkably, he was soon playing accompaniment to every song Dar performed.

While Fenworth dozed against a pile of satchels and parcels, Librettowit and Lee Ark sang the words to the old ballads. Then they spun tales, trying to outdo each other in a good-natured rivalry.

At last Kale curled up in her bedroll. Though she was tired from the journey and the worrisome anticipation of entering Creemoor, her mind dwelt on an unknown mother and destructive spiders. She couldn't banish the image of a beautiful, sad woman the evil wizard Risto had once shown her.

The woman looked like a queen sitting in a castle tower and gazing wistfully across the forested countryside. Risto had said the woman loved her, but Risto was full of lies. Kale knew what to expect from Creemoor spiders. She didn't know what to expect from her parent.

Gymn snuggled against her cheek, but Metta could not relax so long as there might be another song. She skittered up and down Kale's prone figure from her shoulder to her ankle.

From across the campsite, Toopka suppressed a yawn. She got up from the rock where she'd been sitting and came to Kale.

Kale held out the blanket, inviting the little doneel to crawl in beside her.

Toopka shook her head. "No, I'm not tired yet. It's just the rock is hard. Can I sit with you?"

Kale patted the grass in front of her, and Toopka plopped down. She leaned her back against Kale's stomach. The tiny child fit like a small puppy in the crook of Kale's body.

"What kind of dragon will hatch?" asked Toopka, stifling another yawn and wiggling closer.

"I don't know," Kale whispered so as not to disturb Librettowit's "Fable of the Fortunate Farmer." She stroked the side of the little girl's head where long, silky hair grew across her jaw line.

Toopka's small fingers played with the edge of the blanket, pulling at a loose string. "You could ask Gymn and Metta. They might know."

"No, they don't."

"You could ask Librettowit. He knows a lot of things."

"I don't think he can see inside an egg."

"You could ask Wizard Fenworth. He'd know for sure. He can probably see into the egg and into tomorrow or even next week."

"He might be able to, but he doesn't answer questions very well."

Toopka giggled. She leaned her head back against Kale. "I bet it's a girl baby dragon. I bet it's the kind that likes other little girls. I bet it's not as smart as Regidor and not as hard to play with. I bet it's a baby dragon who will want to ride with me most of the time 'cause you're so busy."

"I'm busy?"

"Yep. You're learning to be a princess."

"Princess?"

"No, *a* princess. But I don't understand why Wizard Fenworth is giving Regidor lessons on being a princess too."

"The word is 'apprentice,' Toopka. It means someone who is learning a trade. Regidor and I are bound to help Wizard Fenworth, and in exchange he is obliged to teach us his trade."

Toopka was silent for a moment. She shifted slightly, and Kale moved the blanket over the little doneel's shoulders. The child relaxed into a ball.

"I think it would be more fun to be a princess," she sighed just before her breathing evened out.

Kale ran a finger over one furry, tufted ear. "It depends on whether the princess can stay at home or must go out to save her country." Kale let a long breath flow from her lungs and took another one in. "It depends on a lot of things, like who's the queen, and whether she is good or evil."

18

Mother

Kale wandered through the mushroom grove looking for the particular type Dar wanted for cooking. She repeated the description to Metta and Gymn as they flew around her. Metta, in particular, could not keep the image in her mind. Instead, she sang mushroom songs with such a variety of lyrics that Kale had to shush her to keep her own thoughts clear.

Kale repeated the instructions out loud. "The top of the cap is navy blue, mottled with purple. The fleshy underside is a rich brown, and the stalk is creamy tan with veins of green. A mature specimen will be at least four feet tall, and we are only to bring the cap."

Metta began singing a song about three children afloat on the Pomandando River in the cap of a blue-green mushroom. The words formed clearly in Kale's mind, although her ears heard only a tune sung in the syllabic language of the minor dragon.

"Metta, stop!" she commanded. "Your songs are beautiful, but they are not helping."

The purple dragon let out a long trill. Kale tensed in anticipation. A singing dragon who felt unappreciated could sing arias that scraped across one's nerves.

Gymn flew to hover next to Metta. Kale interpreted the cooing noises Gymn made. The male dragon encouraged the ruffled Metta to put up with the insensitive o'rant.

In mock anger, Kale put her hands on her hips and frowned at the two. "Don't forget I hear everything you say."

Gymn poked the she-dragon with his wingtip. Metta giggled and did a sideways maneuver that unbalanced the green dragon enough for her to race off. He chirruped with glee and gave chase.

Kale pushed the moonbeam cape off her shoulders so that it hung down her back in a narrow curtain. Trying to keep an eye on their quick, darting flight, she squinted in the brightness of the late morning sun. She sent a message that only Gymn would hear.

Thank you, my little friend. Keep her happy and out of the way while I find this blue and purple, green and tan, edible delight for Sir Dar.

With a sigh of relief, she resumed her search. She enjoyed walking among the colorful toadstools. Most were as high as her shoulder and had a leathery texture.

Dar said the younger ones would be more suitable for cooking, and those would be closer to the forest edge, under the shadows of the tall trees.

She made her way toward the woods but without any hurry. She had plenty of time since Dar would prepare the mushroom steaks for the evening meal. The colors and shapes of the growth around her enchanted her eyes. Even the rich, earthy smell pleased her.

An unfamiliar feminine voice spoke with hushed urgency into her mind. *"Kale. Kale, is that you?"*

Who's speaking?

"Over here, Kale, under the armagot tree. I dare not come out in the open. I'm not supposed to be here. Oh please, come to me, Kale. I can't stand the waiting any longer."

The gentle voice pulled at Kale's heart. She took a few steps closer to the towering trees and tripped over a smaller mushroom, breaking the cap off as she fell. She rolled to the side, dusted off the knees of her breeches, and picked up the large, bowl-like piece of mushroom. Dark brown folds of moist and tender substance clung to a smooth, dark blue shell mottled with a deep purple swirl. Kale stood with the prize in her hands.

"Come to me." A sharp note struck in the command. *"Oh, forgive me for my impatience. It has been so long, and still they keep me from you. But I must see you. Kale, I must touch you, and then I can bear the few more days we must wait before we can be together."*

Mother?

"Here, Kale, come quickly. I must return before my absence is noted. There is danger."

The soft words soothed her doubts away. The urgent plea ran through her like a shiver of fear. She clutched the mushroom cap to her chest and hurried to the shade of the huge trees.

A dark-haired woman stepped from the shadows to greet her. Her elegant white dress shimmered in the sun with the radiant softness of a pearl. Trimmed with royal blue cording, the formfitting bodice sparkled with silver threads. An embroidered high collar caressed the woman's pale cheeks. Elaborate sleeves puffed slightly at the shoulder, then followed slender arms to a deep ruffle at the wrists. The full skirt rustled as the woman took a hasty step back into the shadows and beckoned Kale to hurry.

Kale stopped in front of the lady. She wanted to throw her arms around her mother, but the absolute perfection of the person before her stifled the urge.

Her thoughts churned, matching the turmoil in her heart. *I am far too ill-bred for someone so refined as this woman.*

"No, never say so." The woman touched her cheek with smooth, cool fingertips. Her gray eyes latched onto Kale's. "I am Lyll Allerion. You were torn from my arms as a babe, but you are nothing less than a noble Allerion. You were born to greatness. Soon we will be together, and together we will follow that road of destiny."

Kale started to step forward, longing for her mother to embrace her. But the hand that had tenderly cradled her cheek lowered and braced against Kale's shoulder.

"No, I cannot hold you. You are soiled."

Kale jerked back as if slapped.

Lyll Allerion tilted her head and laughed lightly. The gesture erased the momentary stern expression. "I must return to the palace, and I would be hard-pressed to explain smudges on my gown when I was supposed to have retired to my room for a moment of rest."

Kale silently agreed. She'd glimpsed wealthy women, richly dressed, in Vendela. None of them compared to her mother. Her heart squeezed, and she swallowed a lump in her throat. Tears flowed down her cheeks, and she hastily rubbed them away with the back of her hand.

"You've left streaks of mud across your cheeks." Out of her sleeve, the elegant woman pulled an embroidered lawn handkerchief and pressed it into Kale's grubby fist.

Lyll's fairylike laugh rang like winsome bells, and Kale's humiliation increased. Carefully guarding her thoughts as Granny Noon had taught her, Kale fumed. She didn't want this woman to hear her thinking.

She's afraid I'll smudge her fingertips. Granny Noon wasn't afraid of my dirt.

Granny Noon invited hugs. She lived in a hole in the ground and wore homespun clothing. Granny Noon had trimmed Kale's hair and provided food, clothing, and valuable tools for the quest. The old emerlindian had given a frightened o'rant girl assurance with her words of encouragement and sage advice. This woman had given Kale nothing.

A smile lifted the woman's lips. Her eyes shone with affection.

Kale sighed. *I can't give my mother anything. She came looking for me. She wanted to see me. But I'm not much to look at, am I?*

She dropped her head and gazed at the tiny points of blue satin shoes peeking from under the hem of the skirt. Blue satin that hadn't picked up the forest floor's accumulation of decayed leaves. A hem that showed no signs of dust or dirt.

"Kale." A male voice boomed over the grove of mushrooms.

Lyll stiffened.

Again the loud call reached their ears. "Kale, where are you?"

Kale looked up at her mother's face. "It's Bardon."

The woman aimed a cold glare of anger over her daughter's shoulder. Kale shuddered.

An irritated growl rumbled in her mother's throat. "I know this boy." The clipped words felt like pellets against Kale's ears. "Keep him at a distance, Kale. He will interfere with our plans."

Kale whispered, "What plans?"

The fiery gaze shifted to Kale's face, and for a moment Kale withered under its blaze. Then the light under the trees shifted, and with the fickle shadows, Lyll's expression changed. The tenderness flowing from her mother's face was so different from the previous venom, Kale doubted she'd really seen hatred in the woman's eyes.

"Plans for our happiness, dear Kale. We've had our share of suffering, haven't we? It's time for our reward."

The woman gathered her skirts and turned away. She took a step into the darker shadows of the forest.

"Tell no one you saw me, Kale. Paladin would be displeased with me for coming here." Another step, and she was gone. Not just hidden by shadows, but gone. *Soon, dear Kale, soon.*

"Oh good. You found it."

Kale whirled around to face Bardon.

"Found it?"

"The mushroom." He pointed to the cap clamped under Kale's arm. "Be careful not to damage it. Dar would just send you out for another."

Kale nodded.

"Are you all right?"

"Me?"

Bardon scowled and looked around her into the trees. Kale stepped forward.

"I'm fine." She took hold of his arm and turned him toward the colorful grove of mushrooms.

Bardon shook her hand off. "You didn't sample any of this fungus, did you?"

"Of course not." Kale gave him a push and started back the way they had come.

"You're acting strange, and you look kind of odd."

"I haven't eaten any of the mushrooms, and therefore I *am* hungry. Very hungry. Let's get back to the camp."

She trudged through the shoulder-high mushrooms, no longer admiring the wide variety of colors and shapes. To her annoyance, Bardon made two attempts at conversation.

"The minor dragons came back without you," he said.

She didn't answer.

"Wizard Fenworth has been sleeping so much, Librettowit's worried he'll turn into a tree and not be able to turn back."

"Librettowit always frets about something," she answered and then marched on.

Her mother had said not to get close to Bardon. She wanted to talk to him, to talk about normal things, and avoid thinking about what had just happened. Her mother had said not to tell anyone. Kale wanted most to tell Dar and get his opinion of the episode.

Her mother was beautiful, but that didn't make Kale feel good. By comparison, she was a worm. Her mother's eyes had filled with love. But they could also look cold. Her mother's touch had brought feelings of longing and feelings of dread. Having a mother, having *this* mother, complicated her life with too many confusing emotions.

Back at the camp, the minor dragons flew to greet her but veered off before they landed on her shoulders. They sat instead in a nearby rootup tree and made mournful noises like doves cooing before the rain. When Kale bit into the tasty meat pastry Dar served for noonmeal, the egg hanging in the pouch at her neck bumped and twisted. Her stomach felt the same jitters, and she put the food down unfinished.

After noonmeal, she helped Dar with the dishes and then, alongside Leetu Bends, busily polished the major dragons' scales. Celisse stretched out her neck, and the dragon's deep contentment numbed some of Kale's anxiety.

"Are you all right?" asked her emerlindian friend.

"Yes!" Kale moved to the other side of Celisse so she wouldn't have to look at Leetu's puzzled face. Kale concentrated on her dragon and tried to soak in the pleasure emanating from Celisse.

"Kale." Dar came toward her with the mushroom cap in his hands. He carried it with the brown side up and stopped just a few feet from her. "What color was the stalk of this plant?"

"I don't remember."

"Was it a creamy tan with green veins?"

"I said, 'I don't remember.'"

Dar shook his head and looked carefully at the cap. "I don't think it could have been. This smells like a musk melon, and the mushroom I sent you for should smell more nutty."

She shrugged and went back to rubbing Celisse's ebony scales. "Does it matter?"

"One is edible, and another might not be."

She shrugged again and did not look her friend in the eye.

Dar turned the mushroom cap over in his hands, examining it. "This is bruised, and there's dirt in the folds of the underside." He took a step closer to Kale. "What happened out there?"

"Nothing."

"If I could mindspeak, this is one time I'd be tempted to invade your privacy."

"I don't know what you're talking about, Dar. Nothing happened."

Dar gave her a disgusted look and walked away.

A chill ran down her spine, and the hair on the back of her neck stood on end. She cautiously looked around, wondering whether someone was watching her, whether someone who could listen in on her thoughts was doing so at that very moment.

Leetu busily buffed a major dragon's side with a polishing rag.

Fenworth dozed under the shade of the other large dragon's leathery wing. Kale looked more closely. In the tangle of vines and branches that would transform into beard and hair when the wizard awoke, an open eye stared out of a bark-encrusted face. One eye, open and staring. One eye, trained on her, unblinking and eerily focused. The eyelid closed, and Kale let out a breath she had not known she was holding. Fenworth was asleep. He didn't know.

19

Hidden Talents

Kale heard Dar and Bardon fencing long before she wanted to leave her bedroll. The questing party had been camped by the kimen falls for almost three weeks, and each dawn Dar and Bardon engaged in mock combat. She knew Leetu Bends and Lee Ark would soon step in to give instructions.

At first, all of them had tried to get Kale to join in. They might try again today if they knew she was awake. She refused to open her eyes. Birds twittered in the branches of the rootup trees. She covered her head with the blanket.

Metta and Gymn awoke within the folds of their pocket-dens. They squirmed toward the opening, disturbing Kale as they wiggled between her and the bedroll. They reached her clenched fists and butted their scaly heads against her fingers.

I don't want to get up, she told them sternly but loosened her grip so they could slither out. One of them stepped on her nose. Gymn. His tail slapped her cheek as he took off to find a better place to watch the mock battle.

A weight landed on Kale's side. Too big to be a minor dragon. Toopka.

"Dar's going to teach me to use a small sword right after Bardon beats him."

Kale threw back the covers. "What?"

"Bardon always beats him. He's had years more training."

"Not that. What did you say about fencing with a small sword?"

"I'm not big enough to fence. Dar's going to teach me how to duck and jab."

Kale propped herself up on an elbow and glared at the two warriors as they parried and thrust with practice swords, weapons made of wood but capable of leaving nasty bruises. "You're too young to be doing any such thing."

Toopka's eyebrows scrunched together in a serious frown. "We're going on a quest," she said. "It's best to be prepared."

"You aren't going on the dangerous part. You'll stay here in the camp."

"Robbers could come."

"Not in Ordray," said Kale. "The urohms and kimens run a tidy province. There is next to no crime."

"*Next to* no crime. That means there *is* some, and crime is likely to happen where innocent people are unprepared."

"I'm not going to argue with you." Kale threw herself back down and jerked the blanket over her head.

"Bardon says you should be honing your skills as a fighter." Toopka waited for a response.

Kale pressed her lips together.

"Bardon asked you to spar with him. You really should. He might have to report to Grand Ebeck."

Kale pushed back the covers again and sat up, knocking Toopka off her perch. "What made you say that? Did you hear something?"

Toopka gave an exaggerated shrug and purposefully studied the two young men.

"Toopka." Kale poked her furry arm.

She sighed. "Wizard Fenworth says you're mopey. Mopey o'rants don't make a good princess."

"Apprentice."

"Librettowit says you are suffering emotional strain."

"And?"

"Leetu Bends says you need a kick in the pants."

Kale rubbed the sleep from her eyes and studied Bardon and Dar as they circled each other. Dar swept in, attacking the taller man's legs. Bardon leapt in the air and landed out of the doneel's reach.

Kale scowled. *Where have I seen someone move like that? He wasn't an o'rant. Not a marione either. At Lee Ark's! Two emerlindians did a demon-stration match.*

Kale stood and moved closer. She curled her toes against the chill of the dew-drenched grass. The moonbeam cape kept her body warm, but still she wrapped her arms around her torso.

Lee Ark and Leetu also approached the impromptu training field from their tents. Even before they reached Kale's side, Leetu cheered when Bardon lightly jumped over Dar's low swung sword.

"Dar, vary your approach," ordered Lee Ark. "You're too predictable."

Fenworth strode over the rise and advanced upon the two practicing with swords. "Let's see what Bardon does with a pole."

Kale had been among Paladin's soldiers long enough to know that the emerlindians, not o'rants, were masters of the pole and longbow.

Startled, both Dar and Bardon turned to the old wizard. Fenworth held a six-foot prime-pole in each hand. He extended one arm to offer a weapon to Bardon.

Dar looked up with a grin on his face. "Do it, Lehman. I bet you're good at it."

Bardon's usual stoic mien relaxed. He clapped Dar on the shoulder, handed the doneel his sword, and took the weighty pole from the wizard.

"What are they doing?" asked Toopka, clinging to the leg of Kale's trousers.

Kale put her hand on the soft fur between the little girl's ears. "They are going to battle with prime-poles. If they had two shorter sticks, that would be lackey-canes. And shorter lackey-canes that have a strap attached to one end are called dodgerods or dodders."

"I want a dodder."

"They're for fighting. They're dangerous."

"I want to be dangerous."

Kale looked at the big brown eyes staring up at her. She clamped down a grin that would betray her amusement, but she couldn't help teasing.

"Should a bisonbeck warrior ever catch sight of you with a weapon in your hand, he'd turn tail and run for the hills, howling all the way."

Toopka's expressive eyes widened for a fraction of a second and then narrowed. "Harrumph." She turned back to watch Bardon and Fenworth readying.

The tyke sounded so much like old Wizard Fenworth that those standing close enough to hear burst into laughter. Toopka put her hands on her hips and stomped a foot.

Lee Ark, who had many children at home, swooped the tiny doneel up into the air and settled her on his shoulder.

"Watch, little one," he said. "The men are wrapping soft leather around the knuckles of each hand. That's to protect against blows."

"Will Bardon beat the wizard? Bardon always beats Dar."

Lee Ark tilted his head to look up at her. "He's never beaten me."

"You fight with swords and those hadwig thingies."

"Still, he's never beaten me."

"But you are only old. Wizard Fenworth is oldest." The marione general chuckled and patted the doneel's knee with his large, broad hand.

Kale gave Toopka a hard look. Sometimes she suspected the child said things more out of orneriness than innocence.

Toopka, how old are you?

Toopka's head jerked around to find Kale. *"I told you I don't know."*

Did you mean to be disrespectful to General Lee Ark? You should know better than to tell a person he's old. It's not polite.

Toopka's lower lip jutted out in an angry pout. *"I don't think it's fair for you to expect me to know things that we didn't learn on the streets. No one ever talked about being polite. We talked about which shopkeeper had too much fruit in his stand, and when the brown spots were coming on, so we'd know where to forage."*

"Watch now, Toopka," Lee Ark said, unknowingly interrupting. "They'll touch their poles once at the top and then once at the base, then the match will begin."

Wizard Fenworth and Bardon stood straight, gave a ceremonious salute, nodded solemnly, and shifted their feet into the fighting stance. Each man tilted the top of his pole forward. A sharp snap echoed across the meadow as the wood made contact. The men then angled the bottoms of the poles forward. The second snap sounded stronger than the first.

With no more preliminaries, the men attacked with full vigor. The poles clacked and snapped with an occasional thud from a glancing hit.

She winced a couple of times when it looked as though Fenworth was about to land a strike, but Bardon whirled gracefully out of the way and returned a clout against the old man's pole.

The fighting intensified. Bardon began to sweat. Water dripped from Fenworth's brow, and his robe soon bore dark streaks where perspiration soaked the cloth. The more he sweat, the more limber his body became.

Fenworth missed Bardon twice in quick succession and grinned. "You waltz, young man. You should visit the courts of the land, not the battlefields."

Bardon rained a rapid rat-a-tat-tat on Fenworth's well-coordinated defense. "I must admit, Wizard, I expected your moves to be stiff."

"I've always been known for my fluid touch."

Kale shook her head and laid a hand on Lee Ark's arm. "Something is wrong. I've never seen Wizard Fenworth actually fight. Even when surrounded by blimmets."

The general grunted an assent. "I'm amazed by both of them. I've never watched Bardon against such a skilled opponent. Fenworth's right. He has the grace of a dancer. He moves more like an emerlindian than an o'rant."

She nodded, watching Bardon's moves through an intricate attack. "The other students made fun of him because his style of fighting didn't match the instructors' criteria. But he's good. I think they bad-mouthed him because none could beat him."

With her eyes on the bog wizard in front of her, she jumped when his booming voice resounded at her shoulder.

"This is ridiculous!" Fenworth's gnarled hands pushed Kale and Lee Ark aside. The old man glared at the combatants. "Who told you you could borrow my form?"

The wizard sparring with Bardon turned toward the interruption.

Bardon's pole had been positioned for an onward thrust. He could not stay his hand when his opponent suddenly abandoned the match. The young lehman pulled aside, but not enough. The pole struck the old wizard's shoulder. To Kale's horror, it sank into the coarse cloth and on through flesh and bone.

She blinked. As Bardon withdrew his weapon, the wizard's body appeared to ripple outward from the point of impact, much as water does when a stone is thrown into a pond. The ripples reversed to converge on the center. The wizard merely brushed the spot as if he were wiping away dust.

Wizard Fenworth pounded his walking stick upon the ground. Bees swarmed out of the top notch and flew away in a mass.

"I demand you release my form this instant. It's bad enough having two wizards, but two wizards in the same form is ridiculous. Show yourself, man."

The other wizard casually waved a hand in Fenworth's direction. Water sprayed over Fenworth and those standing behind him. "I *would* like to change into something more comfortable."

A mist arose around the stranger until the air was so dense with moisture, he couldn't be seen.

"Aha!" said Fenworth. "Just as I thought, and I can't say I'm happy to see you."

20

A Mixed Bag of Comrades

"Now is that any way to greet an old friend?" A short man emerged from the mist. He strode forward, still holding the prime-pole, which towered above him. The cloud of fog settled toward the ground and trailed away along the drying grass until it dissipated altogether.

Wizard robes in shades of blue covered his small frame. Wire-rimmed glasses perched on a meager nose and did nothing to hide the penetrating azure eyes behind them. He wore a floppy hat like Fenworth's and carried a satchel. Damp wisps of fine white hair hung over his ears and around his shoulders. A thin beard grew from his chin, but no whiskers adorned his cheeks. He had a luxurious mustache that parted directly under his nose, flowed outward around his mouth, and joined the scraggly beard. His eyes quickly took in every member of the assembled party.

Bardon stood with his pole resting against his shoulder and a look of confusion on his face. The wizard thrust a hand toward him.

"Name's Cam Ayronn, lake wizard and cousin to Fenworth here."

Bardon shook the man's hand and then wiped his fingers on his pant leg. Kale couldn't resist the urge to look into the lehman's thoughts. She wrinkled her nose when she realized Bardon's hand had been damp from the moisture he'd gathered from the wizard's palm.

"Harrumph!" said Fenworth. "A *distant* cousin, a *very* distant cousin. Ninth cousin, twenty-two times removed, at least."

Wizard Ayronn cocked an eyebrow at the older wizard and grinned. "Second cousin, not once removed."

"Bah!" exploded Fenworth, with a wave of his hand. A stream of bats hurled out of his bulky sleeve and squeaked piteously in the stark sunlight as they flew away.

Cam Ayronn chuckled and turned to Lee Ark. "You're the commander of this expedition, I take it. Paladin sent me to reinforce your mission."

"I'm the oldest," said Fenworth. "I am in charge."

"Oh yes," returned the newcomer, not in the least discommoded by the old wizard's abrupt manner. "I understand you're in charge of the wizardry elements of the operation, but certainly not the military aspect. How distasteful, to command legions of sweaty, belligerent soldiers."

Kale sent a look of inquiry to Dar. *Legions?*

"Diplomacy," he answered with a look of polite interest on the face he showed his comrades.

Fenworth's head bobbed in one short nod of agreement. "Quite right. Much prefer the intellectual. Astute as ever, Cam. You'll do." He walked away a few steps, but did an about-face to shake his staff at his cousin. "Mind you, you are under me—younger, waterlogged, from a pesky branch of the family. You'll remember I'm in charge."

"Certainly," said Cam with a sober expression. "I wouldn't usurp your authority, not when Paladin has sent me to help."

Fenworth turned again, grumbling. "Where's breakfast? You'd think with the sun in the sky and birds singing, one would smell a piece of bacon frying."

Toopka pulled on Cam Ayronn's blue robe. The wizard looked down, adjusted his spectacles, and smiled at the tiny doneel.

Toopka's eyes twinkled. "Are you wet because you're a lake wizard?"

"Yes, dear."

"When Wizard Fenworth sits still, he grows things. What happens when you sit still?"

"I drip. Leave a puddle. Makes it difficult to have dinner in fine palaces. I'd much rather have breakfast with you beside the campfire."

Toopka hopped and clapped her hands together. "Dar makes fried mullins. You'll love mullins, especially if you like mordat."

"I love mordat, and I know where we can find a mordat grove."

Toopka squealed and grabbed the small wizard's hand. "Let's go!"

"Not quite yet, little one. I must confer with the adults before we indulge our sweet tooths with Dar's delicious mullins."

A gravelly voice interrupted their conversation. "Shouldn't that be sweet teeth?"

The wizard spun around to face Regidor. "My goodness!"

Regidor grinned, his wide mouth opening to show his expansive row of pointed teeth. "My name is Regidor. I'm a—"

"—meech dragon," said Cam Ayronn.

"I was about to say, 'apprentice wizard.'"

"Ah, yes." The wizard pinched his mustache between thumb and knuckle and repeatedly pulled at it. He stuck out his hand in greeting. "Nice to meet you. Do you enjoy mullins? I do hope so, because Toopka has promised us fried mullins for breakfast."

Toopka gasped. "How'd you know my name?"

"I'm a wizard, my dear."

"Do you know everybody's name?"

"I only bother to know the names of important people."

Regidor harrumphed in the manner of Fenworth. He eyed the wizard, who was no taller than himself. Kale frowned at her friend, who peered intently at the visitor.

Regidor cleared his throat. "Are you friend or foe, sir?" he asked.

Cam Ayronn threw back his head and barked a laugh. "That's like saying, 'Are you truthsayer or deceiver?' If I am evil, I will lie about it. If I am benevolent, I would say the same as a malefactor."

"Perhaps, but I am testing out my talents. I believe when you say what you are, I shall know if you tell the truth. I'm glad you've come along, because I am having difficulty testing my theory on those I already know."

"Then I shall say I am friend."

Regidor gave a small nod, and his mouth spread in his toothy grin. "I think you have told the truth."

Librettowit sidled up next to the meech dragon. "What is this, my boy? What talent?"

Regidor's attention shifted to his mentor. "I've discovered if I squint a certain way, I can perceive a haze around living organisms. The haze shimmers with different hues and varying distinctions of clarity. I believe this rainbowlike apparition reflects the purity of the being's soul."

"Incredible." The librarian's face lit with enthusiasm. "That talent is, of course, mentioned in ancient writings, but we've always assumed the ability was myth rather than fact." He hooked his arm in the dragon's, and they walked off, heads bent together. "What are you doing to measure different degrees of attributes? For that matter, how many attributes do you think you can distinguish?"

Kale shook her head. *Just a short time ago, I woke up to hear Metta singing nursery rhymes to a young meech dragon. Now he's developing skills that amaze even Librettowit.*

Regidor and Dar set to work fixing breakfast. Bacon fried in one skillet, mallow brewed in a tin pot, and Dar dropped mullin dough into a kettle of hot lard. Kale's stomach grumbled loudly in response to the delightful aromas.

"Look," called Toopka. "They're coming this way."

She ran to Kale with her arm stretched out and a tiny finger pointing to the eastern horizon. Kale shielded her eyes against the morning sun and saw black specks like flying geese. She first protected her mind from any evil influence and then concentrated to determine what might be approaching.

Her face broke into a grin. "Brunstetter."

"Kimens and urohms," Leetu Bends announced at the same time.

Five beautiful greater dragons, loaded with supplies and warriors, landed in the field. Even after a year of seeing dragons almost daily, Kale marveled over the beauty of these graceful creatures.

Brunstetter threw his leg over the arching neck of his milky white steed, Foremoore, and slid to the ground. In a cascade of bright colors, five kimens alighted from the same dragon.

Brunstetter looked the part of a noble. He wore a crest upon his leather vest, and a circlet of gold held his blond hair back from his patrician face. He bowed formally to the elders of the quest. Shimeran, a leader among the kimens, stood at his ankle, looking equally dignified.

Decorum could not contain the other four kimens. Seezle, Zayvion, Veazey, and D'Shay tripped lightly over the grass and surrounded Kale and Dar. Kale grinned at the kimens she had not seen for many months.

"Who is this?" asked Seezle, patting Toopka on the arm.

Zayvion shook Dar's hand vigorously while Veazey danced around Kale. "Do you have any more hatched dragons? Do you have eight now?"

Kale introduced Toopka and explained how she and Dar were the little doneel's guardians and that another egg was incubating. The rapid-fire questions and the kimens' eager responses made Kale forget for a while that she had been feeling uncomfortable in this bizarre setting.

Brunstetter went off with Lee Ark for a conference, but the rest of the assembly gathered around the cooking fire where Dar and Regidor busied themselves making more of everything. The smells of bacon and fresh frying mullins filled the air. Kimen laughter rivaled the birds' songs in merry notes of pleasure. The sun warmed them as the breeze played among the visitors, fluttering Dar's fancy coattails and lifting the kimens' wild hair.

Kale poured another cup of mallow, stirred to cool it, and carried it to where Toopka sat next to Wizard Cam.

Out of the pleasant peace of the morning came an urgent voice.

"Kale."

Mother?

"You must come to me."

We have visitors, and I can't just walk away. Not without anyone knowing.

"Come."

Kale handed the cup to Toopka and noticed Wizard Cam's piercing blue eyes examining her. She smiled awkwardly and turned her attention to the little doneel, hoping to hide her confusion.

"Toopka, be careful. It's still hot."

"Come, Kale."

Can't it wait? Just a few minutes.

"In the forest, by the mushroom glade, in ten minutes."

Kale sank down abruptly on one of the logs they used for seating. She smoothed her sweating palms across the knees of her pants, then clenched her trembling fingers in a tight curl. If she left right at this moment, she could get to her mother by walking quickly. Another minute or two and she would have to run.

"Come."

Kale looked around at her friends and the soldiers. They sat in groups, talking, laughing, enjoying the breakfast. Brunstetter and Lee Ark sat somewhat apart, but they too were conversing in an easy manner. No one seemed interested in what she was doing.

She stood. A wave of dizziness swept over her. She didn't move for a moment as the feeling subsided.

She looked around once more. No one seemed to notice. Except the lake wizard. She turned her face away from him and strode over to Celisse. She patted the dragon's neck. A shiver coursed down Kale's spine, almost causing her knees to buckle.

"Come."

Celisse jerked under her touch, and her huge head swerved around to look Kale in the eye.

Kale ducked her head. "Nothing's wrong," she answered the unspoken question.

Metta and Gymn flew to her, but instead of landing on her shoulders, they circled her head. Their frantic, jumbled thoughts bombarded her. She waved her hands at them as if to brush them away.

Kale saw Wizard Cam rise to his feet and take a few steps in her direction. She scurried to the other side of Celisse, using the dark dragon's prone figure as a shield.

"Come."

I'm trying.

Brunstetter's deep voice resonated across the camp. "I have news from Paladin. News of more peril in the land."

Kale shook violently. She turned to look at the distant forest.

The urohm noble's message kept her from moving. "We have our mission at last. We will—"

"Come now. Come, before all is lost."

Kale stepped toward the open field. A hand fell on her shoulder and turned her back. Wizard Cam stood before her, his eyes boring into hers. Directly behind him, Fenworth stood rigid and unsmiling. A guttural noise rumbled from matronly Celisse. The minor dragons swooped and called in agitation around her head.

"Come!" the voice shrieked through her mind, making her cringe. The pressure of the old wizard's hand tightened on her shoulder.

He's going to stop me. He's going to do something to stop me. I stand under the authority of Wulder. I call upon His protection!

Her mother's urgent call dropped into silence. The light dimmed around her, and she fell to the ground. Sobs tore from her throat as she grabbed a handful of grass and pulled it from the dirt. The sweet smell of the broken green blades acted as a tonic. She inhaled deeply and looked up to see the others in a circle around her.

"What happened?"

The doneel put a furry hand upon her other shoulder. "We almost lost you."

Wizard Cam helped her stand. "Something evil lured you away."

"No." Kale stepped away from him and Dar. She backed into Bardon's solid form.

She turned and jumped away from him. She didn't like the expression on his face. He looked sorry for her.

"No!" she said again, louder.

Leetu came forward and laid a calm hand on her arm. "You used the name of Wulder to banish it. You'll be all right now, Kale."

No, they don't understand. I broke the spell Wizard Cam had on me. It isn't Mother who is evil. It must be him.

She looked at the smaller wizard's face, his eyes filled with kindness, his mouth barely curved in a reassuring smile.

Or that wasn't Mother calling.

She shivered and let her head drop. "Thank you for helping." Her teeth sunk into her lower lip as she forced the flow of tears to stop. *Just who am I thanking? Who tried to control me, and who made it stop?*

21

Two Tricksters

Kale went through the motions of preparing for the next leg of their journey. She followed Leetu Bends, redistributing the new supplies among the dragons.

Brunstetter assigned the warriors. Three troops would enter Creemoor, each from a different direction, and trap a nest of spiders that had been located. Some spiders would go deep into the mountain and probably escape, but many would be destroyed.

Following Leetu, Kale bumped into a small knot of kimens. They giggled and parted to let her through, watching her all the while. She frowned at them. They giggled more and scurried away. Kale tramped after Leetu. It happened again. A different group of kimens, but the same stares and laughter.

"What's the matter with the kimens?" Kale asked Leetu.

Leetu put down her load, placed her hands on her hips, and looked around. All the kimens were engaged in the business at hand. "What do you mean?"

Kale scanned the busy campground. No one stood idle, and no one stared her way. Still she protested. "The kimens have been coming by to look at me."

Leetu's face tightened. She bent to pick up a bundle she intended to strap on Merlander's saddle. Hoisting the load, she said, "I doubt it. Why would they want to look at you? That sounds rather ridiculous, doesn't it?"

Kale didn't answer. It *did* seem ridiculous.

Leetu nodded toward the bundle she held against the saddle. "Hold this while I strap it."

Kale stepped forward to help. She glanced over at a group of kimens dividing packages of food. *No, they aren't interested in me. Why would they be? I guess I just feel odd because of what happened this morning. What would I think of someone who had been lured away by an evil force? Does everybody think I'm some kind of bumpkin who falls for evil trickery?*

Kale picked up another pack and held it in place for Leetu.

Suppose it wasn't an evil force. Suppose Wizard Cam made me think my mother was calling me. Suppose he wanted me to look ridiculous.

"Kale, grab another bundle," Leetu snapped.

As Kale held another parcel against the saddle, she searched through the crowd and found the short, damp wizard.

He's arguing with Fenworth. Fenworth doesn't trust him. He's probably here to sabotage our mission. If Paladin really sent him, why didn't he come with Brunstetter?

Kale glanced at the urohms. The giant men stood beside one of the major dragons, but they weren't working.

Now they're staring at me. Nobody trusts me anymore, and it's that wet wizard's fault.

Kale glared at the warriors. They immediately went back to work.

A quiet voice entered her mind.

"Come to me now, my dear Kale. Everyone's busy. No one will notice you slip away."

Kale held the last pack in place while Leetu bound it. Then, instead of following the emerlindian across the camp, she strolled to the trees banking the stream. Gymn and Metta zoomed past her.

I'm going for a walk, she told them. *There are too many people here. I'm tired of their staring.*

The little dragons circled her head. She flinched and hurried her step.

They do not *like me. They think I'm evil.*

Their chirrups of alarm raked over Kale's nerves. "Leave me alone. Go back. I want to go for a walk by myself. Is that so horrible?"

Kale felt the hurt and bewilderment from the minor dragons. Their emotions only intensified the confusion in her heart. She wanted to yell or cry or do both. Instead, she kicked over a foot-high toadstool. She stomped into the forest, leaving behind the fluttering dragons, the warm sunshine, and the smell of wildflowers in the field.

Armagot trees towered above her. Last year's foliage crunched under her feet, cushioned by an accumulation of decomposed leaves underneath. The springy carpet released an earthy, pleasant fragrance. Sparse underbrush surrounded some of the older trees. Kale wondered if the tales were true that kimens lived in such trees with their doors hidden by the bushes.

As the tree trunks grew more massive, the distance between the armagots increased. Eerie, diffused green light fell among dappled shadows on the forest floor. Kale slowed her steps.

A squirrel scurried down a trunk, across an old log, and up another tree. A bird cooed. She walked deeper into the gathering of ancient armagot, hearing only the shush of her footsteps through the fallen foliage.

"Mother?"

I ought to turn back. She looked behind her. Walking through the leaves hadn't left much of a path. *Could I find my way?* She stopped. *Mother?*

"Here I am, Kale."

Kale sucked in a breath as the woman stepped onto the path.

A cold smile crept over her mother's beautiful face. "I didn't mean to startle you."

Kale forced her voice to leave her throat. "You called me."

"Yes, it's time to leave that riffraff with whom you travel."

Kale's neck muscles and shoulders tightened. "They're my friends."

Lyll Allerion gestured with an impatient wave for Kale to follow and started away without waiting. "They may be your friends, Kale, but you don't have to follow them wherever they lead. Think for yourself for a change."

Kale hesitated.

"Well, come on. I have to get you tucked away before my absence is discovered, and before your meddling comrades start looking for you."

Kale licked her lips. *Do I want to go?*

She followed. Her mother's heavy dress rustled. The blue and gold cloth of her elaborate gown shimmered. Each time her mother's high headdress passed through thin shafts of light coming through the thick branches, the white material sparkled.

Kale examined her own practical outfit and Lyll's spotless attire. *Well, Mother's not exactly dressed appropriately for a hike in the woods. At least my breeches don't look out of place.*

She hurried to catch up. "Where are we going?"

"There's a secret room in the castle tower. You'll be safe there."

"Safe from what?"

Lyll Allerion stopped so quickly Kale bumped into her. She stepped back, expecting her mother to have a few critical words about being touched by her grubby daughter. Instead, Lyll paused and leveled an inquisitive eye at Kale.

"Risto, of course. What did you think?"

Kale looked at the creamy white skin of her mother's hand. Rings with glittering stones encircled each pale finger. The fingernails curved to delicate points.

Kale clenched her dirty hands into balls and averted her eyes just enough to gaze past her mother to the woods beyond. A clear trail meandered into a thicker gathering of towering trees. A rising wind rustled the dry leaves on the ground and stirred up a spicy fragrance from the forest floor.

Just beyond where Kale stood with her mother, a puff of air laid bare a small patch of dirt. Shadows fell over the path, darkening the soil as if it were wet.

A hiss of movement reached Kale's ears even as the wind eddied among the trees. Slithering out from behind a trunk, a vine grew at a phenomenal rate and headed for their feet.

Kale opened her mouth to speak, but her mother's cold expression stopped her. Lyll's manicured fingers squeezed Kale's arm, then released her.

Her mother whirled around in a rustle of brocade and silk. "Come!"

"Wait!" cried Kale. The path had become a bog.

Her mother took one step and pitched forward, landing in a wallow of mud.

"Oh!" Kale stepped over the thick vine, a vine that had not been there a moment before. Bewildered, she hovered at the edge of the muddy patch and reached to help the older woman in her courtly gown.

Her mother planted her fists in the mud and pushed her face and shoulders up. "Don't touch me!" She sprayed mud out of her mouth.

Kale put her hands behind her back.

Lyll raised up on her knees and struggled to her feet. She turned to face her daughter. Gray eyes glared out of her mud-coated face. Kale blinked and held still as if to avoid an attack from a wild animal.

The woman's gaze dropped to the vine.

Without using her talent, Kale knew exactly what went through her mother's mind. The vine didn't belong. It didn't match any plant growing in the forest.

The sharp caw of a blackbird broke the silence. A large ebony crow swooped between Kale and Lyll. The bird flew directly at Lyll. She threw her hands in front of her face and leaned back. The abrupt movement unbalanced her, and she toppled backward. The bird roosted on a branch above.

"Tut-tut. Oh dear. Tut-tut." Twittering, it preened its shiny wing with a sharp yellow beak.

Kale placed a hand on the pouch that carried the unhatched dragon egg. She felt a thrum from within, and a light, giddy feeling passed through her.

Her mother sat up. The elaborate headdress sat at an odd angle on her head. Clean blue cloth ran down the sides of her dress between swaths of brown mud.

Lyll once again struggled to her feet on her own. She stepped over the vine and brushed past Kale. Lifting her heavy skirts to keep from tripping, she walked away from the wallow.

"Tut-tut." The bird ruffled his feathers, swayed back and forth on yellow legs, and dipped his head. "Oh dear."

The egg under Kale's hand buzzed. A giggle rose in her throat, and she clamped her free hand over her mouth.

"Follow me, Kale." Her mother's command sent a shiver down her spine. The urge to laugh departed.

She saw another rapidly growing vine snake through the trees and across her mother's path. The woman, with her chin held high and her headdress wobbling precariously, did not see it. Once again, she landed flat on the forest floor. When she rose to her knees, leaves dotted her gown, stuck in the layer of mud adhering to her clothing.

She screeched and stood. Turning, she impaled Kale with a wicked glare. "Come," she bellowed and stomped her foot.

Up from the ground where her foot had made its impact, a geyser sprang full force. The spray of water hit Lyll in the face, blasting off a streak of mud. She shook her fists in the air and again stomped a foot. Another geyser erupted. Lyll Allerion whirled in a fit of temper. With each stomp, a new jet of water spurted from the earth. She spun in a circle, shrieking unintelligible words of fury. The air around her crackled and spat sparks, and she was gone.

The bower fell silent. Kale stared at the geysers as they quickly subsided, until the last bubble in the mud disappeared.

She sighed, releasing the tension that had gripped her shoulders. Again the egg in the pouch responded with a peculiar thrum. With the corner of her lip twitching toward a smile, she remembered her mother's second landing in the mud and the oozy brown glop on her face.

She giggled.

The hat had bobbled as her mother stood and pulled her feet out of the thick mire.

Kale giggled a little louder, and the egg answered with a louder thrum.

A sucking noise had accompanied each step her mother took.

She laughed. She sat down on the thick carpet of old leaves and laughed until she cried.

"Do you suppose she's demented?" Fenworth's scratchy voice startled Kale.

"Oh no, I wouldn't think so," answered Cam. "I do believe her egg is about to hatch though."

Kale wiped the tears from her eyes and grinned up at the two wizards. Cam's robes hung damply around him. A lizard darted in and out of Fenworth's beard.

The wizard's words registered.

"Hatch?" She opened the small red pouch and slipped the egg into her hand.

A crack appeared. The wizards sat down with their backs to an armagot tree and discussed the elements needed for a variety of spells. Kale gazed at the egg as it teetered in her hand.

A large piece of shell broke away, and the tiny dragon somersaulted out into her palm. His wet scales glistened in shades of yellow and orange. Kale frowned, trying to remember what the textbook had said about the talents of the orange and yellow. He rubbed his chin against the base of her thumb and then turned and wiggled on his back as if he needed a good scratch.

"Laughter," said Cam's deep voice beside her. "His talent is laughter."

"His name is Dibl," said Kale.

"A good name."

"Of what use is laughter on a quest?" asked Kale.

The dragon flipped over and put his small front legs down and proceeded to do a push-up. He stretched his chin high and yawned. His tiny eyes opened, and he gazed into Kale's. The snap of connection secured their bond. Kale sighed with contentment. The little dragon's lips pulled back, showing two rows of tiny pointed teeth.

"He's grinning!" said Kale.

"So he is," agreed Cam.

Fenworth joined them.

"Best thing to have on a quest," he announced. "Never know when a good laugh will save the day. Glad you thought to bring him along, Kale." He turned to the shorter, wetter wizard. "She's my apprentice, you know. A bit impulsive, but trainable, I think." He patted his beard, and a moth flew out. "Best we get on with this questing. Right, Cam? Can't say I want to spend the rest of my life in this forest. Unpleasant place sprouts geysers and runaway vines."

The old wizard took a look at the dragon stretched out in Kale's hand, then threw back his head and laughed.

22

A Different Direction

As Kale and the wizards returned from the forest, the entire camp came out to greet them. The dragons knew of Dibl's birth and spread the word. Paladin's warriors from the seven high races greeted the small yellow and orange dragon with smiles, laughter, and songs of joy.

Kale sat on a log by a small copse of slender heirnot trees. As the troops of soldiers filed past to look at the dragon, some admirers merely gazed upon Dibl curled in the palm of her hand. Some stretched out a finger to touch him lightly.

As the afternoon progressed, the camp became quieter. Kale pulled her attention away from the newborn long enough to notice that most of the troops had departed. The huge greater dragons carrying supplies and men had spread their wings and lifted into the air with quiet grace.

A shadow darkened her small spot at the edge of the meadow. She looked up to see Brunstetter looming over her. His massive fourteen-foot frame completely blocked the sun.

Brunstetter's handsome face always looked gentle to her. Laugh lines fanned out from his clear blue eyes across tanned cheeks. His lips often twitched with suppressed humor. And Kale had seen this giant man tenderly scoop up a wounded kimen with as much care as a mother lifting a hurting child.

She smiled back at her friend. "Where have they gone, Lord Brunstetter?"

"To their fighting positions." His rumbling voice held a note of sorrow. "We engage the enemy tomorrow."

"Are you leaving too?"

"In a few moments." Brunstetter touched the tip of his finger to her cheek. "We shall not see each other for some time. I have a message from my heart to yours."

She blinked back sudden tears and nodded.

"The gift of laughter before the storm strengthens our resolve. It is good that Dibl came to us now." Brunstetter moved his hand to rest it like a cap over her head. "You, little Dragon Keeper, are important in Wulder's plan. I would give you wisdom if it were like a gem to be plucked from one of my crowns. But I can only whisper caution. I can only say, 'Be still when dark clouds threaten. Listen for the word of Wulder.'"

He stroked Dibl, then stood and strode away to his magnificent dragon.

━━━◆━━━

The group around the campfire that night had dwindled to the same number as before the landing of reinforcements. The peaceful atmosphere occasionally bubbled with friendly laughter.

Kale held the sleeping Dibl in her hand while Gymn lay curled around her neck. His tail flicked up to tickle her left cheek as he kept time to the music. Dar and Regidor had served a cold meal of field greens and sliced jimmin poultry, flavored with a spicy dressing. Now the two chefs played lighthearted tunes on various instruments from Dar's pack.

Toopka danced around them with Metta sometimes balancing on the little doneel's head and sometimes doing her own aerial dance above the merrymakers.

Leetu read a book, holding a lightrock to illuminate the text. Bardon, Librettowit, and Lee Ark played a game of benders. The two wizards rested against Merlander's massive side and could be heard to say things like "Remember old Hoobenanny? I wonder where she is now."

Kale smiled. "I just thought of something funny, Gymn."

The green dragon stretched and lifted his chin to rub against her neck.

"If Chief Councilman Meiger and his goodwife, Mistress Meiger,

were here, they'd be scowling and harrumphing and muttering about all
these people. Master Meiger would say any ninny knows that wizards
don't exist, and doneels and tumanhofers keep to themselves. Mistress
Meiger would say emerlindians don't speak a language anyone can understand, 'cept themselves."

Little Dibl rolled into a ball in her cupped hand and spun himself like
a top until he twirled over the edge and fell into her lap.

"Dibl thinks it's funny too." She lifted him up and held his cool body
next to her face. She giggled. "I assumed the mariones in the village knew
almost everything there was to know. Now that I've been questing, I see
they knew next to nothing, just like me. I'd like to go back and show them
who's smarter now."

Quick as a flicker of flame, Dibl reached out and nipped her chin.

"Ouch!" She jerked him away from her face. "Why'd you do that?"

The little dragon gave a throaty growl.

"What is he trying to tell me, Gymn?"

The impression flowed into her from both dragons.

"Mean-spirited?" She clamped her jaws together. "I think it would
be fun."

This time Dibl bit her on the back of her thumb.

"Stop that!" She switched the dragon to her other hand and put the
tiny wound to her mouth. "You need to go to bed."

She slipped the dragon into the pocket that had once held his egg.

For the second time that day, tears welled in her eyes. "I think we're
all tired."

Gymn jumped to safety as she shifted onto her side on the blanket
pallet and determinedly closed her eyes.

"Good night," she said through clenched teeth.

Kale felt a touch on her forehead like a kiss. The pleasant warmth of the
caress almost woke her. But the cool, damp mist of morning all around

urged her to pull the moonbeam cloak closer and sleep. A thought like a dream told her to rise from bed and search for something. She rolled over and sighed.

Again the urge to get up and seek someone or something disturbed her slumber. She looked around the gray dawn. Only ash-covered embers lay in the campfire bed. She could make out the forms of tents and sleeping comrades. Fog obscured the countryside beyond the camp.

Celisse's head moved from side to side as she kept watch, but the dragon did not reach out to her rider. When Kale told Celisse that something had prodded her awake, the dragon answered that no one had stirred from their beds.

The hush of night hummed like a lullaby. Kale stood and stretched. She wanted to enjoy the sensation alone and walked toward the kimen falls. Following the sound of the stream, she came to the odd cascade.

She sat on the damp grass, her cape protecting her from the chill.

"I wish I could play a flute like Dar or Regidor," she whispered. "I can hear a melody in my heart. The music says Wulder is wonderful, full of peace and wisdom, banishing worry and strife. If I were Metta, I'd know a song to sing."

The gray mist swirled, thinning for a moment on the opposite bank of the rivulet. Kale saw a figure standing away from the bank.

"Who's there? Leetu?"

She rose to her feet, reaching with her mind.

Her pulse quickened, and she took in a sharp breath. In only a moment, she'd found the stepping stones and crossed to the other side. She could now see the flowing cut of a court jacket, the froth of lace at the cuffs, the dark boots that came up past the man's knees.

"Paladin," she whispered.

He turned, and his face shone as if moonlight touched him.

The first time she had seen him, Kale had thought he was very handsome. But now she realized his attractiveness came from his expression rather than his features. Oddly, Paladin and Risto resembled each other—dark hair, blue eyes, a straight nose, a strong chin, and a high forehead.

But Paladin's face held laugh lines and tenderness in his gaze. Risto's brow was furrowed with stern lines, and his haughty expression and cold eyes made her shiver.

Paladin held out one hand, and she stepped into his embrace. She rested her cheek against his chest and listened to him breathe.

"Paladin, I needed you."

"I know, my child, and I need you."

She tilted back her head to look up at his solemn face. "Are we going into Creemoor to rescue my mother?"

"No, Kale, you must go another way."

"But—"

"I knew this would be hard for you to understand, so I chose to talk with you first. You'll go to Prushing."

"Why?"

"Here come the others. We'll talk together."

Out of the mist came Dar, Regidor, and Bardon.

The three men saluted their leader. In spite of the formal greeting, they looked bemused as if they too had come up out of their beds and followed a summons they did not understand.

"Gentlemen," said Paladin, "your talents are needed elsewhere. You will go to Prushing to rescue someone from Risto's clutches. His trail will be hard to follow."

"Prushing?" Regidor tilted his head as he thought. "The capital city of Trese, located north of the Odamee Channel, and noted for a fishing industry and trade with the Northern Reach."

Paladin smiled. "Yes, Regidor."

"Who are we rescuing?" asked Dar.

"Another meech dragon, one almost the same age as our Regidor."

"Another!" Regidor's tail came up around his side, and he grasped it between two scaly hands. "Another? I'm the only meech dragon born in over a hundred years."

"It seems we were mistaken. There is another."

Dar nodded his head slowly. "And Risto has him." He thumped one fist into the palm of his other hand. "That's why Risto let us get away with Regidor. That's why he didn't unleash his wrath."

"I thought Wulder protected us," said Kale.

"Wulder did, but the fight could have been longer. Risto could have caused trouble after the egg was delivered to Fenworth." Dar searched Paladin's face. "I always suspected there was too little hubbub when Risto lost his prized possession. He had another egg. Was Regidor just a decoy?"

"A decoy?" Regidor tugged on his tail. "Nothing as grand as a meech dragon can be a mere decoy."

Paladin placed a soothing hand on the young dragon's shoulder. "Risto wanted you, all right. His plan was to use your life force to create another race. The other meech hatched around the same time as you did, Regidor. From our sources, we know that he bonded to Risto.

"Wulder has been quiet on the matter of this dragon. We proceed with care, seeking His counsel. We won't stand still and wait, since we know that Wulder is ever opposed to evil. But without clear direction, we take small steps, only doing what we know will cause no harm."

He let his gaze move over the selected warriors. "Risto's plan for this other meech dragon is to control all orders of dragon in the land. He will maneuver this meech into a place of leadership and be the power behind the figurehead. With that knowledge, we move into position to stop him."

"Couldn't I stop him?" Regidor grinned at the prospect. "Could I command the dragons to follow me instead?"

Paladin shook his head. "No, Risto has enhanced this dragon's charismatic personality with a spell. At this point he is capable of gaining dominance over the dragons and causing havoc."

Bardon placed his hand upon the hilt of his sword belted at his waist. "Then we find and destroy this meech dragon before Risto can use him for evil."

"No, Bardon, my friend. This is a rescue mission. You are to bring the meech dragon out of the hell he was born into."

Dar shook his head. "I'd rather fight Creemoor spiders. Simpler."

23

Last-Minute Changes

The sun burned away the morning mist.

Paladin had said they would leave this morning. But for now Paladin sat with Wizard Fenworth and Wizard Cam, Librettowit, Lee Ark, and Leetu Bends. Kale resisted the urge to listen in on their conversation using her mindspeaking ability.

I'm glad we're leaving. I'm not sure I could stand this waiting much longer. Kale looked off toward the wood. *But I'm not sure how I feel about going to Prushing.*

"I get to go with you?" Toopka asked again.

"Yes." Kale gave the doneel's solid little body a hug. "Paladin said you would be helpful in the city. Dar knows about the aristocracy, and you know about the street people."

"I'm going to call Dar 'uncle,' but I am not going to call you 'aunt.' No one would believe you're my aunt. You could marry Dar and be my aunt, but that wouldn't be believable either."

"Why wouldn't that be believable?"

"You're so different. You'd fight all the time."

"Not necessarily." Kale tried to remember something she had read in one of the textbooks at The Hall. Something about Wulder making people different so they could work together more efficiently.

Toopka tugged on Kale's sleeve. "You don't know how to cook or sew or play music. Dar can do all those things."

"Wulder gave different talents to people. Imagine if Dar and I fought over who would fix our meals, what a mess that would be. This way I leave him to do what he does best, and he leaves me to do what I do best."

"What do you do best, Kale?"

The question stunned her. *I was a good slave. A hard worker, obedient, quick. And I really liked taking care of the children.*

Kale looked into the trusting eyes of the young doneel on her lap. With a grin growing on her face, she said, "Tickle!" and gently dug her wiggling fingers into Toopka's sides, making her squeal and squirm.

The two toppled over on the grass, and Kale pinned Toopka.

"You're fun, Kale. You'd make a good mommy."

"I'm a long ways away from being a mother."

"Wulder could fix it so you could have babies now."

"Yes, but Wulder wants us to get ready to do a task so we'll be counted good workers—like Dar and Bardon practice for battle. Wulder would want me to learn more before being a mother. He would also want me to have a husband."

Kale let Toopka sit up. Kale smiled as she watched the little girl smooth her blouse and pick grass off her breeches, reminding Kale of Dar's fastidious attention to grooming.

Toopka looked at Kale and wrinkled her nose. "Rules! Wulder should just cross out some. That would make it easier to remember the important ones."

Kale laughed. "Fenworth says Wulder made His rules for good reasons. He doesn't ever rearrange His rules on a whim."

"On a wind? Like a sandstorm? Sittiponder said sandstorms are fierce. They'll shred your skin like sliding down a gravel pit."

Kale tried to capture an elusive memory. "I'm sorry, Toopka. I don't remember who Sittiponder is."

"He's the blind wisdom speaker who lives alone under the stairs at the warehouses in Vendela. I used to bring him food, not just because of the stories he'd tell, but because I liked him."

"How did he get so wise if he lived alone? Did he go to school?"

"He said if he was still, he could hear the words spoken in The Hall, and at night he collected wisdom while he dreamed."

"Someday I'd like to meet Sittiponder."

"So Wulder uses wind to change things when He wants to?"

"What? Where did you get such a strange idea? Oh no! I said, 'whim,' not 'wind.' A whim is a careless idea, one you didn't think about very much, and it is likely to get you into trouble."

"Well, Wulder wouldn't go around thinking whims. I've decided you can't marry Dar."

Bardon's shadow fell across them. "Marry Dar?"

Toopka grinned. "But Kale could marry you, Bardon. Then you could adopt me, and Dar could still be my uncle."

A look of horror destroyed Bardon's usually guarded expression.

Toopka, you said that on purpose.

"Of course I said it on purpose. How can you say something on accident?"

I mean you said that deliberately to embarrass Bardon—and me!

"Kale is t-t-too young to marry," Bardon stammered. "And I, I have no profession."

"You're a servant of Paladin." Toopka planted her fists on her tiny hips. "Isn't that a pro-fes-son?"

"I was training." Bardon ran his hand along the side of his head, smoothing the dark hair that never seemed mussed or at all uncombed. "I never got to the important preparation."

Toopka stepped closer to him. "Paladin said I could go on the quest because I would be useful. *I* didn't have *any* training. So if *I* am useful, *you* must be tons useful."

Dibl came and landed on Bardon, next to his muscular neck. Bardon jerked and turned his head to eye the bright dragon perched on the brown material of his tunic. The warrior took in a quick breath, and as he released it, his face softened. He smiled. Then his shoulders shook gently, and a laugh escaped his lips. He patted the indignant doneel on her furry head and looked to Kale.

"I came to ask you," he said, "if you're ready to go. Paladin says there's no gateway inside the city. We'll have to enter the countryside."

Kale stood as Dar approached with two packs slung over his shoulders. Librettowit followed.

The tumanhofer nodded to Lehman Bardon. "I'm not needed on the Creemoor expedition. Cam will watch after Fenworth. I asked to return to my library, but Paladin sends me with you instead." Librettowit shrugged, shifting the load on his back. "No matter. I believe the rare book shops in Prushing will be worth the bother of trailing a miscreant meech."

Regidor trotted over to join them. "I'll be able to sniff him out. What better person to find a meech dragon than another meech dragon?"

Toopka clapped her hands and bounced on her toes. "A sneaky little doneel. That's me."

Bardon scooped the child into his arms. "You are to stick like a rock pine cone to Kale and stay out of trouble. I am your commanding officer, and you are to obey orders."

Toopka's eyes grew big. "You're in charge of all of us?"

"No, Dar is, but I outrank you, little ninny-nap-conder."

Regidor cleared his throat. "I don't believe I've seen that word in any of Librettowit's dictionaries."

"Ninny-nap-conder refers," said the librarian, "to one who appears to be a ninny, and one who seems to sleep through what is happening, unaware of what is going on. But in actuality, it means a con artist, one who manipulates those around her. In this case, ninny-nap-conder is a term of endearment. Bardon is saying Toopka is a little scamp."

Toopka cocked her head and frowned. "I don't think I like being endeared that way."

Kale chuckled as she snapped her fingers to draw the foraging minor dragons' attention. "Then you'd best deal more honestly with your friends. Gymn, Metta, we're leaving."

The dragons, including Dibl, flew to Kale and pushed their way beneath the folds of her cape to find their pocket-dens. Kale stooped to roll up her bedroll.

In a matter of minutes, the party of questers lined up before Paladin. The second company of adventurers, who would go to Creemoor, stood beside them.

"One more thing before you go," Paladin said. "Kale, I must see the dragon eggs you still have in your keeping."

Kale swiftly lowered her pack to the ground and removed the eggs from the pockets sewn into the moonbeam cape. The three minor dragons came out, chittering excitedly.

Paladin crouched on the other side and slowly examined each of the five eggs Kale lined up along the top of her bundle of belongings.

"This one," he said, picking up the middle egg. He handed it to Kale. "Place this one in your hatching pouch."

The small dragons zoomed into the air and did somersaults above the assembly. Dibl dove into Wizard Fenworth's beard and did not reappear.

"Here now," protested the old man as he patted his beard. "Come out of there. You're eating, aren't you? Take care you eat the bugs and not my buttons. I'll not have my robes falling off because some inexperienced glutton devoured bone buttons instead of beetles. You could be useful while you're at it and eat that drummerbug that keeps me awake at night."

A bumblebee buzzed out of the curtain of gray hair at tremendous speed with Dibl right behind it. The dragon snatched it, chewed, swallowed, and gave out a trill of joy.

"Quite!" agreed the wizard and nodded knowingly at those around him. "Sweet. A delicacy. Very filling. But they tickle on the way down."

24

THE JOURNEY BEGINS

Kale and her friends mounted the dragons. Paladin took the point, leading them to Brunstetter's castle. Flying over the countryside reminded Kale that this rolling prairie held animals larger than in any other part of Amara. Traveling on land, they might have seen chickens as large as dogs, dogs as big as cows, cows as tall as horses, and horses she could have walked under without bending.

The sun reached its peak, and the urohm city of Blisk appeared on the horizon. They landed in a dragon field and rode in wagons to the center of the metropolis.

Lady Brunstetter, a dark-eyed, stately woman, served the questing party a noonmeal. Dar and Regidor savored the meal with a good deal of lip-smacking. Kale kicked the doneel under the table after one especially loud slurp of soup.

"Ouch!" He turned to glare at his o'rant friend.

Lady Brunstetter laughed, her eyes twinkling with merriment. "I know exactly how you feel, Kale. But it's their custom, and doneels think it not rude but complimentary to eat noisily. The problem is when my doneel friends leave after an extended visit. Then I have to retrain our children in the manners of our people."

As if to prove her point, one of the children took a bite of roasted venison and smacked loudly before dabbing grease from his chin with a linen napkin.

The meal was quickly dispatched. Paladin thanked their hostess for her graciousness and ushered the questing party into a chamber behind the throne room.

A gateway shimmered against a solid stone wall. Kale held Toopka with the little doneel's arms wrapped around her neck. Librettowit stood in the shadows against a side wall in the small room. Bardon held a position by the door, his posture stiff, his hand on the hilt of his sword, and his jaw rigid. Kale intercepted a glance her way and smiled at him. He looked away without acknowledging her gesture of encouragement.

It's all right, Bardon. We're all nervous.

He blinked, but didn't respond.

Regidor held his tail in one hand. White knuckles gleamed on each scaly finger.

Kale looked at the stone slab floor and wished for Leetu Bends. *She isn't always friendly, but she sure acts like nothing bothers her. On the last quest, I thought I was safe just because she was there.*

Paladin nodded for Dar to go first. The doneel diplomat stepped before his ruler.

"I pledge again my loyalty to you, my lord. May Wulder keep me humbly in your service."

Paladin rested a hand on Dar's shoulder. "I commission you to stand strong against the enemy of our high and mighty Wulder, to stand true to His word of hope, to stand with wisdom over His warriors entrusted to your guidance, and to seek justice and mercy in this quest."

Dar bowed slightly and strode through the gateway.

Regidor marched forward. "Do I get a commission? Do I get special instructions?"

"Your commission is like Dar's. Each member of the party is to uphold Dar's leadership and to accept his mission as their own." He looked around the stone-walled chamber to include each member of the questing party. "You may decline at this moment."

No one moved to take up the offer.

Paladin turned back to the meech dragon. "Regidor, you will grow in knowledge, stature, and maturity in very short order. Do not think that you outpace your comrades. Wulder has placed each one within your circle of influence for your good and for their own. Be mindful of your rank. You are neither the head nor the tail of this expedition."

"I understand, my lord. We are dependent on each other."

"Precisely." Paladin clapped him on the shoulder. "Go."

As soon as the lights in the gateway faded from Regidor's passing, Paladin held up his arm as a falconer would to invite his bird to land.

"Come, little ones."

The three minor dragons crawled out of their pocket-dens and flew to him. They perched on the elegant sleeve and gazed studiously at Paladin. After looking each one in the eye for several moments, the ruler gave his small subjects permission to fly through the gateway.

Kale realized that some of her anxiety had drained away.

I don't know what he said to them, but it must have been wonderful.

She heard Paladin's rich chuckle in her mind.

"I told them to behave."

Kale grinned. *That's all?*

"I did remind them that Wulder cares whether they do well or not, and will always be with them."

Ah, that comforts me as well.

Paladin gestured for Librettowit to come forward. The librarian shuffled to his position in front of the ruler. Paladin placed a hand on each shoulder.

"My friend, you are always the reluctant hero. What would we do without you?"

Librettowit's head snapped up, and he scowled.

Paladin's face showed no humor, only sincere respect. "Go, my learned comrade. Mind these young rapscallions."

Librettowit jerked his head in an affirmative nod and pushed through the gateway.

"Bardon," called Paladin.

The lehman stepped forward and saluted. "At your command, my lord."

"Trust in what you have already learned, Lehman. Your foundation will serve you well."

Paladin nodded his dismissal, and the young warrior drew near to the gateway. He hesitated only a moment before striding through.

Kale looked at Paladin, wondering if she would be called next.

The ruler's face looked unusually stern. "Toopka!"

The small doneel hopped down from Kale's arms without a word and ran to stand before the ruler of Amara, king to some, bane to others.

She remained silent but looked cautiously at Paladin.

What's going on? thought Kale. *I've never known Toopka to be at a loss for words.*

"I am not so pleased with you as I would like to be," said Paladin.

Toopka ducked her head and stared at the floor.

"I commission you from this day forward to walk in truth, not only in spoken word, but unspoken as well. In deed as well as word. Even in your thoughts, for you deceive yourself as often as you deceive others."

Toopka's small furry head bobbed in acknowledgment of the command. She sniffed and, with one furry hand, wiped a tear from her cheek.

Paladin scooped the child into his arms and embraced her with a warm hug, kissing the side of her face as she sobbed. Resting his cheek against the top of her head, he said, "You must not use your sad beginning as an excuse to travel the wrong path. Wulder has given you much. Give back, dear child, give back. Don't hoard in fear that this is all there is. Give freely, and you will be given to. Wulder has an abundant supply."

He stood her on the floor, pulled a white handkerchief from his pocket, and dabbed away her tears.

He then smiled and kissed her on the top of her head. With a gentle hand on her back, he scooted her toward the gateway.

"You will be fine, Toopka. Trust and be trustworthy."

The doneel disappeared through the gateway.

"Now, my child and friend, servant and keeper of the dragons, it is your turn. Come forward." He held out a hand, and Kale stepped forward to take it.

"Tell me what you are thinking."

"You already know."

"Tell me."

"I don't know my friends as I thought I did. Dar is much more important than he appears, isn't he?"

"I agree."

"Toopka and Bardon have secrets, don't they?"

"Yes. You will need to be a friend to both."

"Librettowit is tired."

"As is Fenworth. We are all tired of the fight against those like Risto. But still, we will persevere."

"What do you charge me with, Paladin? Tell me exactly what you want me to do, and I will do my best."

Paladin smiled and tenderly cupped the side of her face in his warm hand. "As always, Kale, I ask for you to do the good you see right in front of you. That is all."

Kale blinked hard, trying to keep tears from spilling down her cheeks. "Why can't you just tell me?"

"Because then you would know *my* strength in Wulder instead of discovering your own."

Not really understanding, she nodded and turned toward the gateway. She hesitated. "Is there anything else?"

"Enjoy the journey."

Kale took a deep breath, stepped into the thick air exploding with light, and stepped out of the gateway, straight into the arms of Granny Noon.

25

FEAST OF FRIENDS

Kale squealed and hugged the emerlindian, lifting her tiny frame off the floor. "You're here! You're here!" She twirled the old woman around and set her down. "Oh, Granny Noon, you're the very person I wanted to see."

Granny Noon cradled Kale's face with her dark brown hands and looked deep into her eyes. The wise woman's calm joy flowed into Kale, slowing the girl's racing heart and giving her peace.

Then Granny Noon stepped to her side and slipped an arm around her waist. "Come, we must talk."

Kale looked around the room she had entered through the gateway.

A marione home!

Her feet slowed, but Granny Noon gently tugged her toward a square door. The memories of reticent mariones she had known while a slave made her uneasy. But she had also met loquacious mariones in Lee Ark's village.

What type of mariones live here, I wonder. Warm or cold?

Kale breathed a sigh of relief as soon as the heavy wooden door swung open to the sound of laughter and music.

A crowd mingled in the large entryway to a country manor. Dark, rustic beams accented white plastered walls. A huge fireplace dominated one end of the room. Kale saw two massive square doors opened to a front carriageway and lawn.

Along with her eight comrades, many mariones of various ages participated in some kind of celebration. More visitors arrived and were greeted by the host and taken to a buffet of aromatic foods.

"The party is to cover your departure from this house," explained

Granny Noon. "The enemy may or may not know that there is a gateway in the back room. They're definitely suspicious of the family's activities."

Gymn sat in the cupped hands of an elderly woman in a rocking chair. Kale knew he was soothing away the aches of her arthritis. Metta, Dibl, and Toopka had joined the crowd around Dar, who was playing a harpsichord. Regidor eyed the musical instrument as if it were a delectable dessert. Librettowit and Bardon sat in a corner, the librarian holding a tankard and scowling, Bardon just scowling.

Irritated, Kale called to him. *Bardon!*

His eyes flicked her way, and the line of his jaw relaxed.

Stop scowling. These people are risking their lives to help us.

"I'm not scowling. I'm merely observing."

From this side of your face, it looks like you're scowling.

Dibl left the music makers and perched on Bardon's shoulder. The solemn lehman lifted a finger and stroked the yellow dragon's belly. Dibl hummed, closed his eyes in pleasure, and leaned against Bardon's neck. Bardon smiled and winked at Kale.

Granny Noon tugged at Kale's arm. *"Don't frown so, dear. These are your friends."*

She guided Kale through the great hall to a sitting room where three comfortable chairs and a settee surrounded an elegant table.

"I'm really not hungry, Granny Noon," Kale said as she sat down. "We just ate at Brunstetter Castle."

Granny Noon sat as well, lifted the china teapot, and poured into delicate cups. Her homespun dress draped gracefully over her shoulders with soft folds of material.

"Just a cup of tea, then, to settle your nerves."

"My nerves are fine now that I've seen you. Can you go with us?"

Granny Noon chuckled. "No, dear. I'm much too old for adventures."

Kale took a sip of the warm, sweet tea. She closed her eyes as it went down her throat, delighting in the way it refreshed her deep down inside. When she opened her eyes again, she sighed and tackled the subject she most wanted to talk about.

"Granny Noon, I saw my mother."

"Did you, dear?"

"Yes." Now that she had decided to talk to Granny Noon about her mother, even against her mother's wishes, she couldn't hold the words back. "She called to me from a forest near our campsite. She's the most beautiful woman I've ever seen." Kale looked down to the drink in her hand. Beneath the dark amber brew, tiny specks of tea leaves floated near the bottom of the cup.

She shook her head slightly. "But I don't like her, Granny Noon. She told me not to tell anyone that I'd seen her. The second time she called me, it felt awful. When Paladin said I had to come here and not go to Creemoor to rescue her, I was glad."

Her hands shook, and the teacup rattled on its saucer. She hastily put the fragile pieces of china down on the table. Balling her hands into fists, she placed them on her knees.

"What's wrong with me?"

Kale glanced at Granny Noon, but averted her eyes before really seeing the old woman's expression. She didn't want to see her disapproval. "As a slave, I know I'm supposed to obey. I've always been good about doing what I'm told to do. But I didn't obey Mother. And I don't want to find her or stay with her. I'd rather be with Dar and Regidor, Librettowit and Wizard Fenworth, my friends." She sobbed.

"I understand what you're saying, my dear." Granny Noon took another sip of tea. "But I don't understand why you're crying."

Kale peeked at Granny Noon and saw the emerlindian was not looking at her with disgust. She took a deep breath, trying to control the sobs. She must explain how she had failed and was doomed to continued failure. "I'm not good at questing. I don't have any talents that will help my friends. I'll do something stupid and get them killed. I don't have knowledge like Librettowit. I can't fight like Dar and Bardon. I don't even know as much as Toopka does about living in a city. And I'm a bad person. I don't even love my mother."

Granny Noon managed to look sympathetic even with a smile on her lips. "You're not a bad person, Kale. You're not obligated to love a woman you don't know. You're not bound to obey a woman who's done nothing to demonstrate that she's trustworthy."

"But she's a servant of Paladin. She's been doing a dangerous job for years."

"The woman you describe does not resemble the Lyll Allerion I knew years ago." Granny Noon paused to stir her tea. "Living in the stronghold of evil does take its toll on an individual. People change."

"Sometimes for the better," Kale put in, thinking about how much she had learned since leaving River Away.

"Yes, and sometimes not," said Granny Noon. "We will wait and not evaluate her character without knowing more. Wulder will reveal her heart."

Granny Noon stood. Kale jumped to her feet. This sign of respect she did not begrudge her emerlindian mentor.

"Our time for talk," said Granny Noon, "is limited, Kale. I must give you and your friends the things you need to dwell in the city. But you've said some things that I cannot let pass."

She swallowed at the sound of Granny Noon's stern voice. *She is disgusted with me.*

"I am not!" The voice snapped in her mind. "Now listen to me. You referred to yourself as a slave. You are never to do so again. You said you had no talents of worth to your comrades. In this you mock Wulder's wisdom."

Kale gasped.

Granny Noon nodded. "Precisely so. It is a grave error to belittle the talents given to you by Wulder. Judge accurately the value of those talents. You must know exactly what you're worth so that you do not fail your friends. This would be an inadequacy in your spirit, not in your ability." The emerlindian gathered her skirts in her hands and headed for the door.

"We're running late. I want you to be able to enter the city by tomorrow afternoon, which means you must leave before this day turns into night." She stopped with her hand on the doorknob. Her voice softened. "Kale, remember to use to the fullest the talents given you and enhance your skill with every opportunity Wulder provides. You are the Dragon Keeper, and none of your gifts are insignificant."

26

Ambush

Kale rode on top of a stack of trunks and luggage strapped to the carriage roof. Bardon sat beside the driver, a marione named Bruit, with Toopka tucked between them. Librettowit, Regidor, and Dar rode inside. With instructions to stay out of sight, the little dragons slept contentedly in their pocket-dens.

Granny Noon had given the adventurers bags of coins, letters of introduction, lists of contacts, and a key to an upper-class residence. The questing party would not be trooping through mountains, valleys, and hidden caves, but through the streets of a metropolis and the homes of the wealthy. Regidor would be disguised as a foreign abbot whose monastery indulged in trade for the benefit of their demesne. Librettowit, an art dealer. Dar, butler and valet. Bardon would play the part of household sheridan, a special servant armed to protect family and property. Kale and Toopka were ordinary servants.

Granny Noon had given Kale a piece of silver, a rather odd, flat disk with two irregular pie shapes cut out of the sides. Granny Noon said it would help her identify people. Kale turned the shiny silver piece over and over in her callused palm.

"How?" she had asked.

"I don't actually know, dear. But Paladin said it would come in handy, so do your best not to lose it."

Kale kept the disk in the pouch with the egg Paladin had picked. Now, as they bounced along in the warm afternoon sun, the small metal piece was all but forgotten.

A giant draft horse pulled the carriage. The urohm-bred animal had no difficulty hauling the load up and down the cultivated hills. On either side, crops looked ready for harvest in carefully tended fields. Farm carts, tinkers, and smaller carriages passed frequently on the wide, well-graded road.

As they approached a wooded area, Kale relaxed against a softer bundle with her hands behind her head. She gazed at white, puffy clouds drifting lazily in a blue sky.

This isn't going to be so bad. No mordakleeps. No blimmets. No grawligs. No schoergs.

An arrow whizzed by Kale's head and penetrated one of the trunks. The shaft vibrated with a hard hum, causing the hair on the back of her neck to stand up.

Shouts erupted from other travelers on the road. A horse neighed, followed by the sound of hoofbeats galloping away.

Kale heard Bardon yell, "Get down!" and saw him push Toopka off the seat onto the floor of the driver's perch.

Bruit fought to control the frightened horse, pulling it to a stop. In the next moment, Bardon had a bow in his hands with an arrow nocked and ready to shoot. He aimed at a target ahead and released the arrow. With a fluid motion, he pulled another arrow out of his quiver.

Kale peered forward over a ridge of luggage. A band of tattered bisonbecks plowed into the walking travelers. They swung clubs, grabbed parcels, and threw their victims to the side of the road. Women screamed, children cried, and men tried desperately to protect their families and property from the large, brutal robbers.

Bruit still struggled to keep the horse from bolting. Beneath Kale, the doors to the carriage flew open. Librettowit and Dar rushed to lend aid.

Drawing a deep breath, Kale pulled her small sword from its scabbard. The carriage jerked as the horse reared and stomped angrily, protesting the chaos around them. She waited for a still moment between lurches and vaulted over the side of the carriage onto the back of a bisonbeck bandit.

Her blade plunged into the highwayman's shoulder and struck bone. The bisonbeck howled and grabbed at Kale. She jerked her sword free and slid down his back to the ground.

As he whirled around, she braced herself as she had seen Dar do in his mock combats with Bardon. The beast's momentum drove his leg past her blade, slicing his calf. She rolled away, taking her bloodstained weapon with her.

The man fell with a thud to the dirt road. Kale looked back to see him squirming away from the wildly rocking wheels of the carriage. Bardon landed on his feet beside the downed outlaw. Kale turned away.

Librettowit swung a hadwig. The spiked metal ball tore across the side of an attacker. The bisonbeck roared and faced the tumanhofer. With an adept change of the swing, Librettowit clipped the taller man in the face. The brigand leaned forward, grabbing at his wounded cheek. The next swing of the heavy weapon caught the back of his head and laid him out on the road.

Kale joined Dar, who stood between two ugly bisonbecks and a family of farmers. The marione farmer stood his ground with a strapping son beside him. But with no weapons except their walking staffs, they must have welcomed the sight of the feisty doneel. The two scruffy bisonbecks reevaluated the odds against four determined fighters and ran.

Kale, Dar, and the two farmers waded into the battle alongside a tinker fighting to keep his wagon. When those ruffians dispersed, Kale looked back to see Bardon fighting with a sword. She only had a moment to appreciate his grace next to the awkward attacker before a shout called her attention to a bisonbeck man carrying off a tumanhofer woman toward a stand of trees.

Kale followed. Heirnot trees stood with their slender trunks spaced far enough apart that she had no problem catching up with the villain abducting the woman. She launched herself at the man's knees and brought him down with a solid tackle. Then she rolled away and came up again with her small sword ready to swing. Neither the man nor the maiden stirred.

She eyed the mass of disheveled clothing, waiting for some sign of life. She panted from the run, but nothing in the mound moved with any indication of breathing. As she watched, the garments shrunk as if they had lost their stuffing. The woman and her abductor were gone, leaving no more than a pile of ragged clothes.

Kale straightened from her fight-ready stance and glowered. Reaching with her mind, she didn't connect with anything. Taking a cautious step forward, she kept her sword pointed at the curious heap.

A growl warned her an instant before a massive body slammed into her from the side, knocking her down. She managed to keep a grip on the sword as the attacker pinned her arm to the ground. Struggling under his weight, she felt herself pushed deeper into the old leaves. A huge hand pressed against her skull, and she thought she would suffocate in the damp mulch.

She became aware of the distress of the minor dragons trapped in her cape. Metta sang an outraged battle song she had never heard before. Gymn sent wave after wave of strength to Kale, but it was not enough to topple the man off her back. Dibl giggled as images of squashed berries flitted through his mind and therefore hers.

The bisonbeck grunted, jerked, grunted again, and rose off Kale. She forced her arms underneath her and pushed to pry her body out of the muck. She turned on her side to see Bardon deliver a fisted blow to the disarmed assailant. The man sank to his knees and fell over.

Bardon stood with his sword ready, scanning the area around them for other attackers. "Are you all right, Kale?"

She nodded, mumbling, "Yes."

The dwindling sounds of fighting told her the skirmish was almost over.

Dibl flew from her cape and landed on their rescuer. Bardon stroked his orange belly. A twinkle lurked in the lehman's blue eyes. He offered a hand to help Kale rise.

"Next time," he said with a grin, "try attacking your opponent from the top instead of the bottom. It gives you an advantage."

She jerked her hand out of his. "That wasn't funny." She brushed at the leaves and dirt covering her.

"Dibl thought it was."

Her eyes came up to meet his. "You heard Dibl mindspeak?"

Bardon's brow furrowed more, and he shook his head. "No, it was only an impression."

"An impression is all you usually get from a minor dragon," Kale explained. "Images. Thoughts that are almost words, but not quite."

"I don't mindspeak."

She ignored his objection and continued to puzzle over how Bardon had "heard" Dibl.

"Dibl is bonded to me. I can mindspeak with him. He would converse easily with someone else adept at mindspeaking. In a desperate situation, one of my minor dragons could probably get a message through to someone rather inept at the art." Kale studied Bardon, someone she had always considered dense in the ways of wizardry. She shook her head. "But you heard Dibl."

"I didn't."

"Did you think of that quip about me fighting from on top instead of the bottom?"

Bardon nodded with a smug smile tightening his lips.

"What was Dibl's reaction?"

"He laughed."

Kale raised a finger and shook it at the staid lehman. "He didn't laugh out loud."

Bardon's scowl returned, but he didn't speak.

"How many of Paladin's servants at The Hall mindspeak?"

"Some instructors. Grand Ebeck. Maybe a half dozen in all."

"So maybe you never had a chance to develop the talent."

"Maybe you're full of foolishness."

They glared at each other, each with their hands on their hips in a no-nonsense, straight-legged posture.

Dibl flew to Kale's shoulder.

She blinked and relaxed. "Thank you."

"What for?"

She leaned over to wipe her blade in the leaves, cleaning off the blood. "For saving my life."

"Oh, that."

She looked up and giggled. "Yes, that."

Bardon smiled.

She ducked her head, concentrating on polishing her weapon.

He smiled, and Dibl isn't even sitting on his shoulder.

27

Stranded Travelers

"An illusion?" Librettowit considered the matter of the disappearing bisonbeck and maiden. Bardon, Toopka, and Kale had joined Librettowit, Dar, and Regidor inside the carriage as soon as the skirmish with the bandits ended. Dar had ordered Bruit to turn off the main road to take a shortcut avoiding the small city of Tourk. The coach rocked and bounced over rough roads, making slower time than they had earlier.

With each sway of the carriage, the crowded passengers leaned into each other. In his nervous state, Regidor's tail took up more room than usual. The meech dragon had to keep a firm hold on the tail to keep it from twitching in his comrades' faces.

Librettowit interlaced his fingers and rested his hands on his stomach. "The trick was designed to lure someone away from the crowd. Was the trick aimed at just anyone, or at Kale, in particular?"

Bardon nodded. "Was this a random group of footpads, or were they paid to waylay our party?"

Regidor's tail flicked out of his hands and slapped Librettowit alongside the head. The librarian scowled. The meech dragon grabbed his tail and pulled it back into his lap.

Regidor voiced his opinion. "I would have said random had they not lured our Dragon Keeper into the woods."

Dar studied Kale with a thoughtful eye and his arms crossed over his chest. "I agree with Librettowit. I think it was an illusion."

Kale frowned at her friend. "But when I hit the man's legs, they were solid and folded just like you'd expect."

Bardon joined the discussion. "The people disappeared from the pile of clothes, then the clothes disappeared during the fight. Illusion!"

"Yes," agreed Dar. "Kale, did you use the words Granny Noon gave you to protect yourself before you entered the fray?"

Her eyes opened wide. *I stand under the authority of Wulder. In Wulder's service, I search for truth. My thoughts belong to me and Wulder. I haven't repeated those things since before the last encounter with my mother.*

Dar nodded, knowingly. "So you haven't been protecting your mind."

Kale glared at him. *Do you read my mind?*

"No!"

Dar sighed. Since she was already connected to Dar by the brief interchange of mindspeaking, Kale felt his frustration ease out of him. It flowed out of her as well. This was her good friend. She trusted him.

An emotion transferred from Dar, and Kale almost gasped when she realized it was love. The warm feeling embraced her. It resembled the peace she experienced when she was with Granny Noon.

A new realization struck her. *This is how I feel when I'm aware of Wulder's presence. Only this isn't as grand. When I felt Wulder near me, I didn't see His love. It was too big. This small feeling is more comfortable than Wulder's majestic, commanding love.* A shiver of contentment raised goose bumps on Kale's arms. *Wulder loves me.*

She could not recall ever being aware of another's love for her. Lyll Allerion's professions didn't count. Something about that relationship continued to rattle her peace of mind.

"Kale," said Dar, pointing a finger at her, "you're subject to evil influences because you're a spiritual being. You must always be on your guard."

"On guard?"

"The enemy targets one he feels is furthering Paladin's agenda."

Toopka bounced on Bardon's knee. "Maybe Kale should let herself get caught. Then she can mindspeak to us and tell us what's going on from inside."

"Inside where?" Kale asked.

Toopka shrugged. "I don't know. Inside Risto's castle, or inside the prison where they're keeping the other meech, or inside the army head-quarters."

"I've been inside Risto's castle." Kale shook her head. "And I don't care to go back. I don't think they're keeping the dragon in a prison, because he's supposed to be out influencing other dragons."

"And," interrupted Librettowit, "the bisonbeck army's headquarters is in Risto's castle."

Bardon cleared his throat. "Where Kale does not care to go."

The lehman sat scrunched between her and the carriage wall with Dibl on his shoulder. Kale twisted in her seat to look at Bardon's face. She didn't see any amusement in his expression, but a shimmer like an unvoiced chortle passed through her mind. She narrowed her eyes at him, convinced that the ripple of suppressed laughter had come from him.

At that moment, the door to the driver's seat above their heads opened. Kale looked up and saw the back of the driver's boots and trouser legs.

"Begging your pardon," Bruit said with a country drawl, his voice raised over the noise of harness and horse, "but there's a disabled landau in the road some distance ahead. Do you want me to stop?"

Bardon tossed Toopka into Kale's lap, grabbed the top edge of the open window at his side, and slithered out of the crowded coach, climbing to the roof.

His voice came down to them, loud and clear.

"Three o'rant females and a male marione driver. The women are dressed like landed gentry."

"We must stop," announced Dar. "Kale and Toopka, up on the roof with you. Can't have the lower servants riding in the coach. Young Dibl, remember you are to stay out of sight."

Kale pushed Toopka through the window and up to Bardon's waiting hands, then crawled out, clambering to lie on the luggage.

Bruit pulled back on the reins, saying, "Steady, Romer. We're gonna stop for a minute or two and see what these folks need." The horse leaned back against the breeches. The harness jangled.

Kale stared at the fancy carriage, shiny black with yellow wheels. The roof had been lowered to allow the passengers to enjoy the pleasant autumn afternoon. Two young women perched in the seat facing forward. An older lady roosted in the matching seat that faced the rear of the vehicle. The driver sat in the dirt beside a wheel, mending a strip of leather.

The youngest of the ladies lifted a hand in greeting. Kale almost responded before she remembered her place as a servant. Although she couldn't hear the words spoken, Kale recognized when the oldest woman voiced a strong reprimand. The younger girl bit her lip and lowered her head.

Kale explored their thoughts to determine whether this was another ambush.

The mother's mind listed household details that were being ignored because of their delay in returning from afternoon social calls.

The oldest girl bubbled with delight that the exceedingly boring day had ended with an encounter with a splendid man, obviously the household sheridan. This sheridan's amazingly handsome face made her heart flutter.

Kale blinked twice when she realized the young lady was batting her eyelashes at Bardon.

The younger sister, too, found Bardon attractive, so attractive that she could only peek up at him. With each glance, she blushed and demurely looked down to her gloved hands folded in her lap. She hoped their mother would invite the party to their manor so she could watch him all evening long.

Kale studied her companion. Bardon's frame was long and lean, a little taller than the average o'rant. His muscles bulged under the simple garment of a servant. His face held his usual reserved expression. His clear blue eyes under dark eyebrows were startling, but Kale thought they too often looked aloof, not friendly at all. But to be fair, she admitted Bardon had warmed up lately.

Romer slowed and stopped beside the landau. Dar jumped down from the carriage and held the door for Librettowit to descend.

"Good afternoon, ladies," Librettowit bowed. "Trevithick Librettowit at your service. May we be of assistance?"

The oldest woman spoke. "The breeching came loose in the harness. Our driver will have it right in short order."

The driver had risen to his feet as Dar and Librettowit approached. He tipped his hat to the men.

Kale transferred her attention to the thoughts of the driver. His mind was on the impossibility of reconnecting the rotted leather in his hands. Kale conveyed that information to Librettowit.

"Ahem!" said the tumanhofer, looking over to the frustrated driver. "May I have our driver assist? Perhaps we have a piece of leather to graft into the harness."

The older o'rant woman looked to her driver. He nodded, and she looked back at Librettowit.

"Very well."

Bruit handed the reins to Bardon and climbed down from his perch. Kale felt the coach rock as the man shifted from one position to another, but she also felt Regidor move within the carriage after their driver's feet were on the ground. She suspected he sat by the partially opened small door that allowed the driver to speak to those inside the carriage.

It took some time for the two drivers to improvise the connection between the crupper and breeching. Dar remained silent. As a butler, he could not enter into the social exchange of his betters. Librettowit maintained the conversation, though somewhat stiff in his manner.

The mother introduced her girls, Miss Adel Gransford, Peony, and herself, Mistress Gransford. Kale watched as the young ladies tossed flirtatious glances at Bardon.

Librettowit explained their journey to Prushing.

"I'm in search of a rare book I heard has been seen in Dottergobeathan's Antique Emporium. My traveling companion Abbot Gidor remains in the carriage. I beg you to forgive this apparent discourtesy, but he is a religious man from the Northern Reach. He goes about with his head covered and barely speaks."

Mistress Gransford cast a disapproving look to the closed carriage. "What possible business could the man have in Trese?"

"His monastery produces fine glass dishes and articles of art. The trade of these items supplements the income of their modest community."

The woman's eyes lit up, and Kale received an impression of greed. Librettowit had unknowingly touched on a source of Mistress Gransford's pride. She collected fine dishes.

She twirled her parasol and looked at her older daughter before speaking. "Prushing is another day's travel. You will be too late coming into Broadfiord to find an inn. Since aiding us has caused your delay, may I offer you the hospitality of my husband's manor? It is but two miles away, once we turn at the next crossing."

Kale stared at the back of the doneel's head, seeing his ears tilt forward at the woman's suggestion. *Dar, is this good?*

"Yes. We might as well start gathering information from the people about any unusual activity among the dragons. Tell Librettowit I'm in favor of accepting her hospitality."

Kale conveyed Dar's message to Librettowit, and the librarian graciously accepted the invitation.

"I don't like this," said Regidor, mindspeaking to Kale alone. *"The glow that surrounds the girls and the driver seems to indicate nothing unusual, but the mother's luminescence is tinged with a dark undertone."*

Tell Dar.

"I did."

And what did he say?

"Be wary."

28

Quartered with the Enemy

"Bring me some food!"

Kale jumped when Regidor's voice bellowed in her mind. She glanced around the spacious kitchen to see if any of the manor servants had noticed. The mixture of mariones, o'rants, and tumanhofers worked side by side in a friendly atmosphere. They had made Kale, Bardon, and Toopka welcome around their plain wood table.

Kale addressed her meech friend. *You don't have any food?*

"A crust of bread, a hard hunk of yellow cheese, and a tankard of watered-down cider."

She felt the meech dragon's disgust as if it were her own. She knew immediately to whom Regidor attributed his meager meal, therefore, his rant didn't surprise her.

"Dar told them my order of monks rarely eats meat or vegetables or such luxuries as salt and sugar. Only the plainest of food would meet my stringent dietary restrictions."

Kale grinned, imagining the pleasure Dar got from his orneriness. She saw Bardon lift an eyebrow in her direction.

"What are you scheming?"

The question came into her mind along with the realization that she had not initiated the conversation.

You're a mindspeaker, Bardon!

"I am not. I merely respond to what you say."

But I didn't say anything. You asked a question.

"You were looking at me and that opened the communication."

You're stubborn.

"You're wrong and don't want to admit it. That's stubborn."

Regidor's voice bellowed into her thoughts. *"And while you argue pointlessly, I'm starving!"*

From within her moonbeam cape, three more voices radiated to her mind. The minor dragons wanted food too.

All right, all right!

She stood and marched out of the kitchen, not bothering to explain her sudden departure. Quick steps through the cool night air brought her to the stable. She entered the barn and nodded to Bruit sitting with the manor's stablemen around a table lit by a lantern.

Climbing the wooden ladder to the loft, she mentally told Bardon to be quiet as he chastised her for rude behavior. She also told Regidor to be patient. He expounded upon the lack of consideration the others showed him by leaving him alone and hungry in a dreary room in the massive, drafty stone house. At the top of the ladder and out of sight of the men below, she pulled the minor dragons from her cape.

"Stay out of sight," she whispered. "You can forage all you want up here. I'll be back to sleep in the loft. If anyone comes up, remember—stay out of sight!"

Kale climbed back down the ladder and nodded at the men who glanced up from their game of cards.

She shivered as she recrossed the open space between the stables and the huge stone manor. A cold wind whipped under her cape.

Regidor responded. *"Brr. It's cold in here. Be sure what you bring is hot."*

She stomped back into the heated kitchen and went to warm her hands by the hearth.

"See if you can find an extra blanket, too."

First let me see if I can get a bowl of stew. Then I'll think about bedding.

She casually surveyed the other people in the room. Only Bardon seemed aware of her presence.

"I'll cover for you while you take something to Regidor."

Her eyes popped open. His voice in her mind proved her point. Bardon could and did mindspeak. His talent would have to be addressed.

Does he know the etiquette Leetu Bends drilled into me? Does he know how to protect himself?

Kale looked away from the bothersome lehman and spied a clean bowl on a preparation table. She crossed the room, picked it up, and returned to the fire. No one seemed interested in her actions. Many of the workers had finished their chores for the day. They relaxed around a table, enjoying their supper and swapping bits of household news. Other servants still carried trays of food to the dining hall and brought back empty dishes.

The gleaming platters on large polished trays held delicacies she had never seen before. The aroma filled her nose like a promising potion.

Kale ladled stew, chunky with large cuts of meat and vegetables, into the bowl. She then sat in an out-of-the-way corner and pretended to eat, watching the activity around her. At an opportune time, she slipped out the door to the main part of the hall and followed a shadowy corridor to stairs that led to the bedrooms. With her mind on her meech friend, she followed the instinct that would lead her to his room.

I'm coming, Regidor.

"Good. I'm famished."

I've got a large bowl of stew. It's delicious.

"Can you find me?"

I think I could find you in a tumanhofer mine with all its twisting, turning tunnels.

"Kale, your talent is truly remarkable."

She stopped in the dark hallway. *Remarkable?*

"Yes, remarkable, but keep moving. I'm hungry."

Regidor sent her an impression of his rumbling stomach. She grinned and quickened her steps.

Once she had to duck into an alcove to avoid passing a maid coming back from an errand. Twice she passed rooms on tiptoe, knowing someone was working within. A dog rose from guarding another chamber and challenged her with a soft growl.

"It's all right, fella," she said as she approached. "I don't want to go into your master's room."

The dog settled down again. It watched her walk by with only its twitching nose indicating it was interested in the bowl of stew.

She hurried to the end of a hall and turned down a gloomy passageway lit by one flickering sconce. A door at the end opened, and she hastened to where Regidor waited.

"I don't like this place, Kale," he said as he took the bowl. He crossed to a stool and sat down quickly, already spooning the broth into his mouth. "Mmm. This is good."

She sat on the edge of a hard cot covered with a thick, scratchy blanket. "What don't you like about the manor? Is it just because they put you off in seclusion? That's Dar's idea of a joke."

"No." Regidor slurped a big chunk of potato off his spoon and smacked his lips as he chewed. "Remember I told you about being able to see something about people. I think it has to do with how much at peace they are with their existence." He was devouring the stew at an impressive rate, talking all the while.

"But you've been shut in this room by yourself."

He shook his head again. "No, I've been strolling the hallways."

"Regidor!"

"Don't worry. I had my tail curled around and tucked into the belt under the robe. I had the cowl up over my head. My arms were crossed and hidden in the sleeves. I looked just like a monk on a meditative walk."

She'd seen him practicing his disguise. He strolled with a measured step, his head bowed, and his entire person enveloped in the clerical robes. Granny Noon had provided the costume, and Kale felt positive it held secret qualities.

Regidor had grown at a phenomenal rate. He stood taller than she now, and his tail, which had been such a cumbersome nuisance to him when he was just weeks old, now fit the rest of his body. He looked so much like an o'rant it made her wonder where meech dragons had come from. They were neither one of the high nor the low races.

"What did you see?" she asked.

"Most of the inhabitants of this manor are just what they seem, hard-working servants. But a few vibrate with an expectation of great wealth. Some battle with memories of misdeeds. Others shy away from contemplation of what exactly they must do to gain this fortune."

His spoon paused over the bowl. "And the glimpse I got of the master of this manor…" The meech dragon shuddered. "He's evil. The drive to fulfill his desire roils out a hue of turbulent purples and black. The colors clash and spark, setting off streaks of lightninglike disturbance in the air around him."

Regidor set the spoon down in the near-empty bowl. "It troubles me, Kale. There is strength in this man I can't explain."

"One of Risto's minions?"

Regidor nodded soberly. "One would assume."

+=====+

The loft of the stable functioned as guestroom to the visiting servants. Only Dar, as Librettowit's valet, had a room inside.

With their stomachs full of delicious supper, all the travelers were ready for a good night's rest. Bardon and Bruit bedded down at one end where a couple of low-ranking stableboys also slept. At the other end of the loft, Toopka and Kale curled up on a coarse blanket with the moonbeam cape spread over them. The minor dragons hid in their pocket-dens.

In the middle of the night, Kale awoke. She listened for some unusual noise that would have roused her from a very pleasant sleep. Soft snoring filtered between the floorboards. A horse stirred and blew. Another horse stomped nervously, bumped the gate of its stall, and snorted.

She sat up.

A window spread a broad band of moonlight across the loft. Ghostly white hay almost divided the room in half, but Kale could see the men sleeping beyond.

Bardon, wake up!

The lehman hunched a shoulder and relaxed again on his pallet.

Bardon, wake up!

He sat up and looked across the space, directly at her.

There's something down below. Something besides the horses and stable-hands.

Bardon pulled on his boots, drew his sword from the scabbard beside his pallet, and shifted silently to his knees. He crawled toward the edge.

She followed his lead and crept to meet the lehman at the top of the ladder.

At first she saw nothing but shadows.

"There!"

Her eyes followed Bardon's pointing finger.

A shadow moved.

She held her breath.

A form moved away from the wall and crossed to the large barn door. He stood inside with the door slightly ajar, his attention riveted on something outside.

What is he? she asked.

"A ropma."

Kale tried to remember anything she knew about ropmas. Other than they were one of the seven low races and usually occupied themselves herding animals, she knew nothing.

They're harmless, right?

"He could be."

What do you think he's doing here?

"You're the one who can find out."

Me?

Kale felt the ripple of exasperation from her comrade.

"Kale, go into his mind and find out why he's here."

Oh!

She pressed her lips into a straight line and instantly threw up a guard so Bardon would not hear her fuming. Of course, she should have thought of it first.

No more stupid mistakes. My thoughts belong to me and Wulder. I stand under Wulder's authority as I search for truth.

She concentrated on the shadowy form by the door. His thoughts were simple. Only one thing mattered at this moment to the ropma. He must follow orders.

He's waiting for someone, Bardon.

"Who?"

That's not clear. It's someone he's never seen before, and that's hard for him. He has a very simple thought pattern.

"Who is he waiting for?"

She bit back an angry retort. It wasn't easy plucking an answer from a mind that had only a vague notion. Instead of snapping at Bardon, she focused on the man-beast below.

Small.

Covered in hair.

Important.

Nice clothes.

Kale's hand moved over to Bardon's arm. Her fingers dug into his sleeve.

Bardon, he's waiting for Dar.

29

DIRT

What should we do?

"Intercept Dar."

Good idea.

Kale turned away from Bardon and faced the house. Not that she needed to in order to reach Dar with her mind, but Bardon always flustered her. Most of the time his cool, trained attitude reminded her that he had been in Paladin's service since he was a child. And she hadn't even completed three weeks of training.

Dar, where are you?

"In my chambers. Why? What's wrong?"

There's a ropma here in the barn waiting for you.

"He's early."

You're expecting him? She turned to Bardon. *He's expecting him.*

His face looked as though he'd swallowed a peppernut. "Yeah, I heard."

Kale took a moment to gloat. *So are you going to quit denying you can mindspeak?*

He looked away, deliberately studying the dark form below them. "Dar, this is Bardon."

You don't have to tell him who you are. He can tell by your voice.

"Be quiet, Kale."

Kale stifled a giggle. *I am being quiet. I haven't spoken a word.*

"You know what I mean. Leave me alone. This is not the right time to harass me."

Kale allowed the seriousness of their situation to sober her. She nodded.

Bardon ignored her. *"Dar, what do you want us to do with this ropma?"*

"Keep him from getting caught. He isn't the ripest berry on the bush. I'll be there as soon as I can. By the way, his name is Dirt."

Kale furrowed her brow. *Dirt?*

Bardon put his hand over hers. Her fingers still rested on his sleeve, and she felt a flush go up her neck as she realized she'd been holding on to him all this time.

"I've never met a ropma, but according to the books, the parents name their children after things in their natural surroundings—grass, cloud, rock, stone, rain, bird, bug."

Kale listened to Bardon's steady voice in her mind. How quickly he returned to a state of control. Kale knew she was too easily ruffled and stayed ruffled too long.

She decided she could learn to be stoic under fire.

All I have to do is develop the tendency, right? Well, I'm just going to work on it.

"What are you talking about?"

I'm not talking. I'm thinking. And you shouldn't be listening. It's rude.

"How am I supposed to not listen? You're right here!"

He stopped glowering at her and surveyed the area below. He pointed to one of the stalls. A man stood and groped for the latch to the stall gate. He stumbled out of the small enclosure, heading for the back door.

Kale's head swung back to where the ropma had been standing. Dirt had moved. She couldn't see him, but she located him using her talent. He was crouched behind two stacked bales of hay.

The stableman who had awakened went out a door at the back.

Bardon, the ropma is going to run. He's scared.

"We have to stop him. Dar wants to talk to him."

She swung a leg over the top of the ladder, speaking loudly enough to ensure the ropma would hear. "I'm going to go get a drink. You coming?"

"Sure," Bardon responded after only a second's delay. "That stew at supper was good, but salty."

They crept down the ladder. The wooden rungs creaked under their steps. Kale cast an anxious eye to the stall where more men slept and at the door at the back of the barn. The other man would return.

Bardon and Kale walked toward the front door as if they intended to go out to the well. When they passed the ropma's hiding place, Bardon sidestepped to come up behind the man-beast, as she went over the top of the bales in front of the creature.

Bardon clamped a hand over his hairy mouth. The lehman's strong arm encircled Dirt, pinning his scraggly arms to his sides. The man-beast looked like a large rag doll in Bardon's arms.

Kale went before them, opening the door, then shutting it when Bardon had dragged the kicking, struggling ropma outside. A bright moon in a cloudless sky bathed the barnyard with too much light. They hurried to the back of a row of storage sheds to get out of sight.

She did a quick sweep of the immediate vicinity. The only person up and about was the man who had left to take care of a natural need. He now headed back to his bed of hay.

She turned to look at the ropma. His dark eyes, fringed all around with long, black lashes, widened. Kale could see his panic as well as feel it with her talent.

"We're not going to hurt you," she assured the frightened man-beast. "We work with Dar. He wants you to stay here."

Bardon spoke into Dirt's ear. "If I let you go, you must not make any noise. Agreed?"

Dirt nodded. Bardon cautiously removed his hand from the creature's mouth and loosened his grip on the wiry body.

The ropma opened his mouth and squeaked, "Please, please, don't hurt Dirt. Dirt do what you say."

"We don't want to hurt you," Bardon whispered. "Just stay here until Dar comes. He's on his way."

"Sir Dar nice man. Sir Dar save Dirt's life. Help Ma and Da. Sir Dar nice man."

"Yes, he is." Kale patted Dirt's trembling arm, wondering how old he was. Surely he wasn't a child, but he acted like a scared boy. "He'll be here in just a minute, and you can talk to him."

Dirt's head bobbed up and down, and his mouth opened in a wide grin, showing remarkably straight teeth glowing white in the moonlight.

"Sir Dar be happy. Dirt remember everything. Everything. All the little things. All the big things. Dirt remember. Dirt important."

Bardon sighed and put his hand on the man-beast's shoulder. "I'm sure you are. Sir Dar didn't want you to leave before he could speak to you. He's coming out of the manor now. I'm telling him where we are."

Dirt hopped from one foot to the other in his excitement. When Dar came around the corner of the last shed, Dirt fell down on his knees. "Master, master, Dirt tell you everything. You be happy, master. You be happy with Dirt."

Dar gently patted the ropma's head. "Get up now. You don't need to grovel with me."

On his feet, Dirt stood a head taller than the doneel. "Grovel," the man-beast repeated the unfamiliar word. "Grovel. No grovel with Sir Dar. No grovel. Just tell Sir Dar everything. Big things. Little things. Everything."

"Yes. What do you have to report, Dirt?"

"Report?"

"Let's start with the big things."

The ropma shifted from foot to foot and stared at the ground.

Dar laid a hand on his arm. "Don't worry, Dirt. You won't get it wrong. I won't be angry."

"Sir Dar nice man."

"Yes. Tell me about the meech dragons."

"Far away. In the north."

"How many?"

"Ten. Far away."

"Are they free?"

"Can't buy them."

"No, I didn't mean we should buy them. Are the meech dragons able to come here?"

"No. Far away. In the north. Far away. No come today."

Bardon sighed and paced a few steps to the corner of the building. He took up a position to watch the yard.

"This could take a while." His thoughts entered Kale's mind as a gentle whisper.

She agreed. But that wasn't what was on her mind. *Bardon, did you see how well we worked together? I knew exactly when you were going to grab Dirt. I knew you wanted me to block his escape to the door in case he slipped out of your hold. When we came out of the barn, I knew where you wanted to take him. You weren't mindspeaking to me. I just knew.*

"Yes, I noticed."

What do you think it is?

Bardon kept his eyes on the expanse between the manor and the barn and shrugged.

I couldn't even do that with Leetu Bends, and she's always been the easiest person for me to mindspeak with.

He fell silent. Kale reached to his mind and met the swirl of confused thoughts. The impressions she received indicated the lehman loathed everything about mindspeaking.

Why are you so angry?

"I'm not."

You're angry because you can mindspeak, and you can think with me when we do something together, so we don't even have to try to communicate. It makes you mad.

"Mad. Angry. Those aren't the right words, Kale. I've always known what I was going to do in my life. I was going to be a knight, a plain, ordinary knight, serving Paladin to the best of my ability. Now what am I?"

You're still a servant of Paladin. You're a skilled warrior. You're an honorable man. You just don't have the word "knight" in your name someplace.

The ropma jumped up and down. His squeaky voice screeched in the night air. "No, no, Sir Dar. You not go to there. Far away. Many bad people. Bad ropma. Bad bi-becks. Bad grawlies. Bad high people. Not go."

Dar patted the excited ropma's arm. "It's all right, Dirt. I have a lot to do before I could go to the Northern Reach. Tell me about the dragons."

"Bad. Everything bad. Dragons bad." The ropma dug his fists into his eyes, grinding away the tears falling down his hairy face. His nose ran, and he swiped it with a scraggly arm. "Dragons bad. Eat Da's sheep."

"Are the dragons always bad?" Dar asked.

Dirt scrunched up his face, obviously thinking. After a moment, he struggled to put words to his thoughts. "Nice dragons bad. Not happy. Nice dragons not happy. Nice dragons bad."

Dar nodded as if he fully understood the garbled words. "The dragons who used to be nice were happy. Now those dragons are not happy so they are bad, not nice. Right?"

Dirt's eyes brightened, and he grinned. "Sir Dar nice man. Smart man."

Dar patted him on the arm again. "You are a good ropma, Dirt. A good man. Go back to Ma and Da. Tell them Sir Dar is happy."

Dirt made a noise in his throat that might have been a giggle and took off across the field.

In amazement, Kale watched him run. He sped across the grassy pasture and leapt a fence with the ease of a gazelle.

Bardon's voice rumbled at her back. "Dar, you don't look happy."

"I'm not. Dirt has brought us very bad news."

30

Meech Dragons

Kale drew in a sharp breath. How could Dirt with his limited vocabulary convey anything but the most basic information? What could be the bad news? "Dar, are you talking about the dragons turning bad? We already knew that."

Dar shook his head. His ears laid back, a sure sign he was disturbed.

"We expected the dragons to become uncooperative as they fell under Risto's influence. The bad news is that early on a cold morning, the colony of meech dragons was attacked and driven into the Northern Reach."

"There's a colony of meech dragons?" Kale looked at Bardon to see her surprise mirrored on his face.

"There *was* a colony of meech in Wittoom. They secluded themselves in the Kattaboom Mountains. Occasionally, a member of a warm-blooded race was allowed in to quicken an egg. I believe that is how Risto got wind of Regidor, or rather the egg that was Regidor."

"Explain," said Bardon, his voice cool.

"A meech dragon sent out a request for someone to come quicken an egg. This would have been a message to a specific person, not a general announcement. But Risto heard of it, followed, or had the person followed.

"The doneel traveling to assist the meech died on his journey. Soon after, a battalion of bisonbecks descended on the colony. The fact that it was early in the morning aided the attackers. No dragon moves very quickly on a cold morning when woken from a deep sleep. During this raid, Risto acquired the meech egg. The entire cluster of dragons fled to the north."

"And at this time," said Bardon, "the second egg was also stolen?"

"Apparently. My people have not had contact with the meech dragons since they abandoned their homes and escaped. An envoy discovered the disaster on a routine diplomatic visit. Of course, he had no way of knowing two eggs were stolen."

"How did he know one was stolen and where the dragons had gone?" asked Kale.

"There's a tribe of mountain ropma in the same vicinity. He questioned them."

Bardon rubbed his fingers across his chin. "I take it meech dragons are not warriors."

Dar grimaced. "Totally useless in a fight."

Kale's mind went to her meech dragon friend. Regidor slumbered. Kale touched his dream of a table laden with rich foods and dismissed it. She turned to Dar. "So Regidor has parents in exile in the Northern Reach?"

"Yes," Dar replied.

"Will we rescue them?"

"That's a problem for another day."

Bardon put his hand on the hilt of his sword and looked to the manor. "What did Librettowit find out from the Gransfords?"

"That many of the local farmers are having difficulties with their dragon comrades. That is, except the Honorable Mr. Gransford, who claims to have a superior ability to manipulate the dragons. That Mistress Gransford has an unpleasant desire to better herself at the expense of her neighbors. That the girls are empty-headed, vain creatures with no book learning whatsoever. *That* has disgusted our librarian more than the master-of-the-house's pride and greed."

Dar paused. "I suspect we have uncovered a member of Risto's network to debilitate Amara's economic structure."

After a moment, he continued, "The dragons are an integral part of Amara's commerce. Dragons carry messages and products. For centuries, dragons have worked willingly alongside the seven high races. A dragon's nature requires it to develop a relationship with one person or one family.

This bond nurtures their hearts. Without this connection to someone outside its species, a dragon will become depressed and waste away."

Kale leaned against the rickety wooden shed, crossed her arms, and stared at the shining white globe in the almost black sky. "I wonder why Wulder did that? Wulder created the dragons, and He created a deep need in them to connect with the high races. He must have a purpose behind His design."

Dar winked at her. "Wulder always has a purpose. But sometimes His way of doing things is so far beyond anything we can comprehend, we praise Him without complete knowledge. Then there are those things that seem harmful. For those, we must wait for an explanation. And until that day, we trust in His wisdom and goodness."

Bardon spoke with a flat voice. "Wulder is always wise, always good."

Dar looked at the young lehman with a furrowed forehead above his shaggy eyebrows. "Very few people are privileged to learn that in their hearts. We almost always learn it in our heads first, and then Wulder reveals it to our hearts."

Kale turned on Dar. "There! You did it again. Only this time it was Bardon. You heard what he was thinking."

Dar chortled. "No, Kale. I do not have the talent of mindspeaking."

"But you knew Bardon was concerned, because he can say the principles of Wulder but doesn't feel them."

Dar shook his head slowly. "Kale, some thoughts are common to those who seek to follow Paladin. Each individual tends to think that his problems in understanding his role in life are unique. But no. Wulder has made us similar even in the places that cause us to stumble. For that reason, we are better equipped to help one another."

Bardon picked up a stick and examined it. Kale watched him, flooded with the feelings that coursed through the proud young man's heart. The onslaught came too quickly and with too much intensity for her to decipher.

Odd. He looks so detached. So cold. Yet these feelings are fierce. If they were my own, I'd be wailing.

At that moment, Bardon looked over at her. Their eyes met, and she read disapproval. Hadn't she told him earlier that delving into another's thoughts was rude? She turned away, unsure if the reprimand had come from Bardon or her own conscience.

She quoted Granny Noon, *My thoughts belong to me and Wulder.* She shook her head to disperse the confusion of Bardon's feelings jumbling her mind and tried again. *My thoughts belong to me and Wulder.*

Paladin had told her she could always talk to Wulder. *Wulder? Shouldn't Bardon's thoughts belong only to him and You? I don't really want to be this closely entangled with his mind. What's going on here?*

"Discipline." Dar's voice broke through her musing.

Both Kale and Bardon studied the little doneel. Their eyes roamed over the shorter man's earnest face and the way he had his fists shoved up against his waist above the hips.

"I see now why Paladin put you two together. You're going to have to help each other."

Kale saw Bardon's jaw clench at the suggestion and almost laughed. However, the prospect of being called upon to help the lehman set her teeth on edge as well.

"Bardon, have you been reporting back to The Hall on Kale's progress?"

"Yes, up until when we parted from Wizard Fenworth. I no longer have a means to communicate with Grand Ebeck."

Kale bristled. She'd forgotten that Bardon was to keep an eye on her and tell of her development.

Dar continued. "And what was the prevalent theme of your reports?"

Bardon lifted his chin and looked straight at the doneel. "That she lacked…" He hesitated.

"Discipline," Kale finished the sentence for him. "You told them I lacked discipline."

She stomped her foot on the sparse grass and growled. "I have discipline. You can't be a slave for years and not have discipline."

"I agree," said Dar. "However, that discipline was enforced by those in authority over you. Bardon is referring to discipline that comes from within. *That* you still need to develop. And there is none better to help you than Bardon."

She crossed her arms over her chest and glared, first at the doneel and then at the lehman.

Dar grinned. "But to ease your displeasure at such an onerous endeavor, Kale, don't you have something you feel you must bring to Lehman Bardon's attention? An area where he needs instruction?"

She felt her mood lighten. She couldn't help the smug smile that settled on her face. "Yes! Bardon has the gift of mindspeaking and doesn't know how to use it or contain it."

Dar cocked an eyebrow at the strong young man standing so straight in the moonlight. Bardon jerked a nod at the doneel.

Dar turned to Kale. "You remember Leetu Bends's instructions?"

She nodded. "And Granny Noon's."

"Well, then," said Dar. "I think this will be a fair exchange of ability." He clapped his hands together in a gesture of satisfaction.

The diplomat turned to the lehman. "Bardon, you will be surprised at how much self-discipline Kale has developed in managing her talent for mindspeaking." He smiled at Kale. "Kale, you will benefit from applying that discipline to other areas as Bardon reveals to you how that can be accomplished."

He took a deep breath of the cool night air. "Now, let us return to our beds. Tomorrow, we have a long journey to Prushing. And then our adventure really begins."

31

PRUSHING

Kale entered the gates of Prushing on the roof of their carriage. Sitting on top of the luggage gave her an exceptional view. She could see all around the coach, over the head of the horse Romer, and even into some of the second-story windows. She compared the seaside city with the three cities she had seen before, and Prushing lost in the comparison.

Vendela shone like a jewel on the landscape. With gleaming white walls, azure blue roofs, and colorful spheres, globes, spires, and turrets, Vendela looked like a painting of a resplendent royal metropolis.

The stately urohm city of Blisk rose out of the plain with walls of yellow. The shades blended together in perfect harmony—saffron, tawny cream, sunshine, and a deeper color that hinted of sunset. People of all the high races roamed the wide, cobblestone streets. They dressed in neat, clean, colorful attire and greeted each other with good cheer.

In the tumanhofer city of Dael, where Kale had ventured with her friends the winter before, underground lighting made the smooth streets gleam with a charming warmth.

She shook her head when she saw a man shove a pile of debris on the sidewalk out of his way. Her lip curled in distaste. Librettowit had said, "Prushing is one of the oldest cities in Amara." And it looked it.

Dreary gray walls surrounded the fortress city perched high on a rock cliff above the northern end of the Odamee Channel. Darkened beams patched the wooden gate like battle scars. Inside, wagon wheels clattered over the rough streets. Bricks fallen from the ancient walls lay in disheveled heaps in dank alleyways.

Donkeys brayed, street hawkers shouted the merits of their wares, harnesses jangled as people hurried to their destinations without a kind word or greeting to anyone they passed. Mostly mariones and a surprising number of bisonbecks walked the streets. Kale saw only a few tumanhofers and o'rants and not one urohm or kimen.

With every breath, she reminded herself that the sea breeze blew over the city. But in the canyons of gloomy streets, the putrid air almost choked her.

Bruit drove them straight to the house they were to occupy. He unloaded them quickly and bade them good fortune.

"What's your hurry, Bruit?" asked Toopka.

"City life don't suit me," he explained. "I'd as soon be out the gate and down the hill to a little tavern I know outside the Port of Prushing."

"I've never been to a port," said Toopka. She cast a hopeful look at Kale.

"Boats come into the docks on the Pomandando River," Kale pointed out.

"But that was river traffic," Dar responded with a wink to Toopka. "The boats in the Port of Prushing come from all over the world."

Kale tried to imagine the deep harbor with ships from different nations, flying flags she'd never seen before. No clear picture came to her mind. She smiled at Toopka. "We'll go soon. But I don't think it will be today. Let's explore the house."

The square mansion was built around a grassy courtyard with vine-like flowers climbing the walls. On the first floor facing the street, four rooms and an entryway served to welcome guests. In the back, along the alley, the kitchen and three servants' rooms offered sturdy, comfortable furnishings. Upstairs, more bedrooms and a study made up the square. Dar, Regidor, and Librettowit would sleep there, while Kale, Toopka, the minor dragons, and Bardon would sleep on the ground floor.

The comrades congregated in the spacious kitchen.

"There isn't a stable," observed Bardon looking out a back window.

"There isn't a cook," objected Toopka with her arms crossed over her chest.

Dar examined the pantry. "Worse than that, my dear Toopka, there is no food."

Toopka jumped onto a three-legged stool beside a table. "Kale and Regidor can make us cake. They've had *that* wizardry lesson."

Kale looked to the meech dragon, who had pushed his cowl back from his face. He shook his head. She nodded agreement, and then looked with sympathy at the little doneel.

"Regidor and I can't do that without the ingredients, Toopka. We're *apprentice* wizards, after all."

Toopka hopped down and smoothed her blue apron over her black servant's dress. "Then let's go to the market. We'll need food. And I think we should get more servants. This is a big house. I don't want to do all the dusting and washing and scullery things by myself."

"More servants is an excellent idea," said Dar.

"I want to go to the market," said Regidor, putting his cowl back over his head. "I've never been to one."

"It's not going to be as nice as the ones in Vendela, I can tell you that." Toopka grabbed her short woolen jacket from where she'd thrown it earlier and shoved her arms into the sleeves. She headed for the back door and stopped before she turned the handle. "Who's coming?"

Regidor, Kale, and Bardon followed the little doneel into the alley. Toopka skipped down the dingy passage to the front of the house, taking no notice of the debris and clutter. At the main street, she stopped and looked both ways. Without hesitation, she approached the nearest person strolling down the broken pavement.

"Excuse me, Mistress," the little doneel addressed the marione matron. "Could you tell me where the nearest market is?"

"That'd be High Hill, but you'll be cheated there, that's for sure." The old woman stopped and pulled her thick, knitted shawl closer around her bulky figure. With a mittened hand she gestured down the road. "Best to go down a ways to Higgert Street's End. The prices are better, and the produce fresh from the countryside. But don't buy your fish or poultry there. Go to Bless Me Court for your meats and such."

"Yes, Mistress. And the direction?"

"Go to the next corner where the clock tower be sitting in the middle of the road. Turn south four blocks. Turn east two more. That would be Higgert Street's End. I'm glad it's your young feet going the distance this late in the day. I ache from my big toe to my elbow." She sighed and flexed her arm as if working out a kink. "Come back by Dolly Road, and you'll pass Bless Me Court. It's all uphill and down. There isn't a way to get anywhere in this city without stretching your legs."

"Thank you, Mistress." Toopka bobbed a curtsy. "I hope you have a peaceful evening by the fire."

"You're a dear child. Don't be wandering the streets by yourself come dark."

Toopka grinned. "I won't, Mistress. I have friends." The little doneel gestured to Kale, Bardon, and Regidor standing in the alley entry.

"Oh my," the old woman whispered. "That one looks peculiar."

"He's a monk, sort of. But he's no bother. He's always medicating. Even when he's walking around, he's medicating. He just thinks high thoughts and never asks for things the way the others do. And he doesn't get fidgety when it takes you a while when he finally does ask for something."

"I see," said the old woman, keeping her eye on the strange figure. "You staying in number 469?"

"Yes, Mistress. We just arrived today."

The marione straightened and hefted her bag back on her shoulder. "I best be getting on."

"Thank you for the information."

"You're welcome, I'm sure. You have good manners for a serving girl. You'll do well."

Toopka bobbed another curtsy as the woman continued her trudge up the road.

"That was well done, Toopka," said Bardon as he stepped out from the alley. "The information you gave her will be common knowledge by tomorrow noon."

Toopka's head nodded rapidly. "I know."

Kale tweaked her furry ear. "And since you've never once waited on Regidor, it is amazing how much you know about his habits."

Toopka shrugged. "I have great mag-nation."

"That's imagination. And monks meditate. They don't medicate."

Toopka hopped up and down in the cold and tucked her hands under her arms for warmth. "I bet some medicate."

Kale shook her head. "You don't even know what that means."

Toopka tossed her a sassy grin, shrugged again, and skipped off in the direction of the market.

+—•—+

By the time the four comrades trooped back down the street with their arms laden with foodstuff, the sun rested on the horizon. A glow still illuminated the western sky, but the first star had appeared in the darkened east.

"Don't they have a lamplighter in this city?" Toopka asked in disgust.

Kale felt a prickle across the back of her neck. Somewhere in the shadows lurked evil men. She stopped moving in the direction of the house and tried to pinpoint their location.

"Bardon?"

"I know, I feel them."

"Who?" asked Toopka.

"Thieves," answered Regidor.

"I told you I needed a weapon," said Toopka with a stomp of her foot.

Out of the dark alleys came a dozen ruffians dressed in black.

"Toopka," Kale yelled as she drew her small sword, "go get Dar and Librettowit."

Toopka dropped her burden, hunched down, and ran between the legs of the attackers. In an instant, Bardon and Kale were back to back, fighting with their swords. Three men swarmed Regidor.

Regidor threw back his cowl. His eyes glowed green in the semidark. He whirled with both arms outstretched and two of the assailants went down. The long brown monk's robe pulled loose of the meech dragon's frame, revealing his plain tunic, trousers, and muscular body. Regidor's tail lashed out, no longer bound to his torso by the belt. The third thief yelped as the thick, scaly tail knocked him to the ground.

Regidor twisted just in time to bash one more man with a fist and a second with his tail. He kicked high as a third approached, landing a foot on the man's chest and launching his own body into the air. He did a backflip and landed solidly.

Four men with menacing clubs circled the meech dragon. Regidor growled deep in his throat, and the next instant fire streamed from his mouth.

The attackers screamed and bolted for the shadowy alleyways. Even the two fighting Kale and Bardon took off.

Regidor stood with his two feet firmly planted, ready for another assault. His tail whipped back and forth in anger. His shoulders rose and fell as he took in deep, rapid breaths, fueling his body for action.

Bardon and Kale turned toward the rapid footsteps coming from behind. Dar and Librettowit were running from the house to their aid. With their swords drawn, they came to a standstill beside the two o'rants. Toopka, out of breath, joined them.

Up and down the narrow street, men in black garb lay crumpled in defeat. Occasionally, one would moan. Two got up and staggered away.

Regidor reached for his monk's robe, shook it out, and donned it once more.

Kale raised an eyebrow at Dar.

"You saw?"

Dar nodded.

"I thought you said meech dragons were useless in a fight."

"Apparently the traditions are wrong."

Bardon cleared his throat. "He moves like a lizard."

Librettowit nodded. "Agile like a lizard."

"I don't think I'd tell him *that*," said Toopka, eying Regidor with new respect. "He might not like it."

32

Getting Down to Business

"I'm hungry." Toopka picked up the parcel she had thrown down when she ran for help. She stooped for another. "Are we going to eat all this stuff we got, or just stand around in the street?" Her voice quivered. Tucking the second package under her arm, she reached for another. "I want to play with the little dragons. I want Dar to play music and Librettowit to tell stories. I want to eat a whole lot and have fun and go to bed."

Bardon put his sword away and scooped Toopka into his arms. The packages tumbled to the ground as she threw her arms around the lehman's neck, burying her head in his shoulder.

"I'm not big and strong. I'm not brave. Can we please eat dinner?"

Bardon patted her back. "Yes, we can. I think that is a good idea for all of us."

After the meal and the singing and storytelling, Kale tucked Toopka into the bed they would share. The little doneel curled up with the minor dragons. Gymn snuggled next to her neck. Metta nestled on the pillow, crooning into her ear. Dibl played at the foot of the wide bed, doing somersaults and backflips. Kale knew he would eventually settle down. She kissed Toopka and whispered, "Sweet dreams," then went to help Bardon clean up the kitchen.

"You were nice to Toopka tonight," Kale said as she put platters away.

"You told me what to do."

"I did not."

"Oh yes, you did. I just followed your prodding."

"I don't remember any such thing. I do remember thinking she was scared and needed comforting."

"And so I picked her up."

She sat down in a chair by the table. "Bardon, we've got to talk about this. What passes between you and me goes beyond mindspeaking."

Bardon sat down opposite her. He laced his fingers together and rested his hands on the tabletop. His serene expression denied the feelings she felt swirling within him.

"I agree." He spoke slowly, deliberately. "And I must tell you something else I've discovered." He paused and stared at his hands.

She resisted the urge to delve into his thoughts and pull the next sentence out of him. As she blocked the temptation to freely gather information from his mind, she felt an ebbing of the torrent of his emotions.

He stretched his two index fingers out straight so they pointed across the table at her, but she doubted he was conscious of the little gesture.

I'm going to lose all patience and shake him.

A smile twitched at the corner of his mouth. "Sorry, Kale. I've irritated you again." He heaved a big sigh. "I've discovered that I cannot mindspeak if you're not in the vicinity. Whatever ability I have seems to be linked to yours."

"That *is* odd." She drummed her fingers on the tabletop. "I wonder if Librettowit has any knowledge of what's going on between us. His books cover almost every aspect of life. I mean, I wonder if there's a record of it happening before."

"We could ask him. But his books are in the castle in The Bogs."

"So we must practice, or explore, this ability on our own."

"Gain control," insisted Bardon. "But let's still ask Librettowit and Dar for any wisdom they can give us."

"Yes," she agreed. "I think we can learn to manage the ability, given enough time."

"And we should have some time here. Dar says we will gather information about anything unusual happening in the countryside."

She shook her head. "Why can't we just be out in the countryside where things are happening? Why sit in this dismal city when we could be out tracking that meech?"

"Prushing is the best place to collect tales and gossip since much trade comes through here. We can pinpoint the other meech's whereabouts by watching for a pattern."

I don't like it. I'd rather be doing something.

"We have plenty to do. We aren't nearly ready to proceed. We must prepare."

You sound like Librettowit.

"Not such a bad thing."

She smiled at the lehman across the table. They had entered into a conversation by mindspeaking naturally. If Bardon weren't such a pain in other ways, she could enjoy him. She clasped her hands together, trying to keep her nervous fingers still. "What did you think of Regidor's fighting skill?"

"Spectacular."

She nodded. "Surprising." She moved a basket of fruit from the side of the table to the center. She picked up a parnot, turned it over in her hands, and then returned it to the basket. "I think it upset him. He was quiet all evening."

"Maybe that monk business is rubbing off on him." Bardon grinned at her, and she noticed a lock of dark hair had fallen forward, out of place.

She looked away. "When are we going to work on fine-tuning our mindspeaking abilities?"

"Tomorrow."

◆━━━◆

The next day, Dar took on the persona of the butler and hired servants to come in the afternoon and work through the evening.

The band of comrades soon fell into a routine. In the mornings, Dar, Bardon, Kale, and Regidor sparred in the courtyard, perfecting their skills and learning from one another. When Dar suggested the regimen, Kale offered no resistance. Still smarting from Bardon's assessment of her attitude, she determined to show him she had discipline.

Regidor continued to mature at a phenomenal rate. He grew to a foot taller than Bardon and soon outmatched both Dar and the lehman in hand-to-hand combat.

In the afternoon, the servants roamed through the house doing their chores. Librettowit left the house with Dar, and they sought information from the upper class as well as the merchants and academicians. Librettowit used his letters of introduction and his ability to tell a good story to garner social invitations. Dar visited the taverns where the upper echelon of servants took their afternoon break.

After noonmeal, Regidor retired to his quarters along with the minor dragons. The hired help never caught a glimpse of the "monk" during his meditations each afternoon.

Kale and Toopka worked alongside the servants and gathered news. Bardon talked to the maids and occasionally helped with heavy lifting, but as the sheridan he did no housework. Kale thought again how oddly females behaved around Bardon. And it wasn't just the young, giggly maids. The older housekeeper and the cook blushed when Bardon spoke to them.

Also, during the long afternoons, Bardon and Kale sequestered themselves in Regidor's chambers and practiced mindspeaking. Kale demonstrated for Bardon the things that Leetu Bends had shown her. The more she remembered and practiced these exercises, the more her own proficiency grew.

Regidor grew enthusiastic about their endeavors and joined them. He constantly thought of new twists for the old techniques. Some of them were outrageous, and if Dibl were in the room, the results were pushed to absurdity. The meech dragon "confused" Kale's tongue so that anytime she tried to say something, the only thing that came out of her mouth was, "I'm a rapid rabbit." She convinced Bardon his pants were soaking wet through a series of mental pictures that made him think he had spilled a jug of water. He would laugh at their antics, but the serious lehman never instigated any mischief.

Kale insisted they also practice the proper etiquette for mindspeaking. Regidor often had trouble bending his own formidable will to Wulder's principles. He challenged the need to respect another person's private thoughts.

"Article ninety-three," said Bardon with authority. "'Preserve dignity by honoring privacy.'"

The three became very adept with their mindspeaking skills, although Bardon's talent lay dormant anytime he and Kale were separated. Bardon and Kale could meld their minds and work as one, or totally ignore each other at will. She found it much more comfortable than her earlier experiences of being flooded with a maelstrom of his emotions.

In the evening, the companions came together to compile bits and pieces of the information they had acquired. Librettowit had a map on which he recorded their findings.

"Trese is definitely losing the dragons' cooperation." The librarian pointed to the center of Trese, near Bartal Springs Lake. "The latest reported incident was at Bealour, a small village on the eastern shore of the lake. Two dragons destroyed crops and disappeared from the area. Five additional dragons flew off to the north and never returned."

Dar pointed out the last three areas of discontent. "The pattern indicates that someone is moving from place to place. See how they've followed this trade road?"

"Shouldn't that tell us where the meech dragon is?" asked Kale.

"It should, but for one puzzling thing," said Dar. "No one has reported seeing the meech dragon. And a meech dragon is pretty hard to overlook."

"So he's traveling much as I am," said Regidor. "He's in disguise."

"And doing a good job of it," said Librettowit. "Most people would remember you as the monk shrouded from head to toe in your clerical robes. This meech is disguised so that even his disguise is unremarkable."

Toopka squirmed on her chair. "Can we go and look for ourselves?"

"No," said Dar. "First we must gather information from the port. We haven't yet extracted what news they might have."

"Humph," said Librettowit. "The Port of Prushing is dangerous with many unsavory characters lurking about."

"Exactly!" said Dar with a wide grin.

33

FORAY INTO A DEN OF EVIL

Kale tried to leave the minor dragons at home, but Gymn reminded her that they'd proven useful in dangerous situations. Dibl just took up residence in his pocket-den and would not be dislodged. Librettowit stated he was a librarian and did not approve of dangerous expeditions. Toopka strangely did not object to being left at home with the tumanhofer.

Cool mist swirled around Kale, Dar, Bardon, and Regidor as they trod narrow streets heading toward the docks. The atmosphere differed from the bright and colorful markets Kale had visited with Toopka during the day. The Port of Prushing apparently led two differing lifestyles. The one shown during the day resembled a carnival. At night, the air hung heavy with treachery.

Dar led them to The Horn, a noisy tavern in a ramshackle wooden structure. Loud music and the thump, thump, thump of rhythmic and enthusiastic dancing welcomed them.

Inside, lanterns hung along the walls giving a greenish glow to the smoky air. Numerous round tables crowded the edge, while energetic dancers, including some urohms, stomped and twisted in a central area.

Kimens! And minor dragons! Look, Dar. What are they doing here?

"Hopefully, they will be providing us with some much-needed facts."

I mean, what would kimens be doing in a raucous place like this? I always thought of them living in quiet, remote areas.

"Don't you remember that kimens have taken on the role of watchers?"

Yes, and I suppose the best place to observe evil is where evil is active. But Dar, suppose some of these kimens are in league with Risto's forces.

"Then Regidor will sense it. You probably could too, Kale, if you tried."

I don't see auras around people.

"No, but you can enter a person's mind and observe the kind of things they think about."

Dar, you don't know how draining it is to mindspeak. And when it's with someone who's evil, I come out of it with a nasty feeling.

"No, I guess I don't know anything about it except what I've read or been told."

Kale glanced sideways at her friend.

Along with the minor dragons sitting among the patrons of The Horn, other animals sat at a few tables.

What an odd assortment of pets. Some look bored, and some look more intelligent than their owners.

Kale identified two monkeys. A few dogs sat in their masters' laps, and some curled up asleep under the chairs or tables. One bisonbeck had a massive, catlike creature on a leash. Large, colorful birds perched on shoulders. And animals Kale could not begin to identify also accompanied a few of the rougher-looking men in the room.

Kale stepped closer to Regidor where she felt safer. The meech dragon had shown reassuring skill in numerous forms of combat.

From the band in the corner of the room, a drumroll drowned out most of the chaotic noise in the spacious hall. A large curtain across one wall parted in the center and opened in short, jerky movements. Kale saw a stage and knew this entertainment would not be like anything she had ever seen at the tavern in River Away.

"Let's find a table and order some supper," said Dar. "Kale, ask the minor dragons out so they can gather information too."

They sat at the only table available with four vacant seats. Two bisonbecks occupied the other chairs, but they had surrendered to a multitude of hefty tankards of strong ale. One snored, and the other drooled on the table. After the questing party had seated themselves, a urohm came over and hoisted the two bisonbecks out of their seats. He dragged them to a side door and tossed them out. A quick and efficient marione mopped up the table with a limp, grimy rag. Right behind her came a marione wearing superior clothes.

"Rosey, bring a clean rag and wipe this table again. These are fine gentlemen, come from Greater Prushing, no doubt."

He bowed before Dar. "What would be your pleasure, sir? We have fish from the ocean, beef from the pastures of Trese, a duckling purchased only yesterday."

Dar ordered a meal for all of them.

Kale knew Regidor would have been better pleased had their seating been more in the shadows. He could have loosened his tail from the belt that confined it. And he would have been able to eat more comfortably without exposing his reptilian-featured face.

The minor dragons crawled out from the moonbeam cape but didn't venture forth to explore this loud and colorful new place. They sat on Kale's head and shoulders and scowled at their surroundings. Even Dibl hunched his shoulders and dug his tiny claws into Kale's scalp.

"Ouch!" Kale lifted the yellow dragon from her hair and gave him to Bardon to hold.

The performers came onto the stage. Three singers harmonized well and sang loud enough to be heard over the continued chatter of the patrons.

Metta slid off Kale's shoulder and stretched out on the sleeve of her blouse. The little dragon relaxed. Her tail swept back and forth, and her head bobbed to the beat of the music.

Metta! You are not to remember the lyrics to this song.

The end of the purple dragon's tail twitched in annoyance.

Of course you can help it! insisted Kale. *Think about something else.*

Metta sat up and glanced over her shoulder at Kale.

I know the tune is catchy. Why don't you make up words we can share with Toopka while you listen to the music?

The little dragon stretched out her neck and nodded. Then she returned her attention to the stage.

Kale breathed a sigh of relief. Metta did not take correction easily. Kale congratulated herself for steering the stubborn minor dragon away from learning the lurid lyrics sung by the three on stage.

Next, jugglers threw plates, balls, painted clubs, and knives in the air with dazzling skill.

"I'm going to try that," murmured Regidor.

A row of dancers kicked their heels up behind a man singing. Then another man with a female assistant came out on the stage with dogs that performed amazing tricks.

The noise in the room fell during the singing but gained strength during the animal act. Kale had to lean close to Dar to speak in his ear. "Toopka would love this."

"What?"

I said, Toopka would love this.

Dar nodded. *"But soon we should get down to business."*

Kale's heart sank. She'd almost forgotten their mission for the night. Talking to the maids in the safety of the house they had rented did not frighten her. She asked probing questions without one thought of being challenged on her inquisitive nature.

Once she had the young women thinking along the lines that might reveal an important fact, Kale often used her talent to gather any other information that never reached the maids' lips. She found most of the relevant facts flitting through the girls' minds. A cousin moved to town because labor was hard on a farm where the dragons refused to cooperate. No cloth had come from the factory town of Nordante because the dragons would no longer carry the market wares.

But here in this rowdy crowd, Kale dreaded approaching strangers to strike up conversations. She knew she could not probe the minds of so many people with her talent. Such an endeavor would exhaust her.

Regidor reached across the table to put his scaly hand over hers. *"Don't worry about dealing with this riffraff. I'll take care of going from table to table. Probing minds doesn't drain me the way it does you."*

What can I do?

"You keep an eye on the minor dragons."

Dar scooted his chair away from the table. "I'm going to join a card game in one of the back rooms."

"How do you know there are card games back there?" Kale asked.

"My dear, there are always card games in places like this."

"Oh."

Dar winked and strolled to one side where a number of doors led out of the hall.

Bardon stood. "I'll order a drink at the bar."

Kale watched him weave through the tables to a long counter where men served standing patrons. She turned to find her meech friend, meaning to mindspeak with him. She found him alive with curiosity and determined to examine every species in the room. Kale laughed to herself as she observed his tactics.

Regidor, with cowl covering his face and arms crossed and tucked into the opposite sleeve, strolled about the room, pausing at each table. But as he progressed around the room, his attitude changed. From the outside he appeared no different, but even with the distraction of this chaotic environment, Kale could feel agitation rising in Regidor.

She didn't like sitting by herself with only the minor dragons to keep her company. She moved to lean against the wall beside a thick supporting column and felt safe in its shadow.

From this vantage point she noticed that none of the animals roamed the room.

I'm not going to send the dragons out to spy. We'll just view the room from here.

Bardon held a thick mug in his hand. He put it to his mouth and tilted it. But Kale didn't see him swallow. She smiled. Bardon wouldn't be losing any of his sharpness because of a strong brew.

One of the women who had danced on the stage sashayed up to Bardon and maneuvered herself into the small space next to him. She smiled at the lehman and said something.

Kale stopped herself just before she used her talent to eavesdrop.

I don't want to know. I don't want to hear what Bardon is thinking right now. And I certainly don't want to be involved in his feelings.

She turned away to watch Regidor. His lean figure, draped in the somber garb of a monk, stood in sharp contrast to the slovenly appearance of most of the men and women sitting around the tables. His slow, deliberate movements and the air of calm that surrounded him accentuated the incongruity.

Kale noted that several men grew uncomfortable as the cleric stood near their tables. One o'rant poked the bisonbeck next to him and pointed at Regidor. Laughter rose from the table. Another bisonbeck sneered at the robed figure. One man rose to his feet as if to challenge her meech friend, but his companion urged him to sit down.

Kale bit her lip. Regidor concentrated on the task at hand. He was oblivious to the changing mood of the crowd.

Regidor, these people don't like your roaming around the room. They distrust you.

"What, Kale? Why did you interrupt me? These people are wallowing in disturbing lies."

The people, Regidor. They—

"Hey, monk!" A grubby marione stood swaying before Regidor. "You got a reason to be here? You casting a spell on us or something?"

"No," said Regidor in his deep, resonant voice.

Two more men joined the drunken marione, a tumanhofer and a urohm.

The tumanhofer spoke. "No matter. We're tired of you gawking at us. We're throwing you out."

"And what if I choose not to leave?"

No, Regidor, no! Just walk out.

"Curse you! I'm the first mate on the *Rondamoor*. No one crosses me."

A murmur went through the crowd. One man spoke up.

"No one beats him in a fight, either. You best go, monk-man."

Regidor pulled his leathery-skinned hand out of the sleeve. Slowly he raised one finger, its nail almost a claw, and pushed the hem of the cowl up. The hood inched upward, revealing a gleaming smile of many sharp white teeth.

"I choose to stay."

34

A Brawl

The room grew quiet. The band stopped playing. The customers ceased their babble. The workers behind the bar deftly removed glasses and bottles, shoving them under the counter.

Regidor undid the sash around his robe, unfastened the top button, and let the garment fall to the floor. His tail slipped out of the belt at his waist. A plain white shirt covered his torso, but didn't hide the bulging brawn of his back and neck. With his shoulders back and his head held high, he looked more than his seven feet in height. The black trousers he wore had been loose two weeks before. Now they stretched over his muscular thighs and calves. The upper portion of his shiny black boots molded around his legs with supple leather, but the soles and slight heels were hard enough to be lethal weapons.

He tapped his toe on the wooden floor in a slow rhythmic beat that made the hair on Kale's arms stand on end.

"What are you, anyway?" growled the tumanhofer.

"A meech," answered Regidor, his voice a rumble in the quiet room.

The urohm ran a hand through his greasy hair. "You mean, like a meech dragon?"

"Indeed."

The urohm swallowed hard and looked down at his two chums.

The marione bristled. "Ain't no such thing as a meech dragon."

Regidor chortled.

The marione bounced on the balls of his feet, his clenched fists shaking. "We can take him. There's three of us."

The tumanhofer roared, lowered his head, and charged. His two buddies followed on his heels.

Regidor leaned back on his tail, swept one foot up in an arc and struck the attacking man with a clean hit to the side of his head. The meech completed the arc, landing on the same foot. He brought his tail around to land a blow to the marione's midsection.

A dozen men joined the urohm in the fight. Kale grabbed a candlestick and entered the fray, swinging. Before she reached Regidor, the rest of the room erupted into a riot. A few picked up their drinks and made for the front door. Some struggled to pass through the belligerent crowd and leapt onto the stage, disappearing with the performers into the dark nether regions of the building.

Metta and Gymn soared above the ruckus. Dibl flew to a crude chandelier made of six lanterns and an old wagon wheel. He perched on one of the spokes and called out with noises that sounded like cheers.

Kale pressed through the slugfest, still trying to get to Regidor. She soon realized he didn't need any assistance. No one landed a blow on the twirling, lashing warrior. He struck his opponents with fist, foot, and tail.

Two brawling men fell into her, knocking her to the floor. She struggled out from under them and crawled beneath a table. From there, she watched the pandemonium as booted feet scuffled around her. A thud from above warned her someone had landed on the table. The wood creaked, and she scrambled out just before the table collapsed in an explosion of splinters.

Kale jumped to her feet to avoid getting trampled. She dodged where she had to and shoved when she needed to in order to make her way to the bar. Bardon defended himself against two scruffy bisonbeck sailors. Kale jumped on the back of one as he raised his fist to smash the back of Bardon's head. The bisonbeck bellowed and began to spin. She held on, thinking she would be catapulted like a rock in a sling. Bardon dispatched one assailant and turned his attention to the sailor carrying Kale on his back.

Metta and Gymn swooped in, spitting green and purple saliva at the bisonbeck. The sticky goo stung when they projected it into his eyes. Unfortunately, he bobbed and gyrated wildly and made a poor target.

Kale held on with one arm wrapped partway around the man's thick neck. She dug the fingers of her other hand into the fleshy outer ear, twisting and pulling with all her strength.

The bisonbeck yowled. He slowed his spin, making a ham-fisted grab for her hand. Bardon took the opportunity to smash the bigger man's nose. The lehman landed another blow to the sputtering sailor's windpipe. Kale dropped off his back and ran to Bardon's side. The bisonbeck went down on his knees, coughing.

We've got to get Regidor out of here.

"We can't get anywhere near him."

Not physically, but we can with our minds.

"What do you suggest?"

Work together. Both of us tell him to get out to the street.

"And when we get to the street?"

I'm not sure. Oh, where is Dar when we need him?

"We can do this, Kale. You're right. We'll get Regidor out to the street and away from the fight."

Kale poured forth a stream of persuasive prattle.

Regidor, we must get away from here. This is pointless. Stop fighting. Go out the door. Regidor, we must leave. No more fighting. Get out the door. The front door, Regidor, to the street. Leave this riffraff behind. Out. Out! Get out!

Regidor eased toward the door.

Kale and Bardon dodged swinging fists and sidestepped as many of the combatants as possible. Bardon cleared the way for her until they reached the swinging doors. The minor dragons came to roost on the two o'rants as they waited by the exit for the meech.

Regidor burst through a knot of wrangling men and shot out the doors. Kale and Bardon followed, the dragons flying above them.

On the street, men fought with knives.

Oh no! This is worse.

"Don't worry. We're getting out of here. Regidor, to High Street before Kale gets hurt."

Regidor landed a blow to one marione and kicked the knife out of another's hand. The dragon caught a tumanhofer who had the ill judgment to tackle the meech from behind and tossed the short man onto the overhanging roof of a storefront porch.

Regidor flashed a toothy grin at Bardon. "Let's go!" he shouted.

Three ruffians noticed their retreat and began hurling debris from the street. A bottle whizzed by Kale's ear. A small stick bounced off her back. She feared for her minor dragons and wished she carried them safely inside the moonbeam cape.

She heard a thud, a grunt, and saw Bardon stumble. Regidor scooped up the injured lehman and tossed him over one shoulder. They ran until the sounds of pursuit faded.

Regidor ducked into an alley and put Bardon down. The unconscious lehman slumped against the wall.

"You take care of him," the meech ordered. "I'm going back to find Dar."

Panting from her long run, Kale dropped to her knees beside Bardon. The young man slid out of his half-sitting position and fell with his head in her lap. She put her hand on his chest and felt him breathing. "Regidor, those men are probably searching for you."

"They can't hurt me."

"That isn't the point. You'll hurt them. There's no sense in stirring up trouble."

"I'll stay out of sight. When I reach The Horn, I'll mindspeak to Dar. I want him to bring my robe."

"Now you need your robe?" She couldn't keep the sarcasm out of her voice.

"Granny Noon gave it to me."

"Oh."

She watched Regidor slip into the street and dash for another shadowy spot that would hide him.

Metta settled on her shoulder, Gymn on Bardon's chest.

Head wound? At the minor dragon's direction, she felt the back of Bardon's head. She found a lump, and her hand came away wet with blood.

She struggled to reach inside her moonbeam cape. She sat in an awkward position with its folds trapped beneath her legs. As soon as she had the flap pulled back far enough, Kale asked Metta to enter a hollow and find something to use as a pad to hold against the wound.

The purple dragon returned in short order with a wad of linen material. Kale pressed this against the gash with her fingers resting on his scalp. Gymn curled his body around her hand and Bardon's wound.

While the energy of healing moved in a circle between the little green dragon, the injured lehman, and herself, Kale touched Bardon's cold and clammy chin. The dark shadows prevented her from seeing his color, and she wondered how pale he must be. She brushed his straight black hair from his face, and her hand lightly grazed his ear. The shape surprised her.

Exploring with her fingers, she found the ear again and ran one finger around the curve of his lower ear, up the back, and to the top where a distinct point peaked and then tapered down to his temple.

The tip was not as pronounced as Granny Noon's, Leetu Bends's, or Grand Ebeck's, but it definitely did not round off at the top like an o'rant's ear.

She took a swift breath in and whispered as it came out. "Bardon, you're a halfling."

35

Missing Person

Five minutes passed. Then ten. Kale focused on the healing circle. Gymn relaxed as the bond between the three deepened. She felt the pain ease away from Bardon's head. At the same time, a fresh current of life invigorated her spirit. This paradox of renewal while the act of healing drained her physical body brought a strange feeling of lazy peace. She could easily slip into a contented dream state.

Metta sat on one of her shoulders, humming. Dibl sat on the other.

Bardon's eyes fluttered open. "Kale?"

"You got hit on the head with a brick or something."

He sat up.

Gymn rolled off Bardon's head, bumped his shoulder, and slid down his back. When he hit the ground, he stood on wobbly legs, shook his head, and then cast a disgusted look at his patient.

On Kale's shoulder, Dibl did a little dance that ended with a flip. Kale giggled.

Bardon quirked an eyebrow at her.

"Gymn is put out because you dumped him after he healed you. To make it worse, he was almost asleep. Dibl, of course, thinks it's all very funny."

Bardon twisted to look behind him. He picked up the disgruntled green dragon.

"I'm sorry, Gymn. I didn't realize you were napping on my head." With one hand he reached up and felt for the wound. "All that's left is drying blood."

Kale wrinkled her nose. "Sounds attractive."

Bardon looked around. "Where are Regidor and Dar?"

The mist turned into a drizzle. She pulled her hood over her head. "Good question. I never saw Dar during the brawl. Regidor went back to get him and his monk robe."

"Why in the world did he start the fight?"

"You think he started it?"

"He didn't have to challenge those drunks." Bardon stretched his arms out, testing his muscles. "Regidor could have just walked away. But no, he throws off his disguise and starts beating the pulp out of them."

"Are you all right?"

"Yes."

Kale felt her muscles relax as she watched him flex his limbs to restore their vitality. She closed her mind to the incredible link between them and thought of something else.

"Regidor *is* amazing. Have you ever seen anyone that quick?"

"No. He seems to roll into his punches, fly toward an opponent. Oh, I give up! There's no way to describe how he fights—like a circus acrobat and a dancer all in one."

Kale remembered Wizard Cam saying Bardon fought like a dancer. She remembered his ears and quickly shuttled her thoughts down a different line.

"Are you sure you're all right?"

"I feel a bit lazy."

She laughed. The term lazy just didn't fit Bardon.

He stood and stretched. "Let's walk back toward the waterfront and see if we can find Dar and Regidor. I have an uneasy notion."

"Is this notion based on your mindspeaking talent or reasoning?"

"Reasoning. Don't you think it odd that Dar didn't appear during the fight? He's never been shy to lend his sword to a just cause."

"But there was no just cause. It was a senseless riot."

Bardon raked his fingers through his hair, smoothing the sides over his ears.

"Maybe this rain will wash the bloody mat out of my hair."

Again, she kept her thoughts to herself. Bardon had a reason why he didn't reveal his dual heritage. She fought the urge to ask questions.

"Kale, where's my sword?"

"I guess you dropped it in the street."

"Somebody probably picked it up, but let's go back and see."

Kale got to her feet and shook the mud from the bottom of her moonbeam cape. The top now glistened with raindrops. Gymn landed on the front of the cape and darted inside. He apparently was tired and wanted a nap in his pocket-den.

Dibl perched on Bardon's shoulder, and Metta flew above Kale. Briefly, Kale gave thought to the egg in the pouch around her neck. And then she remembered the four eggs still kept in the pockets of the moonbeam cape. She shoved aside the thought of eight dragons flying around her head sometime in the future and trudged after Bardon toward a decidedly dangerous present.

Slick mud covered the remnants of a cobblestone pavement. Where lamplight shone through dirty windows, a pale square of light glistened, reflecting in the puddles.

The rain began to pelt them with greater intensity. Both Metta and Dibl took refuge in the cape. They passed under a streetlamp, and Kale saw a trickle of red water running down the back of Bardon's neck from the blood in his hair.

The cape kept her comfortably warm, but she worried about Bardon. She knew better than to say anything. Even if he realized he would be better off with a cloak, a cloak was not available.

The rain poured as they reached the lane where The Horn faced the docks. No one lingered out in the torrent. Kale shifted the sweep of her gaze. She looked up and down the street, particularly in the shadows, for would-be attackers. Then she surveyed the mucky street for the lost sword. She used her talent to explore the area, hoping to detect any adversaries. But the buildings housed dozens of villains. She could not identify any who had malice in their hearts aimed at her and her comrades.

Bardon!

"What?"

I just realized something.

"You can't pick up on Dar's whereabouts."

She nodded in agreement, even though she doubted Bardon could see her in the dark, rain-laden street. He would know her concern even without seeing her.

And Regidor.

"He's disappeared as well."

Concentrate, Bardon. We should be able to find them.

A moment of silence followed.

Both Bardon and Kale began to run as a glimmer of Regidor's presence pierced the fog of evil shrouding their surroundings. Past two empty docks and three with swaying black hulks of ships, the two raced toward the strengthening beacon. They slowed as the sixth dock came into view. A ship bobbed in the water beside a landing pier. Large crates lined the plank walkway, stacked in uneven rows. Lights flickered from the portholes in the side of the foreign vessel.

Kale and Bardon joined Regidor in the shadows between two warehouses. Regidor mindspoke to them both.

"Dar's aboard that ship."

Bardon identified the type of vessel. *"Frigate, a high-speed, medium-sized, sailing war vessel. Too bad we can't see the flag. But I do know it's from the Northern Reach."*

Kale surveyed the ship. *I don't feel Dar's presence. In fact, I don't detect any occupants.*

Regidor nodded. *"There's some kind of shield surrounding it, blocking our perception. I wonder if we could figure out how to do that. We must try."*

Bardon glanced over at the meech. Kale knew his sentiments matched her own. It wasn't the right time to indulge Regidor's curiosity over the way things worked.

Bardon gave a half grin to Kale and spoke to Regidor.

"Yes, my meech friend. But not now. Now we must figure out how to rescue Sir Dar."

36

Finding Dar

At the foot of the gangplank, a sailor sat on a barrel. Another stood guard at the top. The heavy rain must have driven all hands below. The same rain aided Regidor, Bardon, and Kale in their stealthy approach. The three conspirators hid behind a huge crate not more than six feet from the shivering sailor.

"He's about your size, Kale," Bardon mindspoke to both.

Regidor scowled at the lehman. *"What does that have to do with anything?"*

Bardon is going to knock the man out, Kale answered. *I'll put on his coat and sit in his position, so anyone on board will think the man is still on duty.*

"And you know this because you and Bardon think together." Regidor tilted his head. *"I really want to know why that is. I haven't found a thing in the books about such a phenomenon. But I haven't finished researching."*

The sailor huddled miserably in a large coat, with the collar pulled up around his neck and an oilcloth hat pulled down over his head.

"And what do we do with the man at the top of the gangplank?" asked the meech.

Bardon pointed to the more alert guard. *"Go into his mind, Regidor. Distract him with images he can't resist. Right now I would assume that would be a cozy chair by a blazing hearth with a mug of mulled cider."*

Regidor stared at the man for a moment. *"You're wrong, Bardon. He'd rather be in his bunk below deck. The man's been too long at sea to be thinking fireplaces and comfortable chairs."*

"Can you distract him?"

Regidor snorted. *"Leave him to me."*

Kale edged her way back to where the pier joined the land. She stepped out into the open and approached the first sailor. When the old man noticed her, she projected questions into his mind.

What's she doing out on a night like this? Where's she going? Does she think I'm going to let her board?

She smiled and nodded at the befuddled man and strolled on by. As the guard turned his head to follow her movement, Bardon slipped out and grabbed him. With a hand clamped over the sailor's mouth, Bardon hauled him to their hiding place. Kale followed on the lehman's heels.

Regidor stood in the shadows, his eyes trained on the figure at the top of the gangplank. Kale wondered what method Regidor had used to trick the man's mind into thinking nothing unusual was happening on the dock. Sometimes her friend surprised her with something so innovative she couldn't have predicted his actions at all, and she was supposed to know him better than anyone else. Librettowit said this quality made Regidor a genius.

The meech dragon had matured in a short time. Was she still supposed to "manage" him? She didn't think anyone except Paladin could actually control Regidor. *At least he still listens to me when I reason with him. But he is so much smarter than me, one day my opinions won't matter. He's such a stubborn dragon.*

The dragon watched the snared man struggle. With one finger, he touched the captive's temple. The sailor passed out.

Bardon held the suddenly limp form. "What did you do?"

"Put him to sleep."

"Will he wake up?" Bardon's sharp tone cut through the air.

"Yes, with a headache."

"Where did you learn to do that?"

"From one of Librettowit's old books. But I hadn't tried it until now."

Kale felt tension surge between the two. Bardon didn't appreciate the dragon's interference. Regidor chafed because he knew he should have consulted the lehman before he knocked out the sailor.

"Enough," she said. "We have to get to Dar. Give me the hat and coat."

She settled on the barrel at the bottom of the gangplank. The man at the top remained oblivious to any unusual activity. Regidor obviously controlled his thoughts. She hunched down, assuming the same position as the sailor. She pictured that man in her mind. They'd left him in a heap behind the crate.

One down, one to go. But how many sailors are between us and Dar, once we board the ship?

That thought sent a shiver down her spine.

She waited for Regidor and Bardon to approach the second man. This time Bardon would make the bold advance. Regidor would approach while obscuring the guard's vision of him through his talent.

Kale shivered. *My feet feel like they're encased in ice. My cape and the sailor's coat should be keeping me warm. I bet the goose bumps are from nerves. Why are they waiting?*

A noise behind her answered the question. Someone had come out on deck. Two men stood about twelve feet behind her and some distance above her head. She heard the mumble of voices.

Dar!

Bardon's voice entered her mind. *"He's coming off the ship alone. We'll find out what's going on once he's safely away."*

Dar came down the gangplank, his footsteps sounding light on the sodden wood. She peeked out from under the hat to see the doneel diplomat pass by. The transparent shield he used during a fight was up and repelling the rain. He walked away without acknowledging her presence.

But that doesn't mean he doesn't know I'm sitting here.

"Regidor has you covered," said Bardon. *"Come on."*

Kale hopped off the barrel and joined the two hiding behind the crate. She shed the sailor's coat and hat.

"Let's go," whispered Bardon.

"Wait," said Regidor. He pointed to the crumpled figure at their feet. "We can't leave this old man out here in the cold."

Bardon looked down. "What do you suggest we do with him?"

"Take him to The Horn."

"Why?" The word exploded from Bardon's lips.

"Shh!" Kale hissed.

Regidor sighed. "Because that would be easier than tucking him into his bunk on the frigate."

"But why move him at all?" Bardon's exasperation poured into Kale's feelings.

She shut them off. She was tired of her friends' bickering and wanted to go home.

"I feel responsible for him." Regidor reached down and hoisted the limp figure over his shoulder. "Come on."

Bardon looked at her for an explanation. She shrugged, pulled up the hood of her cape, and traipsed after the meech dragon.

"Oh well," muttered Bardon. "Perhaps we'll find my sword."

Dar had vanished again.

This has to be the strangest adventure I've ever been on. I don't feel particularly frightened, not with Regidor and Bardon beside me. But what is Dar up to? And Regidor? Why did he start that fight? I sure hope someone is going to explain all this. And I hope it's soon.

Regidor marched up the two wooden steps to The Horn, tramped over the wooden porch, and pushed in the swinging doors without one sign of trepidation. Inside, most of the clientele had gone home. Several workers were sweeping up evidence of the fight. They stopped and, with open mouths, stared at the three comrades.

"Look here." The marione who'd taken their dinner order came forward. He carried an unlit, broken candle in his hand. "I don't want any more trouble."

Regidor plopped his burden down in an empty chair and rested the sailor's head on the table. He then turned to the man with a pleasant smile.

"No trouble. Just looking for my robe and my friend's sword."

A sudden movement across the room caught Kale's attention. She'd found the man who'd picked up the sword from the street. She glanced at Bardon, and he nodded.

The marione blocked their way and waved the candle in front of Regidor's face. "You're not welcome here."

The meech dragon continued to smile. "Would you like me to light that for you?" He pursed his thin lips, and with a tiny blow, sent a small stream of fire to ignite the wick.

Regidor stepped around the stunned marione and retrieved his robe from the floor. Bardon crossed to the tumanhofer who had his sword across his knees under the table.

"My sword, please." Bardon's voice sounded smooth and polite.

The tumanhofer swallowed hard. His eyes traveled to Kale and then to the meech dragon. Slowly, he pulled out the weapon and laid it on the table.

"Thank you," said Bardon. He examined the blade, then slipped it into his scabbard.

Kale breathed a sigh of relief. *Good! Now we can go home.*

One of the doorways to the back rooms opened. Dar emerged, immaculately dressed with only a slight hint of dampness around the bottom of his pant legs. He surveyed the shattered hall.

"Seems like you've been busy," he said.

Regidor stopped with only one arm inserted into his monk's robe. "No less busy than you, Sir Dar. I think it's time we had a talk."

Dar cocked his head. "Ah." He looked closely at the faces of his three companions. "Yes, I think you're right. But first let's find a carriage to take us home. I think we can chat best at our own fireside."

37

Good News, Bad News

Kale's stomach rumbled as she rummaged in a chest for her slippers. She'd removed her sodden boots before tiptoeing into the little room where Toopka slept. Kale shushed her tummy, telling it to remember the hearty meal she'd eaten at The Horn. She didn't want Toopka to awaken. The little girl slept soundly, occasionally snoring with a soft snuffling sound Kale had grown to love. The o'rant smiled as Toopka grunted and turned over.

With warm slippers on her feet, Kale found the old pair of trousers Dar had once made for her out of a skirt. She slipped those on, picked her discarded wet ones off the floor, and draped them over the back of a wooden chair. She hurried back to the kitchen, not wanting to miss any of the conversation.

Her comrades met by the warm hearth. Dar placed steaming mugs of mallow and a plate heaped with fried mullins and daggarts on the large kitchen table. He also put out poorman's dessert for the minor dragons. Even with the comforting touches of food and candlelight, the tension around the table could not be ignored.

Librettowit crossed his arms over his chest with his fingers drumming the sleeve of his dressing gown. Bardon held a mug but did not drink. Regidor held his tail in his lap, stroking the scales at its tip. Only the minor dragons seemed unconcerned. They noisily slurped their treat.

Kale looked around the table at her comrades. They all faced the same uncertain future, but they handled the tension differently. Librettowit allowed gloom to settle on his features. Bardon put on a stonelike facade to hide his inner turmoil. Regidor's nerves caused him to visibly twitch. Dar adopted his debonair host persona.

Only Dar and the minor dragons look comfortable. Who do I resemble? She surveyed the different faces once more.

Nobody yet. I guess I get to choose. Paladin is always saying to take care of what is right in front of me. And I know what the problem is right now. I'm hungry!

Kale took a toffee daggart from the plate, which she pushed toward Regidor.

His head jerked up, and he looked at her intently for a moment. Then he sighed, grinned, and helped himself to two daggarts before passing the plate to the librarian.

Dar sat at the head of the table. He wrapped his fingers around his drink as if to warm his hands.

"First, I would like an account of the fight at The Horn." His eyes shifted immediately to her. "Kale?"

"Some of the men took exception to Regidor." She paused, not knowing how to describe the way Regidor goaded the men into the fight.

Dar's eyes moved to the lehman. "Bardon?"

"When the men challenged Regidor, he revealed his identity and instigated the fight."

Dar's eyes narrowed. "And what provoked you, Regidor?"

Kale had grown so accustomed to the unusual pupils in Regidor's eyes, she hardly noticed them. But now the black pupils narrowed to a thick line running down the center of each green iris. The green glowed as if a fire burned within. Kale tensed, wondering if the meech would explode once again.

"They talked of dragons, among themselves and in the stupid rumination of their drunken minds." Regidor's deep voice rumbled like thunder announcing a wild storm still some distance away. "Dragons are to be blamed for every ill of society. Poisonous slander. Malicious lies. These men plot to murder dragons working side by side with the high races. Their words inflame the fears of ignorance. Kill. Destroy. Maim. Imprison. These are their solutions to a nonexistent problem. Crush the eggs. Slit the throats of newborns. Burn the carcass of any slain dragon. Bounties have already been offered in Northern Trese. The slaughter has begun."

Kale tried to stem the panic flooding her. The minor dragons left their dessert and crawled into her arms where she cradled them, holding their fragile bodies as if to protect them from this unseen danger.

"Fools," barked Librettowit. "For centuries Amara's economy has depended on cooperation between the high races and the dragons. The dragons have always been unselfish in their willingness to facilitate the production and marketing of goods. How do these vigilantes propose to conduct business after they have annihilated our worthy friends?"

"Yes." Dar spoke with ponderous gravity. "This narrow-minded propaganda is poisoning the thinking of too many people. The problem escalates by careful planning. Rabble-rousers spread these venomous ideas. And the dragons themselves act in an irrational manner that strengthens the rumors."

Kale cuddled her three dragons. "What are we going to do?" Not even Dibl passed encouragement to her worried mind.

"I have news from my meeting tonight," said Dar. "We can at last leave this depressing city and go in search of the meech dragon. We have a definite lead."

They leaned over the table toward the doneel.

"One wagon of itinerant merchants has been noted to have been in each location where an outbreak of radical dragon behavior has occurred. The meech dragon must be traveling with this band of thieves. They sell elixirs, potions, balms, and concoctions to heal, relieve, and assuage any problem you could name. Of course, it's all a sham. I believe their poison harms men's minds as well as their bodies. We shall track down these swindlers and see what they carry in their wagon besides chicanery."

"First," said Regidor, "we have another issue to discuss."

All eyes turned to the meech dragon. Kale picked up the suppressed anger emanating from her friend. She cast a glance at Bardon to see if he, too, recognized the danger. The lehman's body tensed. He pushed his chair a foot away from the table. His focus remained on Regidor's stern expression.

The dragon glared at the doneel. "Dar, you will not lie to us again."

"Lie?" The doneel clenched a fist. "Explain this accusation."

"You told us that you were going into a back room to play cards." Regidor paused. He ground out his next words. "You were not playing cards."

Dar nodded. His fist relaxed. "I see your concern, Regidor. I'll explain.

"I entered the game of cards, hoping to pick up some useful gossip. However, one of the players was the first mate from the frigate *Breedoria.*

"I knew that a messenger had intended to board the ship in Dascarnavon. So I asked the first mate if they had taken on a passenger from that port. He said they had, but the man was ill. I excused myself from the game and went to the *Breedoria.* I boarded and found our informer was not ill but wounded. He gave me the news I have shared with you."

Dar's cold delivery of the facts made Kale shiver. She did not like this stern, controlled man who had taken the place of her fun-loving friend.

Librettowit slammed his empty mug down on the table. "Good news and bad. Good that we finally have a clear direction for this quest. Bad that we must leave the relative comfort of this house to pursue the reprobates. I prefer my library to the wilds of Trese." He rose from his chair. "I propose we pack in the morning and leave as soon as the dragons are summoned."

He shuffled out of the room, shutting the hall door with a thud. Kale saw a quiver of a smile play on Dar's lips. She relaxed a bit.

"The wilds of Trese?" she asked. "I was raised in River Away in Trese. The countryside consisted of farmland and forest, very tame forest with hardly any wildlife you would call wild. No grawligs, no blimmets, no mordakleeps. In fact, the seven low races are considered to be a fable by most of the citizens of Trese."

Dar chuckled. "Anyplace that has no libraries, no bookstores, no institutions of higher learning is considered uncivilized and wild to our tumanhofer."

"Summon the dragons?" Bardon's eyes glinted with excitement.

"Yes, Celisse and Merlander will fly to meet us, then carry us to our destination."

Kale's heart skipped over the dread of their quest and landed with joy at the prospect of being reunited with the two dragons.

"To bed, then," said Dar.

They stood and cleared the dishes from the table. Each one took a candle to light the way to their chambers.

"Kale," said Dar as he pushed open the door, "there's one thing that I should perhaps mention to you. The first stop on our journey is where the wagon of potion peddlers is expected to visit next. That would be River Away. You shall soon be seeing the masters of your youth."

Kale blinked. *Oh, that'll be just great. The only thing to make this trip better would be if my mother showed up.*

Dar winked at her. "And Fenworth will be there as well. He and his companions have rescued your mother."

38

LEGEND OF THE PAST

In the morning, Dar went out to arrange transportation while the others gathered their belongings. Soon a freighter knocked on the door to speak with Librettowit. The tumanhofer hired the man to take boxes of books to a ship in the harbor. The ship would take the cargo south, around the coast, to be delivered to a friend who lived just outside The Bogs. Librettowit's first thought had been to fly the parcels by greater dragon, but the freighter said the dragons had been unreliable of late.

Toopka skipped around trying to be helpful but actually getting in the way. She hadn't liked being cooped up in the city, and she chattered incessantly about the quest, which would be exciting, and Prushing, which was not.

"It's dreary!" she said.

"But Toopka." Kale packed a chest with their clothing. "You were born in the city."

"This city is different. Vendela's pretty, and most of the people are nice. Here everything is gray and ugly, and most of the people are cranky. Do you suppose they're cranky because they live in a gray world?" She climbed onto the bed and sat cross-legged with a pillow in her lap.

Kale thought it over. She certainly hadn't been as happy here as she had been in Vendela. Could it be that the atmosphere of Prushing had affected her mood? Or was it because she felt they were not making progress in their quest? No matter how often Librettowit said their preparation was important, the delay felt like wasted time. Maybe the grayness enveloped more than just the city.

"Grayness could make people cranky," she admitted.

Toopka sighed. "That seems wrong—to let a gray place make your insides gray too." She rolled over on the bed, propping her chin on her fists. "And I think that the gray insides are too sad to try to make the gray outside any different. So the gray outside stays the same or gets grayer, and the gray insides get grayer too, and pretty soon there's no hope for anything bright and pretty."

"Yes, I guess that could be true."

"And," said Toopka with eyes growing big, "that's why Vendela was different. If I had a fight with someone like Master Tellowmatterden, by the time I'd walked two blocks, I would see flowers and pretty painted carts and people smiling. Then Master Tellowmatterden would have been kind of covered over with better things."

"Does all this have a point, Toopka?"

"Yes." Toopka sprang up on her knees and bounced on the bed. "I'm glad we're going to the country."

Kale chuckled, but her own thoughts were not as cheerful.

I'm glad to leave Prushing, but I don't know if I want to go to River Away. I guess it won't be so bad. After all, I'm not a slave anymore. I have an important job. I've even met Paladin, and no one in River Away has.

Kale stopped folding Toopka's small tunic and stared at her hands. She no longer did daily chores at different houses in a small village. At that time, her palms had been callused and her skin dry and rough. A new callus showed how diligently she had been practicing with her small sword.

As a slave, she had nails that were always cracked, chipped, and stained. Now smooth white ends peeked out over her pink skin.

Granny Noon told me to remember I'm not a slave anymore. Won't Mistress Meiger be surprised? I'm not shabby anymore, either. I'm taller and stronger and smarter, too. And not only that, I'm coming to save River Away from the destructive influence of Risto. I'm not a slave. I am the Dragon Keeper. Between Regidor and me, the wayward dragons will be rescued.

She lifted a shirt from a peg on the wall.

Mother told me I had a destiny. I'm an Allerion. Mother's brave and does wonderful, courageous things right in one of Risto's castles. And she's beautiful.

I'm going to be like her. Someday I'll wear beautiful dresses and smell like a garden full of flowers. Mistress Meiger and all the others will be in awe of my grandeur. Right now they don't know how important I'll be, but I do. I won't act like a slave. I'll act like I'm one of Paladin's most trusted warriors.

Her smile widened as she tucked the last of their meager clothing into her cape. Toopka still prattled on, but Kale's imagination conjured up the gratitude that would be expressed by her former masters.

A carriage pulled up in front of the house just before noon. Bruit grinned at them from his perch. He clambered down and readily helped Bardon, Kale, and Toopka load the luggage and tie it down. Dar then strode out of the mansion and opened the carriage door. Regidor, in his monk's disguise, and Librettowit walked out into the sunshine and climbed into the vehicle. Even at this point the six companions took care to preserve their masquerade.

The ride out of the city put all her comrades in a good mood. Once they had passed through the city gate and begun the slow descent along a broad highway to the valley, Bruit sang at the top of his lungs. They swung west at a fork in the road and angled away from the Port of Prushing. Thick traffic made the going slow, but Kale and Toopka chattered on about the different people they passed, the varied styles of clothes, and the different types of wares piled into wagons and carts. Bardon listened to the old driver's songs and the girls' pointless chatter without participating in either.

The minor dragons came out of Kale's cape and stayed on the bundles above the coach. From below, they could not be seen. Dibl instigated a game of hide and seek with Toopka always "it" and the dragons always hiding. Kale felt sorry for her three comrades who had to ride inside the bouncing, rocking carriage.

In the late afternoon, they stopped at a friendly, clean inn to spend the night. As they traveled north and west the next day, they noticed a subtle depression in the countryside. The crops looked underdeveloped. Fewer carts heavily laden with goods passed them on the way to market. The people did not call out greetings. Riders slouched in their seats. Walkers shuffled along with shoulders stooped.

That night the inn did not seem so friendly. The comrades dropped their pretense of masters and servants. However, Regidor still wore his disguise. They sat in a corner of the public room, having a dinner of good roast beef and farm vegetables.

Almost the entire clientele consisted of mariones, hardworking farmers, and merchants. Bitterness and despair rankled among those dining and drinking and throwing darts at the four-colored corkboard on the wall. The talk in the room disturbed Kale and her companions.

One man waved his tankard as he spoke. "They say there's more of those unnatural beasts north of the border. They stand upright like a man, talk like a man, think they're like one of the high races, but of course they can't be."

"Yet they aren't one of the low races either." A farmer stood to make his point. "So what are these talking dragons?"

"Something made up by one of those evil wizards, no doubt," grumbled a man by the bar. "But it makes no difference, don't you know? I still lost my Clem—a dragon I've known all my life to be cheerful, helpful, and full of goodwill turned sullen. Then he knocked down the barn and trampled my field of winter wheat. Don't have a thing to take to market. And he's gone. Family's heartbroken. And they'll be more than heartbroken in the coming year. They'll be hungry when we don't get another crop in and don't take nothing to market."

"How can you blame that on the meech dragons from the north?" asked the innkeeper.

"Ain't never anything good come from the north," muttered one of the men.

"They's communicating with their minds. That's what it is," said the farmer who'd lost Clem.

"Mindspeaking between dragons?"

The farmer spoke again, "Well, sure, they've always done it."

"But it wasn't a bad thing, Spronder. You know the dragons have never been bad. Just talking more among themselves shouldn't turn the lot of them bad."

"All I'm saying is the more Clem brooded about, the less I could communicate with him. It was like he went away in his mind long before he went on his rampage, knocking things down, and then flying off like he did."

"Maybe it's a sickness," suggested the innkeeper. "Maybe you should take the matter to the wizard of the lake. What's his name?"

One of the patrons rattled off, "Ham? Cram? Cam? Sam?"

"Whatever his name is, no one's dealt with him in hundreds of years. He could have gone over to Risto like Crim Cropper and Burner Stox."

"They didn't 'go over,' man. They've always been evil," said an older, well-dressed man sitting by himself in the corner. "None of you know your history. You must not despair. Wulder will send a champion. Paladin will surface and strengthen our defenses."

"Empty promises, parson," said the innkeeper. "What you speak of is not history but fable."

Librettowit stood up. "I agree with the parson." He turned to the innkeeper. "Identify for me, man, the duties of a parson."

The man blustered, his eyes shifting around the room as if to find someone to help him answer. He snorted and put his hands on his hips. "He talks a lot and does little of anything."

Librettowit stood straighter. "He thinks a lot and says little of anything until he knows what he is talking about."

Several people laughed at the quick response. The innkeeper glared around the room, and the snickering ceased.

Librettowit took advantage of the silence. "A parson examines the books of Wulder. He breaks the passages down into components and analyzes the form, function, and ecclesiastic relationship of each part. He does not do this on his own, but with the guidance of Wulder Himself and under the tutelage of Paladin. And I will tell you, a community prospers in direct relationship to the number of parsons who adequately instruct the populace."

"Bah," said one of the men, a wealthy landowner by the look of him. "There you have it wrong, tumanhofer. Until recently Trese has led the country in economic prosperity. And we have few parsons. This parson here used to be a merchant, but when he handed his business over to his sons, he had too much time on his hands."

A smile curved Librettowit's lips. "He slowed down enough to assess what really is important. Wulder does not count a society wealthy by how many coins change hands. He measures by hearts filled with peace, satisfaction, and joy."

"Oh, I see," said the innkeeper. "You are a parson too." He looked over the party at Librettowit's table. "I should have known. It looks like you travel with some foreign monk and two noble squires, male and female, like the legend of Torse."

"So you know the legend of Torse?" Librettowit's smile grew even wider. "And why did Torse leave his castle and roam the countryside?"

Several in the room sniggered again.

"Got you there, Bickket," said Farmer Spronder. "Torse found a great truth. He wanted to give it away, so he could go back to his castle and live the way he was accustomed. He took the monk with him, for it was he who first revealed the truth. Torse wanted to foist the monk off on some other household. And much to Torse's dismay, the monk kept attracting worthy young people. But even when they took the truth out of Torse's hands, the truth remained in Torse's possession. It multiplied instead of diminishing."

Librettowit nodded, the twinkle in his eye softening his ancient features. "This is true. And when did Torse find peace?"

A young man stood up from the table where he sat with much older men. "When he took the truth home with him and put it in a place of honor."

The eager young man took a few steps forward. "May I go with your band of comrades?"

Librettowit strode forward, put his hand on the young man's arm, and turned him toward the parson.

"Go to this man and learn. In the near future, there will be a great conflict between good and evil. At that time, Paladin will call for ones such as yourself to join the fight. You are of strong body. Prepare your heart to be strong as well."

"A battle?" The question flew around the room on nervous lips.

Librettowit nodded solemnly.

"A war that has been secretly waged will erupt for all to see. You must make your choice. Stand and fight, or do nothing. Choose the higher plane, or dwell on the lower forever."

39

Ardeo

Kale awoke in the middle of the night. She'd curled herself around a lumpy pillow. One hip hurt where it had settled into a crevice in the poorly stuffed mattress. For a moment she didn't recognize the room made of rough-hewn beams and plastered walls. Toopka slept in another narrow bed. Moonlight cast a pale glow through the small chamber. Only the corners hid in shadows.

The inn.

Groggy with sleep, she looked at one window. Curtains hung over a single glass pane.

Dibl's giggle shifted her attention. The three minor dragons perched on the back of a wooden chair, staring at her with joyful expressions. She blinked. *What?* She started to sit up, but a slight weight on her hip stopped her. She craned her neck to see what it was.

A small glowing mass balanced on the curve between her waist and her thigh. It moved. Kale squinted. The ball of white light stretched, elongating into a neck topped with an angular head. Curious dark eyes blinked at her. The small dragon continued to stretch, showing her his small pointed tail.

Kale's hand flew to the pouch that always hung around her neck. No longer round with the egg, the flattened sides and muffled crunch revealed the broken eggshell within.

A rush of joy caught her off guard. She laughed out loud. Scooping the shining baby into her hand, she sat up. Her fingers glowed as if she were holding a white lightrock. Gymn, Metta, and Dibl soared into the air, expressing their delight with a chorus of trilling noises and fancy aerobatics.

Kale watched as the baby performed an instinctive bonding behavior. Gymn, Metta, and Dibl had done this same thing. The young creature rubbed his entire body leisurely over Kale's palm, thrumming contentedly.

"What is your name, little one?" whispered Kale.

The dragon lifted his chin from her thumb and peered at her with eyes that looked too large for his tiny head.

"Ardeo! Your name is Ardeo."

The flying dragons swooped around Kale's head and shoulders. Their excitement transferred to Kale and the newborn. Ardeo rolled in her hand. The dragon's luminescence blurred his features. She couldn't actually see his face other than the dark eyes. A gleaming haze surrounded his entire form.

"Wow!" Toopka whispered her excitement.

Kale looked up to see the little girl standing at the end of the bed. Toopka crawled onto the hard mattress and eased closer to the baby dragon.

"Can I hold it?"

"Him," said Kale. "And you can hold him tomorrow."

"He shines."

The radiance from the newborn reflected off the little doneel's pale fur. The baby settled down on his back.

"Can I touch him?"

"Yes."

Toopka stretched out her hand and stroked the dragon's belly with one finger.

"What do you think his talent is?" she asked.

Kale furrowed her brow. "I don't remember a description in the books of a white dragon who glows. I still have them, though. They're in the hollows of my cape. Tomorrow we'll look him up."

"Maybe his talent is glowing."

Kale held the creature up to her chin and rubbed him softly with her cheek. "That would be enough."

"Oh yes," said Toopka. "But I didn't get to see him born."

"Neither did I. I woke up, and he was already sitting on me."

Toopka heaved a dramatic sigh. "I guess I'll never see a baby dragon hatch."

"I have four more eggs, Toopka. Surely someday you'll be in the right place at the right time."

The little girl nodded but didn't seem to hold out much hope.

Kale scooted over on the narrow bed. "Here, you crawl in with me. We need to go back to sleep. In the morning, you can hold Ardeo."

Toopka scrambled into the warm bed beside Kale. She squirmed a bit to get comfortable and then lay with her head on Kale's shoulder. She stared at the little dragon cupped in Kale's hands and resting on her stomach. "He's beautiful."

"Yes, he is. He looks like the moon, doesn't he?"

⊷⊶

A knock on the door woke the two sleeping comrades and four minor dragons. Bardon spoke from the hall.

"We're leaving early this morning."

"All right," Kale called back.

The dragons nested on top of her and the covers. When she shifted, they flew off with grumbles voiced deep in their throats.

Toopka had to be prodded to get up and move. Kale hurried to dress and get both of them ready to go. The dragons crawled into their pocket-dens even before she put the moonbeam cape over her shoulders. After a bite of breakfast, the party of questers boarded the carriage in time to watch the sun rise over frost-covered fields.

Toopka stood behind Bruit's bench and hung over Bardon's shoulder. A big bump tossed her forward, but she caught herself by grabbing Bardon's neck. He disengaged her with a swift movement and placed her in his lap. She snuggled into the warmth of his chest.

"We have a surprise," she said, with a mischievous grin lighting her face.

Bardon roughed her hair. "What is it?"

"You have to guess."

Bardon glanced back at Kale and then down at the little girl in his lap. He grinned at her. "This isn't exactly fair, Toopka. Kale can't keep secrets from me."

"Will you mindspeak with me? Do you think I could learn how to do it? I mean, start it. I can answer when Kale talks to me in my mind, but I can't start it."

"After I see this new baby dragon, Toopka, I'll mindspeak with you. But I don't think you can learn to do it if Wulder hasn't given you the gift." He stood and stepped over the back of the driver's perch.

Kale pulled out Ardeo as Bardon sat next to her.

"Oh no!" cried Toopka. "He's dead!"

"No," said Kale, but worry trembled her voice. "He's not dead. He's breathing."

"But he's ugly, and he's not moving." Toopka clutched Kale's arm. Her eyes filled with tears.

Blotches of gray mottled the baby's dull white skin. Kale stroked Ardeo's side as he snored softly. Metta, Gymn, and Dibl squirmed out of their pocket-dens and gathered around the littler dragon.

"They say he's all right. He's just sleeping." Kale reported the impressions she had from the minor dragons.

"But he's ugly," cried Toopka. "He looks like a cold lump of porridge."

Ardeo stretched, yawning until his little mouth spread wide enough to cover the end of Kale's thumb. His eyes blinked open, and he gazed around at his audience. He stood and stretched again, arching his back. Spreading his wings, he rocked back and forth on the palm of Kale's hand.

Metta began to sing. Dibl did an uphill roll from Kale's elbow to her neck, then hopped, flipped, and skipped on her head and shoulders. Gymn sprang into the air to dance above their heads.

Ardeo trilled and flew from Kale's hand to her knee and back again. He then pounced onto Toopka, then Bardon, and darted back to Kale.

"He's healthy enough," said Bardon as Toopka clapped with glee. He turned to Kale. *"Why were you worried?"*

Last night he was beautiful. He looked like a dragon formed out of moonbeams.

"Well, he's a little worse than plain in the sunlight. What does your book say about this grayish dragon?"

I haven't looked it up yet.

Kale moved back from the circle of activity and reached into the hollow of her cape. The first book she pulled out was *Training for Performance: An Overall Guide to Dragonkeeping.* She laid it aside and searched again. This time she brought out *The Care and Feeding of Minor Dragons.* Resting the book on her crossed legs, she thumbed through the pages, looking for the list of colors.

"Here it is, Bardon." She pointed to a paragraph near the end of the first chapter.

Bardon moved to sit beside her. He sat on a higher trunk and looked over her shoulder. Dibl landed on Bardon's head. Kale read aloud.

"The dappled white is very rare. An unattractive color in strong light, the minor dragon produces radiance in shadows and darkness. Plainly, its talent is to light the way."

Bardon chortled. "Obviously."

Kale looked at the twinkle in Bardon's blue eyes. "Obviously," she repeated and laughed.

"Is anything about dragons obvious?"

Oh yes. I think most of what they do is logical.

"Only to a Dragon Keeper."

40

A Light on the Subject

Two more days of travel took them past many scenes of devastation. Evidence lined the roadways where formerly placid dragons had used their mighty strength to wreak havoc. The minor dragons expressed their dismay with long, sad chirrs of reproach.

On a sunny morning with brown, crunchy leaves blowing from the trees, they came to a pasture where four dragons awaited them. Kale rejoiced to see Celisse and Merlander. She wondered why the two other dragons had been sent but knew Celisse would explain. One was blue and purple. The other, shades of brown and copper.

Kale ran into the field and threw her arms around Celisse's neck. Dar followed and greeted Merlander with more reserved affection.

Kale turned to wave at Bardon who remained seated beside Bruit. His face flushed, and she heard him with her mind as he declared, *"Not me!"*

Yes, Bardon, it's true. Paladin has sent Greer for you. His rider died in the recent battle in Creemoor. He wants to serve again. Greer's heart will break if he doesn't find a rider soon.

Bardon climbed down from the driver's perch and walked slowly into the field. Grasshoppers and drummerbugs scattered before him.

Greer arched his blue neck and swung his head toward his potential rider. The majestic dragon stretched out cobalt blue wings from a royal purple body and beat the air with one mighty flourish. The draft blew Bardon's hair back from his face.

Kale took in a quick breath. With his hair blown back, she saw Bardon's pointed ears. She glimpsed this oddity all too clearly. She glanced at her comrades and even tested them with her talent to see if they had noticed. No one seemed to have spotted what was so obvious to her.

The dragon bowed his head to Bardon now that the young man stood close. They looked each other in the eye for almost a minute. She held her breath.

Bardon put his hand forward, palm down. The dragon placed his chin next to the hand and neatly nudged it, causing Bardon to turn his hand over. Bardon stepped forward and stroked the huge beast's neck. Greer rested his chin on the lehman's shoulder.

Kale exhaled and squeezed Celisse's neck.

It worked. They're going to be good for each other.

She felt the rumble in Celisse's throat and laughed out loud. *Of course I never doubted Paladin had made a wise decision.*

Toopka ran into the field and jumped into Kale's arms.

"There's one more dragon. Is that one for me?"

"No, Toopka." Kale squeezed the little doneel in a tight hug. "The brown one's name is Bett, and Librettowit will ride him. We need four because we don't want to overburden our dragons with too many passengers and too much luggage."

They transferred their belongings from the top of the carriage to the backs of the dragons. Bruit held his horse in check as he watched the questers take off. He waved his hat in farewell.

"I like Bruit," said Toopka from her seat in front of Kale on Celisse.

"I like him too," answered Kale.

Toopka leaned back, resting her head on Kale's chest, and sighed. "Questing means leaving a lot of people behind, doesn't it?"

"Well, yes. But it also involves meeting a lot of people ahead." *And tomorrow I'll be meeting people from my past.*

They flew until dusk, then landed in a devastated field. Bardon and Kale walked to a nearby farmhouse to gather news. An hour later, they returned to tell the others that the destruction by dragons was even more widespread and more catastrophic in the north. The farmers in the area were nervous.

After supper, Kale sat under a bentleaf tree, close to the trunk. Long slender branches drooped to touch the ground all around her, creating a private bower. Only the sound of insects and a rhythmic call from a beater frog invaded her solitude.

The four minor dragons followed her into her little sanctuary. Her tense body relaxed as Metta began a trilling song. She laughed as Dibl ran up and down her body in his excitement at being in a new place.

"As long as I have you for friends, I won't have to worry about being lonely, will I?"

Ardeo sat in her lap, his glow as bright as the moon. Kale stroked his sides. Metta sat on her favorite perch on Kale's shoulder. The little purple dragon leaned against her neck and nuzzled her chin. She hummed a soothing song that apparently had no words. Gymn sat on the other shoulder, and Dibl chased bugs. Ardeo still hadn't shown any interest in his first meal.

Kale remembered Fenworth's tirades about how uncomfortable quests could be. She agreed. Having an unpleasant mother pop in and out of this quest made it even more uncomfortable. Kale wished she could return to The Hall and escape the complications confronting her. But a little reprieve with only the minor dragons was the best she could get.

The other questers sat around a campfire. But Kale wanted to think and sort through her feelings. Tomorrow they would land at River Away. She would see the people who had raised her from an infant.

"You'll like Dubby Brummer," she told Dibl as he somersaulted in front of her. "I wonder how much he's grown. When I saw him last, he was still in wrappers."

Gymn tumbled off her shoulder and pounced on Dibl. They wrestled for a moment then went after more bugs. "Bolley and Gronmere are fun to watch too. They wrestled in the town square to show off their fighting ability. I wonder if I should offer to go a round with them." She giggled. "Wouldn't they be surprised?

"Then there's Mistress Meiger. If nice means friendly, then Mistress Meiger is definitely not nice. But she's fair.

"And Master Meiger is busy, too busy to be kind or even interested in what a slave is doing."

She scooped Gymn into her hands and snuggled him under her chin. "Just think how their eyes will pop when they see me slide off Celisse's neck and walk toward them in my leecent uniform instead of a slave's tatters."

Gymn warbled in his throat.

"No, we don't have to wear our disguises any longer. Well, maybe Regidor does. But the rest of us will look exactly like what we are—servants of Paladin, sent to help the local populace in their dire need. I intend to look very official and impressive."

She placed Gymn on her knee and pulled the pouch from around her neck. She shoved two fingers in and pulled out a piece of shell. "The first thing we will do is clean out this pouch. Mistress Meiger gave it to me to carry Gymn."

She turned the material inside out, and pieces of shell fell to the leaf-littered ground. A glint of metal warned her that the odd coin she'd been given by Granny Noon had fallen too. Gymn climbed up her body as Kale shifted to her knees and ran her fingers through the mulch. She found the shiny disk. Holding it in the palm of her hand, she examined the two pie-shaped notches cut into its sides.

A breeze whisked Kale's hair. She looked up to see the curtain of bentleaf branches parting. Her mother stepped in. Her velvet dress in shades of purple with gold trim crowded the small bower. She had to stoop, and Kale got the impression this annoyed her greatly.

"Surrounded by your pretty little pets again, Kale? Put them away for the time being. I have important news for you."

The minor dragons scurried to the shadows. Kale plucked Gymn from her shoulder and placed him on the ground, stood abruptly, and bobbed a curtsy.

"Mother."

"Yes, our friends have brought me safely out of Creemoor. My work there is done. There's no need for me to remain in River Away. Fenworth and Cam have the situation well in hand. Now, let's go."

"Go? Go where?"

"Vendela. Isn't that where you wish to be?"

An image of the beautiful buildings, clean streets, and happy people popped into her mind. For two weeks she'd been at The Hall and had a predictable future of training and service. Then she'd followed Dar out the gate.

"No." Kale shook her head.

Her mother's eyebrows arched. "No?"

"I'd like to go back someday, but not today."

"That is neither here nor there. We're leaving." Lyll Allerion held out a hand, waiting for Kale to take it.

Metta flew back to Kale's shoulder. Gymn took up a position on the other. Dibl and Ardeo dove into the front of the moonbeam cape, seeking their dens. The instant Ardeo disappeared under the folds of the cape, the bower fell into darkness.

Lyll's hand snapped back. She hissed a word Kale did not recognize, and a light exposed the area. The harsh glare made Kale blink and shield her eyes.

Her mother spoke another word, and the offensive light dimmed.

Her mother smiled, but the hard look in her eyes remained, making Kale feel wary.

"As you see," said Lyll Allerion, her voice smooth and persuasive, "I have no need for those scrawny creatures. Your collection of beasts will not be necessary in our palace. Instruct them to stay here."

Kale felt a shiver go through her heart, and her hands clenched into fists. The hard metal disk bit into the flesh of her palm. Pain streaked up her arm. Kale released the grip she had on the odd coin and let it fall.

"Oh no." She dropped down to her knees, looking for Granny Noon's gift.

"What is it now?" asked Lyll.

"I lost the coin Granny Noon gave me."

"You won't need that either. Honestly, Kale, step out of this dismal existence. Why be at the beck and call of a motley group of misfits when you can live in the splendor of wealth and power granted by Wulder Himself to the Allerion family? Come!"

Lyll extended her milk-white hand once more, and Kale saw the pointed tips of nails painted a purple hue to match her mother's gown.

She ducked her head and stared at the ground. The coin lay among dry, crisp leaves. A tendril of smoke spiraled up from the edge of the metal disk. With a crackle, the smoke expanded and swirled into a thin tongue of fire. Kale's eyes widened as the small flame encircled the coin and grew taller.

Gymn and Metta squeaked their alarm. With a whoosh of cold air, Kale's mother disappeared. Kale stomped on the fire with her boot. In a matter of seconds, the bower under the bentleaf tree was dark and silent.

She squared her shoulders and fought the fear that almost buckled her knees. Dibl and Ardeo peeked out of the cape. Ardeo gave a trill and dove to the charred ground. He picked up a bug and popped it in his mouth.

Kale gave a nervous giggle. "Roasted roach seems to be Ardeo's preferred meal."

She bent over and carefully picked up the shiny metal disk. No heat remained. She clenched the cold coin in her hand and felt no pain. She tightened her grip and still did not feel the bite into her flesh that had made her drop it before.

Opening her hand, Kale stared at the small piece of metal. "Now what does this mean?"

41

HOMECOMING

Kale stepped out from under the shelter of the bentleaf tree and breathed the crisp, clear air. Stars pricked the velvet sky with brilliant pinpoints. The minor dragons danced in the air, displaying their joyful mood.

She sensed Bardon nearby and searched for him. He stepped from behind another bentleaf tree. Armed with his sword and a bow, he looked ready to defend the camp.

"Are you on guard, Bardon?"

"It's always good to be prepared."

"You were watching out for me."

He nodded.

"Did you see her?"

"I got a glimpse." He hesitated. "She certainly dresses well."

Kale laughed.

Bardon watched the dragons' aerial ballet. "The dragons are happy. Does that mean you are as well?"

"I am. Isn't that odd?"

"Because your mother was here, and she is a…disturbing person?"

"Yes." Kale surveyed the countryside. The devastated field didn't look so harsh in the mellow light of the moon. She sighed at the beauty still visible in the roll of the gentle hills. "I was contemplating how superior I would feel when I see the people I used to serve. Then my mother showed up, and she really is important. And I don't like her."

Dibl landed on Bardon's shoulder, then flew off again. Metta's voice broke into a song of contentment.

Bardon put a hand on Kale's shoulder and guided her to sit on a boulder. He crouched beside her. "So why do you feel so at ease?" he asked.

"Because I didn't go with her. I knew I didn't have to. And tomorrow I'm going to like seeing Mistress Meiger. I'll be seeing friends, not masters."

She gasped as a light appeared out of one of the bentleaf trees. "Kimens," she whispered.

Bardon sat on the grass and leaned against the boulder. They watched as more of the tiny creatures slipped out into the open. They danced beneath the minor dragons and sang with Metta. Their clothing glowed in shades of lavender, yellow, and gold.

Unlike the first time Kale had seen the little people dance, she did not feel compelled to join them. Instead, she basked in the pleasure of their simple song and beautiful dance.

Bardon felt it too. The strong link between them startled Kale out of her reverie. From her perch on the big rock, she looked at Bardon seated on the grass. She expected to see his back or shoulder touching her. But six inches separated him from her knee. Still, a steady vibration emanated from the lehman. The sensation felt like a cat's purr, and she realized it matched, thrum for thrum, a similar tremor in her being.

Harmonizing notes to Metta's song recaptured her attention. Across the stubby field, Librettowit, Regidor, and Dar stood with musical instruments. The librarian played an oboe, the meech dragon played a flute, and the doneel drew a bow across the strings of a violin. Toopka skipped into the open area and joined the dancers.

From the center of the field, among the kimen dancers, a radiance grew. Like the colors of a rainbow, a pool of light ebbed and flowed, pulsating with the chords of music. With each pulse, the borders extended out and returned, but the height of the image grew taller and continued to stretch upward. When the melody ended, a rainbow column soared far above their heads. For a moment the lights quivered, and then the image streaked upward, disappearing like a comet into the heavens.

"What was that?" asked Bardon.

"Worship," Kale answered, her voice still hushed with awe.

Bardon walked with her back to the tents. None of the questers spoke as they went to their beds. The serenity following the musical interlude hovered over them like a peaceful blanket.

Toopka settled on her pallet. But as soon as Kale pulled up her own covers and nestled down to sleep, the little doneel popped out of bed, scooted across the space between them, and slipped under the blanket. Kale cuddled her little friend, and they slumbered peacefully through the night.

The dawn exposed a glistening frost upon the ground once more. The sun's rays infused thin banks of clouds with rich coral colors. The wood smoke from Dar's cooking fire mixed with heavy spices he'd sprinkled in mugs of tea. Toopka hovered close, hoping to be the first to fill her plate with fried mullins.

The dragons tolerated the cold but preferred warmer weather. They stroked the air with their leathery wings to stir their sluggish blood. Anyone who did not know this ritual prepared them for flight might have thought they were doing homage to the rising sun.

After the companions ate breakfast and broke camp, Kale tucked Toopka inside her moonbeam cape for the journey. The other companions dressed warmly in clothing lined with thick, knitted wool. Once they were in flight, the warmth generated by the dragons' labor seeped through the leather saddles and warmed the passengers.

They soared above the countryside for only an hour before they spotted the Guerson River. The dragons descended, landing in a harvested field to the east of River Away. A farmer and his two sons came out to greet them.

Dar led the others to address the marione men.

"Good day to you," he began. "We come in the name of Paladin. He has commissioned us to aid you in your difficulties with the dragons. My name is Sir Dar. My companions are a meech, two warriors, a historian, and a child. I would like to speak to your councilmen."

The farmer looked to his sons for a reaction to this speech. The young men nodded solemnly.

"I'm Farmer Deel. These are my eldest sons, Mack and Weedom. We'll take you to Master Meiger," he said. Then he looked at the four dragons standing in his field. "Your dragons?"

"Safe," Dar assured him. "But if their presence troubles you, they are willing to wait for us elsewhere."

The farmer nodded. He shifted his feet and glanced again at his sons. "Aye, I have a family to protect. Times aren't as they once were."

"This is no problem, Farmer Deel."

Dar returned to Merlander's side and spoke to her. Soon the other dragons followed Merlander into the sky and off to the east.

Kale watched them go, knowing they would come quickly if summoned. She approached the marione men. She had worked as a slave in their household many times.

"Good morning, Farmer Deel."

He examined her face before a light of recognition changed his expression. "Kale?"

She nodded and grinned. Mack stepped forward and pumped her hand in a hearty handshake. Weedom pushed his brother aside and did the same. Neither young man voiced pleasure at seeing her, but her hand felt as if all the bones had been crushed. She massaged her fingers and smiled.

"Enough of this," said Farmer Deel gruffly. "We've business to attend to." Before he turned to lead the way to the village, he patted Kale's shoulder. "You be sure to visit my goodwife. She was mighty fond of you, and it would do her heart good."

Goodwife Deel was fond of me? Kale pictured the farmer's wife stopping during her chores to pick up a crying child. The brusque manner in which the mother administered a hug and a kiss and a word of consolation demonstrated the fashion of her relationships. Not much tenderness flavored her life.

They strode the two miles into River Away at a quick pace. The first things Kale saw among the familiar cluster of humble buildings were the chickens and glommytucks pecking in the yards and roadways. The unpaved streets saw little more than foot traffic, a few goat-pulled carts and handcarts, and an occasional horse and rider.

On market days, either dust or grumbles hung thick in the air. Traffic kicked up dust after a dry spell. Farmers bogged in a rain-soaked road spit out grumbles.

They rounded a corner to the main street through town where the inn, tavern, and mercantile lined up close together. On the bench in front of the tavern sat an old man talking to a tree, which also sat on the bench.

Toopka gave a whoop and ran ahead, throwing herself into Wizard Cam's arms. She hugged him and smacked his cheek with a loud kiss, then turned to the tree.

"Wake up, Wizard Fen. We're here now! Wake up and say hello."

The tree shuddered. Leaves fell on the ground and covered its exposed roots. A bird peered out of the branches with a disapproving glare at Toopka and flew away.

Toopka scrambled down from Cam's lap and took hold of one of the branches. She gave it a little tug.

"Come on, Wizard Fen. Don't you want to see us? Don't you want to hear about our 'ventures? Regidor can spit fire!"

Cam placed a hand on the little doneel's shoulder. "It's getting harder for him, little one. Give him a minute."

The tree rumbled. "You're implying I'm getting old. I'll wrap you in bogweed, Cam, and throw you in a lake! Can't a man rest after slaying 2,356 Creemoor spiders?"

Fenworth stirred himself again. The woody look about him disappeared except for a few stray leaves in his hair and beard.

Toopka clapped her hands and hopped.

Fenworth glared at her, but she just laughed.

"You, child, are impertinent."

"Does that mean hungry? Because I'm starved!"

Fenworth ignored her and turned stiffly to see the others approaching. "Good!" he exclaimed. "There are my apprentices. Thought I'd misplaced you. And my librarian! What I wouldn't give for a tankard of mallow and a good book, a cozy fire and Thorpendipity cawing on and on about Bog news."

He shook his head. "But you've brought that pesky doneel who's always wanting us to do things."

He stood and pointed a finger at Dar. "You, stay here." He pointed the same finger at Kale and crooked it. "You, come with me. Your mother's been worrying me like a dog with an old bone. Let's go meet her."

42

Mother?

As Kale followed Wizard Fenworth across the threshold of the tavern, the dimly lit room brought back memories. Fenworth stepped farther into the room, allowing her a view of the entire first floor. No boisterous farm lads sat at the tables now. No travelers stood at the bar. No solemn men sat with their tankards and discussed the business of market prices and fickle weather.

Kale knew this tavern well. A door led to the kitchen, an addition built onto the back of the establishment. Stairs climbed along one wall. On the second floor, three bedrooms quartered paying guests overnight. On the third floor, two bedrooms and a sitting room accommodated Master and Mistress Meiger. And at the very top, in the attic, a small room housed the village slave. Kale had climbed those stairs countless times.

Noonmeal had not yet been served. Logs crackled and popped in the huge fireplace. In one corner, near the mural, two figures sat in the only upholstered chairs in the room. The lamp on the table between them had not been lit, so Kale's eyes, accustomed to the outdoor brilliance, could not make out who they were.

Two women's voices seasoned the atmosphere with a dash of light-hearted conversation. One of them chortled, her humor evident in the robust music of her laughter. The other's laugh came reluctantly and sounded rusty, as if not often used. Kale recognized the second as her former mistress. The first was unknown to her.

Kale stepped forward to stand beside the wizard. He patted her on the shoulder and left his hand resting there in a comforting manner. She breathed deeply, smelling the old wood and the pine oil polish she remembered rubbing into the bar and banister. The pleasant scent of smoke from the fireplace mingled with a faint fragrance of stew from the kitchen.

The women stopped speaking.

Kale's eyes had adjusted to the dim light. She could now see the squarish form of her marione owner, Mistress Meiger. The other woman stood, and Kale sighed her relief. This was not her mother. This woman was taller by several inches than Mistress Meiger, but just as round. Her brown and gray hair hung over one shoulder in a thick braid. Simple homespun material made up her neat but plain blue dress. A white bib apron covered the front. The woman moved closer with hesitant steps.

In every way that her mother was elegant, this woman was not. Her double chin did not rise haughtily. Her mother's back held her exquisite figure erect. This woman stooped. Her mother's finely chiseled face reflected her moods in beauty. This woman's tears ran down wrinkled cheeks.

She held out a hand. "First, I want to tell you I love you. Second, I must explain why it was necessary to hide you in a safe place."

Kale's eyes shifted to Mistress Meiger and then to Wizard Fenworth. Both wore expressions of concern.

The woman took Kale's hand and pulled gently, guiding her to the seat she had just left. Mistress Meiger vacated her comfortable chair and bustled out of the room through the door to the kitchen. Wizard Fenworth took a seat on a wooden chair by one of the few windows. The woman, still holding Kale's hand, sat in Mistress Meiger's chair.

"You're my mother?" Kale's voice came out in a whisper.

"I'm Lyll Allerion."

"My mother?" Her voice rose in volume by just a little bit, but the squeak made it seem louder in her own ears.

Lyll's face wrinkled in puzzlement. "Yes, Kale, I'm your mother. I had to leave you here when your father was taken captive by Risto. I knew Risto would try to find you, and use you, to coerce your father into following his evil ways."

Kale nodded slowly. "And where did you go?"

"To find Kemry, of course."

"Kemry?"

"Your father."

"Oh."

Kale sat still, absorbing this information. She studied the hand hold-ing hers, then the face of this woman who said she was Lyll Allerion. Laugh lines radiated from the corners of her gentle hazel eyes, but her lips were pursed in a worried moue. Yet even with a frown, this mother looked loving, approachable.

"Did you find him?" Kale asked.

Tears welled in Lyll's eyes. "Yes, but I could not save him."

"He's dead?"

Lyll shook her head. "Asleep—in a trance."

"Risto?"

Lyll nodded.

"Then there's still hope."

The older woman sighed, her shoulders slumping.

Mistress Meiger returned, carrying a stack of linens. She placed these on a table and hurried to the o'rant woman's side. "Lyll, you're exhausted. To bed with you. We'll bring you a tray at noonmeal."

Lyll caught a sob in her throat. She nodded mutely, fighting for a moment with her emotions. She inhaled deeply and squared her shoul-ders. "Yes, you're right, Mern."

Kale helped Lyll stand. The older woman gave her a hug. "We will talk later, dear child." She sniffed and wiped a tear from her eye with a plain handkerchief. "I know you don't know me, and I can't ask you to love me. But I hope we can bridge the gap of too many years apart."

"Of course you will," said Mistress Meiger as she took Lyll's arm and led her away. "Kale's always been the best of children. Her heart's full of grace. I never understood her. But I always admired her warm and gener-ous ways, ways that reminded me of you, Lyll."

Kale watched her former owner walk her "maybe" mother up the stairs, then sank into the cushioned chair. She glanced over at Fenworth. He'd dozed off. Only a stubby tree sat in the chair. The minor dragons slipped out of their dens. Metta climbed to her shoulder. Dibl sat on her knee. Gymn went to the old wizard and took up a post, peering out from Fenworth's branches. Ardeo flew to the table to stand beside the unlighted lamp.

Kale's eyes rested on Dibl, and a smile grew on her lips.

"Yes, it is rather odd. Now I have two mothers when before I had none."

Metta trilled on her shoulder.

She answered. "I like this one better too."

Two young marione girls entered the tavern common room from the kitchen. They looked to be about five and seven. Kale knew immediately that they had come to prepare the room for the dozen or so customers who would soon show up to eat noonmeal. But the girls stopped just inside the door and nudged each other, pointing toward the tree in the chair by the window.

Dibl hopped in delight, and Kale had to stifle a giggle as the two serving maids cautiously crept up to Fenworth. They circled the oddity from a safe distance.

"It's a tree, Cakkue," said the smaller.

"What's that in the branches?"

Both girls stared at Gymn, who stared back, not blinking.

"Is it real?" asked the littler girl.

"I don't think any of it's real, Yonny."

"I think it's a lizard."

Dibl rolled off Kale's knee, down her leg, and continued to somersault once he hit the floor.

Gymn spread his wings and flew to Kale. The two girls squealed. Cakkue yelped, "It's a bat," and both dove for cover under one of the larger square, plank tables.

Between giggles, Kale tried to reassure them. "No, no. Gymn is a minor dragon."

Yonny screeched and wrapped her arms around Cakkue's neck in a death grip. "There's three more over by that girl. They're all over the place!"

Dibl stopped rolling and remained perfectly still. Kale felt his distress as his call for help came into her mind.

"Oh please." She stood and hurried to the table where she crouched and pleaded with the girls. "You're upsetting Dibl. He loves fun, but he thinks he scared you, and that disturbs him very much. Please, come out."

"No, don't," cried Yonny as the older girl started to move.

Cakkue cowered and shook her head.

Kale smiled at them. "The dragons are friendly. Come out, and I'll introduce you."

Both girls shook their heads. With their faces so close together, she could see they were sisters.

Very silly sisters!

She tried to hide her exasperation. "You know you must come out. If you don't get your work done, Mistress Meiger will be most displeased."

Metta began to sing. Yonny and Cakkue exchanged a glance. Kale knew she had made progress with her warning about their mistress, and Metta's song soothed their fears.

The two emerged slowly, still clinging to each other.

"You'll keep them from biting?" asked the older.

"They don't bite!" Kale exclaimed. "Not even in a fight."

"They fight?" squeaked Yonny.

"Only if I'm in danger."

Yonny leaned forward to peer around her big sister. "And the tree?"

"He's a friend of mine, a wizard. He's napping."

The two young slaves continued to eye Fenworth with skeptical frowns.

"Come," said Kale, "I'll help you with your chores. You're behind now."

Cakkue scowled at her. "How do you know what we have to get done?"

She laughed. "I'm Kale. I used to be the village slave here."

With that announcement, both girls relaxed.

"Then I'd like the help," said the elder. She moved to pull silverware from a drawer. "It's because you left that we got to be village slaves. At first, they almost didn't take us, because there are two of us, and they said the village was only pros-per-ous"—she took care to pronounce each syllable correctly—"enough to support one."

Yonny nodded. "Everyone knows about you. You found a dragon egg. You're famous. I'd rather be here than be famous."

"You *wanted* to be the slaves here?" Kale asked.

Yonny nodded again. "We have a home. You don't have a home, do you?"

Before Kale could answer, the older sister explained.

"Yes, we want to live here," said Cakkue. "This is much better than starving out on the farm. Our ma and da died, and we only had one big brother to look after us. As soon as he saw us settled here, he went to work on another place. He knows a lot, but not enough to run an entire farm on his own. We couldn't keep up the rent."

Cakkue gave the silverware and cloth napkins to her little sister. Yonny expertly wrapped a fork and a spoon in each square.

Cakkue went behind the bar to the crockery cabinet and set plates and bowls on the counter. Kale brought out mugs and tankards.

"So you like it here?" asked Kale.

"Sure," said Yonny. "We get to eat."

"And," said Cakkue, "we're learning how to do things for ourselves. Ma died before she could teach me how to do things around the house. When I get married, I won't shame my family."

Kale watched as the girls did the same chores she'd done many times. She helped where she could, but the simple tasks didn't need three people.

Yonny polished the window glass as Cakkue put another log on the fire. Both of them passed the tree and the minor dragons on tiptoe.

"I'll be free to marry," said Cakkue, "as soon as I'm sixteen." She brushed the palms of her hands over her apron to remove the dirt she'd picked up from the log. Kale noticed old fabric patched the worn material of her apron.

A shadow darkened the room. Kale turned to see what blocked the sun. Regidor stood in the doorway and beckoned. In his monk robes, he looked like a dark specter with the sun blazing behind him. Yonny gasped and scuttled next to her big sister.

The minor dragons raced through the air to greet him.

"He's harmless too," said Kale as she moved across the room to follow Regidor. Before she stepped outside, she heard Cakkue speak in a loud whisper.

"Strangers! Lately we're overrun by strangers."

Yonny replied, "It wouldn't be so bad if they weren't such strange strangers."

Dibl did a flip and landed on Regidor's shoulder. Both dragons, meech and minor, laughed at Yonny's reaction to them.

Kale caught up to Regidor and matched his long stride.

"Did you meet your mother, Kale?" he asked.

"Yes, I think I did."

"What did that girl mean when she said she would be free to marry?"

"Slaves are only kept until they're sixteen. By then it's supposed that they've been trained to lead a life without being supported by the village."

"When you talked of being a slave, you never mentioned this."

"Well, the idea is that a slave girl would marry. I never thought any of the marione young men would be interested in me."

"You could have gone to a city."

Kale shrugged. "I suppose."

"So if you had remained a slave, next year when you're sixteen, you would've been freed. Now you're a servant to Paladin, and next year you'll still be a servant to Paladin, still sent on quests."

"I can choose to do something else, Regidor. Paladin explained that to me."

"But you will still be a servant to Paladin?"

"Yes, always. Once you have pledged to follow him, you're his servant, no matter what you do in life."

"This is an interesting concept. Do you look forward to this future?"

Kale thought about the days she had spent with Fenworth, the friends she had made since leaving River Away, and the feeling she had of actually having a destiny, rather than a life ruled by chance.

"Yes, Regidor, I do."

43

Good Night

"I have guests in every room," Mistress Meiger said. "You share a room with your mother, dear. She should be looked after, and who better to take care of her if she be feeling poorly?"

"She's been ill?" asked Kale.

"Not ill exactly, but worn out. I don't understand it all. A lot of things have happened of late that I don't understand. I do know your mother loves you, and I'm powerful glad you're here to visit, myself. Now get on with you, and take those little creatures with you. They're pretty things, but not what I'm used to."

Kale climbed the stairs without the usual candle. Ardeo sat in her hand and lit the way. She wanted the minor dragons for company tonight. She didn't look forward to spending the night with a stranger.

Dibl stomped his hind feet on her shoulder, and she giggled.

"You're right, Dibl, this mother is not as strange as the other mother."

She tapped on the door and opened it when the person within responded, "Come in."

The o'rant woman who claimed to be her mother sat, propped up, in the bigger bed. Wedged between a chest of drawers and the wall, another bed, smaller and harder, waited for Kale. She crossed the room and laid down her bundle. The minor dragons flew about the room, looking for places to roost. Ardeo landed on the sconce attached to the wall. Metta circled the room and then returned to her shoulder. Dibl sat on the pillow of her bed. Gymn landed on the older woman's lap, tilted his head as if examining her, then climbed the front of her gown to curl up just below her double chin.

Lyll patted Gymn tentatively. "Well, I can't say I've had much experience with minor dragons."

"You need healing," said Kale. "Gymn is a healing dragon."

Lyll stroked the little green dragon's sides. He soon turned over to have his belly rubbed. Kale grinned, knowing Gymn enjoyed the attention. The smile fell from her face with the next thought.

If I lie down with them and complete the circle, the healing will be faster and more complete.

She turned quickly away and hung up her moonbeam cape on a peg. Plunging her hand into a hollow, she searched for a piece of pink soap she had bought in Prushing. She'd bought it because Toopka liked pink soap. Tonight Kale thought pink soap sounded like a wonderful way to wash away her troubles.

As if any color soap would clean up this mess in my mind. I could probably use magic glasses so I could see clearly. Or magic hearing so I could sort out the truth and not hear voices that lie. And wouldn't it be nice if Wulder were to write me a note and leave it on my pillow? Or better yet, Paladin could be standing in the hallway ready to explain all this about mothers and renegade dragons. I almost forgot the renegade dragons. That's what I'm really supposed to be worried about. The quest is to find and rescue a dragon caught in Risto's schemes. I seem to be better at finding mothers.

"I'm going to go take a bath," she said over her shoulder.

"That's fine, Kale." The woman's voice already sounded more steady.

Dibl never passed up a chance to play in the water. He flew to land on her head. But she had to call Ardeo to come light her way down the passage to the back steps. Gymn and Metta stayed with the woman in the bed, which did not surprise Kale. She knew the dragons would feel mellow and serene after helping someone. Kale had felt that same contentment herself after being part of the circle of healing.

She stomped down the dark hallway, determined to have a bath, a long soaking bath in nice warm water.

In the kitchen, hot water kettles sat on the stove. Behind a curtain in a roughly constructed alcove, a large wooden tub served everyone in the household.

Kale filled the tub with a mixture of hot and cold water. She used the pink soap and a rough rag. Lying in the tub with her hair clean and her skin scrubbed rosy, she listened to the noises of the tavern.

The slave girls had been sent to bed long ago. A hired maid carried a few items from the kitchen to the tavern room, but the time for supper had long passed, and most of the patrons drank cider and swapped stories. No minstrel performed tonight. On rare occasions, a traveling entertainer spent the night, paying for his lodging with songs and stories. On Friday and Saturday nights, several local farmers would come in and play their fiddles.

But tonight it was quiet, too quiet. Kale had half expected Dar, and maybe even Regidor, to play for the locals. But she hadn't seen them since they ate together several hours before.

"It's *too* quiet!" Kale hissed. She abruptly stood, splashing over the rim of the tub as she climbed out of the water.

"If they won't sing a song to keep my silly brain from asking myself the same questions over and over, then I'll sing a song myself."

She grabbed a large piece of old blanket and scrubbed at the goose bumps rising on her body. Dibl flew around her head, getting in the way. She barely opened her mouth and sang between clenched teeth.

"The general of the day,
He walked among his men.
He called them left,
He called them right,
He called them left again."

Shivering, she slipped a nightshift over her head and wrapped a warm blanket around her thin frame. Dibl enticed Ardeo to join him in a silly dance above her head.

"The king, he came to see,
The men he sent to sea.
He called them up,
He called them down,
He called them back to me."

She sat on a rickety stool to pull on one thick sock. Dibl left the area behind the curtain to go to the less confining space of the kitchen. Ardeo followed, leaving her in semidarkness.

"The cook, she had a duck.
She plopped him in the pot.
She dunked him in,
She pulled him out,
Whene'er the duck did squawk."

Where is everybody when you want a distraction? Toopka chattering in my ear. Librettowit complaining about being a librarian on a quest. Dar whistling or tootling on some fancy noisemaker. Bardon looking like a statue and sending off emotions like a volcano. Fenworth crawling with bugs.

Kale leaned against the wall, sticking her bare foot between the floor and the bottom of the tub. A gap where the floor met the wall let frigid air in from the outside. She found the plug at the seam of the tub with her toes, and then expertly kicked with the side of her heel to pop it out. The bath water swooshed out of the hole and ran out of the building. She wiped off her foot and put on her other sock. She then snatched up the almost empty egg pouch by the leather thong and hurried out of the cold bath closet.

"Come on, Dibl, Ardeo." Kale charged up the back steps and down the hall, stopping before the wooden door. She could hear Metta crooning. Looping the leather thong over her head, Kale tucked the pouch inside her gown, then knocked.

"Come in."

Kale slipped in and quietly shut the door behind her. She put her things away and got out her brush.

"Come sit on the bed, Kale. I'll brush your hair."

"You're too tired," she objected.

"No, I've slept most of the day, and your little dragons have been healing my aches and pains. Come."

The soft tone of her voice coaxed Kale into complying.

She sat rigidly on the large bed. The former slave girl would rather do the brushing herself. She took care of herself very well. And besides, her hair tangled easily, and the wet curls could be stubborn. But the woman eased the brush through the twisted locks. The bristles pulled gently through Kale's shoulder-length hair. She relaxed with each tender stroke of the brush.

"Now, tell me about Dar and Toopka."

Her mother's request startled her. "How did you know about them?"

"Gymn and Metta."

"You can mindspeak with them?"

"Kale, I *am* a wizard."

"Oh yes," she stuttered. "I-I guess I forgot. You don't look like the other wizards I've met."

"Fen and Cam? No," she chortled, "I don't look like those old men."

The good-natured sound of her laughter set Kale even more at ease. *At least Toopka and Dar are easy to talk about. I guess it wouldn't do any harm.*

When she had finished recounting tales of the two doneels, she talked about two of the emerlindians she had met, Leetu Bends and Granny Noon. Then she told of Brunstetter and Lee Ark. Carefully she avoided any mention of where these people were now. And she didn't spell out how they worked for Paladin either.

The woman stroked Kale's hair with her hand. "There. Your hair is dry enough to sleep on now."

"Thank you." Kale took the brush from her hand and laid it on the bedside table.

"Will you tell me about the other woman who said she was me?"

She jerked around to look into the kindly eyes of the older woman. She sighed. "The dragons told you."

Lyll smiled. "Yes."

"She's not like you at all. And I don't like her very much."

"All this Gymn and Metta have told me. They also said she is elegant, refined, and beautiful."

Kale nodded and looked down at her lap.

"Would you like to be elegant, refined, and beautiful, Kale?"

She bit her lip. "Yes," she answered after only a moment.

"But?"

"I don't want to be like her. She's hard and cold and…"

"There are some things that pass from one generation to the next. You have your father's build, strong and lean. You also have my hazel eyes and curly hair. If this other woman were your real mother, you might find that you have the same shape of hands, or arch in your eyebrows, or a dimple in the cheek. But that doesn't necessarily mean you would be cold and hard."

"If you are my real mother, who is she?"

"I have an idea about that, but first I would like you to be convinced that I *am* your real mother." She spread her hands in a helpless gesture and shrugged. "But I have no way of doing that."

"Paladin would know."

"Yes, he would." Lyll yawned and covered her mouth with a sturdy hand.

"Wulder knows."

"Yes, and in time, He will make it clear to you." Lyll leaned back and pushed down into the covers, resting her head on the pillow. "Do you want to sleep in this big, soft bed with me? There's plenty of room."

"No, that's all right. I'm used to sleeping on a pallet. I'll be comfortable over there."

Kale left the warmth of the downy mattress and thick quilts. She snuffed the two candles in the room and padded in sock-covered feet to the darkened corner. Snuggling into the smaller bed, she called the dragons to her.

"Oh dear," said her mother.

"Can I get you something?" asked Kale.

"No, it's just that, well, does Ardeo glow all night?"

Dibl gave a little hiccup of laughter from his place beside Kale's head. She giggled. "Yes, he does. There's no way to put him out. I don't mean put him out like you would a cat or a dog at night, but to put him out like you would a lantern. He can crawl under my covers if the light bothers you."

"I thought it might, but it's rather comforting, isn't it? I think I'll like having his shining presence in the room."

Kale agreed. Gymn stood up, turned in a circle, then settled down again on her shoulder. She knew why he was restless.

"Mistress?"

"Yes?"

"Would you like Gymn to sleep with you? You'll feel better in the morning if he does."

The woman sighed. "Yes, Kale, I would like that."

44

Morning Surprises

"One, two. One, two, three, four. One, two. One, two, three, four."

The chant penetrated Kale's sleepy brain and roused her from a wonderful dream about visiting a palace in Wittoom where Dar was the principal chef. If she allowed herself to wake up, she would miss the banquet.

"One, two. One, two, three, four. One, two. One, two, three, four."

Kale opened an eye to view her mother's bed. Sunlight made a path across the crumpled linens. Dust motes danced above. Metta sat on the far edge and hummed a tune that matched the beat of the unexplained counting. Gymn lay curled up in a comfortable ball on one of the pillows. But no woman lay on the downy mattress.

With both eyes open and her lethargic body propped up on an elbow, Kale watched two feet appear and disappear from the other side of the larger bed.

"One, two." A right foot bobbed up, toes pointing to the ceiling. It dropped out of sight, and the left one replaced it.

"One, two, three, four." Both feet waggled above the horizon of the mattress in a quick flutter of activity.

"One, two." The right foot, left foot performance repeated.

Kale sat up in bed, dislodging a snoozing Ardeo. Cold air hit her neck and shoulders. She shivered and pulled the covers back up to her chin. "Mistress?"

"Did I wake you, Kale? I'm sorry, but it's a beautiful morning, and I'm feeling so much better.

"One, two. One, two, three, four."

This is ridiculous!

Kale threw the covers back and grabbed her clothes. She pulled on her pants and exchanged her nightshift for a shirt. As she shoved one foot into a boot, she heard grunting. Her mother's arms lay across the edge of the bed. In the next moment, she hoisted herself to a kneeling position and stayed there, watching Kale and panting.

Kale felt her eyebrows shoot up as she gasped at the sight of the old o'rant woman. Or rather, the woman who should have been old.

"You're younger!" Kale exclaimed.

"Not as young as I used to be," said Lyll as she struggled to rise. She began running in place as soon as she had her feet under her. "Nothing like a good night's sleep to rejuvenate the old bones. Give me five or ten minutes, and we'll see what a little exercise can do."

Kale collapsed with a thud on her bed. She had one boot on and the other one in her hand. As she watched, the o'rant woman counted to a hundred, lightly prancing in the space between her bed and the window. Then she put her hands on her hips and bent at the knees. Her body descended, only to rise again a moment later. She repeated this action, counting to twenty-five. Next, with her hands clasped behind her neck, she twisted her torso. Then Lyll extended her arms straight above her head, bent at the waist, swinging her arms in an arc. Her upper body bobbed down behind the bed and sprang up again. The thick braid hanging over her shoulder swung like a pendulum.

Kale watched with fascination as Lyll Allerion became younger and thinner with each round of up-down motion.

"There now," Lyll said, as she finally stood still and took a deep breath. "Getting back in shape takes more work the older I get."

She strode over to her dress hanging on a peg. She stopped in front of the garment and seemed to be examining the material.

"A bit soiled," she said.

The dress began to jiggle on its peg. Lyll left it to gyrate and crossed the room to a black bag. She pulled out a brush. Sitting on the windowsill, she undid her long brown braid and spent the next ten minutes brushing and rebraiding the gorgeous fall of dark, curly locks. Metta and Dibl watched with rapt attention. Gymn stretched on the pillow, rolled over, and curled his tail around himself, never waking. Ardeo climbed into Kale's lap, but she saw that he, too, stared in fascination at the lovely wizard.

The dress on the peg ceased its lonely dance. Lyll finished tying a ribbon on the end of her braid, hopped off the sill, tossed the brush in the open bag, and returned to examine the dress.

"What color today?" She tapped a shapely finger on her chin. "I always travel light, Kale. One dress for day, and of course, a nightgown."

As she spoke the dress faded from blue to white and then turned pink, starting with a blush at the hem that rose up the material until the shoulders and sleeves had taken on the cheerful hue. As the color changed, so did the texture of the cloth. A patterned brocade replaced the homespun cotton. Lace frothed out at the neckline.

"Now that's nice," said Lyll and took the dress off the peg. A plain white bibbed apron hung beneath. Lyll took it as well. "I won't need this." The apron transformed into a silk shawl of a deep rose.

Kale blinked and saw her mother was dressed, the nightshirt on the peg, and the dress and shawl on the woman. Dibl rolled so fast in his excitement he nearly missed a turn at the edge of the mattress. He swerved in time and circled the bed once more, this time rolling directly over Gymn. The little green dragon squawked a protest and went back to sleep.

"Well, Kale," said Lyll, "I'm famished. Let's go down to breakfast, shall we? I'm also anxious to see what Fen and Cam have decided we should do about this dragon problem."

✦

"So we just sit here and wait," said Wizard Cam, leaning back in his chair at the breakfast table. His wet hair looked as though it had just been washed, but Kale knew he almost always looked damp. Soon there would be a puddle under his chair, and if he sat in one place long enough, a rivulet would wander away, following any downslope.

Only tea and juice had been served thus far. Dar and Bardon had not yet joined the gathering.

"The suspicious wagon should be here today," said the lake wizard.

"Oh great," said Toopka, a pout pursing her lips. "That means it'll be next week before they get here."

Sitting next to her, Regidor tilted his head. He still wore his clerical robes since the populace of River Away had managed to accept a tumanhofer, two doneels, and three wizards, but still had problems with a walking, talking meech dragon. "What kind of wisdom is that?"

Toopka stood on her chair and put her hands on her hips. "It's wisdom that comes from seeing how things work. Things you want to happen always take a long time." She pointed one little finger at the meech dragon and shook it in his face. "You may read books and know bunches, but I have lived life longer than you."

Regidor's lips twitched as he suppressed a grin.

Toopka stomped one tiny foot. "You may get to be the smartest thing in all of Amara, but you'll never be older than me. That's just the way it is, and you'll have to live with it!"

Fenworth, who was resting in the chair at the head of the table, stirred slightly, rattling his branches.

Cam cleared his throat. "No need to be so pugnacious, Toopka. We are all cognizant of the importance of seniority."

Toopka sent a puzzled look Kale's way.

Kale patted the little doneel's back and guided her to sit down again on the wooden box that had been placed in her chair. "He means, don't be so feisty, and we all know you're older than Regidor, and yes, that's important."

Toopka nodded triumphantly at her meech friend.

Kale glanced around the tavern. In the days when she helped serve breakfast here, a number of regulars sat at the same tables every morning except Saturday and Sunday. Only her friends waited for their meal this morning.

It's because of us, I'd guess. People in River Away don't like to mix with people from outside.

Mistress Meiger came into the room from the kitchen. She carried a pot of tea. Yonny and Cakkue followed with a basket of muffins and a platter of scrambled eggs and sausages.

Kale's former owner put down the pot and picked up a pitcher of fresh purpleberry juice. She refilled empty glasses in front of her guests. When she came to Kale, she said, "How's your mother this morning, Kale?"

Kale glanced over at her mother. With a mischievous gleam in her eye, Lyll spoke up.

"Mern, I'm right here, and I'm feeling more like myself this morning."

Mistress Meiger's eyes popped. "And here I was thinking these wayfarers had brought in another strange person during the night."

Oh dear! That was rude. Mistress Meiger only uses the term wayfarers *to name those guests she believes are disreputable.*

But Lyll Allerion did not take offense. "Now, Mern, you knew me well as a regular traveler years ago and enjoyed our visits to your tavern. Don't be kerflummoxed by a few surprises."

Mistress Meiger's complexion blushed red. "I never would have thought that you and your dear husband were one of them. In fact, you deceived us, Lyll Allerion. I thought you were marione. You disguised your true being."

"Ah, yes," said Lyll, and her face grew solemn. "I wanted to be your friend, Mern, and you would not have let me. You're not fond of things that are strange to your daily living. There are stranger things coming to River Away. Soon you'll have to face the fact that Wulder is real and expects your loyalty."

"Wulder's coming here?"

Lyll sighed. "He's already here."

The innkeeper cast a look over her shoulder as if she expected to see a bogeyman. Cakkue and Yonny moved closer to their mistress's skirts. They, too, peered into the shadowy corners.

Lyll reached out and patted her old friend's hand. "If you took time to know Him, you wouldn't be frightened by the prospect of His presence."

The innkeeper tapped her two little slave girls on the shoulders and waved them off. "Go back to your chores," she said gruffly. She watched until the kitchen door closed behind them.

With a shudder, Mistress Meiger turned back to the elegant lady at her table. "You're talking of things that shouldn't be talked about, Lyll. There're some things best left alone. Talking 'bout the Mighty Good and the Mighty Bad will bring trouble to us all."

"And who do you think is best pleased by this lack of talk?"

Mistress Meiger stared, then shook her head.

"I know," said Toopka. "Pretender."

Lyll shifted her attention to the doneel child and smiled.

"That's right, and can you tell us why?"

Toopka screwed up her face. "Because...because Pretender likes to jump out and scare you. If you talk about him and know he's around, you aren't as likely to be surprised. But I don't know about Wulder."

"Wulder," said Regidor, "likes to be familiar, Toopka. Like a bed you're used to. There you relax, trusting in the comfort and safety during the dark times."

Toopka studied Regidor's face for a moment and then nodded.

The sound of horses clopping down the street interrupted the conversation. The riders drew up in front of the tavern. A moment later Dar and Bardon appeared in the doorway.

Dar doffed his hat and bowed to those present. "Our quarry approaches. Bardon and I went out early this morning to see if we could locate the band of potion peddlers. Their wagon is a few miles east of River Away. Our wait should not be long."

45

Breakfast

Master Meiger strode into the common room of the tavern with three distinguished gentlemen of the district at his back. "We'll have no more riffraff entering River Away and upsetting the order of our lives. The council has met, and we have decided to request that you and your comrades leave our peaceful hamlet immediately. Today!"

The three men behind him nodded their heads.

The companions around the breakfast table stopped eating and looked to the official representatives of the village and the outlying community.

Kale recognized all of them. She'd worked in their homes. *I wonder if they count me as one of the "riffraff."*

The four marione men had prepared themselves for this confrontation by dressing in their best. They didn't look as if they had been up all night, discussing the best course of action. But Kale knew that was standard procedure for accomplishing anything through the council. They loved to meet and would debate matters for countless hours.

Lyll's voice entered Kale's mind. *"Don't be harsh, Kale. These men are concerned for their families. And they don't know what's at stake. Remember, they treated you well. Extend the same courtesy to them tenfold."*

Kale studied her mother's face, serene and gentle. To herself she admitted she had never been harshly used. *The mariones treated me fairly. Their own children didn't get warm-hearted praise, and so I didn't either.*

She examined Master Meiger and his friends, trying to be more objective. The men were not wealthy, but they'd put on their grandest garments to carry out this important mission. Although they still looked countrified, Kale found their determination made her proud. This surprised her.

But it shouldn't. These families gave me a home and taught me to be self-sufficient. They did their best for me even though I'm an o'rant, not a marione.

The tree at the head of the table snorted, shook with vigor, and rose. By the time Fenworth stood, he'd regained the semblance of a man.

"You see!" Meiger's voice echoed in the open space of the nearly deserted tavern. "That's just the sort of thing we don't do around here."

Wizard Fenworth marched around the table. His staff hit the wooden floor with resounding thuds. He certainly didn't appear to be an old man leaning on a walking stick. He looked more like a warrior approaching the front line.

Chief Councilman Meiger stepped back, but only one step. He squared his shoulders and visibly mastered his trepidation. Kale suppressed the urge to mindspeak to her former master. She wanted to say, "Good show!" but knew a voice in his head would completely discombobulate him.

Fenworth towered over the marione men, and Kale thought he'd deliberately added a few inches to his stature. His hat, the point of which never stood straight up, brushed the rafters.

"You dare oppose me. Do you know who I am? I am Fenworth, bog wizard. Do you think to cast me and my party out of your lowly establishment?"

Councilman Meiger's face hardened. "Yes, we'll not be bullied, whether you be bog wizard or king."

Fenworth growled, and this time Kale knew for sure he was casting a spell, for his hat pressed against the blackened beams of the ceiling. The marione men tilted their heads back to look up at the enraged wizard. But none of them faltered. If anything, they looked more stubborn and ill-tempered than before.

Fenworth growled again, and a fog seeped from under the hem of his robe. It rolled across the floor, covering the worn wooden planks. "And who among you do you think can force a great and ancient wizard along with six mighty warriors to leave? Ha! Your words are empty."

Meiger stiffened. "You can strike me down, but there be three behind me, and unseen to you are fields of workers, strong of arm and purpose. You'll not overrun this land without a fight."

A hiss reverberated through the room, Fen shrunk to his normal size, and the fog scudded out the open kitchen door.

Fenworth smiled at the angry mariones and nodded sagely. "Just what I wanted to hear, my good men. You'll do."

He put his arm around the cautious chief councilman's shoulders and called to Dar. "Sir Dar, take these fine gentlemen into our circle of confidants. We shall need men such as these in the trying days ahead."

Tilting his head down to Meiger, the wizard spoke out of the side of his mouth in a whisper loud enough to be heard on the streets. "Dar is an ambassador from Wittoom. A high lee general, in fact. But traveling incognito."

Dar came forward and bowed to the men. "It is my pleasure to enlist your assistance. Your knowledge of the territory and its resources shall be invaluable." He paused to look each one in the eye. "Shall we discuss defense strategies against the impending invasion, gentlemen?"

"Well, now!" Chief Councilman Meiger looked uncertainly at his cohorts.

"It won't hurt to hear what he has to say," said one.

"We could discuss it," said another.

All four men nodded.

Chief Councilman Meiger ushered Dar and the councilmen out of the room.

Fenworth clapped his hands together. Leaves rustled as he walked back to the table.

"Now that's done. First thing on the list for the day crossed off." He nodded to Librettowit. "Make note of that, Wit. Number one—recruit an army. Done."

"Why do we need an army?" asked Toopka.

Fenworth patted her on the head. She grimaced and ducked. The wizard did not seem to notice but moved on around the table. "Once we dissuade the dragons from aiding Risto," he said, "Risto is going to be a bit put out."

Fenworth sat down and surveyed the platters of food left over from the others' breakfast. "Seems a bit of a sloppy way to serve a meal. But no matter. I'm starved. Feel like I haven't eaten in days. Thought I heard a drummerbug. Turns out it was my stomach. Pass the muffins. Pass the juice. Thirsty, too. I could drink a lake. No offense intended, Cam. Cousin Cam's a lake wizard, you know. Pass the eggs. Is that sausage?"

He bit into a muffin. "What's next on our to-do list? Ah! I remember. Confront the wagonload of scalawags, and unmask the villain meech. Gives me a hearty appetite just thinking about it."

Lyll passed him the butter, and as he took it, he looked at her closely.

"Don't I know you, dear girl? No, don't tell me. I'm excellent at remembering faces. Names are a bit of a bother. But I'll get it. I will."

He slathered butter on his bread, took a bite, chewed, and twisted his face in a thoughtful expression.

"Almost got it," Fenworth announced and stabbed a sausage with his fork. He held the link aloft and waggled the fork back and forth as he thought. "Got it! Lyll of the Mountains. Married Kemry Allerion of the Hills. Some say she married beneath her, but of course, that was just nonsense." He polished off the rest of the sausage. "Kemry is a worthy wiz. Excellent Dragon Keeper. Haven't heard much of him lately."

"Risto has him," Kale blurted out.

Wizard Fenworth quit chewing and leveled a serious eye in his apprentice's direction. He pointed his empty fork at her and used it as he would have shaken a finger.

"Tut-tut, dear Kale. Risto may think he has Kemry, but I daresay he doesn't."

She was surprised to see Lyll nod her head in agreement.

Fenworth fed a crumb to a bird that landed on his shoulder. "Now tell me about this expedition to Creemoor where we're going to see who's dropping those ugly spiders on cities."

Librettowit harrumphed. "Already did that one, Fen."

"Really? Did you mark it off the to-do list?"

"No."

"Well, no wonder I didn't remember. But I do now. Rescued lovely Lyll. Only pardon me, dear girl. Tut-tut, you weren't looking nearly so well then as you do now. Almost didn't recognize you."

"Sir?" Bardon interrupted. "Can we hear what happened in Creemoor? Who was responsible, and did you catch them?"

"Most certainly."

Bardon and the others waited expectantly. Fenworth buttered another muffin, took a big swig of purpleberry juice from a tall tankard, and smacked his lips.

Should I remind him of Bardon's question? The trouble with Fenworth is you never know if his thinking is going to go in a straight line.

Just before Kale opened her mouth to prod the old man, he spoke, "Crim Cropper and no."

Lyll giggled. Fenworth glared at her, but she just smiled in return, then turned to the younger members of their party. "Shall we take a walk, children?"

She pushed her chair back from the table. "It only took Bardon and Dar a couple of hours on horseback to return from where they spotted the villains. It will take the heavy wagon a great deal longer to get here."

She looked at Bardon. "I think I can tell you what you wish to know."

Bardon stood abruptly, made polite excuses for leaving before the others were finished, and followed Lyll Allerion out of the building.

"Well, what are we waiting for?" asked Toopka, grabbing both Regidor's and Kale's hands. "She said 'children.' I bet that's anyone under a couple of centuries old. Let's go."

46

A Peaceful Interlude

"Kale, isn't there a little picturesque pond close by?" Lyll pointed north. "I believe in that direction."

"Baltzentor's Pond," said Kale. "It's fed by a cold spring."

"Ah yes, just as I remember." Lyll set off down the street. "I can't be sedentary for too long. I begin to age."

She smiled at the mariones she passed and stopped to pet a friendly dog. The minor dragons flew ahead, making a beeline toward the water.

As she and her companions walked down the main street, Kale saw some of the citizens avert their eyes from the sight of a stately o'rant woman, a strange monk, and a tiny doneel. Now that Kale had traveled, she could see prejudice in her hometown.

In this region of the country, only kimens and mariones mixed. Because of the scarcity of the five remaining high races, mariones looked on them as peculiar. Most of her village friends extracted information about those who lived in the distant parts of Amara from fables and fabrications. Some didn't even believe all the high races actually existed.

Their distrust of strangers flowed out of ancient history with no clear ties to the reality of present times. Kale tried to remember specifics about why the other races were to be shunned and could think of none.

She did know that mariones farmed well and fought well. For fourteen years, her owners drilled the significance of these virtues into Kale's thinking. She still admired her friends for their industry and fortitude, and she now knew of other virtues.

But still, Lyll Allerion managed to evoke smiles from some villagers. Kale thought instantly of Dar's charismatic appeal. The doneel could charm the most unlikely people. Toopka had some of the same quality in her personality.

And they seem happier than I am. I'd like to know what makes them different. It can't just be the smiles.

They reached Baltzentor's Pond. The body of water covered almost two acres. A small stream flowed out of one end, and the surface constantly rippled from the pulse of a spring beneath.

The village men had built several wooden benches around the shore. Many used them for fishing, and some of the fancier ones were used for courting. Bentleaf trees lined one edge, and late-blooming bushes of ernst brightened the view with tiny, starlike, pale yellow flowers. Their cinnamon fragrance mingled with the smell of autumn leaves crunching under the comrades' feet as they walked.

Kale thought the scene was as peaceful as she remembered, but the waters looked darker. She glanced at the sky to see if a cloud had cast a shadow on the pond, but the skies were clear.

Lyll sat on one of the carved benches and pulled Toopka into the seat beside her. Bardon and Regidor stood, but Kale sat at her mother's feet.

Lyll smiled at the standing men. "You, no doubt, want to hear all about the battles. For details you'll have to consult Cam. Of course, Brunstetter and Lee Ark will join us at some time, and they'll have more precise information. I can tell you that three forces converged on the Creemoor spiders' favorite haunt and wiped out as many as they could before the creatures disappeared into the depths of the Dormanscz caverns.

"Now I know from my work in the Creemoor region—mind you, I wasn't in the mountains but among the populace—that Crim Cropper is intent on developing means to control all beasts. He figured out how to gather the spiders without injuring either those who herded them or the spiders themselves. He bred them in captivity, producing many more than nature would have allowed. You see, as soon as the little spiders emerge from the egg sack, the parents devour them. About one-third escape the feast and skitter off to hide and mature.

"Much to his disappointment, Cropper couldn't control them. He wanted them to march as an army under his direction. He got tired of the experiment and decided to be rid of them. But instead of releasing them back into their natural habitat, or slaughtering them, he thought it would be more entertaining to drop them on a city. Then word came that Kale was at The Hall. He chose Vendela, because he didn't want the Dragon Keeper to interfere with his plans to subvert the dragons."

Regidor threw back his cowl. "So it was an attack on Kale."

Lyll nodded. "Basically, yes."

For a moment, Kale found it impossible to draw a breath. She flexed the fingers of the hand that had been poisoned by the Creemoor spider. Her stomach lurched.

His plan almost succeeded.

She turned to Bardon and saw his expression of concern. She swallowed hard but could not speak.

Bardon—

He abruptly looked away. "May we ask what your mission involved, Lady Allerion?"

Kale consciously took a deep breath. Bardon's question had released the overwhelming grip of fear that had squeezed her lungs.

"I gathered information, which I sent to Paladin, and I encouraged those few poor souls who follow Paladin in secrecy in that region. Of course, I was imprisoned during my entire service."

Kale gasped. "Imprisoned?"

"Yes, a nasty place. But it was the most wonderful place to foil Cropper's plans and, of course, Risto's."

"I don't understand," said Regidor. "If you were in jail and could not move around the country, how could you be of use?"

"All the information came to me. Right under Cropper's nose. None of our underground workers had to figure out where I was. I was always in the same place. Cropper's soldiers guarding the prison also were a fount of information. Don't forget that I mindspeak."

"Didn't they realize you were a wizard?" asked Toopka.

Lyll laughed. "I told them I was Lyll Allerion, a great and powerful wizard, but then when they asked me to do something to prove it, I…well, I just never did. So they thought I was a bit loony. To them I was a meddlesome old lady who liked to visit all the other prisoners."

"But why did you have to stay there?" Sympathy crumpled Toopka's face.

"Because, as wonderful as Paladin's army is, they're woefully inadequate in communication. But then Risto's forces have the same problem."

"Why did you get out?" asked Toopka.

"Because Crim Cropper is brilliant, but not very focused. His wife, Burner Stox, is not quite as smart, but more practical. The last time she visited the southern castle, she noticed me. That was the end of my usefulness."

"And the last job you had to do before you could be rescued?" Regidor tilted his head.

"Arrange for my replacement to be accepted by my network of contacts."

A thought invaded Kale's mind, and she tried to shake it off. She looked to her mother and saw the woman watched her closely.

"Leetu Bends?" Kale whispered.

Lyll nodded.

Kale shivered. She rose to her feet and pulled the moonbeam cape closer.

"Ugh!" said Toopka. She pointed to the reeds growing at the edge of the pond. "I saw something ugly in there."

Everyone turned to look. The water on this side of the pond glinted black like a sheet of rippled ebony. The water on the other side sparkled blue under the sun's rays.

The entire pond was dark before, but not as black as it is here.

Metta, from the nearest bentleaf tree, called out a shrill warning. Gymn echoed the alarm.

Lyll rose from her seat. "Mordakleeps."

Regidor shed his clerical robe and drew his sword. Kale and Bardon also unsheathed their weapons. Lyll took two steps forward, twirling as she did. Her dress transformed into formfitting leggings, tunic, and shirt. Oddly, these garments suited for fighting were still the blushing pink color.

Kale stared at her mother. Lyll held out her arm as if ready to wield a sword, but her hand held nothing.

Three creatures sprang out of the water. Black, huge, and menacing, they covered the few feet of grassy bank in a bound.

"Cut off their tails," shrieked Toopka as she dove over the back of the bench.

Regidor and Lyll each fought a monster. The third rushed at Bardon. Kale and Bardon fell into a pattern of synchronized attack. Bardon attracted the mordakleep's attention and angled it around so that Kale could wield a savage blow to sever its tail. The huge body dissolved into a puddle and disappeared into the ground.

Another monster loomed out of the pond. Kale ran to confront it. This time, she managed to maneuver the creature so that Bardon had a clear swipe at its tail.

Regidor danced around his opponent. He flipped into the air, landed behind the monster, and severed its tail. The mordakleep melted away.

With the stance of a fencer, Lyll approached a mordakleep intent on the o'rant woman's demise. The lack of a sword diminished her credibility as a warrior. Kale tensed, ready to rush to her mother's side.

Lyll leapt forward and swung her arm. A gash appeared on the mordakleep's hand. Its mouth opened in a soundless roar. Lyll skipped back and circled to the left. She plunged the invisible sword into the monster's side, then withdrew and circled to the left again. The nightmarish creature turned with her, keeping its tail away from the swift and deadly blade it could not see. Lyll twirled with blurring speed to the right. Her arm swept downward over the snakelike tail. It fell away from the mordakleep's body. Both the deadly creature and its separated tail oozed into the earth.

Two more mordakleeps surged out of the watery reeds.

Kale and Bardon took on one, and by the same method of distraction, killed it. Lyll and Regidor dispatched the other. The four warriors moved to form a group. For a moment they stood alert and ready.

Toopka peeked out from behind the bench. "Are they gone?"

Lyll answered, "For now." She took out a cloth from a small satchel attached to her belt and made the motions of wiping a blade. It looked as though she laid the sword carefully across her chest, cradled by the other arm. She whirled. When the blur became recognizable again, she wore the dress she had donned that morning.

Regidor turned to look directly at Lyll and bowed with the same grace Dar often displayed. "I admit I held some doubts as to Lady Allerion's ability. I beg your pardon."

She nodded graciously.

He paced to the edge of the pond and peered into the reeds. The sandy bottom showed through the water now sparkling and clear. "Although we know the enemy is encroaching upon this territory, with no bodies it will be difficult to convince our hosts that danger is imminent."

47

WAYFARERS

The companions returned to the tavern. Fenworth and Cam had taken over the kitchen where they created elaborate culinary delights. Mistress Meiger muttered that she didn't think her customers would take to such fancy food, but she sat at the table and sampled everything that appeared. Toopka joined her since food always claimed her interest.

Kale led Bardon, Regidor, and Lyll to a stand of trees near the road. She pointed to an empty field next to the last building, the Widow Ord's cottage, on the edge of the village.

"Most wagons stop here, and the people walk into town. This is where the market is held once a month. We can't see it from here, but there's a sign facing the road."

Twenty minutes later, a colorful wagon rumbled toward the village of River Away. Just as Kale had predicted, the driver pulled the house-vehicle onto the grass and stopped. She had seen these odd wagons before, but they still fascinated her.

On top of a rectangular wagon bed, a house built like a barrel on its side provided shelter for the peddlers. Red wheels carried the blue box. Yellow stars and blue stripes decorated the rear wheels. Green curlicues adorned the blue box and the driver's perch.

The top had windows cut in the side, and elaborate swirls and stars in blue and purple crowded every spare inch. Yellow curtains flapped out of the open windows. In the back, a red door allowed access to the odd home. Beneath this, a pan box hung. Kale knew that the pan box folded down to make a step, but it also held the cook's instruments for fixing meals over an open fire.

The driver of the caravan passed the reins to a young man sitting beside him. He stood and stretched before jumping to the ground. He patted the horse closest to him on the rump and walked to its head.

"The driver certainly isn't a meech," observed Bardon from their hiding place behind thick ernst bushes. "Nor the young man. They look like father and son, don't they?"

"Has anyone been able to penetrate their minds?" asked Regidor. "I've tried with no success. This feels much like the shield around the core of the ship Dar visited."

"I can't get in either," said Kale. "But I have detected Toopka trying to sneak up behind us."

Kale turned and gestured for the little girl to abandon her hiding place.

"Fenworth said I could come," she explained as soon as she plopped down beside Kale.

"You tricked him, then," said Kale.

Regidor slanted a disapproving glance Toopka's way. "Pestered him until he hollered at you to leave?"

She nodded solemnly, then smiled. She squirmed between Regidor and Lady Allerion, so she could see through the bushes.

"Where's the meech?"

"We haven't seen him yet," said Kale.

"The door's opening," said Bardon.

The older man left the horses and came to the rear of the wagon. He let the fancy steps down, and an older woman with a colorful scarf wrapped around her head climbed out. She looked critically around the open field and spoke. The old man frowned and gestured toward River Away.

"What are they saying?" asked Toopka.

"I don't know," answered Kale.

"Just a minute," said Lady Allerion. "I think I can fix this." An intent expression invaded her eyes.

Kale's efforts to penetrate the shield had been so great that when her mother broke its power, a flood of impressions burst with a clamor into

Kale's mind. She fell backward and landed on her backside. Bardon snickered, and Regidor laughed.

"Shh!" hissed Lady Allerion. She looked over her shoulder at Kale. "I'm sorry I didn't warn you, Kale." She cast a look of disapproval at Regidor and Bardon who were still smirking. "We'll just have to assume that some of us were not as intent on doing our jobs and didn't need a warning."

Kale grinned at Bardon's look of chagrin and Regidor's thin-lipped grimace as she returned to her position.

"Where's the meech?" asked Toopka, her head still pushed into the bushes. "I don't see the meech."

"I think our meech is now coming out of the wagon," said Lyll.

The five became silent. Kale pulled her lips between her teeth and held her breath. A tall woman dressed in a deep purple gown descended the steps. A round hat with a wide brim covered her head. A dark blue scarf draped over the hat, completely covering the woman's head and shoulders. She wore gloves and carried a small, beaded reticule.

"Well," said Toopka. "Where's the meech?"

Regidor answered with a whisper of air, "That *is* the meech."

"He's a girl meech?" Toopka turned unbelieving eyes to interrogate her elders. "How can he be a girl?"

"Maybe it's a disguise," suggested Bardon.

"No," said Regidor. "He is a she."

Lady Allerion eyed her companions. "Let's gather information before they realize their ring of containment has been penetrated. Kale, you take the woman. Bardon, the two men. Regidor and I will concentrate on the meech. Do not forget to protect your own mind before you delve into theirs."

Kale asked for Wulder's protection and claimed her status as His servant searching for truth. The woman's anger smacked Kale, and Kale had to mentally back up and approach more cautiously.

"When did that man stop listening to me? If he'd done what I'd told him, we wouldn't be in this mess. Don't deal with that sleazy wizard. Don't take in that unnatural creature. Have we sold any potion? Not hardly! Not enough to

cover our expenses. Yet he thinks we're going to be covered in money and liv-
ing in a castle when we finish this 'job.' What job? Carting her *all over the*
country?"

The younger of the two men had unhitched the horses. He constantly
turned his eyes to the meech but continued to do his chores. The older
man got a padded chair out of the wagon and then placed it in the shade.
The woman pulled supplies out of a hidden cupboard beneath the barrel
house.

"Look at those men. Like father, like son. Crazy men! Obeying orders she
doesn't even speak."

Kale glanced over at the female meech sitting motionless in the shade.
A breeze stirred the scarf veil. The urge to know what the mysterious figure contemplated tempted Kale to abandon the angry woman and explore
the meech's thoughts.

Toopka sighed. "Aren't we going to *do* anything?"

"Yes, we are," answered Lyll.

Toopka's ears perked up.

Lyll turned away from the scene of the wagon and its load of villains.
"We're going back to the tavern and report to Wizard Cam and Dar."

Toopka's shoulders slumped. Kale suppressed a giggle when she saw
Regidor's shoulders do the same.

With Lyll in the lead, the comrades crept out of the wooded area and
circled the village to enter from the other side. They found Dar and the
two wizards sitting out on the benches in front of the tavern.

Kale furrowed her brow in puzzlement. Knowing the councilmen of
River Away, she couldn't imagine Dar had been able to bring them to a
decision this quickly. Dar lifted a hand in greeting as they approached.

"No, Kale," he said. "They are not convinced, but Librettowit has
taken over for me for the time being. He's giving them the history of the
problem."

Kale planted her fists on her hips and turned to Lyll. "Does he read
my mind?"

Lyll laughed, a hearty laugh unlike the musical tinkle of the other mother's. "I can't answer that. I will say doneels are *not* known to be mindspeakers, but *are* renowned for their diplomatic skills. I imagine their success in diplomacy stems from an acute discernment of others' temperaments."

Wizard Cam laid a hand on the sleeping wizard next to him. "Fen, wake up, old man. We have news of the culprits. You won't want to miss this."

"Who are you calling old?" The voice rumbled out of the leaves, but Fenworth did not resume his manly form.

"You," answered Cam. "Come now, Fen. We have work to do."

Kale watched as the wizard opened his eyes. His other facial features emerged from the bark, moss turned to hair, sturdy branches to arms and legs. Leaves became cloth and a pointed hat.

No wonder the mariones of River Away are goosy about having wizards around. Cam leaves a puddle of lake water wherever he pauses for more than five minutes. Fenworth transforms into a tree. And he always has small creatures skittering about, climbing through his hair and clothing, some flying out at unexpected moments. I think a year ago, I would have cowered at the sight of him.

"Precisely so!" said Fenworth, looking her straight in the eye. "I'm almost as much of an oddity as you are. Tut-tut. How narrow we are in our thinking! Tut-tut, oh dear."

"The report?" prodded Dar. "Ladies first."

He stood up and gestured for Lady Allerion to take his seat.

When she was settled, she took Fenworth's hand as she spoke. She didn't direct her words to him in particular, but clasped his hand in a friendly manner. The old man beamed at her, and Kale remembered Fenworth had said Lyll had once been his apprentice.

"We have found the culprits. There are two marione men and two ladies. One woman is also a marione. The other is our meech. She has a tremendously strong personality. She believes in what she is doing. Her drive to succeed is reinforced by her insatiable desire to win Risto's approval." Lyll turned to Kale. "Kale?"

"The marione woman is bitter and angry. She resents the devotion her son and husband show to the meech." Kale turned to Bardon.

"The two men respond to the meech differently." Bardon reached up and pulled a lock of dark hair. He smoothed it over his ear, a gesture Kale had seen him do many times. Now she understood the subconscious habit had a significance that probably even Bardon didn't realize.

I'm glad Grand Ebeck sent him with us. Bardon has secrets, and I think he'll be better off once he gets rid of them. I have secrets too. Only my secrets are hidden from me as well.

She looked at the woman who claimed to be her mother.

There's one mystery.

"The father," continued Bardon, "is motivated by greed. The son adores the meech with an unnatural devotion."

Regidor unclenched his fist and rubbed his palm down the rough material of the clerical robe. "Her name is Gilda. She's proud, vain, and deluded. She believes Risto is the savior of the people of Amara. She derives pleasure from her power over men and dragons. She enjoys giving orders to destroy."

Kale's mind had been puzzling over a problem, and she had to ask her question. "How does she influence the dragons as a fortuneteller?"

"She sets up the farmers to distrust their dragons. She foretells the dragons' defection. She warns of their treacherous ways coming to the surface. Then at night, she visits the dragons and sows seeds of discontent. She has a poisonous tongue." He grimaced. "She then confuses their thoughts so her victims have no clear memory of where they acquired these errant ideas."

Regidor shifted his feet and took in a deep breath. "What I find most disturbing is the smile on her face as she contemplates evil."

"You could see her face?" asked Toopka.

"No, I could feel the euphoria in her physical being as her mental images conjured up destruction."

"Not a nice lady," said Toopka.

"But one Paladin wants us to rescue," said Bardon.

Regidor clenched his fist once more. "It would be easier to destroy her than to change her mind."

"Well then," said Fenworth as he came to his feet, "let's go. Sounds like a delightful challenge before supper. Stimulate the appetite, or kill it. Interesting either way."

48

Confrontation

When the companions reached the market field, they discovered two tents had been set up. One sold potions. The other, an elaborate green-and purple-striped canopy over yellow sides, was marked *Fortuneteller.*

"She's in the fortuneteller tent," said Regidor.

"I suggest," said Dar, "that Regidor and Kale go in to have their fortunes told."

Lyll raised an eyebrow at the two. "I take it you do not believe in such nonsense."

Both Regidor and Kale shook their heads.

"Good!"

Dar looked up at his two warriors. "I'm sending you because you have the best chance of influencing Gilda. Regidor, obviously, because he's a meech. Kale, because she's the Dragon Keeper. Take the minor dragons with you."

Lady Allerion placed a hand on Kale's shoulder. "Gilda's clever, and she'll likely uncover your true identity quickly. Deal in truth, and she cannot hurt you. Any deceit will give her the advantage."

While the wizards, Bardon, and Dar went to the potions tent, Regidor and Kale approached the fortuneteller.

Regidor stopped at the opening, held the flap up, and gallantly gestured for her to proceed. "After you," he said with a twinkle in his eyes.

"Thanks," said Kale and stepped into the gloomy interior. With relief, she felt Regidor follow. His tall presence behind her gave her courage.

The veiled figure sitting at the back of the tent did not move. In front of her, one lantern sat in the middle of a black table. The flicker of the flame reflected in the highly polished top, making the table look as though fire danced beneath its surface.

"So you are the mighty Dragon Keeper." The meech dragon's sultry voice floated across the room. "I am disappointed."

Kale took two steps forward. In spite of the fact she knew Regidor had not followed her farther into the tent, she spoke boldly. "Paladin sent us to find you. He doesn't want you to live in bondage to Risto."

"Oh, I see. He wants me to be in bondage to him. How nice."

"If you choose to break away from Risto, Paladin offers you freedom. He does not offer another form of slavery."

"Strange, but your words seem attractive." She remained motionless for a moment, long enough for Kale to wonder whether or not she should say something to fill the silence.

But Gilda spoke again. "Perhaps this inexplicable attraction is the lure that makes you the Dragon Keeper. However, *I* am not overwhelmed by your influence."

The shadows in the room pulsated with her words. Although the lantern had not dimmed, the darkness grew. Kale held her breath as the dragon continued.

"I perceive that you speak out of an honest belief. Perhaps *this* is the strength behind your persuasive words." Again the female meech retreated into silence.

Abruptly she spoke once more. "What a pity your belief is ill-founded. You are a slave to Paladin whether you are aware of it or not."

The atmosphere in the room thickened as if a mist had infiltrated the tent. Kale looked down at her arms expecting to see dew clinging to her skin. Goose bumps rose as the hair on the back of her neck stood on end.

She tried to keep her voice calm. "It's a little dreary in here, isn't it?"

She wished Regidor would step up and take over. Since he seemed determined to stay in the background, she'd call upon the minor dragons for moral support. She pulled her cape over her shoulders from where it hung down her back. "I brought some other dragons for you to meet."

Gymn and Metta came out and perched on her shoulders. Dibl took his place on her head. Ardeo snuggled in the crook of her arm, letting off a reassuring glow. The whole interior of the tent brightened.

"So," said Gilda after a moment, "does the Dragon Keeper keep pets or slaves?"

"Neither," she snapped back. "These dragons are my friends." She lifted her chin. "And I'm not Paladin's slave. But I don't expect you to be able to understand that."

She heard Regidor prompting in her mind. *Wulder or Pretender? The Creator or The Destroyer?*

Kale nodded slightly and spoke more gently. "I follow Wulder, who created the world. You follow Pretender, who seeks to destroy Wulder's creation."

The female meech stiffened. "I follow only Risto."

"And Risto follows Pretender."

"You are wrong. Risto is our leader."

Regidor stepped forward. "Now that's a fine tangle."

He removed his cowl to expose his distinctive meech features. Kale heard the sharp intake of breath by the female.

"What you have," explained Regidor, "is a usurper whose servant is planning to usurp him. Pretender tries to seize Wulder's authority, and Risto tries to move into Pretender's position. That's going to be a nasty bit of business." He tilted his head in a gesture Kale knew well, and he spoke even more deeply. "And where are you in all this, Gilda? You are a pawn."

He moved around the table, closer to the other meech. "But Kale was making a point before we got sidetracked." He knelt beside her. "You can choose, Gilda, whom you will serve. Creator or Destroyer." Regidor looked down at the hands she kept so still in her lap. "Put your hand on the table, and I will show you the difference."

Kale expected her to refuse, but after a moment's hesitation, Gilda put her gloved hand on the shiny black surface.

"Will you remove the glove?"

Again, the hesitation. Again, the compliance.

As they focused on the meech's hand with its scaly skin and fingernails that came close to being claws, an image formed in the palm. A small plant unfolded. A stem stretched upward, topped by a bud. The bud opened with pale pink petals uncurling around a golden center. A shadow fell over the beautiful blossom, and the plant shriveled to black stubble. The image vanished.

"Creator or Destroyer?" Regidor whispered. "You can choose, Gilda."

Gilda clenched her fingers into a fist. "You are a fool, meech dragon." She snatched her hand back from the table and held it against her chest. "You have to clear the field before you can till the soil. You have to break up the ground before you can plant the seed. Destruction is a part of the process."

Regidor stood with a sigh. "You do not plow down a field of corn to plant weeds, Gilda. Open your eyes and see."

Gilda stood. The top of her hat came to Regidor's chin. With her shoulders squared, she looked poised to attack. Kale felt energy building within the female meech's body. Kale tensed, ready to spring into action should the woman strike Regidor.

Regidor spoke with urgency. "Why do you wear the veil, Gilda?" He paused for an answer, but the female did not give him one. "Risto told you these people would shudder at the sight of your face, didn't he? He destroyed your self-confidence with a few words. He chained you to his side with lies."

"You wear a cowl." Gilda's words resounded in the tent like hammer blows.

"I have friends from each of the high races. My appearance does not frighten them."

Kale felt Dibl stomp his little feet on her head, and she giggled. "I can tell you Regidor was kind of cute as a child, and now I think he's rather handsome—for a bald man."

Regidor relaxed, threw her a grin, and waggled the hairless ridge that passed for eyebrows. "I didn't know you befriended me for my stunning appearance."

"It's the charm of your smile," she answered.

"Go!" The word exploded from Gilda. "I do not welcome your presence. I do not believe this act of camaraderie, meech dragon."

"My name is Regidor, and I am at your service." With a swift movement, Regidor lifted Gilda's clenched fist to his lips and kissed it. "Open your eyes, fair lady. Do not be afraid of what you will see."

She pulled her hand away from him and turned her back to the intruders. Regidor looked for a moment as if he would lay his hand upon her shoulder. Instead, he shrugged and marched out of the tent. Kale followed.

The three wizards, Bardon, and Dar joined them as they strode away from the tents and toward the village.

"What did we learn?" asked Dar.

"They are very second-rate potion makers," said Fenworth.

"But none of their products is truly poisonous," added Cam.

"They *are* overpriced," said Bardon.

Lyll smiled. "The poor mother is justified in her complaints against her husband and son's foolishness."

Dar nodded. "These tidbits are interesting, but our main focus during Kale and Regidor's visit with the fortuneteller was to keep them safe."

Regidor looked back at the two men now standing beside the ornate wagon. "You kept them from attacking?"

"No, we spoke to Wulder, requesting His protection be invoked on your behalf." Dar turned to his o'rant comrade. "Kale, what did you learn from the meech?"

"I learned nothing except I'm no good at diplomacy."

Dar touched her arm. "Often the results of our confrontations do not materialize immediately. You more than adequately engaged her interest while our meech friend did his best on our behalf. Regidor?"

"Risto has gathered an army of bisonbecks and grawligs to the west of Bartal Springs Lake. Over five hundred dragons have joined his forces. He intends to swoop south three days hence. His goal is to annihilate anyone who gets in his way."

Kale stopped in her tracks, seized Regidor's arm, and forced him to face her. "Where and when did you get all that information?"

Regidor smiled. "Directly out of Gilda's sweet little mind while you were first speaking to her. She could barely contain her glee, knowing soon your annoying little person and your senseless prattling would be eliminated forever. She's got a heart of lead, that one does."

"Humph! I couldn't get past the block she had on her mind," Kale admitted. "You followed up with a mighty pleasant speech for one who knew what she was thinking."

Regidor shrugged. "Well, Paladin expected us to try to persuade her away from Risto."

Fenworth spoke up. "And what would you say was your level of success in that endeavor, my boy?"

"Next to nil."

They began walking toward the tavern once more. The minor dragons flew about Kale's head, trying to draw her attention. She ignored them.

This means a battle.

"So after we have a delicious meal," said Fenworth, smacking his lips, "and a round of relaxing entertainment—music, I think—"

What kind of forces do we have to meet such an army?

"—and perhaps a few good tales and a good night's sleep—"

Fenworth said the mariones would turn out as an army to defend their land.

"—what do you fine comrades suggest we do with this startling information?"

Cam patted his damp beard. "Oh, I think we should go stop Risto's army, don't you?"

Stop them? Just us? What about the marione army? What about Paladin? Where are Brunstetter and Lee Ark?

"Quite," agreed Fenworth. "There's nothing like a mission to save the world to liven up a vacation."

"We aren't on vacation, Fen," said Cam.

Vacation! Ha! And this isn't exactly a quest, either. For a quest, you go find something and, hopefully, bring it back.

"No, that was last week, wasn't it? Or perhaps the week before?"

"Last century, maybe."

"Was that before or after that uncomfortably cold spell, Cam? I do have to say my memory is getting worse."

"Could it be that you are getting old, Fen?"

Senile! Both of you!

"Never!"

49

PLANS TO PROCEED

"The problem," said Lady Allerion to the group crowded into the River Away meeting house, "is that once we've made a gateway, there's no way to seal it up. And the size of the gateway we're proposing…well, hiding it is going to be a problem."

"And what about those peddlers?" interjected Master Meiger. "We don't want them here, causing more problems. We need to concentrate on our defense. With the peddlers and that fortuneteller in our midst, we'd have to keep an eye on them."

Regidor nodded. "We should take Gilda and her cohorts with us to the battlefield."

Kale sat at the head table, quietly observing her former neighbors. The assembly consisted of mostly men and older boys, but a few women had turned out to hear Master Meiger define the threat and recommend following the leadership of Ambassador Dar.

With their propensity for long discussions, Kale feared the mariones would talk for days and not get to the point before the invading forces were at the door. But the people had surprised her. Once convinced of the danger, they took action. The boys grabbed the charge to ride throughout the country, raising the alarm and delivering a message concerning where the volunteer army was to assemble. Baking and packing occupied the women not at the meeting. Older men, who would not be going to the front, promised to care for the women and children, property and animals, of those who must defend the land.

A farmer stood in the back of the room and waved his hat to get Lady Allerion's attention.

"Yes sir?" Lyll nodded in recognition of his right to speak.

"I have a little bog land that runs along the river. Worthless bit of property, but no one goes there. Could that be used for this giant gateway you speak of?"

"Tut-tut. Bog land worthless, did he say? Not a very intelligent fellow, I'm sure."

"Hush, Fenworth," said Lyll. "Not all people understand your affinity for bog."

Another farmer spoke up. "I'll vouch for the site being inaccessible, but how we gonna get men, equipment, and these dragons of yours through the bog to get to the gateway if we deliberately put it someplace nobody can go?"

"We have a bog wizard with us, sir," said Dar. "Are there any other suggestions for the location of the gateway?"

No one offered a word.

"Fine," said Dar. "That's settled. Let's turn to another problem. We need four volunteers to go with Lehman Bardon, Regidor, and Leecent Kale to capture the peddlers."

Four young men stepped forward, Bolley, Gronmere, Mack, and Weedom.

Dar nodded his approval. "Right. Report to Lehman Bardon when this meeting adjourns. Now, the boys who've taken the charge to spread the alarm and orders of procedure, meet with Wizard Cam for instructions. The gateway will be functional in three hours. Those of you who will be fighting, gather at the bog. Any questions?"

Dar waited a moment, surveying the room full of mariones, looking many of them in the eye. "This meeting is dismissed."

The marione farmers and merchants rose from their seats and solemnly shuffled out of the building. Soon they would travel to a battle, the likes of which none of them could imagine. Master Meiger had presented the call to arms. Dar and Librettowit had done a good job of preparing the men in short and vivid speeches. But the concept of battling bisonbecks and grawligs seemed a nightmare, a nightmare they didn't want to see materialize in their own fields.

Kale pushed past the boys gathering around Cam and hurried outside. A large armagot tree spread its bare branches over one end of the road leading to the north of River Away. Kale strode over to lean against the wide trunk.

The minor dragons climbed out of their pocket-dens. Gymn sat on her shoulder and cuddled his head underneath her chin.

"You're right," she said, stroking the side of his belly with one finger. "I feel sick. But I don't think it's anything you can cure."

Dibl and Ardeo foraged for bugs among the purple fall leaf blanket beneath the tree. But Metta abandoned the hunt and flew to Kale's other shoulder.

"We're talking about going into battle, and I'm scared." She glanced around at the mariones dispersing to do what had to be done and tried to swallow the lump in her throat. "Do you think they know, Metta, how awful it's going to be? I've only been in skirmishes. I can't imagine a full battle. I don't want to."

"Do you remember how I got my medal, Kale?"

She jumped at the sound of Dar's voice at her elbow.

"Your medal? For fighting the Creemoor spiders at The Hall?"

"Yes."

"I remember."

"Do you remember I said I got the medal when I was just trying to stay alive?"

She nodded. "Yes."

"That's what it's like in the big battles. You've fought before. You don't think about your fear. You just try to stay alive. And if you see a chance to help a comrade, you take it."

She nodded again, but her throat had closed around that lump again, and she couldn't speak.

Dibl came to roost on her head, his little claws digging into her hair. Dar patted her arm. "Don't worry. Wulder has given you what you need for this encounter, and He's given you a place to go if you don't live through it."

Dibl pulled slightly on the hair wrapped around his toes. Kale rolled her eyes at Dar and allowed a small smile to lift the corners of her mouth. "Thanks for the comforting words, Dar."

"Anytime." He winked at her.

"Come on, Kale," Bardon called. He and Regidor and the four marione men stood across the road, ready to march to the market field.

She shoved away from the tree. *I'll get right in the middle of that knot of warriors and let them protect me.*

"That's a plan, Kale!" Dar beamed at her. "Your intelligence is a better weapon than your brawn."

She compared her skinny arms to the muscles rippling over the mariones' backs and arms. "What brawn?"

"Exactly!" said Dar as he waved her off and headed back to the meeting house.

She took a few steps toward Bardon, stopped abruptly, and turned back. Dar strolled toward the meeting house.

Did you just read my mind?

He didn't even turn. *"Kale, you have more important things to occupy your mind."*

Did you?

"Of course not. Bardon is waiting."

"Won't they know we're coming?" asked Bolley. "That female meech can tell what you're thinking, right?"

Kale gladly answered. "Regidor can block her ability to know what our plans are."

Bardon led his men to the potion tent. Without waiting to watch that confrontation, Kale and Regidor entered the fortuneteller's tent with the minor dragons flying in attendance.

Gilda remained seated and did not move.

Regidor stood by the door. The dragons swooped around the room, inspecting all the darkest corners. Gilda ignored them all.

A surge of impatience rose in Kale. The woman swathed herself in thick clothing, moved only when forced to, spread discontent among people who had done her no harm, and acted as if she were a queen.

But Paladin said the meech dragon must be treated with mercy. She was born into this situation and needs to be rescued. Regidor made an attempt on our last visit. I suppose before we disable her powers, tie her up, and haul her off with us, I ought to give kindness a try as well.

Kale walked around the black table and stood beside Gilda's still form. "I would like to see your face."

Gilda didn't move.

"Really," said Kale. "I think if I could look in your eyes, I might be able to at least begin to understand you."

Still Gilda did not respond. Kale put her hand on the female meech's shoulder, and the clothing collapsed.

Dibl did somersaults in the air, and Metta squealed her surprise.

"Very clever," said Regidor.

"Where is she?" asked Kale.

Regidor tilted his head and surveyed the room. After turning slowly in a complete circle, he answered, "She's in this room but not in her own form. Let's look around and see how she may be hiding."

"She's changed herself into something?"

"I don't know if she has the skill to do it herself, or if this is Risto's doing. Pick up that pile of clothing and shake it out. See if anything falls to the floor."

Kale did as Regidor suggested. The hat fell out of the layer of veil. She peeled a blouse from inside the dark purple jacket. Petticoats slipped out of the purple skirt. The half boots contained empty stockings. She sighed with disappointment.

Dibl abandoned his jovial air dance and set to work. He crawled along the floor, nibbling on bugs as he looked for clues. Metta sat on the back of Gilda's chair. Kale picked her up. The little dragon shivered with dismay over the disappearance of the meech. "We'll find her, Metta. It doesn't look like anyone hurt her."

Kale continued to stroke Metta as she walked around the room. "What are we looking for?" she asked Regidor.

He spoke over his shoulder as he examined a pillow. "Well, I'm looking for that shimmer of light I sometimes see around people. Hers was a particularly disheveled pattern."

"I've never seen any lights."

"Then I suppose you should look for something that's out of place, or something that's here now that wasn't before."

"Wouldn't it be most logical for her to change herself into a living thing, like a cat or dog, a bird or mouse?"

"That would be the easiest transformation, but Risto is above doing something simple."

"Still, I'd be happier if Dibl would quit eating those bugs. Dibl, stop it. You might eat Gilda."

Dibl rolled on the floor and bumped into a table leg. He lay there with his sides jiggling as he laughed.

"It's not funny!" She pursed her lips and tried not to smile at his antics.

"I hardly think she's a bug, Kale." Regidor prowled the room, looking in various boxes, trunks, and under cushions.

"No, I guess you're right. She doesn't have the personality to allow herself to be an insect."

Ardeo and Gymn investigated the corners of the room. Ardeo's light brightened each dark cranny. Gymn trilled in excitement.

She hurried to where the minor dragons danced around some object. "They found something."

A coin lay on the canvas flooring of the tent next to the cushions that must have been Gilda's daybed. Regidor picked up the large disk and examined it as Gymn and Ardeo hovered around his shoulders.

"No, I don't think so," said Regidor. He flipped it in the air and tossed it on the table.

"What about this?" Kale pointed to a small, standing mirror on an upright trunk. "This seems out of place. Why would Gilda want a mirror?"

Regidor started to cross the room.

"Never mind," said Kale. "Metta says it was here before."

She put her hands on her hips and surveyed the interior of the tent.

"This is hopeless, Regidor. What makes you think she's still here?"

"I know she is. I can feel a sort of vibration in the air, one that I noticed when we were in the tent before. I thought it came from her." He shook his head and grimaced. "Maybe I was wrong."

She almost chuckled. *I doubt that! He just needs to focus.* "Stop and be still, Regidor. See if you can tell whether that feeling is stronger in one part of the tent."

Regidor stood motionless for a moment with his eyes closed. Kale watched him breathe in and out. It occurred to her that Regidor, in this almost motionless state, reminded her of Gilda's restrained presence.

Regidor moved to the shiny black table. The lantern burned with a flickering yellow flame. A handkerchief of white linen lay on the table where Gilda had been sitting.

Regidor picked up an earthenware jug with a cork stopper. He gently tilted it from side to side. Water sloshed within.

"A plain jug of water," he said, his teeth gleaming white in the combined light of the lantern and Ardeo's glow. "Or the essence of one meech dragon."

Kale smiled. "You found her."

"Yes, and unless we spill her, she should be easy to keep track of."

Dibl gave a tiny hoot. Gymn landed on Kale's shoulder and flapped his wings.

"I believe she did this herself, Regidor," said Kale as she looked at the finely shaped clay bottle. "If Risto had been here and changed her, wouldn't he have taken her away?"

"That's a thought, Kale. But what if he wants her to travel with us and for us to think she is harmless in this state?"

She considered the possibility. "So we'd best be wary."

"It is always best to be wary."

50

Building the Gateway

A wide lane built atop a levee stretched into the bog from the main road. Neither the lane nor the levee had existed several hours before. Men, ready to fight for their homes, gathered on the main road. Women and children stood by their men, waiting to say good-bye.

Kale saw Master Meiger, and for the moment he didn't have someone demanding his attention.

"You gave a good speech today, Master Meiger."

He blushed and looked away from her. "Not as fancy as some, but I said what I knew to be true."

"You said just the right thing, and these people believed you."

"They've known me all my life."

She wanted to say more, but words didn't come to mind, and he looked uncomfortable at her praise. She thought of another topic to broach.

"The wizards haven't called you into the bog?"

"No, they told us to wait here until they had the gateway constructed. Evidently it's a rather complicated business, and it will take all three of them. That one wizard, Fenworth, he did that road all by himself. Amazing to watch."

She nodded. "I'll go in and see how close they are to finishing."

"Should you?" asked Master Meiger. "I mean, interrupt them?"

"I won't bother them." Kale started toward the lane, but turned back. "Master Meiger, it might be a good idea to warn these people about mordakleeps. Remind them they have to cut off their tails to kill them."

The old marione looked startled. "Yes. Yes, of course."

She gestured to Regidor and Bardon. "I'm going into the bog. Want to come along?"

The two men exchanged glances. Regidor grinned. "Decided you didn't want to run into any swamp creatures on your own, huh?"

She grinned back at him. "That's right. Dar told me to use my brain."

"We'll come," said Bardon. "I'm curious, too."

They passed several groups of men and a few families before they set foot on the new path. The springy road looked like logs of various diameters woven together with sturdy vines. The minor dragons flew about them as they walked. A feast of bugs swarmed over the murky bog water.

"Where's Gilda?" asked Kale.

"In my pocket," answered Regidor.

Kale looked at the smooth lines of his clerical robe.

"It's a hollow," explained Regidor before she could ask. "How did you give Toopka the slip?"

"She was helping Cakkue and Yonny. She didn't even seem particularly outraged that we didn't plan to take her along."

"That sounds suspicious." Bardon laughed.

"I agree," said Regidor.

Kale shook her head, half agreeing with her friends yet still believing her own eyes. "She was changing beds on the second floor when I left. Mistress Meiger finds Toopka just a bit unnerving because she's not had any dealings with doneels. But Toopka is doing her best to impress her. I do wonder what's going on in that furry little head of hers."

"Well, she can be a good worker," said Regidor, "but she's also conniving and too curious for her own good."

"And what would she say about you?" asked Kale.

Regidor laughed. "That I'm bossy and stubborn."

Bardon slapped him on the shoulder. "She'd be right then."

A ballyhoo bird cried out an objection to the invasion of its territory with a distinctive "ballyhoo, ballyhoo." Kale craned her neck, trying to catch sight of the blue and white bird. The small, quick bird perched on a limb covered with cascading moss. Kale watched as it flitted from branch to branch.

Dry winter leaves rattled as they still clung to vines draped around the trees. With a deep breath, Kale recognized the same damp smells as in Bedderman's Bog.

But here, no cygnot trees linked together to make planking. These trees stood far apart. Patchy, gray bark hung loosely on the trunks as if the trees were shedding an outer skin.

Maybe the winters are too harsh here for cygnot trees. I don't think it snows as far south as The Bogs.

The lack of cygnot trees also meant no roots provided natural stepping blocks. Away from Wizard Fenworth's floating road, the foot-deep water combined with a reedy vegetation. After they were finished with the lane and it was destroyed, the bog would be difficult to trudge through.

But now, Kale almost felt as though she were on an afternoon stroll. A breeze stirred the vines on the trees, and the afternoon sky above provided a blue canopy. The road beneath them creaked and swayed in an easy rhythm.

It all seems too comfortable to be the pathway to war.

"There's the gateway." Kale pointed at the three wizards, Librettowit, and Dar gathered at the end of the temporary road. "It looks as though they've finished."

"No," said Regidor, "the smaller one is complete, but the larger has one edge that needs to be more tightly woven. Why are there two gateways? I only heard of plans for one."

Librettowit and Dar conversed solemnly while Fen and Cam sat on logs resembling roughly hewn chairs. Lyll paced in front of the unfinished gateway.

Afternoon shadows stretched long across the makeshift road. Remembering that they had recently been attacked by a peaceful pond, Kale shuddered and kept a wary eye on the dark splotches.

Dar greeted Kale and the others. "We're just about to send Wizard

Fenworth and Librettowit off to summon Brunstetter and Lee Ark. This will be one for the history books. If it works as planned, Librettowit and Fen will bring troops through the different gateways to this central one, which will take them all to the battle. Time is short."

"And Paladin?" asked Kale.

"He may show up," answered Dar.

"We can't summon him?"

Dar shook his head. "Wulder will send him if he is needed. We've no authority over either Wulder or Paladin. We cannot command them to appear." Dar's expressive eyes brightened. "But we will not be abandoned by them, that I can assure you."

"Are you coming?" Librettowit called to Fenworth. "I can do this myself if you're too tired."

"Tired? Harrumph! I only did a third of the work building these gates, and I could have done it all. Of course I'm not tired."

Fenworth got to his feet stiffly. Mice, lizards, and bugs skittered out of his hair and beard. He took no notice of their departure, but smiled warmly at a large blackbird flying through the widely spaced trees. He landed on the bog wizard's shoulder.

"There you are, Thorpendipity." Fenworth lifted a shaky hand to stroke the bird's glossy back. "I'd begun to think you'd taken up with some other wizard. I'll be needing you. Glad you came."

Fenworth strolled to the smaller of the two shimmering gateways and stepped through, still talking to the bird.

Librettowit addressed Cam and Lyll. "I'll try to keep him in the background, but you know there's no bending that will of his once he's decided to do a thing."

Cam's jaw clenched before he spoke. "We shall hope he doesn't think of leading the forces on the battlefield."

Lyll wrung her hands. "Try to convince him of the importance of gathering reinforcements. He's too frail for the rigors of war." She pressed her lips together and blinked rapidly.

Librettowit put his hand to his hat and tipped it slightly. "I'll do my best, my lady." He entered the gateway and disappeared in sparkling light.

Wizard Cam turned to the large, unfinished gate.

"What do you think, Lyll? Can we finish this off?"

"I think we need help."

Cam and Lyll turned to look at Kale, Bardon, and Regidor.

"Come," said Lyll, "we need you three apprentices."

Regidor and Kale stepped forward quickly, but Bardon hung back.

"Excuse me, my lady, but I am not one of Fenworth's apprentices."

"Be that as it may," said Cam, "come, my friend. You may observe."

Kale's head jerked around to see Bardon's reaction. Wizard Cam had said almost the exact words Fenworth had once said when he wanted Bardon to take part in a wizardry lesson.

Bardon wore his inscrutable expression, and when she reached to his mind, he had a block up that should have had a sign reading, "Go away, Kale!"

She made a face at him, and of course he didn't respond.

Lyll touched Kale's arm. "Stand by me. Regidor, you go next to Cam, and Bardon, take the middle position." She waited only a moment for them to follow her instructions. "Now, look at this wall on the right side. Do you see the threads that have not yet been woven together?"

Kale's mouth dropped open as she nodded. Always before she had concentrated on the center of the gateway where the air seemed to ripple, distorting the image meeting her eye. Now she could see long, thick strands of almost transparent color dangling as if the edge of a huge cloth had frayed.

She felt Bardon's excitement surge and knew he saw the threads. His reaction overtook his determination not to share this experience with her, and his guard fell.

"Now watch carefully, children, as Cam and I weave the loose cords. You can join in and help as soon as you see the pattern."

Regidor joined in first, followed by Kale. She knew Bardon saw the pattern soon after. But he hesitated, because he didn't quite believe he could do it.

It's like the beat of a drum behind the music, Bardon. Just react to the rhythm.

He didn't answer, but soon she felt his energy flowing in time with the others in the group. When Lyll tied off the last strand, the five let out a collective sigh. The feeling of working in harmony dissolved, but Kale felt a sense of satisfaction. She turned to see if Bardon felt the same way.

His face had taken on the stonelike expression she hated. She almost yelled at him. *Can't you just enjoy something?* The question tried to leave her tongue, but she clamped her lips over it.

"How can that happen?" he demanded. "How can I be part of something like that?"

"It isn't such a mystery," said Wizard Cam. He turned away from Bardon to ask Kale a question. "Do you have the talent of healing?"

"No, Gymn does."

"Yet you assist him when he has need of your help. Your presence boosts his natural talent."

"Yes, I think that's how it works."

"And you share in the joy, the satisfaction, after the work is completed, even though it was not your talent that achieved the end?"

"Yes, and I feel very close to Wulder."

Cam nodded and refocused on the stiff lehman. "Bardon, you are to Kale as she is to Gymn in this instance. You sustain her ability. Actually, during this enterprise you supported the four of us. And nourishing the talent is just as valuable as having the talent yourself. When you and Kale fight together, it is she who is bolstering, or one might even say multiplying, your skill and ability."

Bardon cast a skeptical glance at Kale. Dibl chose that moment to circle his head, flying around and around Bardon's crown like a bee deciding to land on a flower. Kale grinned.

Bardon's glare hardened, but Dibl plopped down on his head.

The lehman sighed, his stiff shoulders relaxing. Kale heard his voice in her mind. *"It's difficult to stand on your dignity with a yellow dragon in your hair."*

Maybe dignity isn't always important.

A smile broke Bardon's grim expression.

Dar signaled Kale, Bardon, and Regidor to come to him. "I'm going back to talk to Master Meiger and his friends. Cam and Lyll will continue to fortify this gateway so that the dragons can safely pass through. I want you three to go ahead. Scout the lay of the land, the location of the enemy camps, and their strength. Then return. After you report, we should be ready to begin transporting the warriors. If I'm not here waiting for you, Kale, send one of your dragons to locate me."

"Yes sir. Dar?"

"Yes?"

"Are you really a high lee general as Fenworth said?"

Dar laughed and shook his head. "No, he was thinking of my father."

"Are you an ambassador?"

"We are all ambassadors, Kale. We represent something to someone every day of our lives."

"Come on, Kale." Regidor tugged at her arm. "We've a mission. Let's go see where the enemy is camped."

51

In Enemy Territory

"That felt different, didn't it?" Kale said as soon as she passed through the gateway and faced Regidor and Bardon. They stood in a wooded area against a rise of rocks.

Regidor nodded. "It did. I didn't feel like the air was squeezed out of my lungs."

"I thought maybe I was just getting used to pushing through gateways," said Bardon. "I didn't feel the weight and stickiness of the light as I have before."

Regidor tilted his head and studied the gateway etched in the boulders. "I suppose it has something to do with the dimensions."

Kale took hold of the meech dragon's sleeve. "No, Regidor! We are not going to stop and analyze the gateway."

Bardon chuckled. "She's right, you know. We have a mission to perform."

Kale coaxed the minor dragons out of her cape. "Come on, you can help. Just be careful not to be seen." Dibl trilled at her. "Very funny, but I don't think it will work."

"What?" asked Regidor.

"He's going to pretend to be a bird if any bisonbecks spot him."

"This is serious business," Bardon spoke firmly to the little yellow dragon as he zipped back and forth across the small clearing.

"It's useless to reprimand him." Kale glared. "He knows the situation is dangerous."

"I don't want him to compromise our mission."

"Yelling at him won't change his temperament."

"All right," interrupted Regidor. "The two of you bickering won't help our attempt to scout the area either."

Both Kale and Bardon clenched their teeth and answered, "Right." Realizing the synchronization of their response, they stared at each other with widened eyes.

Dibl did two backflips in the air and then buzzed around Bardon's head. The lehman didn't even bother to wave him off. He looked at the western horizon. "We have about an hour of sunlight left. Shall we split up and meet back here?"

"Fine," said Regidor. "I'll take this mountainous terrain since I'm the most surefooted."

Kale squared her shoulders. She didn't want her two companions to know how much she disliked the idea of going alone. "I'll go due north."

"And I'll take the east," said Bardon. "We'll travel until sunset and then retrace our steps. There should be moonlight tonight, enough to navigate by. Kale, watch where the moon comes up, and use that to keep your bearings on your return."

"I know that." She signaled the dragons to come and started into the woods before she unintentionally revealed her fears to Bardon.

"Be careful." Regidor's voice gave her a measure of comfort.

"Don't do anything foolish." Bardon's voice made her jaw ache as she ground her teeth together.

She carefully guarded her thoughts as she stormed away.

Why is he so bossy all of a sudden? By now he should know I am at least competent.

To refocus her mind on the task at hand, Kale planned her next moves. She sent the dragons ahead of her, telling them to look for bison-becks and grawligs and renegade dragons. Gymn came back first with a report she could hardly believe.

She veered off to the left and followed him. She smelled wood smoke before they came to a ridge where Gymn urged caution. Lying on her stomach, she inched into a position to peer over the top. Her stomach knotted as she surveyed the wide valley below. Campfires dotted the darkening landscape. Thousands of bisonbeck warriors crowded the eastern side, clearly organized in military units. A river marked a dividing line. On the western banks and all the way to the hills below the Morchain Range, grawligs camped in their typical helter-skelter manner. Kale examined the chaotic scene and located knots of ropmas and schoergs here and there amid the grawlig encampment.

Gymn grumbled deep in his throat.

"Yes, I see them," she answered.

At the other end of the valley, dragons roved over a hilly landscape.

Kale gulped. "How many warriors are there? How many dragons? How do we determine where the leaders are?"

Metta landed on her shoulder. She had come across the same scene and traveled along the top of the ridge to rejoin Kale. Soon Dibl and Ardeo skimmed over the rocks and bushes to land on her as well.

To the west, the sun dipped below the peaks of the Morchain Range. A blood red streak of clouds announced the end of the day. A grawlig chant rose from the valley, making Kale's skin crawl. Even though she could not distinguish the words, the beat of the tuneless mantra sounded like a war cry.

"Well, we've got something to report. We might as well go back."

Kale pushed herself away from the edge and slid down the slope. Standing, she brushed debris from her cape and trousers.

This is so much bigger than I imagined. How can a small, untrained army of farmers stand up to that gigantic army? I hope Wizard Fenworth and Librettowit find Brunstetter and Lee Ark.

She started back through the woods. Ardeo flew just ahead, lighting the way. Metta, Gymn, and Dibl sat on Kale. Not even Dibl found any humor in the situation.

Kale's thoughts were on how to phrase the enormity of what she had seen.

I'm sure Bardon and Regidor saw the same thing from their positions. I wonder if they went closer to the enemy.

She tripped over a half-buried, rotten log. As she stumbled a few feet, the underbrush caught at her legs.

"I don't remember the forest being this overgrown."

She peered upward but could not see the sky. "Well, that eliminates using the moon as a guide."

Kale reached with her mind to find Regidor or Bardon, but found her emotions and the nearness of so many of the enemy hampered her ability.

Or maybe Risto knows we're here and has done something. The minor dragons found me easily. Maybe they'll lead me to Regidor or Bardon.

Kale made the suggestion, and each of the dragons agreed they could find Regidor. When they started off at a southwest angle, Kale got an impression of the meech dragon's location and breathed a sigh of relief. She didn't want to spend the night alone and lost in the forest, especially if Risto knew she and the others had infiltrated his territory.

"No!" She giggled as the minor dragons bombarded her with objections. "Of course I know I'm never alone when I have you around. And remember, Granny Noon said Wulder is always with us too."

She trekked confidently through the woods, but still tried to be as silent as she could, hushing Metta when she hummed a marching song. The thought of running into an enemy patrol prompted her caution.

She heard Regidor speaking before she saw him. She urged the dragons to return to her, and together they crept up on the situation, not knowing to whom the meech dragon could be speaking.

She hid behind a boulder and peeked at Regidor.

He sat on the ground with the clay bottle between his knees. Hovering above him, Gilda appeared as a translucent, cloudlike figure. She was dressed in a white, gauzy flowing gown. Her profile showed the squarish nose and jaw like Regidor's. But all her meech features held finer lines than the male dragon. Kale thought her strikingly beautiful.

"You say I was born into a bad situation, Regidor." Gilda's voice dripped with honey. "How do you know you are not the one being deceived? You and I are meech dragons. We shouldn't be fighting each

other. We have a kindred spirit. I can be your true friend. I can understand you like none of them. Their brotherhood is a pretense."

"You're wrong again. And you've pinpointed what makes the 'brotherhood' unique. It has nothing to do with being of similar lineage. The
quality of relationships among this band is the key, Gilda. I am trusted,
respected, and even cherished by those I associate with."

"Risto trusts me."

"He does?" Regidor shook his head. "He trusts you so much that he
put a spell on you. Should you waver in service to him, you become a
vapor in a jug. That doesn't sound like trust to me."

"The spell is to protect me from the likes of you."

"And what horrible thing am I supposed to do to you?"

"Destroy me."

"Well, if you want to know the truth, I've figured out how to do away
with you in this form, but I don't plan on doing it."

"You twist things, meech dragon. Come with me to meet Risto." She
hitched a shoulder and looked down on Regidor with an expression of
disdain. "You don't dare see him face to face, do you? You know he could
prove you're wrong."

"I know he's wicked and very clever. I'd rather not deal with him at all."

"Aha! You're afraid."

"I'm intelligent, Gilda. Only a fool would throw himself into Risto's
clutches."

"I don't have any more time for this ridiculous discussion. And since
you know my weakness, I'll admit I'm beginning to dissipate. I must
return to the bottle."

Regidor pulled the cork from the top. Gilda drifted toward the
opening.

"Think of what I've said, Regidor. You and I could be an invincible
team under Risto. Your friends offer you nothing but hardship ahead."
She detoured from her descent into the bottle to curl around her male
counterpart. Her mist draped around his shoulders and slid toward the
bottle. The sultry quality of her voice deepened. "Perhaps if we joined

forces under Risto, we could one day surpass even him. Perhaps this is the only way for you to defeat him. With me, Regidor. With one of your own kind." Her cloudlike image condensed and swirled into the bottle. Regidor firmly pushed the cork into the top.

"You can come out now, Kale," he said.

She straightened and walked around the rock. "Hi."

"Hi."

She waited awkwardly while Regidor stood and tucked the bottle inside his clerical robe.

"You think I shouldn't be talking to her," he said.

"I didn't know you could talk to her, so I hadn't formed an opinion on whether it's wise or not."

"Do you have an opinion now?"

"I think it's dangerous for the same reasons you're reluctant to casually visit Risto."

Regidor's lips twitched into a smile.

"So you give me my own advice—stay away from evil."

"It does sound like a good plan."

Regidor shrugged. "Let's go join Bardon."

"Certainly."

Kale followed the surefooted dragon over the choppy terrain. The rough rocks provided traction beneath their boots. Slipping resulted from crumbling flint, not from a smooth surface. They reached more even ground, and she allowed herself to think about what she had just seen. Regidor might be tempted to follow Gilda to Risto, just to prove her wrong. Regidor would never succumb to Risto's convoluted reasoning, but he might be captivated by Gilda's charms and let down his guard. In the conversation she'd heard between the meech dragons, Regidor didn't seem particularly antagonistic to Risto's minion. Kale worried about him being caught in an attractive trap.

Two of the minor dragons squealed an alarm at the same moment. The other two echoed the cry. Kale whipped her head around to see what had caused their shrieking. She smelled it first, the sickening, rotten smell of a grawlig.

She pulled her sword.

Regidor roared. "Behind you, Kale."

She heard a swishing sound. Something slammed into the back of her head, jarring her body and buckling her knees. The ground in front of her turned black with tiny bursts of light circling in erratic patterns. A rough hand grabbed her hair. She closed her eyes and managed to utter, "Help!" before total darkness took away all the pain.

52

Mother's Love

A tender hand bathed the back of Kale's aching head with cool water. She lay on her side in a soft bed. The linens smelled fresh. A soft pillow cradled her head.

"Is she awake yet?" The harsh voice pricked at her memory.

"I think she's coming 'round, my lady." Kale knew she'd never heard those mellow tones before.

"Then move, you fool." The first voice clanged in her brain.

Who is that?

A swish of fabric and a stirring of the air told Kale that the two women had changed places. Cool fingers touched her brow.

"Kale, dear."

Now she recognized the voice, now that the speaker used a honeyed manner to drench her words. *Mother Number One.*

Kale kept her eyes closed.

"Kale, dear, are you all right? We've rescued you from a band of grawligs."

Did Regidor escape? Oh no! She'll listen to my thoughts. Block. Block. Wulder block. Under Your authority. Seeking truth. Wulder protect me. My thoughts belong to me and Wulder. There, that's it. My thoughts belong to me and Wulder.

"You are coming around, aren't you, dear? Don't be afraid. I'll take care of you."

Kale opened her eyes to gaze at the beauty of the perfect face so close to her. Mother Number One definitely outshone Mother Number Two in exquisite elegance. Kale looked into the cold gray eyes and turned her head.

"Are you in pain, dear Kale? The medicine I put in the water should have eliminated any discomfort."

"Where's Gymn?"

"Having a resplendent supper. The others are as well. They're in the cook's tent. Can you sit up, dear?"

Kale struggled to rise on her elbow. "My cape?"

"Really, Kale, I haven't stolen it. You were filthy when the men brought you to me. You have a fresh gown, and you're clean. You could say thank you."

"Thank you." *The cape wouldn't be dirty. It sheds dirt. And at The Goose and The Gander, Magistrate Hyd said a moonbeam cape cannot be stolen. Where is it?* "Where is it?"

"Now I know you aren't well. Fussing over such a petty detail. The cape is in the covers with you."

"Why?"

This impressive and autocratic Lyll Allerion stood abruptly. "Why?" Her voice shrilled. "Because the nasty thing stings anyone who tries to touch it."

She turned to the door, her skirts rustling with the swift movement. "I have work to do. Tayla, call me when my daughter is in a better mood."

Kale sat up and contemplated the servant. The tumanhofer looked old enough to have children but not old enough to be a grandmother. But a tumanhofer's age was hard to determine.

"Could you bring my dragons to me?" Kale asked.

"Not and live to see tomorrow, Miss Kale."

"I want to get dressed. Where are my clothes?"

"Burned. My lady didn't like them. She'd have had the cape, too, but as she said we couldn't get it."

"My boots?"

"Burned as well."

So I am without clothes and shoes. She pulled her knees to her chin and surveyed her very nicely furnished prison. She didn't see an obvious means of escape. Beyond the flap of the tent, two sturdy legs stood at attention.

They probably belonged to a guard. *And my muscles feel like noodles. I wonder if I've been drugged to keep me out of trouble. I don't think Tayla can help me without risking her life. And I don't want that.*

"Surely your name isn't Tayla. I've never known a tumanhofer with such a short name."

"Well, that would be right, but my lady doesn't like to say it all."

"What is your name?"

"Taylaminkadot."

"Thank you, Taylaminkadot, for taking care of me."

The woman started and frowned at Kale. "Well now, that was nice, and you're welcome. Are you sure you're the daughter of my lady?"

Kale chuckled and rested her forehead on her knees. "I prefer to think I'm not."

"Well, I don't blame you there." Tayla looked nervous. "I can get you something to eat. Would you like that?"

"Are my dragons truly in the cook's tent?"

"Aye, they are, but I can't fetch them for you."

"I understand, Taylaminkadot. And yes, I would like something to eat."

Tayla started to leave, but she turned back to warn Kale. "There's a nasty bisonbeck guard at the door," she whispered. "Don't try to go anyplace."

Kale nodded even though she hardly heard the words. She concentrated on the servant's mind. She had done this trick before. She could pick up the images the woman saw. As the woman walked from the tent and then through the maze of the camp to the cook's tent, she marked her progress. By the time the tumanhofer servant came back with a bowl of soup and some bread, Kale had a pretty good idea where the tent was located. She also knew her dragons were healthy but locked in cages.

"Now," said Tayla, nervous again, as if being in Kale's presence was a dangerous thing, "if you're feeling all right, and don't need anything, I'll be going about my other chores."

"That's fine, Taylaminkadot."

The woman curtsied, gave her a pitying look, and rushed out of the tent.

"Well, it's about time." Toopka crawled out from under the moon-beam cape.

"Toopka!"

"Shh! Didn't she say there was a guard right outside?"

"How did you get here?"

"I've been with you all along. In a hollow. In the cape. Really, Kale. Quit staring."

"You were in there for hours!"

Toopka went to the small table and picked up the spoon. After taking a slurpy taste of the soup, she grinned at her.

"Why not? It's a little stuffy, and you bump into things, but other than being too dark, it's not all that bad. You can't hear very well in there though, so I had to keep poking my head out to find out what was going on. This is not a good situation you've gotten us into, Kale." She broke off a bite of bread and popped it in her mouth.

"Well, I didn't do it on purpose."

"And I don't like that woman who is 'my lady.' Who does she think she is, anyway?"

"She thinks she's my mother."

"Nah, take the wizard that hangs around with Cam and Fenworth. She's much better."

"I think I will, *if* I can get back to her."

Kale stretched her aching muscles. A fatigue enveloped her, and she found any movement a strain. If only she could feel wide awake. If only every single speck in her body weren't so very tired.

Toopka took another lip-smacking scoop of soup. "As soon as I finish this, I'll go get the dragons."

"And how do you propose to do that?"

"I'll borrow your moonbeam cape. No one will notice me cause I'm so sneaky and short. It might be a problem to locate the little dragons though. This is a big camp."

Kale smiled. "I know exactly where they are."

53

Gathering Together

Kale monitored Toopka's progress. The doneel child slipped from one hiding spot to the next without ever raising an eyebrow from any of the many soldiers roaming about the camp. Sometimes she moved only one step at a time, letting the cape's camouflaging ability hide her from people standing within a few feet of her. Kale held her breath and marveled that Toopka didn't shake in her boots.

I'm nervous enough for both of us, Toopka.

"Don't be silly, Kale. None of these bullies are any worse than Henricutt Tellowmatterden."

Oh, I think they are. I think they're killers, every last one of them. You be careful.

Something jolted Toopka, and she sidestepped between two stacks of wooden crates. Kale heard someone swearing.

Toopka?

"I'm all right. A bisonbeck oaf bumped into me from behind. I didn't see him coming. His friend says he tripped over his own feet. They can't see me. I'm all right."

Kale heard the slightest bit of a quiver in the little doneel's voice.

Toopka, you can turn back anytime you want to. We'll find another way out.

"I'm all right. Really."

Kale bit her lower lip and tried to send Toopka some courage through her talent, but she wasn't feeling very brave herself.

You're almost there. Turn to the right. The other way, Toopka. That's your left! Good, now—

"I can smell it, Kale. I found it."

The cages are right inside the front door.

"You told me that already."

I'm sorry.

"Just a minute. I'm going to walk in behind these three soldiers."

Be careful.

"You've told me that a hundred times already."

Kale watched the inside of the tent appear as Toopka slipped through the front door. She chose to hide in a corner.

"This is impossible!" complained Toopka. *"The dragons are like a side-show at a carnival. The cages are right where everyone can come and gawk at them."*

I have an idea, Toopka. I'm going to tell the dragons to make a lot of noise, then I'm going to tell the cook to cover them to make them be quiet. You have to pick out which man is in charge. Can you do that?

"Sure. Wait a minute."

Kale watched as Toopka's eyes swept the room, examining each of the men who worked in the tent.

"Him."

Kale told the dragons to set up a ruckus. The four hooted, shrieked, trilled, and squawked. They flapped their leathery wings as if they could break the bars of the cages.

"What's all this?" Through Toopka's mind, Kale heard the cook holler. "What's got into them?"

"Cover 'em like you would chickens. They'll settle down." Another voice gave the suggestion Kale had intended to put in the cook's mind.

With satisfaction, Kale and Toopka watched the man bring out a large cloth and drape it over all four cages. In only a few moments, Toopka crept under the edge and began picking the locks on the doors. One after the other, she freed the dragons. Each one climbed into a pocket-den in the cape. Toopka finally started the perilous return journey to the tent where Kale waited.

Toopka crawled under the back of the tent and opened the cape to let the dragons fly to Kale. Gymn, Metta, Dibl, and Ardeo did not go to their usual perches. All four dragons landed safely in Kale's arms.

"Now," Toopka whispered, "how do we get out of here?"

"I don't know." Kale cuddled the minor dragons. She eyed the opening in the front of the tent where a guard stood sentry, then examined the small opening at the base of the tent.

Could we cut that tear to make it larger? They took my sword, but I have a small knife in one of the hollows. Then of course, we could just walk out of here. Could we? With the cape? If only I weren't so tired.

Kale patted the mattress beside her. "Come sit with us. You've had a trying evening."

Toopka rolled her eyes and hopped onto the bed. She undid the cape and laid it inside out next to her. "I brought some more food."

She reached into a hollow and pulled out loaves of bread and hunks of cheese. She smiled at Kale. "I thought we might get hungry."

"When did you get this? I didn't see you reach for anything."

"I told you I was sneaky." Toopka's grin spread over her face.

A noise outside the tent caught Kale's attention. She heard Tayla speak to the guard.

Kale lifted the moonbeam cape and turned it over so the pockets were underneath. "Everybody under and don't move!"

"I've come to see if you need anything else for the night," said Tayla as she pushed the tent flap aside and came in. Her eyes went immediately to the loaves of bread and cheese. The tumanhofer servant looked at the partially eaten food on the bed, the empty bowl on the tray, and then Kale's face.

"No, Miss Kale, I don't know anything about the hills around here. My father was a fisherman. To me, a boat is the only way to travel."

Kale stared at the woman for a moment and then blinked her eyes.

Is she telling me how to escape? If she is, she's risking her life! I hope the guard believes I spoke first, and she answered. I can fix that! Kale sent a thought to the guard. Now he would have a vague memory of having heard Kale say something he couldn't quite hear right when the tuman-hofer woman entered the tent.

"I'm afraid you won't be able to sleep for another hour or so," the servant continued, "but after that your mother insists this part of the camp be quiet. She wants her rest, she does. She's very strict about no one prowling around. You'll have peace and quiet then."

She is *helping us. Oh, Wulder protect her.*

"Thank you, Taylaminkadot." Kale kept her voice calm. *The guard must not suspect anything is amiss.* "I don't need anything else tonight."

Tayla curtsied, picked up the tray, and left.

"What was that all about?" asked Toopka in hushed tones as she slithered out from under the cape.

"The river is just a few yards from here, isn't it?"

"Yes," answered Toopka.

"When everyone is asleep for the night, we're going on a boat trip."

A smile spread over Toopka's face.

"Now let's get this food out of sight," said Kale. "My mother may come to tuck me in."

⊢⊨⊣

Kale didn't regret that her mother did not return for a good-night visit. She believed that some drug had been given to her, for now that she had held Gymn for a couple of hours, the crippling lethargy had left. She felt strong and able to make a good attempt at stealing away.

When the only noises they heard were from the distant tents, Kale slit the small tear into a nice large hole to climb through. With the dragons in their pocket-dens and Toopka held in Kale's arms with the moonbeam cape wrapped around them both, she tiptoed on bare feet toward the sound of the river. She passed a few tents and a couple of sentries, but the darkness and her cape kept them safe.

At the river they could see a number of boats tied up to docks a hundred yards down the bank. Kale crept along the river, keeping her eyes open for soldiers. She started to get in the first boat they came to, but a hand on her arm stopped her.

"Not this one, Miss Kale."

"Taylaminkadot?"

"Follow me."

"You scared me."

"Follow me." The tumanhofer servant ran to a larger boat at the end of one of the docks.

"Get in." Tayla motioned to Kale as she knelt on the dock and held the boat steady.

Kale did as she was told. Tayla scrambled into the boat after her, the mooring rope in her hand. She shoved off.

"You're going with us?"

"Aye."

"Why?"

"I would be blamed in the morning whether I helped you or not. Have you ever rowed a boat, Miss Kale?"

"No."

"Then that's another good reason for me to go along, isn't it?"

"Yes, it is."

Kale sat on the wooden seat stretched across the stern of the little craft.

"Where does this river go, Taylaminkadot?"

"To the lake." Tayla sat on the middle seat and began to ply the oars.

"Is that a safe place to go?"

"If we get there before sunrise."

"Do you think we will?"

"If Wulder be willing."

54

Another Mother's Love

The small river meandered in gentle curves. For the first half hour, grawligs could be heard on one side, with their raucous songs and loud snoring. Dibl thought the combination so funny he had to be popped inside Kale's cape to keep him quiet. On the other side, bisonbecks loomed in the shadows between tents.

When they passed the last tent and slid between banks of trees, Kale's breathing slowed to a normal pace, and her hands unclenched. A few minutes later, she spotted lighted figures darting along the river. One came to the shore and waved to the passing boat.

"Taylaminkadot, we must speak to the kimens."

Taylaminkadot steered the boat toward the bank. As soon as they were within hearing distance, a kimen called, "We've been sent to bring you to Lyll Allerion."

"Which one?" asked Toopka.

"It would be Mother Number Two," answered Kale. "Mother Number One doesn't associate with kimens."

Several kimens gathered behind the first. "May we come aboard?" asked the first. "We'll go down the river toward the lake and join Lady Allerion."

The kimens jumped into the large rowboat as soon as it scooted into the shallow water. Tayla and the kimens propelled the boat to the other side where five more kimens hopped in. They bombarded Kale with their names, politely introducing themselves to her and referring to her as the Dragon Keeper. She remembered clearly the name Azalone and connected it with the one she thought might be the leader.

With a dozen kimens in the boat, you'd think we'd be going slower. She studied the small people sitting around her. *What are they doing to make us go faster?*

She never solved this puzzle and determined to get Regidor to think it through. If anyone could find the answer, he could.

"Azalone?"

"Yes?"

"Do you know what has happened to my friends, Regidor and Bardon? Regidor was with me when the grawligs attacked."

"Both men went back through your gateway. They returned with many mariones, Wizard Cam Ayronn, and Wizard Lyll Allerion. Lady Allerion sent us to find you."

"The mariones are not a large enough force to face Risto's army."

"More have come. An army under General Lee Ark. Our friends the urohms, led by Lord Brunstetter. Dragons are coming as well. Some through this gigantic gateway. Those who are close enough, fly in."

They glided downstream for many minutes before Azalone spoke again. "We are close to the field in which your Celisse awaits. You must hurry now to the camp of your comrades. Your mother is injured and requires you and the healing dragon."

"Injured?" She spun around on her seat, rocking the boat. "How did she get injured?"

"The wound is serious, but not life-threatening. When she heard you had been taken, she rushed out to save you. She charged into a trap, facing Risto and Burner Stox without assistance. Wizard Cam and the meech dragon Regidor soon arrived. It is likely Lady Allerion would have died without their assistance."

She turned quickly away. Tears stung her eyes, and she found it hard to breathe.

Toopka took her hand and squeezed. "It'll be all right. You and Gymn can make her well."

Kale peered ahead, trying to spot the place where they would land.

Tayla's short, muscular body blocked some of the view. Her shoulders strained as she pulled even harder on the oars. Kale sensed the tumanhofer woman wanted to help Kale get to her mother quickly. The woman had done much for a stranger, an o'rant girl who had done nothing for her except expose the servant to danger.

"Taylaminkadot, will you be all right? Do you have someplace to go?"

"I was hoping to go with you, Miss Kale. I'd like to be your servant."

Kale turned to Azalone. "Can you escort Taylaminkadot to our camp?"

"We will go with her downstream. It is a shorter distance to walk from the lake to your camp."

"Can you protect her?"

"We will try."

The boat pushed ashore where the trees thinned to reveal a meadow. Celisse paced over the winter pale grass, wearing a path. The moon reflected off her silver scales. She lifted her head and greeted her rider with a low call.

Kale leapt from the boat, waving good-bye to the others. The minor dragons flew ahead of her. Toopka pumped her little legs to keep up.

After a swift hug around the dragon's neck, Kale scooped Toopka into her arms and clambered on board. As soon as her knees were snug in the saddle hooks, she gave the signal to fly. Celisse flapped her large wings and vaulted into the night sky.

A cold wind blew in Kale's face. Not at all partial to frigid temperatures, the minor dragons hid in the moonbeam cape. Kale bent her legs back as far as she could and pulled the cape down over her freezing feet.

From the sky, she could see the sprawling Risto encampment, Bartal Springs Lake, and a camp just forming. Celisse banked and headed for the new settlement of warriors.

Celisse gave the warning. Behind them a dark dragon raced toward them. The smaller dragon flew at a faster speed and would soon catch up. With horror, Kale saw a stream of fire bolt out of the dragon's mouth.

Kale reached with her mind, trying to send a clear message.

Bardon, Regidor, I need help. Dar, Wizard Cam, can you hear me? I'm being followed. Regidor, I need help. I'm being followed by a fire dragon, and it's catching up to Celisse. Regidor, can you hear me?

She looked over her shoulder. The dragon was gaining. She couldn't make out a rider on its back, but she remembered that the twelve fire dragons who had confronted Paladin were riderless. Celisse abruptly banked to the left. The other dragon kept close on her tail. She shot up, flying higher. So did the pursuing dragon, and he spit a blaze as if to say he was annoyed.

Bardon, help! There's a fire dragon after us.

"I'm on my way, Kale."

She looked to the south and saw a dragon rise from the small encampment. Another sprang into the air after it. A few seconds later, a third followed. Turning her head, she gasped when she saw how much the fire dragon had gained on them.

Hurry, Celisse!

The fire dragon spewed out flames. The heat of the blaze came close enough that Kale felt the force of it on her back. The next projection singed Celisse's tail. Celisse screeched and beat her wings harder.

I should be able to do something.

Kale tried to pick up the enemy dragon's thoughts. When she touched its mind, she backed away from its fury for only a moment before she closed in and sent a message.

You've picked the wrong target. Risto will be furious.

The fire dragon faltered, then roared and sent out another flame. But its hesitation gave Celisse enough lead to avoid being hit again.

They were close enough to the oncoming dragons for Kale to make out who they were. Bardon led the charge on Greer, Brunstetter followed on Foremoore, and Dar brought up the rear on Merlander. Both Bardon and Brunstetter held lances ready to throw. They swept past Kale on either side of Celisse. Kale whipped her head around to see them hurl their weapons at the pursuing fire dragon. Both lances hit their marks. The dragon bellowed. Dar bolted past her, and she saw him swinging a hadwig. The spiked ball soared through the air and hit the fire dragon square on its head. Brunstetter and Bardon turned in a wide circle and prepared to make a second assault. The fire dragon had had enough. With its wings beating an irregular rhythm, it lost altitude.

Foremoore, Greer, and Merlander took up positions to escort Celisse home.

Thank you. Her gratitude went to each dragon and their riders.

"I'm glad you returned to us," Dar's voice warmly greeted Kale.

Thank you, Dar. And thanks to you, Bardon. Brunstetter, it is very good to see you! Where's Regidor?

Bardon answered, *"Regidor has been acting strangely. At first I thought he was ashamed because he was unable to protect you from the grawligs and prevent them from hauling you off. But I don't think that's really why he's disappearing all the time. When he shows up again, he's very morose."*

He could be worried about me. He's bonded to me.

"You talk to him after you've seen your mother. Maybe you can determine what's wrong with him."

A thought occurred to Kale, and with it came a pang of apprehension. She kept these thoughts to herself as she speculated. Would Regidor consider joining forces with the beautiful, beguiling Gilda?

They landed in an open field. Brunstetter and Bardon offered to unsaddle the dragons so Dar could take Kale to her mother.

"Celisse's tail!" Kale ran back to see whether her dragon's hindquarters had been injured from the one blast of fire that had made a hit. A layer of soot covered the glistening scales, but no real damage had been done. Kale gave the black and silver dragon a hug and followed Dar across the field.

"Is my mother badly injured?" Kale asked as they hurried past mariones, kimens, o'rants, and tumanhofers sleeping on makeshift cots and bedrolls.

"Yes, she was," said Dar, "but Fenworth and Cam repaired much of the damage. You and Gymn will bring her back to good health, I'm sure."

They entered a large tent. Kale rushed to the figure lying on a nice bed, took her wrinkled hand, and pressed it to her cheek. Lyll Allerion looked as she had the first time Kale met her in Meiger's tavern.

"Mother?"

Lyll opened her eyes, and a tired smile traced her lips.

Gymn came out of his pocket-den and hopped onto Lyll's chest. Kale put one hand on the little dragon, and the other held her mother's hand.

"I have something to give you, my child." Lyll fumbled in her bed-clothes and pulled out a disk on a chain. "I thought for a minute this afternoon that I had been foolhardy enough to lose my life. If that were to happen, you would be an orphan again. It is my hope that we might rescue Kemry. Take this disk. It will help you identify your father lest Risto try to trick you."

"I have a disk like that."

"You do?" The surprise in her mother's weak voice made Kale smile.

"Granny Noon gave it to me, but she didn't tell me how it works."

"Do you have it now? I can show you how it works."

Kale let go of her mother's hand and pulled the thong around her neck, lifting the red pouch from beneath the nightgown she still wore. She emptied the coinlike piece of silver into her palm.

Lyll held out her hand. "Give it to me and watch what happens."

Kale placed the notched disk into Lyll's palm. At first, nothing happened. Then the shine of the metal grew brighter. As she continued to watch, one of the notches foamed at the cut edges and closed together. When the shine diminished, the coin had only one notch.

Lyll Allerion opened Kale's fist by gently prying on her clamped fingers. She put the coin back in her daughter's hand. "When you find your father, the other notch will heal."

Kale stared at the one-notched disk and slowly closed her fingers over it. She looked up at the tired old woman in the bed.

"You really are my mother," she whispered.

"Yes, I am. How do you feel about that?"

Tears rolled down Kale's cheeks. "I don't know."

"Are you sorry I am not as beautiful as the other mother you found?"

She shook her head. "No, I always liked you better."

"Do you think you could love me?"

Kale nodded and threw herself into her mother's arms. She sobbed for a moment, but a jolt of energy passing through the circle of healing made her jump back. Still holding onto her mother's arms, Kale looked into the young face of Lyll Allerion.

She giggled. "You're young again."

Lyll laughed. "Yes, that was a mighty potent healing. Now I must get up and get dressed. Bardon has been telling me Regidor is having problems. Shall we go see about our friend?"

Kale saw the morning sun peeking through the tent flap. She'd been up all night. But her mother was right. They must talk to Regidor.

"What color should I wear today?" asked Lyll. "Yellow or blue?"

"Yellow," said Kale. "It's going to be a bright day."

"Is it, dear? I predict problems, and thus, yellow is the perfect choice." She nodded at the dress slung over a chair. "Yellow!" Lyll examined her daughter's attire. "I do believe you could use a dress as well."

55

TREACHERY

Lyll's prediction of trouble was validated as soon as they walked out of the tent. Dar and Bardon stood with Wizard Cam. Toopka hovered at their heels. All of them looked as though someone had died.

Cam stepped forward. "In the hour before daylight, all the dragons aligned with our camp took flight. It is reported that they headed north."

"Which would take them to the enemy," added Dar. "It seems our dragons have gone over to Risto's camp."

Bardon looked at Kale only. "And Regidor is nowhere to be found."

She blinked. "He and Gilda persuaded the dragons to defect?"

"Subterfuge *is* Gilda's specialty," said Cam with a sigh. "I'm afraid her brand of persuasion was too much for Regidor to resist. Remember, Risto enhanced her natural abilities. Once Regidor was converted, the two of them must have been a formidable pair against our dragons' trusting dispositions."

"All the dragons?" Kale realized the magnitude of the treason. "Celisse? Merlander?"

Bardon nodded. "All the dragons."

Kale felt the pressure of Metta's claws in her shoulder. "Not the minor dragons," she said. "The minor dragons are still here."

"Yes," said Cam, "but the minor dragons cannot carry soldiers into battle or transport wounded men. They cannot deliver supplies or give a commander an aerial view of the battlefield. Risto now holds an unbeatable hand."

"Will he attack today?" asked Bardon.

Cam looked old and sad. "If he wanted to win just this battle, he would. But he's smart enough to know we're amassing a fair-sized army to block him. If he waits a day, instead of crushing five thousand men, he can crush ten thousand."

Kale twisted the pouch hanging around her neck. "We have to rescue the dragons. If I talk to Celisse, I know she'd come back."

"Invading the enemy camp would be too dangerous, Kale," said Lyll Allerion. "I'm hoping Wizard Cam will have a trick or two up his sleeve. After all, he is a lake wizard. And Bartal Springs Lake just happens to be his home lake."

Cam nodded. "We'll go to my castle under cover of darkness."

"What are we going to do all day?" asked Toopka.

"Sleep!" said Cam. "At least some of us. Others will mingle with the new recruits, bolster their spirits and squash rumors."

"Am I one of the ones who gets to squash rumors?"

"You're one of the ones who gets to sleep."

"I slept some in the boat."

"You'll sleep more in a bed."

"I could—"

A bucket of water appeared over the little girl's head and dumped its contents.

Toopka sputtered.

"That was warm water," said Cam. "But you shall soon be cold. A nice warm bath and a snuggly bed are the best thing for you at the moment." He turned to address the tumanhofer servant. "Taylaminkadot, would you be so kind as to escort this little doneel to the tent that's been made ready for Kale? See to her needs, if you will, and don't let her out of your sight! Not even when you think she's sleeping."

"I won't be able to sleep," protested Toopka as she was led away.

Kale didn't think she would be able to sleep either, but a warm breakfast of porridge and hot mallow, a soothing bath, and a cozy bed invited slumber. She woke up hours later with no more aching muscles, no headache, and a hearty appetite. Gymn rested on her shoulder. When he saw her awake, he perked up.

"Heal their minds?" Kale sat up and contemplated her green dragon. "Whose minds?"

Gymn trilled and the explanation unfolded in Kale's mind. "The other dragons. They are deluded, and you think it's an illness. Maybe it is, Gymn. We'll try almost anything to get them back. How would you treat an illness like that?"

Gymn hummed in his throat and squeaked as he thought.

"Isolate the bad and nourish the good?"

Kale spied a new set of clothes. Forgetting about Gymn's theories, she jumped out of bed and raced to put them on. The pants and tunic reminded Kale of her mother's outfit she'd worn to fight the mordakleeps, except they weren't a flashy pink. The supple boots were black. Creamy soft material made a formfitting undershirt. The breeches and tunic were an earthy brown like the uniforms of The Hall.

Toopka stood in the doorway, pouting. "You're supposed to come eat."

Behind her Taylaminkadot nodded approvingly. The tumanhofer followed Toopka with the air of someone who would pounce if the child strayed so much as an inch. Kale grinned to herself as she watched the thwarted mischief maker march to the dining tent.

They rushed through supper. The winter sun had already set, and dusk shrouded the camp. Kale and Bardon, Dar and the two wizards, Brunstetter and Lee Ark, Taylaminkadot, Toopka, and several kimens marched down to the lake. The hike covered at least three miles of rough path through timber and rocky hillside. No one spoke unnecessarily, but concentrated on where to place the next step.

Two kimens guarded the boat tethered to a shoreline pine. Azalone took the point position, sitting astride the prow.

Dar sat on the next seat with Dibl on his knee.

Kale sat with Wizard Cam.

Brunstetter took the rowing bench and wielded one oar while Lee Ark and Lehman Bardon plied the other.

In the back sat Taylaminkadot with Lady Allerion and a half-dozen kimens.

The remaining kimens on the shore untied the line and shoved the boat out onto the lake. Gentle waves rocked the boat. The oars dipped in and out of the water. The three men propelled the skiff toward deep water.

"Where to?" asked Brunstetter.

"Oh, toward the middle in clear sight of the enemy camp, I should say," answered Cam.

Kale hoped they would not have to set up their fortress in full view of Risto's henchmen. "Is that where your castle is?"

"Well now, it's anyplace I want it to be, isn't it? But we do want to draw Risto's attention."

"We do?"

"Yes, we do. I must ask you to be quiet now, Kale. I am plotting all sorts of devious surprises for the wicked wizard and his cohorts."

Kale didn't mind being quiet. Fenworth would have been more blunt in ordering her silence. She found she missed the old wizard. A dozen topics of conversation sprang into her mind, but they all led to what would happen tomorrow and who would win the battle. How did she get in the front line of a war?

The quest was to find the meech dragon and save him—her—from Risto. To rescue those dragons already under the influence of Risto. And to thwart Risto's evil plans. We found Gilda, but didn't lure her away from Risto. Not only did we not rescue any dragons, we lost the ones we still had. And as for thwarting Risto—

Her eyes surveyed the western shoreline where the camp of bison-becks sprawled for miles.

If Wulder sends Paladin, Paladin could obliterate the whole army. What can we do alone?

She glanced back at the shore. Were soldiers gathering on the banks of the river? Had they been spotted?

We certainly aren't doing much to hide. Azalone is lighting the prow. At least the kimens in the back are subdued. The moon's path across the water seems to be pointing right at us.

The mural! This is the painting on the wall of the Gander!

"Bardon!"

"That has occurred to me as well, Kale, but remember you're being quiet."

Bardon!

"It doesn't really mean anything that I can see."

But it's happened to me before. On the last quest, there was a point when we looked just like the mural in the River Away tavern.

"I still don't see that it means anything for us today. What would be significant is if you were to see another mural that has us all doing something else. That might mean we'll live through tomorrow."

Oh, Bardon, do you think it's possible?

"We work for Paladin, Kale. Anything is possible."

"This will do," said Cam.

He stood and looked at the water some distance ahead of them. "There it is."

A spire broke the surface of the water and pushed upward. It was attached to a central turret, which soon became visible. The white stone edifice shone in the moonlight. Water cascaded out of the windows and off the balconies. The castle continued to thrust toward the sky, revealing a massive structure as it rose out of the water.

The eruption of a castle in the middle of the lake attracted attention from the shore. The water pouring from the building formed a roaring waterfall. If the bisonbeck soldiers hadn't seen the spectacle, they surely would have heard it.

Cam turned and handed Dibl to Kale. "Thank you for the loan of him, Kale. He has inspired many interesting events to unfold within the next twenty-four hours."

The rush of falling water subsided. The whole castle sat, apparently, on the lake.

Cam signaled the rowers to proceed. "To the front door, if you please."

They hitched the boat to a dock and climbed damp stairs to an ornate double door. Cam turned to frown at the sky.

"Feels like snow, wouldn't you say?"

Kale looked at the stars shimmering in a clear sky and thought, *Not in the least.*

"Well, there are extra blankets in each bedroom. You'll be warm enough. Shall we get some sleep? Big day ahead of us, you know."

From the shore a flaming arrow arched over the water. It fell far short of the castle target and sizzled as it plopped into the lake.

Cam put his hands on his hips. "Now that was optimistic. Had the fellow actually been able to shoot the arrow that great distance, did he expect one lone firebrand to demolish a castle still dripping water?"

He looked again at the masses of bisonbeck soldiers milling around on the shore. "On the other hand, it does portend well for us. They don't seem to solve problems well on the spur of the moment, do they? Yes, that bodes well for us."

56

Action

A dry bed surprised Kale that night, and so did the blizzard in the morning. Cam seemed a bit unhappy with the view out his dining room window.

"Well, Cam," said Lady Allerion as she buttered her toast, "you have to expect the wind when you gather together such a storm on short notice."

"Yes, but let's subdue it, shall we? I'm sure it's done its work, and we don't need it any longer."

"As soon as I've finished breakfast, Cam."

"What work did the blizzard do?" asked Toopka.

Cam sat down again at his place and poured himself another cup of tea. "The ropmas, grawligs, and schoergs all like their cozy little dens and hovels. They particularly like to be in them when there's inclement weather."

"In-clem-at?" Toopka scrunched up her face over the new word.

"Inclement, wet, in this case, wet *and* cold. I, personally, find inclement weather refreshing." He frowned. "Wind can be a bit bothersome."

"So the grawligs and others won't like the snow?"

"Hate it."

"What will they do?" Toopka leaned forward.

"Go home."

"Oh! That's good, isn't it?"

"Good for us. Annoying for Risto. He's not going to be pleasant to work with today."

After breakfast, Lyll and Cam combined their skills to tame the wild wind. In a few minutes, the company could see farther than four feet out the window. Snow blanketed everything on the shore.

"Listen," commanded Cam.

From a distance they heard whizzing and thumping noises.

"An eerie sound," said Lyll, a smile curving her lips.

"What is it?" asked Kale.

Cam smirked, looking pleased with himself. "Hundreds of dragons stirring their blood. If we were on the land, we could feel the vibrations under our feet."

"I'm sure the bisonbecks won't like the ground shaking," said Brunstetter.

"No, they won't, and the earthquakelike feeling will be the last straw to send the less disciplined warriors home before the battle begins."

Cam patted his damp beard. "Time for us to make a morning call."

"Where are we going?" Toopka dogged the wizard's steps.

"You're staying here with Taylaminkadot."

"I amn't."

"You can't say 'I amn't.' That isn't a proper contraction."

"Regidor says I can't say 'ain't.' What do you want me to say?"

"I want you to say, 'Yes, Wizard Cam, I shall do as I am told.'"

"Aargh!" growled Toopka between clenched teeth.

An hour later, Toopka stood on the front steps of the castle with her hand firmly clasped by Taylaminkadot. The rest of the party shoved off in the skiff and headed for shore at the northernmost end of the lake.

Kale looked back at the castle and started. At every window, at every parapet, an armed soldier stood sentry.

"The castle is manned!"

"Illusion, my dear. Risto will tell his soldiers it is just illusion, but the sight will weaken their resolve. It's so hard to believe your ears over your eyes, especially when appearances line up with expectations."

"Will you tell us where we're going now?"

"Oh, didn't I say? We're going to call upon the dragons."

Her heart skipped a beat. Soon she would touch Celisse. All her efforts to mindspeak to the dragon had been useless.

If I can see her and touch her—if she sees me, I know she'll want to come back.

The oars pushed through the water, and again she suspected the kimens somehow sped the boat over the waters. When they approached the shale-covered beach at the northern end of the lake, she marveled at the colorful array of dragons. Against the white backdrop of snow, the brilliant colors looked like colored panes in a stained-glass window.

Regidor stood on the shore as the boat skidded across the shallow water and scraped the coarse bottom. He greeted them with a smile. "Mission accomplished, Wizard Cam."

"Splendid. Lord Brunstetter, Lee Ark, you'll find your mounts ready to take you back to your troops."

Lady Allerion shook a finger at her fellow wizard. "This was a ruse, Cam!"

Cam did nothing to hide the smug look on his face.

Kale bounced out of the boat and threw her arms around Regidor. He looked surprised and then caught her up with a hug, whirling her around the snowy beach.

"Where would you have me, sir?" Bardon's voice sobered Kale.

A battle still loomed ahead of them. Regidor put her down, and they faced the elders.

Cam eyed Bardon solemnly. "You go with Lee Ark, Lehman."

"Yes sir."

"And me?" Kale was glad her voice didn't squeak.

Lady Allerion put her arm around her shoulders. "You're with me."

⊹⊱══⊰⊹

Lee Ark, Brunstetter, Regidor, and Bardon took off on their noble steeds with most of the dragons soaring into the sky and following. The plan devised by Cam and Regidor had worked. Gilda had been overconfident in the influence that Risto had gained over the dragons through her persuasive personality. She'd scoffed at the possibility of Regidor taking the loyal dragons into Risto's camp and winning back those under his influence.

The gentle dragons mingled with the dragons gone wild, and the voice of reason won. The dragons would return to the men they had deserted only weeks before. Many men under Lee Ark's command would now ride into battle.

"I wish Toopka were here to ask some of her endless questions," said Kale as the battalion of dragons shrank into the distance as they flew to the south.

"What questions do you have?" asked Lyll.

"Will the farmers accept the dragons after their betrayal?"

"Yes." Lyll gently squeezed Kale's shoulders and began to walk, guiding her daughter across the beach. "It may take time for the wounds to heal, but there's an immediate need for cooperation. Fighting side by side will do much to mend the past."

"Are we going to win this battle?"

Lyll laughed her deep, throaty laugh that somehow comforted Kale. "We've already won, Kale. We've chosen right, and that's victory in itself. Now whether we come out of this engagement alive is another matter. But no one can take away the personal conquest of good over evil that we waged in our own hearts before the war began. And in the bigger scheme of things, if our side is defeated here on this battlefield, others will stand and fight tomorrow. As long as Wulder reigns, and He reigns forever, there will always be those who choose right over wrong."

"Still, speaking of the smaller scheme of things, I wish you could just say, 'Yes, we will win.' "

Lyll laughed low and quiet as she leaned to press her head against Kale's. "I would like that too."

57

Test of Fire

Kale didn't ask where the dragon saddles came from. She knew Cam and her mother were capable of fabricating what was needed out of what was there. While the two master wizards got ready, Kale spent the time apologizing to Celisse.

"I should have known you would not abandon me. I know now the desertion had to appear genuine so that no suspicion of a deception would get back to Risto, but I should have listened to the doubt in my heart and believed in you instead of what I saw."

Soon Wizard Cam, Lady Allerion, and Kale set off on dragons, heading for the very center of Risto's camp.

Where are we going? Kale asked Wizard Cam.

"*To Risto's doorstep.*"

Why?

"*To stop him. Once he's out of the picture, his army will disintegrate. In the long run, we will save many lives.*"

She took a deep, calming breath and surveyed the land beneath them. The grawligs, ropmas, and schoergs had indeed deserted. Tracks in the snow all headed toward the Morchain Range. To the south, the two forces battled fiercely. Kale thought she saw Paladin's distinctive black dragon on the front line of warriors in the air. Their army was successfully pushing back the bisonbecks.

With Cam in the lead, the dragons began their descent. They landed in a crowded area, knocking down tents and laundry lines, regiment banners, and a weather sock as they tried to squeeze into the pathways of the enemy encampment.

Cam and Lyll slid from their mounts and charged toward the largest, most elaborate tent. Kale jumped to the ground, pulled her sword, and followed. She burst through the doorway and skidded to a stop right behind her mother.

Risto stood on a raised platform where a table littered with maps dominated the room. The wizard's dark hair brushed the shoulders of his well-tailored coat. His lean and muscular body tensed as he spied the visitors, but no alarm registered in his clear blue eyes. His lips curved in a smile that sent chills down Kale's spine. She had noted once before that Risto's face uncannily resembled Paladin's. But the evil wizard's sly expression annihilated the similarities.

Seated across from Wizard Risto was the woman Kale had referred to as Mother Number One.

Mother Number Two spoke. "I believe you've met Risto before, Kale. But let me formally introduce his companion. This is Burner Stox."

Burner rose with a cunning smile on her lips and coldness in her eyes. "I'm so pleased to see you here."

Kale sidled closer to the Lyll Allerion she claimed as her real mother. Burner Stox made her skin crawl.

Risto laughed. "With all your artfulness, Lyll, Cam"—he nodded at each wizard—"you still managed to play right into my hands. You see, all this"—he waved his hand over the battle plans and gestured toward the surrounding countryside—"was contrived for the sole purpose of bringing the Dragon Keeper to us. How nice to also have two annoying wizards delivered at the same time. I must admit that I'm disappointed Fenworth and the meech dragons aren't here as well. But it's only a matter of time before they, too, fall into my hands."

He gave Burner Stox a wink and a sardonic grin. "Shall we, my dear?"

She nodded, and both turned evil glares upon their company.

A fire burst around Cam and Lyll. Cam merely raised his arms, and a torrent of water cascaded over the flames. He moved to stand directly in front of Risto while Lyll approached Burner in an agile, catlike prowl.

Burner sneered. "We wanted you, Lyll Allerion, and Risto's brilliant plan worked. Once rid of Paladin's elite inner circle, we can easily control Amara."

"Where is Crim Cropper in all this, Burner?" asked Lyll. "Surely your husband should be here for this triumph."

Burner's twisted smile deepened. "He's playing scientist in a southern region. He doesn't care for 'field work.' He'll be grateful enough when I bring him more specimens for his experiments."

Kale's head swiveled back and forth as she watched the male wizards fight. Bolts of lightning, balls of fire, whirlwinds, hornets' nests, and anything else the combatants captured from nature hurled across the small space between them. The female wizards tossed words back and forth and edged closer to each other. That in itself unnerved Kale.

Instinct told her that Burner Stox must not lay a finger on her mother. She edged around the side of the tent. When she managed to get to a flank position, she screeched out a warning.

"There's two Ristos and two Burner Stoxes. You're looking at a reflection. The real Risto—" She didn't get to finish.

Simultaneously, Risto and Burner Stox grabbed their opponents. Cam and Lyll stiffened. The color drained from their flesh and clothing. When the evil wizards withdrew their hands, only statues remained.

Kale screamed.

Risto turned to her. "Dealing with you should be a lot simpler. But first I want my troops to see I have you in my power. It should do wonders for their morale."

Kale raised her small sword, only to have it jump from her hand at Risto's command.

He grabbed her by the arm. "Burner, keep that dragon of hers from following us."

He dragged Kale out of the tent. Celisse let out a cry, and her huge head swung toward them. A light flashed, and Celisse wailed. Again the dragon stretched out her neck to intercept Risto's departure. The light flashed, and Celisse fell.

Kale kicked at her captor, to no avail. Once on the back of a dragon and in the air, she dared not pull away from him. But she vowed she would flee at the first opportunity.

They landed on a hillside overlooking a heated battle of ground troops. Burner Stox followed. When she dismounted, she took hold of Kale's arms in a viselike grip.

From the vantage point of the hill, Risto shouted encouragement to his men, pointing out the capture of the Dragon Keeper. He muttered spells, and his men fought with renewed vigor. He leveled his evil eye at a line of marione warriors, and they collapsed, to be slain by the brutal bisonbecks.

"No, no!" cried Kale. *Oh, where is Paladin? What is it I should do?*

"You? Ha!" Risto smiled in her direction, and she stiffened. "You can do nothing. You're an apprentice wizard. What resistance can you muster? You're untrained and have gained no power since we last met, especially under the tutelage of a decrepit old has-been like Fenworth! What could you learn from a wizard who's more often a tree stump than a man?"

"I've never liked him, Thorp." Fenworth stood on the hill behind them, staff in his hand, leaves clinging to his clothing, Thorpendipity on his shoulder, and a mouse climbing up his sleeve.

Risto laughed, sinking onto a boulder and leaning back as if Fenworth offered not a threat but only a great deal of amusement.

Burner's harsh laugh rent the air in a series of hard-edged slashes. "May we offer you refreshment, old man? A cup of tea? A daggart?"

Fenworth turned a baleful glare on her. "Silence!" he commanded. Burner Stox stopped, gasped, and disappeared. A smell of sulfur lingered in the air.

Kale gasped. "Is she dead?"

"No," said Fenworth with a grimace. "Just silent. In a room full of quacking ducks. She won't like that."

Risto bellowed. "You're a fool. More of a clown than a wizard."

Fenworth shook his head. "Now, Risto, just because I prefer not to be nasty about things."

Rage transformed the evil wizard's countenance, and Kale shrank from his fury. She collapsed on the ground, clenching her hands into fists. She wanted to disappear to a place of safety, as Burner had, but knew there just might be a chance for her to help.

Risto thinks I'm no threat. He doesn't even remember I'm here. That's good. Perhaps that will give me an opening.

Risto sprang to his feet at the same time the top of Fenworth's staff burst into flame. Thorpendipity squawked and flew to perch in the bare limbs of a tree. Wizard Fenworth stormed across the space between him and the evil wizard. The old man threw his arms around the younger wizard, gripping him with sinewy arms.

"I know you think I am too old to be any real danger to you, Risto. But you have not considered this—I would rather die with you than let you live."

Risto struggled, knocking the staff from Fenworth's hand. Fenworth's arms wrapped around the younger wizard in a grip that proved hard to break. Kale bounced to her feet and raced forward to snatch up the crooked branch that served as Fenworth's walking stick.

As soon as she lifted it from the snow, the flame flared from the top of the staff. Instead of surging upward, it spurted out toward the heads of both wizards and cascaded down to engulf Risto and Fenworth. Kale shrieked and tried to drop the staff, but her fingers would not release the old wood.

Risto writhed within the blaze, and Fenworth released him, stepping back. But the inferno still clung to the old man's clothing. The fire consumed Risto but danced around Fenworth.

Kale shook her hand and threw the staff down on the ground, then raised her arms to cover her eyes. She heard Risto's piercing scream. The heat from the ball of fire grew, snapping and crackling. She stumbled backward and fell, then peeked over her arm and saw Fenworth reach out his hand. The staff leapt from the ground to his outstretched fingers. In another moment, Fenworth was gone. His staff stood for a second and then toppled.

Risto fell as the flames gathered into a tight ball around him. The sphere of flames dwindled until only a small flicker at the end of the fallen staff remained.

Sobbing, Kale ran to snatch up the unburned rod. The fire went out as soon as her fingers wrapped around the wood.

Holding all that was left of the old wizard, she looked around for help. A short distance away, men continued to battle.

Her knees buckled. She sat on the trampled snow, rocking the staff in her arms and sobbing.

"The trick is to pop inside the safety of the rod at the last possible moment." Fenworth's voice broke through her lament.

She looked at the staff in her hands. It thickened and grew heavier. She rested the end on the ground, and it bent in two places while she cradled the top in her arms.

"Can't believe I'm stuck. No, I'll just rest a moment and try again." The voice came from the swelling stick.

She giggled and wiped tears from her eyes. She heard the staff take a deep breath, felt it expand, and watched as it turned into a familiar tree-like figure.

"Metta, Gymn, Ardeo, Dibl, come out," Kale called. The minor dragons cautiously crept out of the cape. "Help Fenworth."

Gymn, Metta, and Dibl sat in Fenworth's branches. Ardeo nestled on Kale's shoulder, glowing faintly in the muted light of an overcast winter day. Metta sang softly. Gymn wrapped himself around what might be an old man's arm. The tree lost its wooden stiffness and grew warm as Fenworth reclaimed his body. He sat beside her on the cold, wet ground with his upper body and head resting in her lap.

He opened his eyes and smiled at her. "Ah, sweet girl, I think I shall retire. I wouldn't want this to be known, but I believe I may be getting too old for this adventuring business."

He looked around. "Where are Cam and Lyll?"

"At present they are statues in Risto's headquarters."

"Tut-tut. Oh dear, I shall have to put off retiring for a day or two, I see. We've a few problems to take care of."

"You can take care of them, Wizard Fenworth," she said, giving him a hug. "You are a great and powerful wizard."

"Oh dear, tut-tut, I must get around to giving you a few more lessons before I retire. First, hugging wizards is not at all the thing to do. Second, I am not a great and powerful wizard. There is no strength in that. I am a devoted and trustworthy servant, as you shall be someday."

58

Where Is Home?

Wizard Cam had no servants at his castle, so they all made dinner, served it, and washed up. Taylaminkadot fussed about people who didn't know their place. She would've done all the work if the others had let her. When she learned the extra guest for the meal was Paladin, she threw her apron over her head and sat in the corner until Librettowit coaxed her out.

Kale moved sluggishly with Gymn draped around her shoulders like a scarf. They had spent most of two days giving aid to wounded soldiers, most of whom were marione farmers who had valiantly traveled the distance to meet evil head-on. All who were able helped the wounded. Of course, Kale and Gymn were greatly needed. They treated the wounds of injured dragons as well. The dragons sometimes embarrassed her with their obvious adoration and their pleas for forgiveness.

"Just do what's right from now on," she said over and over. "You need to deal with Wulder. Show Him you're sorry by doing right by your families."

She returned to the wizard's lake castle with a sigh of relief.

They sat around a plank table in the castle's kitchen. A fire blazed in the hearth, fish jumped in the stream flowing through the room, and Dar had placed mugs of hot mallow on a tray with plenty of daggarts.

He leaned back in his chair, pulled out his harmonica, and provided restful music for their digestion.

"You've done well," said Paladin as he looked around the company of his servants. Candlelight highlighted the reddish tints in his dark brown hair. His smile eased the hardness of his strong features. Kale felt the friendly warmth of his gaze and knew this important man actually liked her.

He set his mug down on the table and addressed those relaxing around the room. "What do you wish to do now that the threat to Amara has been crushed?"

"I want to go home," said Librettowit. "The shelves will need dusting. And the books I bought in Prushing will have arrived by now."

Paladin nodded. "Wizard Fenworth, Librettowit, Kale, her dragons, Taylaminkadot, Toopka, and Regidor shall go back to Bedderman's Bog."

He smiled at Kale. "I've seen that Bardon has shown you how to defend yourself. I suspect you both learned from Regidor as well. You must concentrate on your skills as a wizard now."

Wizard Fenworth twitched, sending a scurry of beetles out of one sleeve. "I'm retired, you know."

"Yes, I had heard that. Who will teach wizardry skills to Kale and Regidor?"

Cam raised a finger. "I'm not overly occupied at present."

Paladin winked at the wizard. "Do you wish to stay in your castle or at Fenworth's?"

"Here now!" exclaimed Fen. "Pesky cousin. A distant cousin. Ninth cousin, twenty-two times removed, at least. He hasn't been invited."

"Yes," said Paladin in a reasonable tone, "but if he were there to handle the small things that come up, you could enjoy your retirement more fully."

Fenworth harrumphed but did not voice any further objections.

Cam smiled at his cousin. "I'll spend some time with Fenworth in The Bogs. I'm sure he'd miss the hubbub if he found himself alone with only Librettowit and Thorpendipity. But I will take the students on field trips. Nothing like on-the-spot instruction."

Paladin nodded and raised an eyebrow in Regidor's direction. "I haven't forgotten Gilda."

Regidor's hand dropped to cover a spot on the side of his robe. "She's safe."

Paladin's eyebrow rose a notch. "Do you mean she's safe to be around, or she's safe from harm in your pocket?"

Regidor's thin lips puckered. He looked Paladin in the eye. "I would like to be responsible for her. She bonded to Risto, and now Risto is dead. I feel I can help her."

"So be it," Paladin said and turned to address Kale's mother. "Lady Allerion?"

"I should like to travel. I didn't really enjoy being restricted to that dungeon. And I might just uncover a way to free Kemry." She laid a hand on Fenworth's arm. "I do hope you will allow me to visit often, Fen. I would like to get to know my daughter."

Fenworth arched an eyebrow at her but did not answer.

"Thank you." Lyll leaned forward and kissed the old man's brow as if he had graciously invited her to come at any time.

"Harrumph! Seems I neglected that lesson for you as well. Your daughter hugs me. You kiss me. Not at all the thing. Wizards must be held in great respect. Unapproachable. Awe-inspiring."

A mouse slid out from under his hat and scrambled down his sleeve, across his lap, and down to the floor.

"Nothing," said Fenworth, "should detract from a wizard's dignity."

Paladin stroked his chin with his long fingers as he nodded solemnly. "I couldn't agree more, Wizard Fenworth."

He turned to the warriors. "Lee Ark and Lord Brunstetter, where do you wish to go?"

"Home," they said in unison.

"So be it." Paladin's eyes held sympathy. "Dar?"

The doneel took the harmonica from his mouth long enough to answer. "Home, Wittoom."

"And Bardon?"

Kale held her breath and looked down at the daggart in her hand. Where could Bardon go? He didn't answer, and she peeked across the table in time to see him shrug.

Paladin drummed his fingers on the table for a moment before he spoke. "I think you've learned what Grand Ebeck wanted you to know when he sent you from The Hall. Are you ready to begin training as a knight?"

Bardon jerked up straight in his chair. "Yes sir." He bit his lips and blinked. Kale saw his hand move as if to reach up and pull the locks covering his ears, but he stilled the movement.

Was he supposed to learn something about his mother and father as I have? Was he supposed to learn to accept his roots? Because if he was, I don't think he did!

Bardon sat a little straighter. Kale watched the familiar resolve sharpen the contours of his jaw.

"Sir, I don't know what it was that Grand Ebeck expected me to learn."

Paladin smiled the slow, relaxed smile that somehow made Kale trust him and his wisdom. "I'm not surprised. Often the lessons in life that are the most meaningful are the hardest for us to sort out. Wulder blessed you with a great potential. He used your parents to gift you with unique traits. Grand Ebeck saw those inherent talents bound by your rigid adherence to rules. He threw you out of the austere environment of The Hall so that you would have a chance to become more flexible."

Paladin swung his arm around, his sweeping gesture indicating the members of the quest sitting around the stone kitchen. "In the company of this motley crew, how could you help but unbend a little?"

Kale grinned as Librettowit and Fenworth harrumphed, Dar and Cam chortled, and Toopka laughed out loud.

Bardon's lips spread into a smile, and his body relaxed. "So I was to learn to be more yielding before I entered a discipline that is unyielding?"

Paladin clapped him on the shoulder. "Precisely! You must learn to be malleable before you're formed into an instrument of justice. Otherwise you wield a sword with no mercy, no discernment."

Bardon nodded thoughtfully, then glanced at Kale and winked.

You have changed, Bardon!

"And I intend to change even more. In three years I will be a knight, Kale. And if our paths do not cross again until then, I promise I will seek you out so you can marvel at the Snitch."

Kale gasped, and then smiled. He knew the name they had all called him back at The Hall.

Paladin nodded as if he understood their exchange. "You will need something I believe our venerable Wizard Fenworth has been keeping for you." He stretched out his open palm to the old man as if he expected Fen to hand over the object.

"Oh dear, tut-tut. Where did I put that? Tut-tut, oh dear." The wizard sat up straight and began patting his beard and robes. Tiny creatures skittered in all directions. The minor dragons jumped on the scampering feast of bugs, ignoring lizards, birds, and rodents as they escaped.

Wizard Fenworth's hand dug into a fold of his robe. "Aha!" He pulled out a closed fist, turned it over, and slowly uncurled his fingers. A tiny sword lay across his palm.

Bardon stood, and so did Amara's leader.

Paladin picked it up between his thumb and forefinger.

"Fen, you constantly amaze me. I believe this would be more useful to our future knight in different proportions."

The sword shimmered and grew at a steady, unhurried rate until the hilt became a size Paladin could wrap his hand around. The silent audience watched the shining blade stretch out to a gleaming point.

Paladin swished the sword through the air, testing its balance. "A finely crafted weapon." He deftly reversed the blade and offered it to Bardon. The young man took it without a word.

Kale thought she would burst with pride for her friend. She started to enter his thoughts and congratulate him, but the look on his face stopped her. This moment was too important to Bardon for her to intrude upon.

Paladin laid his hand on the stunned lehman's shoulder. "You shall go with Dar to Wittoom. Sir Dar will train you."

Kale's mouth dropped open, and her head whipped around to find the doneel relaxing in a chair with his legs draped over the arms. She slammed her fists against her hips. "You really are a knight?"

Dar ran his mouth over the harmonica, making a loud scale of notes trill through the cavernous kitchen.

He winked at her and grinned, his face splitting almost in two. "Yes, dear Kale, but only a very little one."

Glossary

Amara (ä´-mä-rä)
Continent surrounded by ocean on three sides.

armagot (är´-muh-got)
National tree, purple blue leaves in the fall.

ballyhoo bird (băl´-lē-hoo)
An insect-eating bird with dappled brown feathers. It is rarely seen, but its distinctive ballyhoo call is frequently heard in all types of woodland.

beater frog (bē´-ter frôg)
Tailless, semiaquatic amphibian having a smooth, moist skin, webbed feet, and long hind legs. Shades of green; no bigger than a child's fist; capable of making loud, resounding boom.

benders
A game played with a deck of cards.

bentleaf tree
Deciduous tree having long, slender, drooping branches and narrow leaves.

bisonbecks (bī-sen-beks)
Most intelligent of the seven low races. They comprise most of Risto's army.

blattig fish (blat´-tig)
Freshwater fish often growing to a length of two to three feet, voraciously carnivorous, known to attack and devour living animals.

blimmets (blim´-mets)
One of the seven low races, burrowing creatures that swarm out of the ground for periodic feeding frenzies.

bodoggin (bō´-dŏg-n)
A breed of short-haired dog with a large head, short bowed legs, stocky body. Strong jaws with dewlaps, useful on farms for curtailing vermin.

Bogs, The
Made up of four swamplands with indistinct borders; located in southwest Amara.

borling tree (bôr´-ling)
Having dark brown wood and a deeply furrowed nut enclosed in a globose, aromatic husk.

bornut (bôr´-nŭt)
Nut from borling tree.

brillum (bril´-lum)
A brewed ale that none of the seven high races will consume. Smells like skunkwater, stains like black bornut juice. Mariones use it to spray around their fields to keep insects from infesting their crops.

broer (brôr)
A substance secreted by female dragons through glands in the mouth. Used for nest building, it hardens into a rocklike substance resembling gray meringue.

chukkajoop (chuk´-kuh-joop)
A favorite o'rant stew made from beets, onions, and carrots.

cygnot tree (si´-not)
A tropical tree growing in extremely wet ground or shallow water. The branches come out of the trunk like spokes from a wheel hub and often interlace with neighboring trees.

deckit powder
Yellow crystalline compound used for explosives.

doneel (dō´-nēel)
One of the seven high races. These people are furry with bulging eyes, thin black lips, and ears at the top and front of their skulls. A flap of skin covers the ears and twitches in response to the doneel's mood. They are small in stature, rarely over three feet tall. Generally musical and given to wearing flamboyant clothing.

Dormanscz Range (dôr-manz´)
Volcanic mountain range in southeast Amara.

druddums (drud´-dums)
Weasel-like animal that lives deep in mountains. These creatures are thieves and will steal anything to horde. Of course they like to get food, but they are also attracted to bright things and things that have an unusual texture.

drummerbug
Small brown beetle that makes a loud snapping sound with its wings when not in flight.

eberbark tea (ĕb´-er-bark)
Tea made of dried root bark from the eberbark tree, a deciduous having irregularly lobed leaves and aromatic bark, leaves, and branches. Contains a volatile oil used as flavoring and for medicinal purposes.

emerlindians (ē´-mer-lin´-dēe-ins)
One of the seven high races, emerlindians are born pale with white hair and pale gray eyes. As they age, they darken. One group of emerlindians is slight

in stature, the tallest being five feet. Another distinct group is between six and six and a half feet tall.

ernst
An evergreen shrub, flowering in late fall. The tiny, starlike, pale yellow flowers give off a fragrance similar to cinnamon.

ersatz (er-zäts´)
Imitation, substitute, artificial, and inferior to the real thing.

Fairren Forest (fair´-ren)
A massive forest of mostly deciduous trees in southwest Amara.

fire dragons
Emerged from the volcanoes in ancient days; these dragons breathe fire and are most likely to serve evil forces.

fortaleen (for´-tuh-leen)
Bush with two-inch long thorns.

gaperlot (gā-per-lŏt)
One who stares rudely.

glean band (gleen)
A bracelet delicately woven by kimens out of vines from the glean plant. It wards off wasps and other stinging insects, as well as poisonous reptiles.

glommytucks (glŏm´-me-tŭks)
Large aquatic birds with a long slender neck and shorter, rounder bills than ducks. Lay large clutches of eggs and are wonderful birds for roasting.

grand emerlindian
Grands are close to a thousand years old and are black.

granny emerlindian
Grannies are both male and female, said to be five hundred years old or older, and have darkened to a brown complexion with dark brown hair and eyes.

grawligs (graw´-ligs)
One of seven low races, mountain ogres.

greater dragon
Largest of the dragons, able to carry many men or cargo.

gum tree
Tree with sticky leaves and yellow, rayed flower heads, the center of which may be plucked and chewed.

hadwig (ad´-wig)
A sling-type weapon with a spiked ball at the end.

halfnack bird
Brightly colored, medium-sized bird.

heirnot tree (âr´-nŏt)
Slender, white-barked, pole-like trunks with light green, round leaves attached by a flattened stem, which causes them to rustle in the slightest breeze. People often say the trees whisper or chatter.

jimmin (jĭm-mĭn)
Any young animal used for meat. We would say veal, lamb, or spring chicken.

kimens (kĭm´-ens)
The smallest of the seven high races; elusive, tiny, and fast; under two feet tall.

lightrocks
Any of the quartzlike rocks giving off a glow.

major dragon
Elephant-sized dragon most often used for personal transportation.

mariones (mer´-ē-owns)
One of the seven high races. Mariones are excellent farmers and warriors. They are short and broad, usually musclebound rather than corpulent.

meech dragon
The most intelligent of the dragons, capable of speech.

minor dragon
Smallest of the dragons—the size of a kitten. The different types of minor dragons have different abilities.

moerston bark (môr´-stun)
When chewed, it soothes hunger and freshens the mouth; bumpy, brown and thin.

moonbeam plant
A three- to four-foot plant having large shiny leaves and round flowers resembling a full moon. The stems are fibrous and used for making cloth.

Morchain Range
Mountains running north and south through the middle of Amara.

mordakleeps
One of the low races, a shadowy creature with a long tail.

mordat (môr-dăt)
A tree that produces sap, out of which a sweet syrup is made.

mullins (mŭl´-lĭns)
Fried doughnut sticks.

mumfers (mŭm´-fers)
A plant cultivated as ornamentals for their showy flower heads of profuse petals and brilliant colors.

ninny-nap-conder (nĭn´-ē-năp-cŏn-der)
A type of con artist who uses the appearance of naiveté to dupe his victims.

nordy rolls
Whole-grain, sweet, nutty bread.

o'rants
One of the high races. Five to six feet tall.

parnot (pâr´-nŏt)
Green fruit like a pear.

pnard potatoes (puh-nard´)
Starchy, edible tuber with pale pink flesh.

Pomandando River (po´-man-dan´-do)
River running along the eastern side of Vendela.

quiss (kwuh´-iss)
One of the seven low races. These creatures have an enormous appetite. Every three years they develop the capacity to breathe air for six weeks and forage along the sea coast, creating havoc. They are extremely slippery.

razterberry (ras´-ter-bâr-ee)
Small red berries that grow in clusters somewhat like grapes on the sides of mountains. The vines are useful for climbing.

River Away
Marione village in eastern Amara.

rock pine
Evergreen tree with prickly cones that are as heavy as stones.

rootup tree
Appears to be upside down. A dense bush surrounds the base. In the center, leafless branches intertwine tightly. From a distance, they appear to be a solid trunk. At the top, these limbs spread apart, looking just like a root system.

ropmas (rōp´-muhs)
One of the seven low races. These half men, half animals are useful in herding and caring for beasts.

scarphlit (scar´-flit)
An oily substance used in medicinal potions.

schoergs (skôrgz)
One of seven low races, much like grawligs; shorter, less playful.

Sheridan
A household servant, armed and designated protector of the family and property.

Torsk Tower
One of three towers at The Hall. Four clocks adorn the top. It is rumored that a gateway through time exists in the tower.

trang-a-nog tree (trăng´-ə-nŏg)
Smooth, olive green bark.

Trell Tower
One of three towers at The Hall. This one houses gateways.

tumanhofers (too´-mun-hoff-ers)
One of the seven high races; short, squat, powerful fighter, though for the most part they prefer to use their great intellect.

tumpgrass
A tall grass that grows in a clump, making its own hillock.

urohms (ū-romes´)
Largest of the seven high races; gentle giants; well proportioned and very intelligent.

Vendela (vin-del´-luh)
Capital city of the province of Wynd.

Wittoom (wit-toom´)
Region populated by doneels in northwest Amara.

About the Author

DONITA K. PAUL comes from a family of storytellers and teachers. So it is only natural that she loves spinning imaginative tales interwoven with lore. A retired schoolteacher, she keeps her hands in the mix by being one of the professional storytellers in the Sunday-school department of her church.

Donita enjoys keeping in touch with her readers through www.dragon spell.us. This interactive Web site has more details about the land of Amara, plus games, recipes, a fan gallery, and much more.

She has two grown children, two grandchildren, and two dogs. She currently lives in Colorado Springs, Colorado, in the shadow of Pikes Peak. When she's not writing, she enjoys reading all genres, from picture books to biography.